BLACKOUT

ALEXANDRIA CLARKE

❀ Created with Vellum

I looked over the side of the roller coaster as it climbed to the top of the first hill with a series of loud clacks. The night was dark and cold, but the theme park was lit up with fairy lights and neon arcade games below. The nippy breeze flirted with the hems of sweaters and blew hats off the heads of unsuspecting park guests. Soon, the seasonal theme park would close, as it would be too cold to run the rides, but for now, I could enjoy the brief view of Denver from one hundred feet above the ground. Screams built around me—some scared, others excited—as the first car of the coaster crested the top of the hill. I craned my neck, savoring the liberation of the sky, even if I was strapped into a padded harness, and put my hands up. My boyfriend, Jacob, reached up and linked our fingers together.

My stomach floated as the coaster careened downward at a steep angle. I let out an involuntary whoop of joy. The wind tore through my hair, freeing it from its messy bun. The air was so cold that my eyes streamed with tears. The coaster zoomed up into the first half of a cobra roll and hurtled down the other side before taking us upside down in a big loop. Jacob's fingers tightened around mine as he brought our entwined hands down to grab the handle of his harness, a deep yell reverberating in his throat.

This was freedom, however fleeting. It was forgetting about the trivial issues in your life for ninety seconds of metal track at sixty-five miles per hour. It was letting the smell of cotton candy and turkey legs and funnel cakes rush by in quick succession to overwhelm your taste buds and make you momentarily forget about the whole unprocessed diet you so obsessively stuck to every day of your life. It was letting the sting of the wind strip the warmth from your pores and chill the tip of your nose in a way that made you feel more alive in that minute and a half than you had since the last time you got off this ride.

And then every light in the city extinguished itself, dousing the world with an inky-black blanket. The roller coaster rushed forward, but when it leveled off on the platform that was meant to slow it down before it glided into the next drop, the automatic brakes did not engage. It thundered on, diving into the dip with such intensity that it whipped the heads of its riders unceremoniously about on their necks. My heart drummed against my chest as we plunged into the darkness at a reckless pace, the black night pressing against my pupils. I squeezed Jacob's hand in mine as the screams of pleasure turned to terror.

EARLIER THAT DAY

IT WAS A CLOUDLESS MORNING, and the sky stretched out to either end of the city to blanket our little corner of the world. The end of October beckoned November in with pink cheeks, chapped lips, and leaves the color of fire. It was my favorite time of year. Summer was long gone, and winter was on its way. At dawn, I slid out of bed while Jacob was fast asleep, made a cup of coffee, wrapped a blanket around my shoulders, and sat in the creaky rocking chair on the fourth-floor balcony of our apartment. I liked Denver best first thing in the morning. The people were slow to wake, and everything was quiet and calm. The sun cast a pale pink tint across the sleepy city like something out of a neon-colored eighties movie. On a clear day, the white-capped mountains layered themselves in hues of blue in a background that almost looked fake behind the buildings of downtown. Somewhere out there, my childhood memories flitted in and out of the trees, looking for a place to touch down. My mind wandered to meet with them sometimes, but I was never alone long enough to get lost in a land of the past.

"Georgie?"

I liked Jacob's voice best first thing in the morning too. It was slow and rough with sleep. His enunciation slipped, the letters looser on his lips. It was a welcome change from his prim, polished daily manner of speaking. Jacob was born and bred into an upper-class family, and his staccato elocution was a product of private schools and international travel. Drowsiness leveled the playing field for us, and I savored the conversations whispered between yawns and stretches.

"Morning," I said, drawing the blanket tighter around my shoulders as the wind swept the long violet hair on the left side of my head about.

Jacob shivered as his bare toes met the cold concrete of the balcony. His fingers combed through my tangle of hair, attempting to tame the wild purple locks, before he gave up and stroked the patch of baby-fine, white-blond fuzz shaved close to my scalp on the other side of my head. The partial buzzcut and the wild color were products of an on-air dare for my talk radio show. I covered the same news stories and current events as the major networks, but the fact of the matter was that people our age, in their late twenties, needed an incentive to invest any amount of interest in politics and related matters. I hoped that the stunts I pulled on the show were enough to get listeners to tune in on their way to work or to at least check out my website later for more information. Jacob, however, wasn't always a fan of my methods.

"It's freezing out here," he said, perching on the arm of the rocking chair.

I braced myself as the chair rolled backward and knocked against the sliding door. "I like it."

"We're both going to catch pneumonia. Come inside."

The faintest shadow of golden scruff coated Jacob's cheeks and chin. His dusty blond hair stood up at haphazard angles, not yet subdued by his morning ritual of mousse and gel. His eyes, the same creamy golden-brown color of my coffee, were partially hidden behind drooping lids, and his pink cheek bore an etching of the bed quilt's lacy pattern. I smiled and cupped his face. Unrehearsed, he pressed his lips to my palm. His hand found mine, and he played with my fingers, warm from being wrapped around the hot mug of coffee.

"You're not wearing your ring," he said. "Where is it?"

"On the bedside table," I told him. "I don't wear it to sleep."

"You don't wear it ever."

"That's not true."

"Do you not like it?" His lethargy quickly faded, and I wished there was a way to slow his route to alertness. "Is it not big enough?"

"No, no. It's beautiful."

I trailed my fingers down the side of his face. His ears were already pink with the cold, but his cheeks were pink with the mingling hues of pride and insecurity. The ring in question—my engagement ring—boasted a gigantic diamond, but I had never been the kind of girl to flaunt such a display of wealth to any of my friends. Most of my friends at the radio station were guys anyway. They didn't know the difference between a real gemstone and cubic zirconia, and they didn't care. Quite frankly, neither did I, but Jacob had presented the piece of jewelry with an air of triumph when he'd proposed, and to tell him that I preferred a less expected route of matrimonial symbolism might have wiped the jubilant grin right off of his face. Jacob came from a traditional family, and he followed the traditional rules, though I suspected that his father, rather than his freelance photojournalism career, had bought the ring. As far as size went, I couldn't wait for the day I could exchange the conspicuous rock for a simple wedding band.

Jacob tilted my chin up to kiss me. "Are you sure? It's not because you're still mad about last night?"

My lips stiffened against his. I sipped my coffee instead. It had gone cold. "I'm not mad."

"Really? Because you said—"

"I know what I said."

"I just think that getting married in a church is the best way to please my parents," he went on, clearing his throat. He flattened his hair to the best of his abilities, and his day-to-day demeanor rose to the surface. "I know you aren't really religious, Georgie, but—"

The charming quiet of the morning hours had been broken, like tossing a boulder into a glass pond. I stood up from the rocking chair and went inside. "Can we not talk about this right now?"

The sliding door clicked shut as Jacob followed. I liked to keep it open to let the fresh, mountain-scented air flow in and out of the apartment, but he claimed that it was impractical to run the heat if I was going to let the warmth escape outside. In a few hours, the sun would be high enough to warm the apartment through the glass doors and windows, and it wouldn't matter anyway. I didn't understand why Jacob was so conscious of money. His father owned the building we lived in, so he didn't pay rent or utilities. He had never scrounged a day in his life. He had never clipped coupons or swiped change out of a public fountain to buy a slice of pizza at a corner store. He had never siphoned gas from a parked vehicle in the middle of the night because he couldn't afford to fill up his own tank. He also didn't know that I had done all of those things and worse at some point in my life, but I wasn't the one chiding the other for accidentally leaving the bathroom light on.

I put my mug in the microwave to rewarm the coffee and opened the fridge. I had a few minutes before I had to get ready to go into work, which meant I had just enough time to make myself a decent breakfast. I rifled through my materials. Eggs, spinach, tomatoes, mushrooms—

"If you're making omelets, can you leave out the mushrooms?" Jacob asked, straightening the ever-growing stack of newspapers on the island counter. "You know I don't like them. Do you need all of these?"

I put the mushrooms back in the fridge. "Yes, I do. Please don't touch them."

He peered at a yellowing page. "This one is from three weeks ago. You can probably recycle it by now."

I snatched the newspapers out of his hands, tapped them into straight lines, and placed them at the far corner of the island beyond his reach. "I need them to reference previous articles, which I've told you a hundred times."

I felt his eyes on me as I heated a skillet over the stove and cracked a few eggs. "They're piling up. About the wedding, though, we really do need to talk about it. Mom wanted a ceremony early next year, but Pippa's going to pop in the next month or so, and she said she doesn't want to look fat in the pictures. You're still going to let her be a bridesmaid, right?"

The heat from the stove rose. Despite the chilly morning, sweat beaded at my temples. My cheeks reddened, and a drip of moisture rolled down my back between my shoulder blades. "Yes, of course your sister can be a bridesmaid, but we've only been engaged for a few months, babe. Besides, I wanted our wedding to be in the fall."

"That's, like, now," Jacob said, confused. "This isn't a shotgun wedding."

"I meant next year."

"That's forever!"

"It's one year." I sprinkled salt and pepper over the sizzling eggs then gave the pan an experimental shuffle in preparation for the flip. The omelet slid easily across the smooth silver. "It gives us the time to figure everything out. Why are you in such a rush anyway?"

"Because I feel like you're going to change your mind."

I missed the catch. The omelet landed half in, half out of the pan, splitting in the middle. The eggs splattered against the pristine white tile of the kitchen floor. A piece of hot spinach plastered itself to the top of my bare foot. I hissed and shook it off then dumped the pan on the stove. "Fuck me. Seriously?"

Jacob blanched as he grabbed a roll of paper towels and knelt down to collect the ruined omelet. "I hate it when you swear."

"Sorry. That's your half, by the way. I'm late for work."

Since there was no hope of saving the omelet, I scooped the rest of the eggs into a whole wheat tortilla, wrapped it up like a burrito, and shoved half of it into my mouth as I stripped out of my pajama pants and made a beeline for the bedroom.

"I thought Nate took over the morning show on Fridays," Jacob called after me.

I pulled on a pair of jeans and a sweater. "He usually does," I said, juggling the burrito as I laced up my boots. "But we hired a new intern, and Nate's not a people person. I told him that I'd be there today. We've got a lot to cover."

Jacob leaned against the door of the bedroom. A piece of scrambled egg was stuck to the back of his hand. "I was thinking that we could go to the park today to spend some time together. You've been so busy lately, I feel like I haven't seen you in years."

"You see me every night."

"You know what I mean. Come on, I promise to get on the roller coasters with you since I know how much you like them."

I tied off my laces and shoved them under the tongue of my boot so that they were invisible. I finished off the breakfast burrito in three humongous bites then stood in front of Jacob and put my hands on his shoulders. With my boots on, I was a good inch taller than him. He was a stocky guy, well-muscled but compact. That worked for me—I didn't have to stretch to kiss him—but he took offense whenever I wore heels around him.

"I promised Nate that I'd come in today," I said. "But what if we go to the park later? I always like it better at night anyway. Everything looks so pretty lit up. Here." I picked up one of his cameras from the collection on his desk. "There's a charity run downtown today to raise awareness for cystic fibrosis. You should cover it."

He expertly flipped off the lens cap and raised the camera to snap a picture of me. "Those are generic photos. I want danger and intrigue. I want grit and trench warfare. I want the Hells Angels as security at the Altamont Free Concert, not sweaty people in garish tracksuits."

"Be glad you're not photographing trench warfare," I said. "I hear typhus sucks."

I smacked a kiss to his cheek and sidestepped him to get to the coat closet. Then I pulled on a denim jacket, straightened out the collar, and grabbed my keys from where they hung on the inside of the door.

"So what time tonight?" Jacob asked, following me through the kitchen. Somehow, he'd managed to wipe the egg from the floor, wash the frying pan, and put the dirty spatula in the dishwasher in the same time it had taken me to change my clothes. That was another thing that set us apart. Jacob was a neat freak, while I operated best within organized chaos.

8

"I don't know. I have dinner plans with Nita that I'll have to cancel."

His shoulders slumped. "It's fine. We can go another day."

I shoved my phone and wallet into a messenger bag and slung it across my shoulders. Then I snaked my arms around Jacob's neck and pulled him close. He always smelled like cinnamon and cloves when it got cold out, compared to his citrusy summer scents. "Nita's easygoing. She'll understand. I'll text you when I'm on my way home, okay? And then we'll go ride the roller coasters until you puke."

"Now I'm having second thoughts."

I grinned and kissed him goodbye. "Too late. See you later."

A FEW BLOCKS from the apartment, I realized that I had forgotten to put on my engagement ring once again. Jacob was probably in the bedroom, staring at the little ceramic cup on the bedside table that cradled my meager jewelry collection. Maybe he'd take a few photos of the ring, zoomed way in on the diamond, the focus on the gold band blurry to make the stone look as bare and lonely as possible. Or I was just being dramatic and he had already left the apartment to meet his buddies at the gym.

The radio station was about a thirty-minute walk from our building. The one thing I loved about living downtown was the lack of need for a car. I didn't own one. Not only did I save on gas, but it was one less bill that I had to rely on Jacob's parents to pitch in for. Offices, restaurants, bars, and gyms were all just a stroll away, and if I needed to get any farther, the bus and light rail systems worked like a charm. The city was so different from the wide-open spaces of my youth, and while I sometimes found the tall buildings and fast pace alarming, I preferred it to the alienating silence of my previous life.

A gush of warm air made my cold nose and ears tingle as I

pulled open the door to the station. It was a modest business, with just a control room, a studio, and a storeroom that doubled as our break room through the back. Nate sat at the desk in the control room, staring through the window into the studio. Kenny, our mild-mannered control technician who wore noise-canceling headphones at all times and spoke to no one ever, sat next to him. The on-air light flared red as the new intern, a girl I'd found at the local university who'd majored in broadcasting and dubbed herself Aphrodite, chattered away into the mic.

"Next we've got the new single from Walk the Moon," she announced. "And when we return, Nate and Georgie join us for a discussion on gun control. This is QRX First Watch. Stay tuned, folks."

The on-air light flickered off, and Aphrodite gave us a hesitant thumbs-up through the window. Nate returned the gesture with a smile so wide and startling that his cheeks looked as if they might crack. Then he flicked off his headphones and swiveled in his chair to look at me, his expression completely flat.

"She's boring," he declared.

"Talk-back's on."

Nate whirled around to check the button that transmitted sound from the control room to the studio. It was unlit. "That was mean."

I chuckled, shrugged out of my jacket, and draped it over the spare chair. "Give her a chance. You weren't exactly a prize when I recruited you either."

"Excuse me?" he said with faux indignation. "Whose listener count doubled when I was added to the show?"

"So you pulled in a percentage of the male market. Big whoop."

The door to the studio swung open, and Aphrodite stuck her head out. "Sorry to interrupt your little powwow, but the song's almost over. The two of you should probably get in here."

"Sure thing," Nate said. The intern retreated, and he fixed me with an incredulous stare. "She's been working here for five minutes, and she's already bossing us around. I can't deal. I know you're a feminist, but—"

I flicked the shell of his ear. "Don't even try to finish that sentence. Come on. Let's get in there before our new boss fires us."

We left Kenny to manage the controls and joined Aphrodite in the booth. Before I could sit down in front of the mic, she wrung my hand so fiercely that the bones in my wrist cracked.

"Georgie," she said. "Nice to see you again. I love the hair! I always thought about dying mine purple, but it's already red, so I'd have to bleach it and then dye it, and it would probably be a big mess and a waste of time. Did you shave the side yourself?"

"Nate did it, actually," I told her, settling into one of the plush red rolling chairs that we kept in the studio. He caught my eye across the table and made a face. "Have a seat, Aphrodite. Kenny's got the countdown for us."

Through the window, Kenny held up five fingers and put them away one by one. When the last one joined his fist, I leaned toward the pop filter.

"Gooooood morning, Denver, and welcome back to QRX First Watch," I crooned into the mic, dropping my voice into a smoother, more personable version of its original. "I'm your host, Georgie Fitz, and joining us for today's Dirty on the Thirty is our own Nate Vega, who you know and love—"

"What's up, Denver?" Nate interjected.

"—and our new intern, Aphrodite," I went on. "Before you call in, folks, she is *not* the Greek goddess of love and beauty in disguise. I already asked."

"Sorry about that," Aphrodite chimed in.

"The subject for today's Dirty is gun control," I said. "What with the unfortunate and tragic incidents that have occurred in the recent history of this country, the question remains: Should the average American have the power to purchase these weapons? Aphrodite, why don't you start us off?"

Aphrodite cleared her throat. "Well, I'm a pacifist—"

Automatically, Nate groaned. "Here we go. There's always one hippy-dippy peacemonger who thinks we can save the world with positive energy and chakra candles."

Aphrodite pursed her lips, cocking her head and aiming a stare at Nate like a loaded gun. "If you'd let me finish. I'm a pacifist, but my motto has always been 'Do no harm. Take no shit.' That being said, gun control isn't a question of banning all firearms like most people think. People should be allowed to protect their homes and families with a modest handgun, but when it comes to semi-automatic rifles, it's a different story. The average American doesn't need high-power weapons."

"When was America ever about 'need?'" Nate countered. "We want guns, so we have them. I'd agree that the process of procuring high-power weapons is a bit lax—"

"A bit?" Aphrodite repeated.

"*But* there's no point in banning rifles entirely," Nate continued as if he hadn't heard her.

"No point?" Aphrodite said. "What about preventing another mass shooting?"

"People are going to get their hands on guns no matter what," Nate said. "Even if they have to go through illegal means. There might come a time when we really do need them, and I'd rather be safe than sorry. All I'm saying is that when the zombie apocalypse rolls around, I'd want that AR-15 to blow a few faces off."

"Okay," I said before Aphrodite could jump in again, her face reddening with rage. "Let's take it back to examine these points one by one. Then we'll take a few calls from our listeners."

I LEFT THE STATION EARLY, unable to take much more of Nate and Aphrodite's bickering. While it was great to have representation for both sides of a debate, a lot of the useful information that I wanted to spread to the general public got lost in the heat of disagreement. Dirty on the Thirty was a segment that I'd specifically tailored for intelligent, opinionated conversations, and I didn't want it to devolve into a verbal ping-pong match on par for drama with one of the various *Real Housewives* reality shows. Either Nate and Aphrodite needed to learn how to argue effectively, or they'd both be out of a job.

In the stairway of the apartment building, I ran into a short, olive-skinned woman with smooth black hair. I smacked my palm against my forehead. "Nita! Crap, I'm so sorry. I totally forgot to call you earlier. I have to cancel our dinner plans tonight."

Nita was a few years younger than me, but as a first-year med student, she had more maturity and determination than most of my and Jacob's mutual friends. She hoisted an armful of anatomy textbooks higher in her grasp and shrugged. "No big deal. I should put in some extra study time anyway. You got a hot date or something?"

"Yeah, actually," I said. "Jacob's got a night at the park planned."

"Aw, are you going to share a funnel cake on the Ferris wheel?"

"Hell no. I want my own funnel cake."

Nita laughed, dislodging a binder from her grasp. It hit the floor and spat notes down the stairs. "Damn it."

"I got it." I trotted down the steps to collect the papers then tucked them back into the binder. "There you go."

"Thanks," she said, perching her books between her torso and the wall of the stairway. "Is everything okay with you and Jacob?"

"Of course. Why?"

"The walls are thin, Georgie."

I chewed on my bottom lip, a nervous habit from childhood

that I'd yet to kick. "You heard us yelling at each other last night."

"I think the whole floor heard you."

"Ugh." I slumped against the wall, the safety handrail jutting into my side. "We keep arguing about stupid stuff. Last night's fight started because he didn't squeeze the toothpaste to the top of the tube."

"What an animal."

"I don't know what's wrong with me," I told her. "I love him, you know? But ever since we got engaged, I keep noticing more and more of his flaws. Then I think to myself, is this really the guy I want to be with for the rest of my life?"

"Well, divorce is one in two these days, so odds are it won't be for the rest of your life."

I looked up at her from the step below. "Usually, I'm all for the dry humor and sarcasm, but I need some rom-com level bridesmaid enthusiasm and reassurance from you right now."

"Right. Sorry." She shifted her stance, perched a hand on her hip, and pursed her lips in her best impression of a duck. "It's just nerves, Georgiana! Don't you worry. Jacob is *such* a wonderful guy. And he's hot. And he's conveniently rich."

I rolled up a page from her notes and swatted her playfully over the head. "Not helping."

She snatched the paper back and smoothed it out. "I'm kidding. Seriously, you and Jacob are good together. You've told me a million times that his quirks even yours out. You fell in love with him for a reason. Try to remember why."

I sighed as I held the door to our floor open for Nita. "You're right. If he's being clingy, it usually means that he thinks I'm pulling away."

"Are you?"

"I don't know," I said. "I guess we'll find out tonight."

. . .

14

IN MY BOOK, it was a perfect night to spend at the park. The wind was chilly enough to justify the purchase of hot chocolate, but not so cold that it was miserable. Jacob and I held hands as we strolled through the park, smiling as little kids whacked moles and raced horses at the brightly lit arcade games. Their parents stood farther back, supervising at a distance. Most of them nursed a cheap beer. Overhead, the thrilling hoots and hollers of the roller coaster riders pierced the air. The lights were too bright to see the stars, but a radiant silver sliver of the crescent moon decorated the navy sky. We rode the merry-go-round and the tilt-a-whirl, playing like middle schoolers, but when we got on the Ferris wheel and it took us above the bustling crowds where no one was watching, Jacob couldn't help but take advantage of his captive audience.

"So you want a fall wedding."

I kept my eyes trained on the horizon, trying to ignore the ominous creaking sounds that emanated from the swinging hinges of our pod. "It's my favorite time of year. We could have the reception outside."

"What is it with you and the cold?" Jacob asked, trapping my knees between his. "An outdoor wedding in October? All of our guests would freeze."

"It doesn't have to be October," I countered. "September would be nice too. Just as long as the leaves have already started to change. Those are the colors I want. And no one's going to freeze. They make space heaters for a reason."

"You want orange as your wedding color? My mother's going to die."

"This isn't your mother's wedding," I said, a sharp edge to my tone. "And I didn't say orange. I said fall colors. Hues that remind me of autumn. Red, gold, brown—"

"*Brown?*"

"Yes, brown."

The Ferris wheel jolted to a halt as our pod approached the

top. We swung a little back and forth. I peered over the edge, but Jacob pushed me against the padded cushion. "Don't do that."

"Why not? It's not like I'm going to jump."

"It's dangerous."

"I laugh in the face of danger."

"Okay, Simba," Jacob countered. "But I like having you alive. Why the hell did we get on this thing? I hate heights."

"You thought it would be romantic to kiss at the top."

"I was wrong," he said. "It smells like corn dogs up here."

"Oh, sorry. That's me."

He cracked a grin at the joke as the Ferris wheel lurched into motion again. As it rounded the top and floated toward the other side, Jacob traced the bones of my knee through my jeans.

"So," he said tentatively. "Are you going to invite your parents?"

My spine stiffened. "What?"

"To the wedding," Jacob clarified. "They should be there. It's a huge step, Georgie. Don't you think your parents ought to be around on the most important day of your life?"

The Ferris wheel was a trap. It stopped and started to let people on and off at the bottom, the pace at which we neared the exit infinitely too slow. The rickety metal contraption wasn't a fun romantic ride. It was a way for men to ensnare their girl-friends—sorry, *fiancées*—in order to talk about things that didn't need to be addressed. Not now and not ever.

"How many times do I have to tell you?" I said. "I'm not in contact with my parents."

"I haven't even met them—"

"Because I don't talk to them," I told him as we bumped another space closer to the exit of the ride. "Why are you so caught up on this? Not everyone has a family like yours, Jacob."

"I just think that this is a perfect opportunity to reach out to them," he pressed. "Don't you agree? It would be a gesture of decency—"

I clapped a hand over his mouth. "Stop. Okay? Just stop. I don't speak to my parents for a reason. They will not be at our wedding. It's not a discussion. It's fact. Leave it alone."

We finally bounced down to the platform below, and I jumped out so quickly that the ride attendant, a gangly boy with greasy black hair, had to steady the swinging pod so that Jacob could exit too.

"Hey." Jacob caught me and spun me around in front of a stand selling snow cones. "I'm sorry, all right? Can we just have a nice evening for once? I feel like all we do is bicker with each other."

"Because *you* keep bringing up things that make me want to fight with you," I said, crossing my arms. "I don't want to repeat myself once I've told you something."

"I know," he replied. "That's my fault. I haven't been listening to you."

"No, you haven't."

A yell of joy echoed overhead as a roller coaster zoomed over top of us. Jacob glanced skyward and grinned. "Are you ready?"

"For what?" I asked.

"I promised you that I'd ride the coaster until I puked." Jacob winked and coaxed my arms out of their taut positioning. There was that charm I loved, the brazen confidence that made me fall for him in the first place. "And I don't break my promises."

2

My pulse raced as quickly as the coaster sped along the tracks. Something was terribly wrong. My head roared with the screams of our companions and the rumble of the wheels against the track. The power to the city was out as far as I could see, and the moon overhead wasn't enough to illuminate our path. Without light, there was no telling which way we were headed next. We blasted through a corkscrew at top speed and hit another loop, but as the coaster train headed up the next hill, gravity worked its magic. The train slowed, coasting toward the top of the hill, but at the peak, we stopped and began to roll backward.

The shrill screams increased, and I crushed my eyes shut as the coaster reversed its route. Jacob let out a yell that tugged at my heartstrings. I had practically forced him to get on the ride. He had never been a fan of roller coasters, and now it was my fault that he was experiencing the one thing that he feared the most. Thankfully, the train lost momentum at a rapid pace. It rolled up the hill that we had just come from, switched direc-tion, and rolled forward again. As it continued to trundle back and forth, the riders stopped screaming, until we finally came to rest in the valley between the hills.

I groped for Jacob in the darkness. "Babe, are you okay?"

I wasn't the only one checking in on their loved ones. Worried murmurs broke out all along the coaster, filling the air with a buzz of concern. Some of the younger kids were crying. I strained to catch a sound from Jacob, anything that would let me know he was all right, but all I heard were the rapid, shallow breaths of hyperventilation.

"Jacob," I said firmly. My eyes started to adjust to the pitch-black night. His ghostly fingers gripped the handles of his harness tightly enough to cut off the circulation. I pried open the hand closest to me. His fingers were freezing. "Jacob, breathe. Just breathe. Everything's going to be okay."

But panic had begun to set in on the train. Voices lifted into the air.

"Help! Help us!"

"We're stuck!"

"I'm going to sue this place for everything they're worth."

"Don't listen to them," I ordered, tightening my grip on Jacob's hand. "I'm sure it was just a fluke. The fire department will come and get us out soon, okay?" He stared straight ahead, gasping for air. "Jacob, I need you to talk to me. Look at me. *Look at me!*"

When I pinched the skin on the back of his hand between my finger and forefinger, his head jerked in my direction, and he peered over the cumbersome neon-green harness. His eyes were impossibly wide, pupils blown so big that his irises looked black.

"Good," I breathed. "Are you okay? Are you hurt? Your neck maybe?"

He shook his head.

"Good," I said again. "Can you talk to me?"

His lips parted. A sprinkle of powdered sugar, left over from our indulgement in funnel cakes, dusted his top lip. His voice came out in a hoarse whisper. I leaned forward, struggling against my harness to catch his question.

"What the hell is happening?" he whispered.

It was the question on everybody's mind. The world had gone dark but not silent. Crash after crash echoed from the nearby interstate, the crunch of fenders unmistakeable. People cried and yelled and spoke over one another. Other than that, everything else was eerily quiet. The whir of the theme park attractions had died off. The arcade games quit their eerie tinkly tunes. The buzz of the street lights was noticeably absent. Phones didn't ring and car engines didn't turn over. Above all, the cold black night pressed in on all sides.

"I have no idea," I whispered back.

The worst part was the waiting. The minutes ticked by, and no one came out to tell us what was happening. It was the type of situation that warranted an announcement over the ride's audio system, but the speakers perched over the tracks remained silent. I knew enough about roller coasters to know that we shouldn't have stopped anywhere other than one of the block brake platforms stationed throughout the ride. The coaster was programmed to land on those platforms in case of damage or system failure. The fact that we were stuck at the bottom of the track was a bad sign. Something had completely fried the coaster's system, and from the looks of things, it had fried the rest of Denver too. My phone was inaccessible, tucked securely into the back pocket of my jeans to keep it from flying away during the ride. In the row in front of us, another guest managed to wiggle his iPhone free, but when he pressed the home button, the screen remained blank.

"My phone's not working," he called out to the rest of the train.

"Mine either!"

"Same up here."

"Does anyone have the time?" I asked, keeping a firm grip on Jacob's hand to let him know I was still with him.

"My watch is dead," someone called back. "Anyone else?"

"Mine's out too."

"It's ten to eight," another voice, light and young—a little boy's maybe—floated up from the front of the train.

"Your watch works? How?"

"It was my grandfather's," the boy replied. "It's old. Mechanical. No electronic components."

No electronic components. The kid had been the first to realize it, or at least the first to say it out loud. Someone pointed into the black sky.

"Look!"

Everyone's heads tipped upward. Behind the clouds, a white light mushroomed in the atmosphere and radiated outward. It was almost as if the heavens were opening up, the world gone dark to call attention to their presence, but in all of those stories, the angels never showed up before the ultimate destruction of everything on earth.

"It's a solar flare!"

"It's a bomb!"

"It's a what?" Jacob asked, his voice trapped in an interminable whisper. The coaster had swept his golden hair away from his forehead. It stood straight up like a cartoon character's. I would've giggled if the moment weren't weighed down by the mysterious light in the sky.

"It's not a bomb," I said automatically, but the words felt heavy and wrong on my tongue, and a pang of guilt ricocheted across my conscience, the same way it always did when I told a lie. "It can't be. We would have heard it."

And because this wasn't a world where bombs detonated while people were enjoying a pleasant evening at a theme park. This was Denver, where the Rocky Mountains met the sky, and the crisp air staved off the smell of exhaust in the city. This was

First World America, where we lived in excess of material goods and relied on the country-wide grid to function from day to day.

I didn't know how long it took for the light to subside. It could've been minutes or hours. The harness rubbed against my sweater, chafing the skin of my shoulders. A prickling began in both of my legs as the deep bucket seat restricted blood flow to my lower half. I wiggled my toes and straightened my legs, trying to get everything moving again. How long had we been sitting here? Someone should have done something by now. At the very least, the employees that ran the attraction should have updated us on the situation. Restlessness set in. The other guests grew uneasy, complaining and commiserating about our terrible luck. Next to me, Jacob was hauntingly quiet.

"Still with me?" I asked him, giving his hand another squeeze.

"Mm-hmm." The whites of his eyes reflected the moon overhead. "How long do you think we're going to be here for?" His tone was steadier than before. He was calmer now that there was no immediate danger other than being confined to the coaster, and his claustrophobia hadn't kicked in full blast yet.

"I don't know," I said. "Probably a while if the power's out everywhere."

But another voice shouted at us from out of sight. "Hello! Is everyone okay?"

The entire train clamored at once, shouting pleas for help. From the darkness, two park employees, dressed in silly patterned sweaters and khaki pants, approached the coaster. They were young—college students who probably worked at the park to make rent or pay tuition—and they definitely didn't look like they had the ability to free all of us from the coaster's locked harness system.

The first employee, a nimble young man with a scruffy ginger beard, set a ladder against the track, carefully climbed up, and stepped on the front car of the coaster so that we could all see him. He cupped his hands around his mouth. "Hi, everyone.

I'm Dave. This is Hayley." He gestured to the other employee, whose platinum blond hair served as a beacon in the moonlight as she waved. In her free hand, she held a sturdy metal bar shaped kind of like a tire iron. "We're going to try and get you out of here."

"What's going on?" someone shouted.

"Where's the fire department?" asked a deeper voice.

Dave waved his hands to settle the crowd. "We don't know what happened either. From what we can tell, the whole city is out of power. A lot of the cars in the parking lot won't start, so we're guessing that the fire department can't get here either. We don't want to leave you in the coaster while we wait for them since we don't know how long it will be, so we're going to do this like a routine evacuation."

"And we're supposed to trust you?" Jacob asked, raising his voice for the first time since the coaster had failed.

Dave squinted toward the back row where we sat. "Sir, I can assure you that we've been trained to handle this sort of situation, and we routinely evacuate this ride without issue."

"From one of the safety platforms," I called. "What about from a random part of the track?"

"I have to admit this is a new one," Dave acknowledged. "But it's the same procedure. We have a tool that unlocks each row of harnesses manually, and we're going to evacuate one row at a time. Hayley and I will help each of you down the ladder to the ground. Once we finish a row, we'll escort those four people back to the loading area and come back for the others. It's important that you follow our path exactly. There are a lot of dangerous components on the ground out here, and we don't want anyone getting electrocuted if the power comes back on. There's another train stuck at the beginning of the tracks that the other attendants are helping, so it's just the two of us. It's going to be slow going, folks, and I apologize in advance. Please just bear with us."

"We've had word that the park's medical team is making their rounds as quickly as possible," Hayley added, shouting up at us from below the track. "Before we begin, does anyone on the train need emergency assistance?"

A general murmur reverberated through the crowd. I glanced over at Jacob, who now looked more aggravated at how long we had been sitting in the train than scared about the situation.

"You're good, right?" I asked him. "You're okay to wait?"

"Yeah," he said. "Let the medics tend to the people who really need it. I can stick it out."

"Are you sure?"

He tucked his chin to look at me over the bulky harness. "Georgie, I'm fine. Stop freaking out."

"I'm freaking out because *you* were freaking out," I reminded him.

"Well, stop."

I rolled my eyes. Of course we were arguing again. Even in the midst of a city-wide blackout, we managed to find the ability to bitch at each other.

"All right," Dave called. "We're going to get started with row one. Everyone sit tight."

"Like we have a choice," Jacob muttered.

There was nothing to do but wait as Hayley handed the hefty tool bar mechanism up to Dave. He balanced along the edge of the track, his sneakers between the metal piping and the bottom of the coaster, and inched toward the first row, stepping carefully between the coaster's wheels. Hayley supervised from below, moving the ladder to match his pace. The lowest part of the track was about ten feet from the ground, not high enough to cause a life-threatening injury, but if someone misstepped, it might mean a broken arm or leg. Dave seemed well aware of this. His gaze kept flickering toward the ground as if to check that Hayley was keeping up with the ladder. He leaned into the coaster as he reached the first row and bent out of sight with the tool bar.

"One, two, three," he grunted, and with a pneumatic hiss, the first row of harnesses sprang free. The four guests, two teenagers and two adults, tried to stand up at the same time, but Dave waved them back in their seats. "One at time, please. We need to do this as safely as possible. Ma'am?"

He rested the toolbar against the coaster, leaned against the train to secure his footing, and offered his hand to the first woman seated in the row. She staggered to her feet, grasping Dave's shoulder for balance. He helped her step over the lip of the coaster car and onto the waiting ladder then continued to hold her from above as Hayley coaxed her down from below. The woman's hands shook as they left Dave's shoulders.

"This is going to take forever," I mumbled, watching as Dave encouraged the next guest out of his seat.

"They already told us that," Jacob said.

"Yeah, but we could've sat in the front seat," I countered. "I wanted to. If we had, we would've been the first ones off the coaster."

"I don't like the front," he replied. "You have to wait longer, and it's nerve-wracking to ride up there. The back's better."

I tugged the seatbelt free of the harness. It dangled uselessly between my legs, which were now completely asleep. "The back's rougher and faster."

"No, it's not."

"Yes, it is, because the front of the coaster pulls the back, which means there's less resistance when you whip around the turns." I sucked in my stomach and wiggled around, testing the space around the harness to see if I could free myself without Dave's assistance. "Or has the ache in your neck not set in yet from the whiplash?"

"That's from the lack of brakes. And I didn't know you were suddenly an expert on physics," Jacob fired back. "Is that what you do after you finish the morning show at the station? Because you sure as hell aren't working on the radio."

"It's common sense," I snapped. "And what's that supposed to mean? Where else would I be other than the station?"

"Can the two of you shut up?"

I looked over at the seat at the end of our row, where a teenaged girl with heavy black eyeliner and fading green hair rewarded me with a dramatic sigh. She had been quiet for the duration of the unfortunate event. If I remembered correctly, she hadn't let out so much as a whoop of excitement during that first drop.

"Excuse me?"

"Shut up," she repeated, enunciating the *P* sound with an emphatic pop of her lips. "God, you two bitch more than my separated parents when the mortgage bill hits. It was bad enough that I had to stand behind you in line, but this is just straight-up torture."

Thankfully, the seat between me and the girl was empty. No one else played witness to me and Jacob being chided by a teenager.

She pointed to the ring on my finger, which I had finally remembered to put on before we left for the park. "Please tell me that's not from him."

Jacob strained to get a look at what the girl was referring to. I stuttered and lowered my hand, but there was nowhere to hide the incriminating diamond.

"Honey," the girl said, her tone dripping with condescension. "He's clearly compensating for something."

"How old are you?" I managed, acutely aware of Jacob's stare.

"Old enough to know when two people shouldn't get married."

"You don't know us."

She rolled her eyes. "Thank Wonder Woman for that."

I huffed and turned away from her, only to realize that Jacob was studying me with a glare as honed as a laser pointer. I faced front, pretending to monitor Dave's progress. He had just freed the third row. The quartet waited on the ground with Hayley as he climbed down, and the group disappeared again to return to the attraction's loading zone. There were eight rows to the coaster. The rescue process wasn't quite halfway through. With a groan of frustration, I jiggled the harness. It moved a fraction of an inch up and down, making more of a racket rather than helping my case.

"Are you trying to break the ride?" Jacob asked with a wry turn of his lips. "It won't get us out any faster."

I pushed the harness up as far as it would go and attempted to worm out. "At least I'm trying."

"What would you even do if you managed to get out?" he went on. "Jump to the ground? It's a good ten feet."

"Ten feet never hurt anyone."

"Actually—"

"I've jumped from higher than that before."

"Off a diving board and into a pool—"

"*Ahem!*"

We both looked over at the teenage girl, who pointedly picked at her polished black nails.

"What happened to shutting up?" she asked.

Jacob and I fell silent. I tipped my head back against the headrest, looking up at the sky. The strange mushroom of white light had dissipated, and now that the whole city had been extinguished, the stars blinked overhead in a myriad of patterns. As Dave and Hayley returned to continue the evacuation procedure, I lost myself in the constellations. There were stories written in the sky, legends and myths that most people read about in high school. I had learned about them earlier, studying them each night through a massive telescope as they became visible in our hemisphere. I remembered my first date with Jacob years ago. We had driven out to a park to have a picnic under the stars. After, we lay out on the blanket, cuddling together to stay warm, and watched the sky together.

"Which one's your favorite?" Jacob had asked.

I considered my options before pointing to a cluster of stars. "There. Lyra. The harp."

Jacob squinted up at it. "How come?"

"In Greek mythology, the harp belonged to Orpheus," I'd explained. "He used it to play love songs for Eurydice, his bride. When she died, Orpheus couldn't stand the loneliness, so he went to the underworld to bargain with Hades to get her back. Hades was so impressed with Orpheus's music that he agreed to let Eurydice return to Earth."

"So it was a happy story?"

"Not quite," I said, nuzzling beneath Jacob's strong chin. "Hades had one condition. Orpheus had to return to the upper world without ever looking back to check if Eurydice was following. Otherwise, Hades would take her back to the underworld. At first, Orpheus could hear her footsteps behind him, but then they faded as Hades led them through a pine grove. You can imagine what happened next."

"Hades tricked him?"

"It wasn't a trick," I'd replied, musing over the story. "It was more of a test of faith. Anyway, Zeus placed the harp in the sky to honor Orpheus's music and his love for Eurydice."

Jacob pulled me closer. "Were there any Greek myths that ended happily?"

"Not many."

Dave's face popped up over the edge of our row, ending my jaunt through a simpler time in my relationship. The rest of the coaster had finally been unloaded. Dave fit the toolbar into a notch underneath the seats and asked, "Everyone ready?"

"Beyond ready," Jacob answered.

"Here we go then. Hands up, heads back."

The three of us obliged, and Dave heaved the toolbar into

position with a grunt. The harnesses released at long last, floating upward to free us. I groaned and stretched then lifted my butt from the seat to get the blood flowing again. My legs felt as though they had a thousand pins stuck in them.

Dave helped Jacob out first. Jacob's hatred of roller coasters fueled his efficiency. He had no trouble swinging one leg, then the other, over the edge of the car and stepping out onto the ladder. When I heard the soft swish of his boots in the grass, I breathed out a sigh of relief. Dave reappeared at my level.

"Ready to go, ma'am?"

At long last, I stood up, letting out an involuntary hiss as my wobbly legs crept and itched as the blood rushed back to my limbs. I made to step over the edge of the car but misjudged the distance, and my foot caught the underside of the coaster's decorative accents, sending me sprawling forward into the open air.

"*No!*" Jacob yelled. "Georgie!"

Dave made a wild grab as I tumbled past him, but the silky fabric of my sweater slipped from between his fingers. A panicked yell escaped from my lips as I hurtled headfirst toward the dark ground. Self-preservation instinct took over, and I tucked my chin into my chest, flipping myself as quickly as possible so that I wouldn't land on my head. Less than a second later, I crashed into Jacob's firm chest, his knees bent to absorb the impact, and we both fell to the grass, bruised but ultimately unharmed.

"Holy shit," a voice said from above, and we both looked up to see the teenaged girl peering over the side of the coaster. "That was the coolest thing I've ever seen. Maybe you two really are meant for each other."

Hayley knelt beside us, forgetting to hold the ladder steady. "Oh my God, are you okay?"

Jacob helped me shakily stand to my feet, running his hands along the lengths of my body to check for injuries. "Baby, is anything broken?"

Experimentally, I wiggled my fingers and toes. A sharp pang radiated through my left hand. My pinky finger jutted out at an unnatural angle. "Just a finger."

Jacob brought my hand closer to his face for a better look. "Shit. Come on, let's get you to First Aid."

The teenager jumped from the last few rungs of the ladder, followed shortly by Dave, which signaled the end of the lengthy rescue mission. Dave immediately approached me. "I'm so sorry about that. It was all my fault. I should've had a better hand on you."

"No, I misstepped," I countered. "I don't blame you at all."

Dave patted me on the shoulder. "Even so, we should get someone to look at your finger."

"No need." I took a firm hold of my pinky finger with my uninjured hand, and with no more than a grimace, yanked the bone straight. I held it up for everyone to see. "All better. Just needs a splint."

Jacob's jaw dropped. "I can't believe you just did that."

"It's not the first time I've broken a finger. Let's get back."

Hayley led us through the yard beneath the roller coaster, which loomed like a great mythical monster overhead. The teenager walked behind me, chattering away about Jacob's heroic catch, and Dave brought up the rear. We were the last ones to climb up the rusty metal stairs to the loading platform. Everyone else had already left, and the queue house was empty. The track looked oddly vacant without a train to occupy it.

"What are we supposed to do now?" I asked.

"Go home," Dave suggested. "There's no point in staying. The whole park is down." He pointed down the exit ramp of the loading platform. "Make a left out of the ride then a right at the ice cream stand. It's a shortcut to get to the exit. We have to go help get people off of the other rides."

We parted ways, thanking Dave and Hayley for their assistance. Then we followed the teenager out of the coaster's queue building and into the rest of the park. Immediately, we were shunted in with the rest of the crowd heading for the exit. All around, people tapped their phones against their palms, urging them to turn on. What kind of power outage took out cells as well as landlines? I grabbed the back of Jacob's jacket so that we wouldn't get separated then instinctively reached for the girl.

"What are you doing?" she asked, tugging her hand free of mine.

"You shouldn't be alone," I said as the crowd jostled us along. "Is your mom here?"

She scoffed. "My mom? I'm not twelve. I have to go find my friends. Good luck, lady. Hope your shit works out."

And then she disappeared into the swarm. I lost sight of her at once. In the darkness, everyone looked the same. I tightened my grip on Jacob's jacket, pulled myself level with him, and linked my arm through his in a more secure grip. Someone bumped against me, jostling my broken finger, so I tucked it against my side as we made our way out to the parking lot.

The lot was a mess. Cars blocked the aisles, frozen in place on their way to the exit. Dads sat in the driver's seats of their minivans with the doors open, coaxing keys into the ignition and muttering words of encouragement to the cold, silent engines, while their wives kept track of the kids. Some engines turned over, eliciting both cheers from their owners and groans from those who were less fortunate. There seemed to be a trend in which cars got started. They were all of an older variety, beaten-up clunkers driven by sixteen- and seventeen-year-olds with fresh licenses. The shiny newer cars remained ironically taciturn, refusing to turn on as the few older cars navigated carefully around the cemetery of vehicles. However, when they reached the exit to the main road, they ran into another problem. The entire street was clogged with unmoving cars, some of which had run into each other. Drivers yelled at each other, at their phones, and at nothing at all to vent their frustration.

"I'm glad we took the bus," I muttered as we surveyed the chaos.

"Yeah, which means we're walking all the way home," Jacob pointed out.

"It's better than sitting in this traffic."

We passed the welcome sign for the theme park and resigned ourselves for the long walk back to the apartment. With the sun long gone, the temperature had dropped drastically. I leaned into Jacob, worming my way beneath his jacket, and he hugged me against his side. Our positioning made for an awkward gait, but at least we were warm. I took my phone out of my pocket and clicked the home button.

"Any luck?" Jacob asked.

"Nope. Yours?"

"Not even a flicker. What do you think it means?"

The buildings of downtown Denver materialized like rectangular titans, looming over the pandemonium in the streets. A wayward toddler wobbled toward us, waddling as fast as possible on his chubby legs. Up ahead, a teenager looked frantically through the crowd, her eyes aimed at knee level. I swept the toddler up in my arms, which prompted an immediate spit take over my shoulder, and made my way toward the teenager.

"Does he belong to you?" I asked, presenting the toddler.

The teenager slumped with relief. "Yes, thank God! I looked away for a second. Miss Stark would've killed me if I'd lost him in this mess."

I handed over the squalling child. "Be careful. The two of you should head home. It's not safe to be out right now."

"You're telling me."

The teenager and her charge escaped into a tall brick apartment building. Jacob pulled me closer again, and we continued through the city. The number of car accidents tripled at every dark stop light, but there were no ambulances or squad cars to supervise the madness. Good Samaritans assisted those in need, pulling bloodied women and children from wrecked sedans and trucks.

"This is bad," I said to Jacob. "What the hell happened?"

"I don't know. Do you think it's like this everywhere?"

"God, I hope not."

The light rail had stopped too. Transportation officials, drivers and workers alike, pried open the doors of the train manually. The reflective patches on their neon yellow vests glowed feebly under the starlight as they strained to free the people trapped on the metro.

"I should check on my parents," Jacob said, unable to tear his eyes away from a portly man lifting a small child from a ruined minivan. "And my sister."

"How?" I asked. "The phones are out."

"There has to be a way."

"Your parents are smart people," I told him, squeezing his arm in reassurance. "And they don't really go out on Friday nights, right? They're probably safe at home."

He relaxed slightly. "What about Pippa?"

"Pippa is a seventeen-year-old who's eight months pregnant," I reminded him. "If I know her at all, she was in the process of downing a pint of mint chocolate chip in her bedroom and calling all of her nonpregnant friends to remind them that she exists."

"You're probably right."

I swallowed hard as we passed another crash, averting my eyes from the bloodstain on the asphalt. "Let's just get home. We can buckle down and figure out what to do from there."

3

*B*y the time we reached our apartment block, a fixed sense of nausea had moved into my stomach with no intention of relieving itself. No matter where I looked, someone was hurt or in trouble. People cried for help, and no one answered. We had personally stopped a number of times to assist someone. Jacob had teamed up with another man to lift a fallen tree trunk off the legs of the man's wife. Farther along, I patched up a gaping gash in a ten-year-old's forehead with decrepit bandaids from the glove compartment of his mother's demolished car. He had been sitting in the front seat when the car stopped and smashed his face against the dashboard. As I stanched the blood with a roll of gauze and pinched his skin back together, his mother cried in horror over the fact that she'd let him sit up front. Twenty minutes later, Jacob shrugged off his jacket and draped it around a shivering five-year-old as she waited for her father to free another child from a car seat. In a sense, Jacob and I had gotten lucky at the theme park. I would probably never go on another roller coaster again, but at least we had escaped with minimal injuries.

When the door shut behind us, enclosing us in the lobby of

our building, it muted the clamor of the outside world. I rubbed my eyes, wishing I could unsee the blood and the pain. Jacob jabbed the button for the elevator, but it stayed dark.

"Right," he muttered. "No electricity. I'm an idiot."

"No, you're not."

He rubbed his hands together. The cold had already begun to penetrate the glass doors of the lobby. "I guess it's the stairs then."

We headed up, plodding along at a lazy pace. My feet ached from the miles between the park and our home. All I wanted to do was fall into bed. A few people passed by us, recognizable from the mail room and other floors. We exchanged polite exclamations about the situation and wished each other luck but didn't linger long in the stairway. When we reached the door to our apartment, I silently thanked whoever had installed manual locks in the building, rather than the fancy expensive keycard pads that relied on electricity to let you into your home. Jacob unlocked the door and held it open for me. Out of habit, I flicked the light switch up.

"Damn it."

"I have a feeling we're going to be doing that a lot," Jacob said, tossing the keys onto the kitchen counter. The apartment was chilly but not unbearable. For once, I was glad of Jacob's anal obsession with keeping the balcony door shut. He vanished into the bedroom, reappeared wearing a cashmere sweater, and opened the fridge to look inside. "Are you hungry?"

"You should probably keep that shut," I said. "Keep the food cold for as long as possible. Honestly, after everything that we just saw out there, I don't think I have the stomach for dinner."

"I'd usually agree, but I bought fillet medallions to grill for our anniversary dinner next week, and hell if I'm going to let those go bad."

I wrapped my arms around his waist and perched my chin on his shoulder as he took the package of meat from the fridge. "I'd like to take this opportunity to tell you how grateful I am that you so adamantly insisted on learning how to use a charcoal grill this year."

"Gas grills are cheating," he replied. "Go wash up. I'll manage out here."

I left him to it and headed for the bathroom, keeping one hand on the wall to lead me through the pitch blackness. When I flipped up the tap, a few drops of water trickled out before it went totally dry.

"There's no water," I announced in the kitchen as Jacob seasoned the medallions with a flurry of spices.

He groaned. "You're kidding."

"Nope. Don't worry though." I swung open the cabinet beneath the kitchen sink, revealing three big five-gallon jugs that fit into our water dispenser, along with several packages of smaller bottles. "I stocked up last week when I went to Costco. We're good for a little while at least."

Jacob planted an appreciative kiss on my cheek. "Bless you and your weird doomsday tendencies."

The word "doomsday" stirred something in the pit of my stomach, but before I could lend too much thought to it, someone rapped on the door. I put my eye to the peephole and caught a glimpse of long black hair.

"It's Nita," I said, pulling the door open.

"Hey, Georgie." For once, my friend wasn't carrying an armload of books. She waved at Jacob over my shoulder. "Hi, Jake. I knocked earlier, but no one answered."

"We just got back from the park," Jacob said.

"I'm glad you made it back safely." Nita hugged me tightly. "How's it look out there?"

I rested my chin on the top of her head. "Not good. Pretty terrible actually."

She drew back, her brow knitting together. "I wish I could do something. That's the problem with med school. You read a ton of books on biology and theory and all that, but it's useless until you get into the field."

"Don't beat yourself up," Jacob said. "If the power's out to the whole city, there's only so much the hospitals can do. You're better off here with us."

"Totally," I agreed.

"I guess," Nita said. "Anyway, a bunch of us are having a party on the roof to grill all our food before it spoils. Do you guys want to join? Everyone brought whatever booze they had, so it's bound to be a good time."

"A blackout party?" Jacob asked. "I haven't been to one of those since we vacationed in Miami during hurricane season." He held up the plate of steaks. "What do you think, Georgie? Should we share the wealth?"

"I'm not so sure it's a good idea."

Jacob tilted the steaks toward him and studied the raw meat with a wistful sigh. "Yeah, I guess we only have two of them."

"Not the steaks," I said. "The party. It doesn't feel appropriate. There are people out there in the streets who are hurt and bleeding. We have no idea how far this blackout reaches. Do you really think it's wise for us to get drunk and not care while everyone else is trying to figure out what's going on?"

Nita leaned her head against my shoulder. "It's like you said. We can't do anything about it now. It's late, and it's dark out."

"I say we enjoy ourselves tonight," Jacob added. "We might as well have some fun and then get a good night's sleep. Who knows? Maybe the power will be back on by the time we wake up in the morning."

"That's the spirit." Nita gestured for us to follow her. "Come on. I'd grab a jacket though. It's pretty windy and cold up there, even with the grills lit."

"Actually, Nita, could you do me a favor first?" I held up my left hand. My pinky finger had started to swell. "I broke my finger at the park. Think you could help me splint it?"

"Sure. You got the stuff?"

"In the bathroom."

"I'll get some things together," Jacob called after us.

Nita followed me into the bathroom, where I extracted our first aid kit from underneath the counter. Nita popped it open and rifled through the contents, pulling out a splint and medical tape.

"Finger," she requested. I held it out for her to examine. "Did you set it yourself?"

"Yup."

"Wow. Nice job. We should probably take this off." Nita wormed my engagement ring off of my third finger to make room for the splint. The gold band clinked against the countertop. "Your hand's going to swell even more, and you don't want the ring stuck on there. Believe me."

"Good looking out."

Nita trapped her bottom lip between her teeth in concentration as she positioned the splint against my finger, her face inches from my hand in the darkened bathroom, and wrapped the medical tape around my knuckles.

"Are you worried?" I asked her.

"About what?"

I nodded toward the flat black canvas of the bathroom window. "This. It doesn't feel like a normal power outage. Jacob and I saw this weird white light in the sky while we were at the park. And what's with the phones? And the cars? My dad always said—"

I cut myself off, realizing where I had been going with the sentence, but Nita didn't seem to notice, absorbed in the patchwork of my injury. She finished off the tape and patted my hand.

"All done," she said, packing the supplies back into the first aid kit. "I'm going to be real with you, Georgie. Most days, you are the most laid-back person I know, but you're a bucket of anxiety about things that most people don't bother to blink at."

I released an indignant huff. "I am not."

"Oh, really?" Though she was just a silhouette, I could imagine her answering smirk. "What about last year when that storm hit? You knocked on my door at two o'clock in the morning because Jacob was out of town on a business trip and you didn't want to sleep alone. I've never seen anyone so worked up over snow."

"Excuse me. It was a *blizzard.*"

"This is Colorado, honey," she replied. "It snows."

"I did grow up here, you know."

"Never would've guessed."

Jacob popped his head in from the hallway. "You girls almost done? I'm starving, and this meat isn't going to cook itself. I also managed to unearth a few six-packs of beer. Do you like dark brew, Nita?" He glanced at the bulky metallic splint on my finger. "Edward Scissorhands?"

I stuck my fingers together in an imitation of pincers and pinched the collar of Jacob's sweater. He ducked and darted forward to tickle me. I dodged his attack, knocking into Nita, and the three of us tumbled into the bathtub, laughing. I landed squished between Jacob and Nita.

"Let's not break anything else, okay?" Nita suggested.

"No promises," Jacob said.

A faint scream from the street below ruined the lighthearted moment. Our giggles died out. Jacob's grin vanished as he lifted himself away from our dog pile then helped first me then Nita out of the tub.

"We should go," he said, ushering us out of the bathroom.

"My coat's in the bedroom," I said.

"I'll get it."

Nita picked up one of the six-packs and tucked it under her arm as Jacob reemerged from the bedroom and helped me thread my injured hand clumsily through the sleeve of my army-green coat. It was technically a ski jacket, but the slippery material would keep the biting wind on the roof away from my body. Jacob tugged a black knit hat over my uneven hair.

"Ready?" Nita asked, waiting by the door.

"Right behind you," Jacob said. As Nita left, he gave me the steaks to hold, knelt beneath the kitchen island, and pulled out a package of water bottles.

I stopped him before he could follow Nita. "What are you doing?"

"I figured we should probably try to keep everyone hydrated," he said, hefting the package over his shoulder. "Knowing our friends, none of them thought to bring anything other than booze."

"Leave that here."

A mixed look of belligerence and confusion crossed his face. "Why?"

I thought of the screams on the streets below. "Because I think we're going to need it."

Jacob let out a quick puff through his nose, a sign that he was losing patience with me. "We're out of power, Georgie. It's not the end of the world."

"You don't know that."

"Yes, I do," he insisted. "This isn't Castro's Cuba. We're not going to waste away in one night. And don't you think it's better for us to take care of our friends than selfishly hoard all of the water for ourselves?"

"Our friends are mostly your friends," I corrected him. "And they should have been responsible enough to buy their own water in case of emergencies. Hell, they should be responsible enough not to get wasted on a night like this."

"Not everyone is as paranoid as you," he shot back.

"Jacob—"

"Fine!" He slammed the package of water on the ground, picked up the other six-pack instead, and grabbed the steaks from me. "I'm leaving the water. Can we go now?"

"I'm just trying to be practical."

"And I'm trying to make the best out of a crappy situation," he replied, heading for the door. "Are you coming or not? I can always give the other medallion to Nita instead."

"I'm coming."

He didn't wait for me to lock the door behind us, breezing by Nita so quickly on his way to the staircase that his passage ruffled her hair like a light breeze. She shot me a look.

"What was that all about?"

"Don't ask," I sighed, zipping up my jacket as we followed in Jacob's wake. The staircase was cold and quiet.

Nita linked her arm in mine. "Don't worry. This will blow over."

"The power outage or my relationship woes?"

"Both, hopefully."

At the top of the staircase, we pushed open the door to the roof together. The sight was a refreshingly affectionate one. Several residents from the building huddled together in intimate groups around three different barbecue grills. Two of the grills smoked with the enticing scents of cooking food, while the third had been lit for the sake of warmth. Everyone was bundled up in hats and scarves, talking and laughing as they traded hamburgers and beers. It was like an unplanned neighborhood potluck, except that the festivities were lit by the orange burn of the charcoal coals rather than the fairy lights strung overhead. Someone had brought their guitar up to provide a soundtrack, strumming the chords to "American Pie" out of sight. A few people hummed along to the verses, but when the chorus rolled around, the voices rose to deliver the deceivingly buoyant melody to the missing moon above.

"Bye, bye Miss American Pie. Drove my Chevy to the levee, but the levee was dry. Them good ole boys were drinking whiskey and rye, singin' this'll be the day that I die."

Jacob had already found his way to a grill. He was one of the few who knew the lyrics to the verses. He sang proudly as he tended to the steak, and his performance was so impressive that the others quieted down to listen.

"I didn't know Jacob sang," Nita said to me.

"Neither did I," I muttered.

The music slowed as we joined Jacob at the grill, and he turned away from the steaks to sing the last bit of the lyrics to me instead.

"In the streets, the children scream, the lovers cried, and the poets dreamed," he crooned, putting down the metal grill tongs to take my hands in his. "But not a word was spoken. The church bells all were broken." Somewhere down below, a cry rang out, but Jacob sang on. "And the three men I admire most, the Father, Son, and the Holy Ghost. They caught the last train for the coast the day the music died. And they were singing—"

The tempo picked up again, driven by the guitar player, and everyone joined in for the last few repetitions of the chorus, drowning out the faint sounds of struggle and discomfort in the streets. My throat tightened as I focused on the fervent request in Jacob's warm eyes to just exist in that moment with him, to revel in the humanity of it all. He drew me closer and closed out the last line of the song in complete silence, the guitar and other voices fading out to let Jacob's deep and resonant tenor echo through the night on its own.

"Singing this will be the day that I die…"

A moment of silence followed before the rooftop burst into cheers and applause. People clapped Jacob on the back and praised his impromptu gig. He thanked each of them, but his gaze remained fixed on me as I ducked my head and wiped the moisture from beneath my eyes. He waited for me to say something.

"Your steaks are burning."

"Ah, shit."

He whirled around to rescue the meat from the grill, giving

me the time to disappear into the crowd. Someone offered me a beer, but I shook my head, bypassing each group until I reached the edge of the building. I rested my elbows on the frigid concrete and peered over. It was too dark to see anything in the streets other than the phantom outlines of cars stuck in place, but the wind whispered with tragedy. A baby cried. A dog whimpered. The shatter of breaking glass cued what probably wasn't the first of a long list of criminal activities.

The others didn't understand. A citywide blackout was not cause for celebration. The morning would shed light on the severity of the situation. People grew desperate very quickly. We relied so heavily on modern day accommodations that we had forgotten the basics of how to take care of ourselves without things like running water and electricity. Reality would set in soon, when everyone realized that their toilets wouldn't flush and they had nothing to eat but peanut butter and kale chips. The grocery stores and supermarkets would get bombarded, but with no way to pay for goods, people would turn to theft and looting. The shrewd and the brutish had the best chances of survival. Everyone else would be collateral damage.

I hung my head, releasing a sigh as I stared at the speckled flecks in the concrete. Maybe Jacob and Nita were right. Maybe I was paranoid and anxious, but that was how I had been raised, with the inveterate thought of ultimate ruin fixed in the back of my brain. After all these years, I figured the real world might have dampened the lunacy I'd grown up with, but parents shaped their children, and I was the last person to deny that my father had chiseled me out of the same damn block of stubborn rock he'd been born out of.

A paper plate bearing a blackened fillet appeared beneath me.

"It might be a little overcooked," Jacob said. "Also, no one bothered to bring any forks or knives, so—" He produced two hamburger buns, one for me and one for him. "Creative problem solving, right?"

I mustered a smile, put together my burger, and took a bite. Despite Jacob's claim, the meat was juicy and tender on the inside.

"About earlier," he said, arranging a piece of lettuce on his bun so that it sat just right. "I'm sorry. You're probably right. We should make sure we have enough supplies for ourselves before we start handing them out to everyone else."

I wiped a dribble of juice from my chin. "Have you ever noticed how often we apologize to each other?"

"I guess so—"

"Why are you guys all the way over here?" Nita asked, sidling up next to me. She handed me a styrofoam cup of instant hot chocolate. The powder hadn't entirely dissolved yet, revolving slowly on top of the drink. "Thought you could use a hot drink. We boiled water on the grill. Clever, right?"

I stirred in the rest of the chocolate and took a sip, reveling in the warmth of the beverage as it made its way down my throat and into my belly. "Thanks."

Nita nudged Jacob over my plate. "Hey, where'd you learn to sing like that?"

He took a bite of his steakburger and grinned. "Church camp."

"I didn't know you went to church camp," I said.

"Yeah, I went every summer as a kid. I never told you that?"

"No."

"Oh."

Nita cleared her throat to fill the uncomfortable silence. "It's freezing over here. You guys should come back over to the grill. We're making s'mores next. It'll be just like Girl Scouts. Come on."

"You go," I told Jacob as Nita bounded off. "I think I'm going to head to bed. It's been a long day."

"Are you sure?" he asked, polishing off his burger. "I could come with you."

"No, you should stay," I said. "Have fun while you can."

He cocked an eyebrow at my unfortunate wording but didn't comment on it. "Okay. I'm coming to check on you in an hour though."

Jacob leaned in for a kiss. His lips tasted like salt and beer, but they were soft and reassuring against mine. I pulled away and let him return to the party, ducking my chin into the front of my jacket to ward off the wind. Nita's eyes followed me as I walked across the roof to the door. I pretended not to see her, and she wisely did not call attention to my hasty exit.

In the apartment, the silence was more profound. The usual whir of the heating unit in the bedroom was absent, along with the general hum of functioning electronics. I pulled the duvet off of the bed, wrapped it around my shoulders, and wandered into the walk-in closet that Jacob and I shared. Three-quarters of the space belonged to him. Rows of neatly pressed pants, suit jackets, dress shirts, and vests were hung equal distances apart. Beneath that, his collection of fancy leather dress shoes gleamed in the darkness. A storage compartment hid all of his casual clothes and workout gear. I knew that if I opened the top drawer, I'd find every T-shirt and muscle tank folded flat along the seams.

At the rear of the closet, my small assortment of faded jeans and practical crewneck sweaters paled in comparison to Jacob's stunning wardrobe. Shopping had never been my thing, although I had indulged in amassing an impressive array of Vans's all-weather shoe line. With the snow and the rain, it was nice to have a little variety while I kept my feet warm and dry. I sat down on the floor of the closet and shoved aside the pile of shoes, reaching way in the back beneath our hanging coats to get to what I was looking for. My fingers closed around a cold metal corner, and I drew out a fat, rusty ammunition can. Inside, encased in a smaller cardboard box, was an old antique radio. I lifted it out, closed my eyes in silent prayer, and flipped it on.

It fizzled to life, filling the closet with fuzzy static. My half-assed Faraday cage had kept it safe from whatever blast had fried the rest of the city. I fiddled with the dials, pausing on each channel to listen for signs of communication. Chances were low. The radio towers had probably felt the impact too, but if someone had managed to set up a working signal in the time since the blast, then I was determined to find it. After several passes through the white noise, I finally caught something and turned up the volume on the feeble speakers.

"If anyone's listening out there, this is Diane and Lacy from Cherry Creek," a woman's voice, distorted and imprecise, said. "We've made contact with amateur operators in the District of Columbia, who have information from government officials. From what we can tell, the entire United States and the southern part of Canada have been affected by the blackouts. Whether it was a solar flare or the result of a nuclear EMP blast, people are already claiming that the act was one driven by terrorism. Electricity is not expected to return anytime soon. We recommend that you get out of the city before it's too late. Areas with less population density will be safer at a time like this. Ration your supplies. Make intelligent choices. Remember your humanity. And good luck out there."

An EMP blast. The white burst of light in the atmosphere. The acronym triggered a hazy memory. My father's voice echoed indistinctly, almost as if it were coming out of the radio.

"An electromagnetic pulse, George," he'd said, wire cutters working furiously to shape a cage out of layered chicken wire. He was the only person who ever called me George. I always thought it was because he'd wanted a son rather than a daughter. "It's a nuclear bomb. North Korea's got 'em, and when they detonate 'em, it's gonna take out the entire grid. Gotta be ready for anything."

"If anyone's listening out there, this is Diane and Lacy from

Cherry Creek," the radio chirped again. "We've made contact with amateur operators in the District of Columbia..."

The message was prerecorded and programmed to repeat. Diane and Lacy were probably on their way out of Denver already. If this really was a terrorist attack, there was no point in sticking around. Major hubs would be the most dangerous places to be. The women on the radio were right. We needed to get out of the city.

I set the radio down and kicked myself free of the duvet, fumbling around in the dark to find the exit to the closet. When I reached the hallway of our floor, I tripped over a raised corner for the carpet, nearly twisting my ankle. Bracing myself against the wall, I forced myself to take a long, deep breath. Panic and rushed decisions weren't going to help us. I needed to be calm. Levelheaded. And just a tiny bit paranoid.

The blackout party on the roof was still in full swing. The alcohol had kicked in, and I barged into a drunken rendition of "Bohemian Rhapsody." The guitar had lost a string and dropped out of tune, but its owner played on unaware. People danced around one grill like participants in a bizarre ritual while others toasted marshmallows around another. Someone else balanced on the edge of the roof as if it were a tightrope. I rushed over and pulled the inebriated partygoer to safety by the pocket of his coat then sent him downstairs to think about what he'd done. Then I scanned the roof for Jacob and found him sharing one of the patio chairs with Nita.

"I need to talk to you," I announced, marching up to them.

"What's wrong?" he asked. Thankfully, he was sober. "I thought you went to bed."

Nita reached out to draw me closer. "Is everything okay?"

"No, and it's going to get worse," I told them. "We need to leave."

Jacob blinked. "Leave what?"

"The city. Denver. We should get out now before the rush."

Jacob and Nita exchanged worried glances. I gusted a sigh.

"Remember the white light?" I asked them. "It was either a solar flare or an EMP attack, both of which are bad news for all of us. The entire country's black—"

"How do you know?" Jacob interrupted.

"I found a working radio. Someone was broadcasting."

"Where? If everything's toast?"

My teeth worked at my lip, trimming the skin. "I hid one in a crappy Faraday cage in our closet."

Nita squinted up at me. "What's a Faraday cage?"

"It's a shield that blocks electromagnetic fields," I explained impatiently. "I used an old-school ammunition can. Anyway, listen—"

"Hang on a second," Jacob interrupted, shifting forward in his seat. "You've been hiding some weird doomsday device in the back of our closet all this time?"

"It's not a *doomsday* device—"

"Damn it, Georgie, I thought we were past all this!" Jacob rose to his feet, kicking an empty beer can across the roof. It clattered against someone else's shoes, causing a few heads to turn in our direction. "It was cute in college, okay? All the prepper talk and bugout novels. But this is real life now. You can't hide shit and not tell me."

"You didn't tell me you went to church camp."

"My mother and father are devout Christians! *Of course I went to church camp!*"

"Guys," Nita said as the growing volume of our voices began to draw the attention of the other partygoers.

"Why can't you listen to me just once?" I demanded, stepping into Jacob's personal space. "I kept telling you that something like this was a possibility. Yeah, sure, the chances were one in a million, but guess what? Here we are! And you know what? I'm one of the only people who's going to know what to do when everyone else is scrambling like idiots trying to survive the apocalypse."

"Are you listening to yourself?" he shot back. "This isn't the apocalypse, Georgie. It's a blackout. We'll wait it out here at the apartment, where it's safe, and when the power comes back on in a few hours or a few days or however long—"

"You don't get it, do you?" I said over him. "The power's not coming back on, Jacob! The grid is gone. Gone! This country runs on over two thousand transformers. Do you know how long it will take to replace them all?"

"*Guys,*" Nita said again, maneuvering herself between us. She was so short that we glared at each other over her head. At this point, the entire party had gone silent to watch our flare-up. "Calm down."

"You're jumping to conclusions," Jacob argued. "Just because one random person on the radio said it was an EMP or whatever doesn't actually mean it actually is. They're probably trying to capitalize on fear."

"Or they're smart enough to know it's time to get out of town and nice enough to warn everybody else to do the same."

"God, I can't take this anymore," Jacob said, running his hands through his hair. "Georgie, this is not one of your end-of-the-world books. This is not *The Walking Dead*—"

An explosion rent the air, cutting Jacob off midsentence.

4

$\mathcal{I}$nstinctively, everyone hit the ground. I flattened myself out on the roof between Nita and Jacob, covering my head with my hands, but the explosion settled quickly. A transformer on a nearby telephone pole had burst into flames. The wires around it fizzled with leftover electricity. The purple-white light lit up the rooftop and illuminated the sky. For one moment, I could see every horrified face around me. Then the power surge fizzled out with another loud bang, and darkness descended again.

Silence blanketed the rooftop. Then one lubricated voice uttered:

"What. The. *Fuuuuuuck.*"

Jacob lowered his hands from where they cradled his skull and looked around. "Georgie. Nita. Are you guys okay?"

"I'm fine," Nita said, coming out of her tucked position too. "Georgie?"

"Oh, I'm good," I told them. "Do you believe me now?"

Jacob pushed himself to his knees. "Let's not panic. It was probably a fluke."

"It wasn't a fluke." I grabbed Jacob before he could get to his feet and pulled him closer, grasping his face between both hands. "Look at me. I know I've told you some crazy stories over the years, but just this once, I need you to believe me. I know about this kind of stuff. Please. This is not your average blackout."

I wasn't sure what helped to shift Jacob's perspective—my insistence or the exploding transformer—but I saw the change in his face. His lips parted as if he was going to say something. His brown eyes grew darker. He pressed his mouth to my palm.

"Okay," he said against my skin.

"Okay? You believe me?"

"I believe *in* you," he modified, clutching my hand to press it against his chest. His heart thumped beneath my fingertips, adrenaline racing through his veins. "If you think we should leave the city, then we will."

"It's that easy?" I ventured.

"No," Jacob admitted. "First of all, there's no point in leaving now. We have hours until dawn, and marching around in the dark and the cold is not going to make for good attitudes. Plus, it isn't safe. We don't know who's wandering around down there. I'd rather have clear visuals."

"Agreed," I said. "We'll leave tomorrow morning."

"That's not all," Jacob went on, kneading the pads of my fingers. "I can't leave Denver without checking in on my family. I need to know that they're okay, and we should ask them if they want to go with us."

"They should come with us," I insisted. "The city won't be safe, especially for Pippa. We need to get her somewhere secure, quiet, and clean."

"Which brings me to my third point," he said. "We need a plan. We need a way to get out of the city, since cars obviously aren't an option, and we need a place to go. Any ideas?"

My teeth found my lip again. The skin split, and the familiar tang of blood touched the tip of my tongue. "I know a place," I told him. "Somewhere I used to go when I was a kid. It's up in the mountains, off the grid. If we can get there, we have a pretty decent chance of waiting this thing out."

"What about supplies?"

"We'll need a few things to get out of the city, but the place I have in mind is practically a fortress. It should be fully loaded."

Jacob worked my lip free of my teeth and blotted the dot of blood with his thumb. "If I ask you why you know a place like this, are you going to tell me a true answer?"

"Probably not."

He gave a resigned sigh. "I thought not. Nita?"

The other partygoers had begun to disperse. The explosion had put a damper on the festivities, and everyone was ready to call it a night. As they collected empty beer bottles and trash from around the grills, Nita appeared at Jacob's shoulder.

"I was listening," she said. "You guys are leaving?"

"Yeah, and you should come with us," I told her. "You don't have any family here, do you?"

"Nope. They're all in Barcelona."

"Good." I tugged her into a hug. "That means they're safe. Is there anyone else you need to check in on?"

She put her hands into the pockets of my jacket to warm them. "Not really. I don't talk to anyone at school. Everyone I know here lives in this building."

"Speaking of which," Jacob began. "Hey, everybody!" He climbed up on one of the patio chairs and waved his hands above his head. Those who remained on the roof turned to look at him, quieting their conversations. "This blackout's not going to go away anytime soon. The longer you stay in Denver, the more dangerous it's going to get. If you have the ability to leave the city, you should do so as soon as morning hits. Stock up on water and supplies. Go somewhere safe and stay inside. There's going to be a lot of crime on the streets, and I don't want to come back to this building a few weeks from now and find out that any of you got hurt." He cleared his throat uncertainly. "I guess that's all. See you later."

Jacob jumped down from the chair and clapped shoulders with a few of his muscled friends from the gym. I was glad that he hadn't invited them to join our escapade out of the city. More people meant more trouble. As much as I hated to admit it, bringing Jacob's family along was going to be a challenge in and of itself. The Masons were used to luxury cars and expensive hotels. I couldn't picture them in flannel and hiking boots as we trekked through the mountains. His parents would have to power through, but Pippa was going to present a unique problem. It wasn't wise to put a pregnant high school senior through this kind of stress. We needed someone to look after her.

"Hey, Nita," I said, pulling her aside. "What do you know about pregnant women?"

"Uh, I did a few rounds in obstetrics."

"Perfect."

Jacob finished his goodbyes and joined us, his arms laden with empty beer bottles and the empty steak package. "Ready to head to bed? We should probably try to get a decent night's sleep."

We followed the others into the stairway and made our way down to our floor. Outside our apartment, Nita hesitated before moving along to her unit at the other end of the hall.

"Do you mind if I stay with you guys?" she asked. "I don't want to be alone tonight. Not in this craziness."

"Who's the scaredy cat now?" I teased.

Jacob pinched my arm. "Hush, you. Of course you can stay with us. Come on in."

We ushered the younger woman into the apartment first. Despite my mocking, the thought of Nita sleeping over comforted me. Safety in numbers and all that. Moreover, Jacob's and my unit was the best one in the building. His father had made sure of that, renovating each room until the apartment could have passed for a New York City loft. The rest of the units in the building were fit for college students and recent postgraduates rather than anyone with a plentiful salary. I'd seen Nita's apartment. It was nice, but it lacked the extra touches that we were fortunate enough to have in ours. A twinge of remorse flickered through me. Tomorrow, we would leave our homey apartment behind without concrete knowledge of whether we would ever return to it.

Jacob dumped his armload of trash into the bin. "You two can take the bed. I'll sleep on the couch."

"Oh no, I couldn't do that to you," Nita said. "You guys should both sleep in the bedroom."

Jacob flopped down the couch and pulled the throw blanket over his legs. It only covered from his waist to his shins. "Too late. I'm already asleep."

I smiled, shucked off my ski jacket, and knelt down to free a few water bottles from the plastic package that Jacob and I had argued over earlier. "It's a losing battle, Nita. Here, take these to wash up. We're going to have to make do for now."

Nita accepted the water bottles and headed down the hallway. "You're too good to me."

As the door to the bathroom clicked shut, I looked over to Jacob. He had one arm slung over his face, and his chest rose and fell in a steady rhythm. I envied his ability to fall asleep so effortlessly. Every night, I tossed and turned and stared at the ceiling and let a barrage of thoughts tumble through my mind like an untuned radio. I couldn't remember the last time I'd gone to sleep like a normal person. It had been this way since I was a kid, and I had learned to function on six hours instead of the prescribed eight.

"Stop staring at me," he said suddenly.

I jumped a little. "I thought you were asleep. And I wasn't staring."

"Yes, you were." He peeked out from beneath his arm. "I can feel your eyes on me. Get over here."

I walked over to the sofa and perched myself on the edge. Jacob wrapped his arms around my waist and pulled me on top of him until I was flush against his chest. My hand sank into the cushions as I propped my head up to look at him. The wind on the roof had stripped his golden hair of product. I combed my fingers through it, laying it flat across his forehead in a style he never wore. He blew upward, and the whoosh of air sent the blond strands out of his eyes.

"Everything's going to change tomorrow, isn't it?" he asked, taking my face in his hands.

I closed my eyes, focusing on the rough feel of his calloused palms against my cheeks. "Everything already has changed. You just haven't realized it yet."

His touch drifted to the hair buzzed short to my scalp. When I'd first shaved it off, he'd grimaced at the lopsided style. Now he gravitated to that side of my head, as if the soft fuzz acted as a curious comfort.

"What do you think it's going to be like?"

"Hmm." I rested my head against his chest, buzzed side down. "Do you remember when you told me that you wanted to go backpacking through Europe?"

He played with my long violet locks. "Yes…"

"And then when we got to the first hostel, you told me that there was no way you were going to stay in that filthy room or share a bathroom with the other travelers?"

"And then we booked a four-star hotel room in Rome," he finished. "Which you loved. Just putting it out there."

I poked his side, just beneath his rib cage, one of his few ticklish areas. He squirmed beneath me. "I did love it, but that's not the point. You know what it's going to be like? It's going to be like that hostel but worse. At least that place had running water.

This time you won't be able to turn your nose up at the accommodations and run off to a hotel."

"I am perfectly capable of roughing it."

"Oh, really?" I reached past the waist of his jeans and snapped the band of his designer boxer briefs against the sensitive skin of his hips. "And what happens when you run out of clean underwear?"

"I don't know. We'll wash them in a stream or whatever."

"Can't wait to see that."

"Hey, I read *My Side of the Mountain* in fifth grade," he argued. "I'm ready to go all Sam Gribley on your butt. And speaking of butts…"

His touch wandered south. For all the arguments and the bickering, that was one area of our relationship that never suffered. From the beginning, our connection had been based in physicality. When we'd first met at a crowded club near the University of Denver, we hadn't bothered to introduce ourselves to each other. A raw undeniable energy sparked between us as soon as we spotted each other across the bar, and a minute later, I was pressed against the wall of the club mezzanine, hands in his hair and legs around his waist. It was a fiery moment fueled by neon lights, a pulsing backbeat, and the taste of margarita salt on Jacob's tongue. That was over five years ago, and while Jacob and I had had our ups and downs—we even broke up for a while —the urgency and enthusiasm for each other's figures never wavered.

Unfortunately, as much as I wanted to take advantage of our last night in our own place, we weren't alone. The bathroom door creaked open.

"All yours!" Nita called, her footsteps padding down the hallway.

I rolled off of Jacob, dislodging his eager touch, and stood up as Nita came into the living room. She stopped short when she saw us and delivered a sly grin.

"I said I'd take the couch," she offered.

Jacob rolled over, groaning his embarrassment into the couch cushions. A blush crept up my neck and cheeks, but the darkness hid the rush of color.

"Sorry," I said to Nita.

"Don't apologize." She swept her damp hair away from her forehead. "I'd probably do the same thing if I had someone to do it with. Seriously, take the bedroom—"

"No, it's fine," Jacob said, facedown in the cushions. He wasn't the type of guy to boast about his boldness in the bedroom. He remained poised and respectful in front of other people and saved anything blue for behind closed doors. "I've already died of shame."

Nita caught my eye and mouthed, "*Smack his butt.*"

I obliged.

"*Georgiana Elizabeth Fitz!*"

Nita and I burst into laughter, and Nita tossed a throw pillow at Jacob's head. "Relax, Jake. We get a kick out of messing with you."

He used the throw pillow to hide his ears, which turned bright red when he was embarrassed. "I'm going to sleep now."

"Night." I kissed the back of his hand since his face wasn't available then looped an arm around Nita's shoulders and led her down the hallway. "I'm glad you're around. We're going to need your sense of humor during all of this. It's a good way to stay sane."

She leaned against the doorway of the bathroom while I washed my face with the bottled water. "You really think it's going to get that bad?"

I dried my face and reached for my toothbrush. "I think it's better to expect the worst. That way, either you're prepared for whatever shit comes down the stream, or you're pleasantly surprised by the working raft."

"Pessimist."

"Realist," I rectified.

A few minutes later, after I'd retrieved the duvet from the closet and given Nita a pair of pajamas to borrow, we climbed into the king-sized bed and curled up on opposite sides. The sheets were cold and unforgiving. I curled my toes in and drew my knees up to my chest, hoping that my own body warmth would make up for the lack of heat in the room. I closed my eyes. A minute passed. Then another. Then several more. I rolled over and stared at the blank ceiling. Usually, the street-light outside the window cast the pattern of our curtains across the white paint like a piece of abstract art. Tonight, my makeshift gallery was gone. The ceiling was dark, and the skinny moon outside wasn't enough to penetrate the cotton fabric of the window treatments. I turned over again.

"Georgie?"

"Yeah."

Nita flipped over to face me. "I can feel you moving."

"Oh. Sorry."

"I wasn't scolding you," she said, fluffing the pillow that usually belonged to Jacob. "I just feel bad because you can't sleep. Come here."

"What?"

She patted the empty space between me and her. "I know I'm not Jacob, but there are studies that say sleeping close to someone reduces stress and encourages feelings of safety. It has something to do with lowering your cortisol levels and blood pressure—"

"Nita, I don't need the rundown on the whole study," I told her, but I scooted closer to her side of the bed. She cuddled up behind me and draped an arm casually across my waist. "Hey, shouldn't I be the big spoon since I'm taller than you?"

"No," she said. "Now shut up and go to sleep."

We fell silent again. I didn't expect Nita's trick to work. Sleeping next to Jacob did nothing to ease my nighttime anxiety.

Then again, we tended to leave several feet of space between us since he ran hot at night. As I listened to Nita breathe, the ebb and flow of it like waves against a shore, my eyelids drooped, and I drifted off in a matter of minutes.

THE SUN WOKE US, streaming through the bedroom window with something like boastfulness. I shifted against the pillows as it glowed red behind my eyelids, forgetting for a few moments the events that had transpired the night before. Then I realized that the timer on the coffee pot in the kitchen hadn't automatically brewed my usual Saturday morning cup—the aroma of dark roast was missing from the air—and the person sleeping next to me was small and soft. Jacob's snores, loud enough to rouse me from the deepest of REM cycles, did not reach their customary air raid siren volume but rather traveled lightly into the bedroom from down the hallway.

Grudgingly, I opened my eyes. Nita was still asleep, huddled under the covers to keep the cold at bay. The chill had worsened overnight, but the rug was warm from the light of the sun as I stepped out of bed, tugged on another layer over my pajamas, and slipped into a pair of boots with a fuzzy inner lining.

In the kitchen, I tiptoed around, trying not to wake Jacob as I rummaged through cabinets and drawers that we rarely opened. A collection of items grew on the island counter: canteens, camping cookware, hand-crank flashlights, bug repellant, citronella candles, matches and lighters, et cetera. Jacob and I had not been camping once together—it was too reminiscent of my childhood, and Jacob wasn't exactly an outdoorsy guy—but I hadn't forgotten the basics.

Jacob found me out on the patio, curled up in the rocking chair and drinking coffee as if it were any other morning. He peeked into the mug. "How did you make that without a working pot?"

I pointed to the grill that we kept on the patio. "Boiled water on the grill like Nita did for the hot chocolate last night. Then I mixed in the coffee grounds and poured it through a filter. Want a sip?"

"No, thanks. I can't drink it black." He dropped a kiss on the top of my head. "I noticed the stuff on the counter. What's the plan for today?"

"Pretty simple," I said. "We pack up, head to your parents' place, and try not to get caught up in the bullshit in the process. As soon as we pick up your family, it's out to the Rockies."

"But how are we supposed to get there?"

"We didn't buy those expensive road bikes for no reason," I reminded him. "They're perfect for getting through the city. It's about thirty blocks to your parents' apartment. We could cover that in less than an hour. And Nita has a mountain bike, so she's good too. Are you sure you don't want some coffee? The caffeine kick might help."

Jacob caved in, took a sip, and wrinkled his nose at the bitter taste. "I wasn't so worried about making it across town. I was more wondering how we're supposed to get up to this place in the mountains without a working vehicle."

"We'll cross that bridge when we come to it, but it might come down to a good few weeks of hiking," I told him.

A flash of panic crossed his face. "Weeks?"

"We're taking Pippa, remember?" I looked out over the city toward the mountains, trying to ignore the clamor at street level. "She's going to need to rest more often than the rest of us."

"Georgie…" Jacob fiddled with a splinter in the wooden arm of the rocking chair. "I want to ask you one more time. Are you sure that getting out of the city is our best option?"

I glanced up at him. He tried to reset his expression but couldn't mask the top layer of doubt. "You're having second thoughts."

"No," he said. "Fine. Yes. I just keep envisioning all six of us trekking through the mountains like the Donner Party before someone's cell phone rings and we all look back at the city to see every light in town on."

"The Donner Party resorted to cannibalism to stay alive."

"So not the point."

"I don't know how to convince you that this is the right thing to do," I told him. "Do I have doubts? Yes. But when it comes down to it, my plan is the safest one. If the power comes back on when we're halfway to the hills, then it will be a pleasant surprise. Until then, I think it's better for us to take as many precautions as possible."

Someone knocked on the glass door, bringing the conversation to an end, and Nita stepped out to join us on the balcony. "Ooh, coffee! Do you mind?"

"Go for it," I said. "There's no cream though."

"Please. Cream is for amateurs." She poured herself a cup and squinted into the sunlight toward the mountains. "We're really doing this, aren't we?"

"Yup," I said before Jacob could jump in. "We should try to get out of here in the next hour or so. The streets are pretty quiet. We need to take advantage of it."

"What should I do?" Nita asked.

"Pack a bag," I told her. "Not a suitcase. Something you can carry on your back. Make sure you bring enough stuff to keep yourself warm, but not so much that your back's going to hurt after a few hours of walking. Meet us back here with your bike. Sound good?"

Nita saluted me. "Yes, sir. See you guys in a bit."

She left with her coffee, leaving Jacob and me alone once more. I finished off my drink and stood up. "Let's get started."

OVER THE NEXT HOUR, Jacob watched as I packed up the essentials for roughing it in the woods. At first, he tried to help, but he didn't even know to roll and arrange his clothes to fit them all in the packs that we had left over from our backpacking attempt. I quickly showed him the ropes so that we could expedite the process, but it was almost painful to watch him painstakingly roll every single Ralph Lauren sweater into perfect cylinders before attempting to stack them in his pack. I left him to it and returned to the items in the kitchen, fitting everything into my own backpack or attaching it to the outside. As I tightened up the straps, Nita knocked on the door.

"How's it look out there?" I asked her.

"In the hallway? Pretty tame." She propped the door open with her foot and rolled her bike in. I was glad to see that she wore a practical duffel bag strapped to her back. "I don't think the people in this building are taking things very seriously."

"I guess they're mostly college students who don't have anywhere else to go." I hefted my backpack up and down, testing the weight. "Got everything you need? Winter jacket, snow pants, toiletries?"

"I think so," she said, patting her bag. "That's the good thing about going to school outside of your own country. You don't lug a whole bunch of unnecessary crap across the ocean."

"Good to hear."

Jacob emerged from the bedroom, dressed head to toe in the ski gear we usually used during our Christmas ski trips out to Breckenridge. One of his cameras—a film one, not a digital one —swung from a lanyard around his neck. He balanced his pack on his back and extended his arms out. "Eh? What do you think? Prepared enough?"

"Beautiful," I said. "But it's not cold enough out for that jacket yet. You're going to start sweating as soon as we start walking."

"Yeah, I couldn't fit it into the pack."

"Give it to me."

I squished Jacob's jacket into a spare pocket of my own pack and patted it down. Then the three of us looked around the apartment for anything we could have missed.

"What about the water?" Jacob asked, nudging one of the big five-gallon tanks that I'd pulled out from underneath the counter. "We can't carry that on a bike."

"And once people see that we have it, they'll go nuts," I mused.

"I have a wagon," Nita announced.

"A wagon?"

"Yeah, like to pull kids in," she clarified. "I babysit for one of the ladies on the first floor for extra cash. We could tie it to the back of someone's bike and lug the water like that."

"And we could throw a tarp over it so no one sees it," Jacob added. "Right, Georgie?"

"That'll work," I said. "As long as people don't get too curious, we should be okay. Are we ready to go?"

We all performed one last scan of the apartment. Jacob looked forlorn, shoulders slumped, mouth tilted downward. He didn't want to leave. Nita, on the other hand, buzzed from her coffee jolt.

"I'm good," she said.

"I guess I'm good too," Jacob said.

I hefted one of the five-gallon jugs over my shoulder to carry downstairs. "We can load up the wagon in the lobby. Let's go."

FIVE BLOCKS LATER, I realized that I had left my engagement ring on the bathroom counter. Briefly, I considered going back for it, but in the grand scheme of things, the diamond wasn't worth it. Hopefully, Jacob wouldn't notice its absence from my finger for a while, what with the metal splint wrapped around the next one over. The argument was inevitable, but I filed away the thought. We had bigger things to worry about.

In one night, the streets had already been reduced to havoc.

The wrecked cars had finally been abandoned by their owners, picked clean by scavengers in the night. Shop windows were no more. Shattered glass crunched beneath the tires of our bikes as we rode through the wreckage. People hopped in and out of the broken windows, emerging from the stores with bags full of nonperishable food, toiletries, and medication. Most places had already been picked clean, the shelves in the dark businesses starkly empty. In one alleyway, two mothers argued over a gallon of water, each claiming that their children needed it more. Our red plastic wagon, leashed to the back of Jacob's bike seat, bounced over the cracks in the sidewalk with the weight of the water jugs. I swallowed hard and faced front. We couldn't afford to hand out our limited supplies.

The bikes had been a good idea. While everybody else patrolled the city on foot, we whizzed quickly through conflict. We passed three street fights in two blocks, speeding by the aggravators before they had looked up from their fists. But when we proceeded through the busiest part of the city on our way to the Masons' expensive uptown apartment, where the intersections grew larger and more dangerous, we met our first bout of trouble. Without warning, Nita skidded to a stop, dropped her bike, and darted through the maze of stone cars, disappearing behind a white Mercedes with the hood bashed in.

"Nita!" I called, nearly running the front wheel of my bike into the demolished Mercedes. "Where are you going?" She didn't reply, so I swung my leg off the bike and put down the kickstand. "Stay here," I told Jacob. "Don't leave the bikes. Try not to talk to anyone. If someone asks you if you have water or food, say no."

"Georgie, you know I'm a terrible liar—"

I hopped over the hood of the Honda that had gone toe to toe with the Mercedes. "I can't leave her by herself. I'll get her back as soon as I can."

"But—"

I left him there. As a stocky guy, Jacob was less likely to get harassed in the streets, but Nita was a petite woman, and her firecracker attitude wasn't an infallible defense should someone attempt to take advantage of her.

"Nita!" I called out into the junkyard. No answer. I climbed on the hood of a delivery truck, shielded my eyes from the sun, and looked around. There. Nita knelt on the ground a few cars over. I leapt down and slipped through the fenders to find her. "Nita, you can't do that—oh my God."

Tears shimmered on Nita's olive skin as she looked down at the body of a middle-aged woman. The pavement was stained dark with blood. My stomach roiled, threatening to eject my caffeinated breakfast. I swallowed a mouthful of bile.

"I thought she was still alive," Nita said, weeping freely. "Why is she here? Why didn't anyone help her?"

I tried to pull Nita away from the body, but she shrugged me off. "Nita, I'm sure someone tried, but it was probably someone who had no idea what to do to save her. The paramedics wouldn't have been able to make it out here."

"It's wrong."

I knelt beside her, trying my best not to look straight at the body. "I don't want to be the one to tell you this, but we'll probably see more like her. We can't stop for everyone. The more we stop, the less safe we'll be."

Nita fiddled with something at the back of her neck beneath her long dark hair. She unclasped a necklace, a gold chain with a matching cross, and laid it on the woman's chest like an offering.

"Come on," I said, lifting Nita from the ground. This time, she let me help her up. "We should keep moving."

5

"What happened?" Jacob asked when Nita and I emerged from the pile of cars. He had been snapping photos of the debris in the streets, but when he saw the tear tracks on Nita's face, his camera fell to bounce against his chest. He took Nita by the shoulders. "Are you hurt?"

She shook her head, picked up her bike, and rode a few feet away from us. Jacob turned to me with a questioning look.

"There's a dead woman," I said. "Nita didn't realize. She thought—" I couldn't finish the sentence. The image of the woman's bloated face was etched into my memory. "Have you seen anyone?"

"A couple kids ran by, but that was it." He studied my expression, looking for hints. "Are you going to be okay? You look pale."

"I'll get over it. She won't be the last. Kids?"

"Teenagers," he replied. "They went into the corner store, but they're gone now. I think they came out with a few packages of donuts. Do you think we should grab some food too? I'm getting hungry."

"Not here," I told him, straddling my bike again. "We shouldn't go into the stores unless we have to. It's not safe. I'm sure your parents have something to eat."

"Good point. Let's keep moving."

We continued on, catching up with Nita. She let us drift ahead of her. Jacob led the way, most familiar with the route to his childhood home. We rode in silence, unable to voice our dark thoughts aloud. Every so often, I caught sight of another unlucky soul that hadn't made it through the night. Each time I did, I glanced over my shoulder to check on Nita, but she kept her gaze trained on the back tire of my bike, unwilling to accept the dysphoria of the world around us. It was real now. There was a body count.

A few blocks later, we reached the radio station. Miraculously, the windows were intact. I stopped pedaling as we cruised past it then planted my feet altogether. Nita drifted to a halt beside me. Jacob looked over his shoulder, saw that he had lost us, and pulled a wide U-turn to compensate for the play wagon's poor turning radius.

"What's up?" he asked.

"I was just wondering if there's anything salvageable inside," I said. "I have my key. I can get in."

"Why would we need radio stuff?"

"No phones, remember?" I hopped off the bike. Jacob held it upright by the handlebars. "Radio's the most basic method of communication. If I can find some spare parts—" I tested the handle of the door. It was unlocked. Someone had already been here.

"Georgie, I don't think this is a good idea," Jacob said.

"Shh. I'll be right back."

I pulled the door open and peeked inside. The windows were heavily tinted, blocking out most of the sunlight. I peered through the gloom. The control room was empty. The station had evaded most of the trouble from outside, though someone had tugged the control panel free from the desk. I inched forward to look through the glass into the studio. No one there. I exhaled the breath I'd been holding.

Something shattered in the back room. I knocked into one of the rolling chairs, sending it spinning across the room. The wheels skittered across the plastic covering over the carpet. It stopped in full view of the door to the break room. I waited, feet staggered, ready to make a run for the door if I needed to.

"Who's there?" I called out.

There was a beat of silence. Then:

"Georgie! Georgie, help—!"

"Nate?"

Without thinking, I kicked open the door to the back room and barged inside. Nate cowered on the opposite side of the room, hiding beneath the shelves where we kept all the extra bits and pieces to keep the station equipment running.

"Nate! Hey, are you okay?"

"Behind you!"

His warning came a second too late. Someone stepped out from behind the door I'd just come through, and the indisputable click of a cocking handgun echoed in my right ear.

"Don't move," ordered a low, deep voice. Too deep, almost as if the person it belonged to was trying to sound tougher than he actually was.

I slowly raised my hands to eye level. "Okay. Take it easy. You don't have to hurt anyone."

"Do you work here?" asked the voice.

"Yes."

"You know how radios work?"

"Yes."

"I need you to build me one. Your friend"—Nate quivered across the room—"is useless. Doesn't know his ass from a hole in the ground."

That wasn't true. I knew Nate. His knowledge of radio was immediate and unchallenged. He could've built a basic radio with the materials in the back room in less than five minutes. The only reason he wouldn't have done it was if we were running low on parts and he needed them for himself. I guessed that the owner of the gun had absolutely no idea what he needed for a working radio. Even if we did hand over a crystal radio, he'd need to find or build a transmitter to reach anyone.

"Now!" shouted the voice, brandishing the gun. The weapon flashed in my periphery.

"Okay," I said, keeping my tone level. "Just relax. I'll do it. I'll build you a radio."

Several things happened in the next second. The person behind me sighed, the gun dropped a fraction of an inch toward my shoulder, Nate's eyes widened, and I blinked before turning my head just enough to gauge the placement of the firearm.

In the following second, I reached back, grabbed the wrist that held the gun, and yanked it forward, planting my right foot. Using the gunman's own momentum, I flipped him over my hip. He was surprisingly light. I slammed him so hard against the floor that the impact shook the walls of the break room. His breath whooshed out of his chest in a sharp gasp. The gun came up, and for one wild moment, I stared directly into the barrel. Panicked, I aimed a kick to the side of the gunman's head. When the toe of my boot connected with his temple, he immediately went slack, and the gun clattered to the floor as the person passed out. My chest heaved as I stared down at him.

"He's just a kid," I muttered, kneeling next to the unconscious teenager. He was seventeen or eighteen maybe. His long hair and dirty jeans implied that he'd seen trouble long before the blackout started.

"Is he dead?" Nate breathed.

"No!" But I checked his pulse to make sure. It beat firmly against my fingers. One blow to the head wasn't enough to kill someone, but the kid would wake up with a roaring headache. "He won't be out for long. We should get out of here." I looked up at Nate, who was still frozen under the shelves. "Are you okay?"

"Give me a second. I just had a gun pointed at my face."

"So did I."

"Yeah, but I'm not harboring secret jiu jitsu skills," he replied, backing up against the wall as I approached him. "Where the hell did you learn to do that?"

I held out a hand to him. "My dad taught me basic self-defense. What are you doing here anyway?"

Nate grabbed my hand and let me pull him to his feet. "Same thing you're doing, I'd guess." He turned to the shelves and began rummaging through the cardboard boxes of spare diodes, copper wires, capacitors, and speakers. "This shit is going to blow over in a couple of days. Phones are down, which means everyone's totally screwed communication-wise." He held up his handful of goodies. "Except for people who know how to work a radio."

As he shoved the parts in a messenger bag over his shoulder, I noticed that the cardboard boxes behind him looked too empty. I grabbed his wrist. "Nate, you can't take all of those. I need some."

"I got here first."

"This is my station," I reminded him. "You're essentially stealing from me."

"Come on, Georgie."

I held out my palm. "Hand it over. I'll give you what you need to get a radio up and running. Everything else belongs to me."

Nate stared at my outstretched hand, hiding his messenger bag behind his back. His eyes flickered toward the exit door.

"Don't even think about it," I warned. "You saw what I did to the kid."

He bolted anyway, making a flying leap for the door. Unfortunately for him, I'd been anticipating the move. I slipped my foot in between his legs and hooked it around his calf. He stumbled, failed to catch himself, and hit the ground. I sat on his back and pulled his messenger bag toward me.

"Told you."

"Get off!"

"Nate, I like you, okay?" I said, fishing through the things he had taken from the station. As I'd assumed, he had taken way more than necessary. My guess was that he planned on selling the stuff he didn't need to the highest bidder. Nate wasn't exactly moral. "I told you. I'll give you what you need to get by." I placed the basics for a crystal radio by his nose as he struggled to eject me from his back. "Everything else is mine."

As I finished sorting through the materials, a glint of metal caught my eye. The teenager's gun—whether it belonged to him originally or not—had settled near the baseboards of the wall, inches from Nate's reach. Carefully, I wrapped up the radio parts in a spare bag I'd brought inside with me. Then I lifted myself off of Nate, darted across the room, and picked up the pistol before he could figure out what I was doing.

"God, Georgie." He sat up and rubbed his jaw. A red burn decorated his chin from where the skin had dragged across the gray carpet. He watched as I clicked the pistol's safety into place and tucked the gun into the back of my jeans. "You can relax. I don't need that, and I wouldn't stoop so low as to shoot you over a few radio parts."

"Sorry," I said. "You can't really trust anyone but the people closest to you in a situation like this."

"You're right about that." Nate sifted through the parts that I'd left him. "I guess this stuff will do."

"Are you staying in the city?" I asked him.

"Hell no. My granddad's got a place out in the boonies." He packed up his messenger bag and got to his feet. "You think it's something big too, don't you? I can tell by the look on your face."

"What do you mean?"

"This blackout isn't because of some thunderstorm or fluke," he said. "There was a blast."

"You saw it too?"

"That big-ass light in the sky?" Nate asked. "Yeah, I saw it. You and I both know what that is. We've talked about it on the show before."

"An EMP bomb."

"Yup. Guess someone finally had enough of us."

"I just didn't think we'd ever be alive to actually see it happen," I told him.

Nate drew his messenger bag on over his shoulder. "That's the thing, isn't it? We never think." He jerked his head at the teenager on the floor. "He's waking up. We should leave."

As the teenager moaned, we hurried out through the exit door. In the alley behind the station, we clasped hands.

"Good luck," I told him.

"Listen for my call sign."

"Will do."

When he disappeared around the corner, I snuck back into the radio station. The teenager sat against the wall, his head between his knees. When he saw me in the doorway, he waved a hand in surrender.

"I'm sorry!" he cried, his head wobbling on his shoulders as if he hadn't fully regained control over it. "I just needed—"

"I get it," I said. "Desperate times, desperate measures. I'm sure you had your reasons, and I have mine. Do you have an extra magazine on you?"

"What?"

"For the gun. Do you have extra bullets?"

"Yeah, why?"

"Hand it over."

His face bunched up in anger. "No. Why should I?"

"Consider it a trade." I set something down on the floor

between us. A crystal radio that I'd made years ago when I'd first started up the radio station. Usually, it sat on my desk in the control room. "You get your radio, I get your gun."

He eyed the device. "That's a radio?"

"Sure is. You wanted one, right? You did hold a gun to my head for it."

The teenager hesitated then said, "I have to find my mom. This is the only way to do it."

"Take it," I said, nudging the radio toward him with my foot. "You'll have to find a working tower. I heard a broadcast last night from Cherry Creek, so you might be in luck. Be gentle though. It's fragile."

He stretched out along the floor to grab the radio, his eyes never leaving me as I stood over it. "Thanks."

"Now the magazine."

The kid reached into his jacket pocket, pulled out a black rectangle, and slid it across the floor. I stopped it beneath the toe of my boot and bent down to pick it up.

"Did you ever read *Wonder Woman?*" I asked.

"Never read much at all."

"The Amazons had a saying," I told him. "Don't kill if you can wound, don't wound if you can subdue, don't subdue if you can pacify, and don't raise your hand at all until you've first extended it." I gestured toward the crystal radio in his hand. "If you'd asked, I would've given it to you. Remember that for next time."

I left before he could reply, this time heading toward the front door through the control room. Outside, Jacob had gotten off his bike to pace nervously back and forth in front of the station's windows. Nita picked at the rust on her handlebars, staring blankly at the ground.

"Finally!" he said when I emerged. "What took you so long? I was about to come in there myself. Did you get what you needed?"

I held up the bag of trophies. "Yeah, let's go."

We continued on, turning onto the street that led up to the nicer block of apartment buildings in the area. The sun worked its way higher. It warmed my back, bringing a layer of sweat to the surface of my skin, but the chilly wind made me clammy and cold. My nose ran, and my eyes streamed constantly. I had to keep wiping my face on my sleeve, which grew damper and damper the farther we rode. Finally, we made it to the Masons' building, but we had to wait for the doorman to let us into the lobby since Jacob's spare key card had been rendered useless.

"I can't believe you're at work today, Frank," Jacob said, clapping the doorman on his shoulder. "Shouldn't you have had the day off?"

"I worked the night shift," Frank replied as he helped Jacob steer the tricky wagon across the lobby. "I got stuck here."

"Lucky for us," Jacob said. "Listen, do you think you could keep our bikes and supplies in the storeroom for us? I'm not keen on the idea of lugging everything up twelve flights of stairs."

Frank made a gruff noise of affirmation, taking mine and Nita's bike at the same time to wheel out of sight behind the front desk. Part of me felt a twinge of insecurity. Sure, Frank had been working in the building since Jacob was a kid, but that didn't mean he wouldn't take advantage of us. It would be easy for him to ride off on Jacob's bike with the water and our backpacks.

"I'll stay down here," I said.

"Why?" Jacob asked. "We're going to need you. If you thought I couldn't pack a bag, wait until you see my parents. Come on. Thanks, Frank."

I had no other choice but to leave Frank with our things and follow Jacob and Nita up the stairs. It was slow going. We were all tired from the night before, and the lack of breakfast was starting to get to us. On the seventh floor, my legs started to burn while Jacob marched upward like a toy soldier, all of his time at the gym paying off. By the time we reached the twelfth floor, I felt as if my legs might turn to jelly, and if the wobble in Nita's step was any indication, she felt the same way. Jacob knocked on the door to his family's suite, which occupied the entire floor. A second later, it swung open.

"Jacob!"

My boyfriend's mother, Penny, was a tall, lean blonde with arms and legs sculpted like a Greek goddess from hours of yoga and kickboxing. She always smelled slightly of salon chemicals and Chanel Number Five. She was also a good twenty years younger than Jove, Jacob's father. When Jacob had first introduced me to his parents, I'd wondered if Penny was his real mother. Here was a woman accustomed to luxury, married off to an older guy with a lot of money to feed her shopping addiction. That had been my first impression of her, and while the details had not changed, I'd learned that there was no kinder or more giving soul.

"Oh, I'm so glad the two of you are okay!" she said, unwrapping herself from Jacob to throw a hug at me as well. She noticed Nita behind me. "And who do we have here?"

I held my breath until she let go to avoid the tidal wave of perfume then gestured for Nita to come inside. "This is our friend, Nita. She lives in our building."

"Wonderful!" Penny said, beaming. "Would you three like some breakfast? Leti is grilling on the balcony."

She ushered us through the suite. The place was so large that it could have fit four of our own apartment in it. This was where Jacob had grown up, high above the city in a suite that looked more like it belonged on the top floor of a New York City skyscraper than in Denver. It had four bedrooms and an office. Priceless artwork hung on the walls. The furniture was bright white, a sign that the family did not anticipate having to clean the pristine fabric themselves. It was so radically different from the setting of my own upbringing that I didn't feel comfortable visiting the Masons. I didn't belong in a place like this, with its shining tile floors and sweeping ceilings, but Jacob dragged me here once a week for dinner with his family anyway.

Leti was the Masons' combined cook and maid. Like Frank, she had never made it home the night before. That was lucky for the Masons. I doubted that they had ever cooked a meal on their own. Jove, Jacob's father, supervised Leti as she flipped bacon like a pro on the gas grill. He was a large, rotund man, over six feet tall, with a head of curly white hair that blended in with a matching beard. He lived up to his name. With his holier-than-thou demeanor and quick temper, all he needed was a lightning bolt to complete the picture.

"You're going to burn it," Jove was saying to Leti.

"Mister Mason, please, the grease—"

"I'm just saying," Jove interrupted. "The bacon should come off. Ow!"

A shower of grease popped up from the frying pan on the stove and splattered across Jove's forearm. As he swiped a dish towel from Leti's shoulder to wipe the hot oil away from his skin, a tiny smile lifted her lips before she stowed it away again. I turned a laugh into a hacking cough, and Jove glanced up.

"Jacob, my boy," he said, shaking hands with his son. He completely ignored me. "You made it."

"Hi, Dad." Jacob shifted me forward. "Georgie's here too. And this is Nita, one of our friends."

"Mm-hmm. Do you want breakfast?"

"Is there enough for all of us?" Jacob asked.

"Of course there is!" Penny answered for her husband. She steered Jove inside. "Come on, honey. Have a seat at the table. I'll make your plate."

I thanked Leti as she finished up the bacon and arranged the breakfast on a ceramic plate for me, then waited for Jacob and Nita before going inside. I sure as hell wasn't going to eat breakfast with Jove alone. I maneuvered myself to put both Jacob and Nita between me and Jove. Jacob's father and I had never really gotten along, but we pushed through by avoiding each other as much as possible.

"Where's Pippa?" Jacob asked as he settled in next to me and started eating. "Shouldn't she have something to eat?"

"She's still at school," Jove replied, biting into his buttery roll and showering the glass table with bread crumbs.

Jacob's fork clattered against his plate. "She is? Why didn't you go get her?"

"Have you been living under a rock, son? Our cars don't work, and even if they did, the traffic down there is ridiculous."

"Dad, she's pregnant!"

"Don't remind me."

Penny stepped in from the balcony with Leti, holding two plates. She placed them both on the table. "Sit down and eat, Leti. You deserve it. Jacob, honey, I'm sure Pippa is fine. Saint Mark's is probably well-prepared for something like this."

"It's a private school, not a fort, Mom," Jacob said, his bacon and eggs going cold. "We have to go find her. She could be in trouble."

"She's the one who wanted to keep going to school after all of *this*." Jove circled a hand around his own ample stomach. "If she agreed to be homeschooled like I wanted—"

"Pippa is responsible for her own decisions, Jove," Penny said.

"Yes, so she's responsible for this one," he replied. "She can wait this out at the school. When the power comes back on and the police clear off the roads, we'll go pick her up."

I swished orange juice around in my mouth, letting the tang against my taste buds wake me up. It wasn't quite cold enough, but the Masons' gigantic stainless steel fridge had at least maintained its temperature long enough to keep the juice from spoiling. "Sir, I hate to break it to you, but the power isn't going to come back on," I said to Jove. "The blackout was from an EMP."

"A what now?"

"An electromagnetic pulse—"

Jacob squeezed my thigh under the table, a silent request to stop talking.

Jove peered at me from across the table, one eye squinting more than the other. "You know, I listen to your radio show, Georgiana. It boggles my mind that you can spread such inane propaganda like that. It shouldn't be legal."

"It's not propaganda—"

"Jacob's told me all about your little doomsday prophecies," Jove went on as if I hadn't spoken at all. "He might entertain them, but I won't."

"Dad," Jacob warned. His fingers tightened on my leg, but I wished he would let go. "Stop talking."

"This is my house!"

His fist fell upon the table, causing the plates to clatter against the glass. A sausage rolled off of Nita's plate and onto her lap. Penny cleared her throat, and Jove fell silent at once. The color drained from his ruddy face as he made eye contact with his wife.

"Dear," she said. "Perhaps we might want to consider listening to what the kids have to say. You have to admit it. This is all a bit funny."

"We're leaving the city," Jacob announced. "We're heading up into the mountains where it's safe, and I want you to come with us."

Jove barked out a laugh. "Come with you? Where are you going? What supplies do you have? How are we supposed to get into the mountains without a car? Goddamn it, Jacob, I thought you were a smart kid. What the hell happened to you?"

My face burned as the unspoken answer weighed down the dining room. *I* happened to Jacob. I was the one who'd convinced him to leave town. I had agreed to stop by his parents' house. Granted, I cared more about Penny and Pippa than I did for Jove, but he was Jacob's father, so I naturally had to include him. Now Jove was being an ass, as usual, and Pippa wasn't here, further stunting our progress.

"We should go get Pippa," I said, pushing my plate away from me. I'd lost my appetite. "She needs to be with her family, especially now."

Nita rose with me as I left the table and escaped into Jacob's old bedroom. She closed the door behind her, anticipating my explosion.

"I should have known," I said, pacing between Jacob's twin-sized bed and the chin-up bar mounted to the wall. "I should have known better than to come here. That man—"

"Georgie, relax," Nita said. "How far is Pippa's school?"

"Ten blocks maybe?"

"That's not far," she assured me. "You and Jacob can go get her. I'll stay here with his parents and get them ready to go."

I flopped down onto Jacob's old bed and pressed my face into the pillows. Somehow, they still smelled like him even though he hadn't slept here in years. "They don't even want to go!"

"I'll convince them," Nita said. "Believe me, I can be very persuasive. Don't worry, okay? By the time you get back with Pippa, I'll have them ready to get out the door."

I peeked out from beneath the pillow. "Really?"

She sat down on the bed next to me. "I trust you, okay? Jacob's dad may be boneheaded, but I'm not stupid enough to ignore the signs. We're getting out of here, and if Jove wants to stay behind, I say we let him."

Someone knocked on the door. "Georgie? Nita? It's me."

"Come in," Nita called.

Jacob slipped inside. "I'm sorry about that. My dad—he's an idiot. Just ignore him. I already told him that we're going to go get Pippa no matter what. I have to know that she's okay. Are you ready to head out?"

I got up from the bed. "Boy, am I ever."

"You coming, Nita?"

She shook her head. "I've got a mission here."

So it was just Jacob and I that braved the twelve flights downstairs again and headed out into the cold. We left the bikes with Frank since Pippa wouldn't be able to ride one on her own anyway. Jacob held my hand as we walked through the streets, though it was more for his comfort than mine. What Jove had said irked me, and the thought that Jacob was talking to his parents about me behind my back didn't sit well. We were engaged, for Pete's sake. Jove and Penny were going to be my in-laws. Penny, I didn't mind, but I had a feeling that Christmases with the Masons were going to be really fun with Jove around.

The streets weren't getting any better. In fact, it was getting worse. Multiple times, Jacob pulled me down behind a car or forced us to duck into an alley in order to avoid someone. People took baseball bats to car and shop windows. They fought with each other over the simplest things like hand sanitizer or a package of baby wipes. I flinched each time a punch landed against someone else's cheek. The teenager's pistol from the radio station pressed against my spine. I had to stop myself from instinctively reaching for it. No one else knew that I had it—Jacob didn't know that I could shoot a gun at all—and I wanted to keep it that way for as long as possible.

We kept moving through the surreal landscape. In less than a day, Denver had disintegrated into madness. I could only imagine what it would look like in a week. At this rate, the death toll would skyrocket in a matter of days. I'd seen enough death already, bodies splayed out across the hoods of their cars or slumped over the steering wheels. The stench would grow worse with each passing hour unless someone organized a removal of the corpses. I almost took my hand from Jacob's, but silent tears streamed down his cheeks as we continued up the block toward St. Mark's, so I let him squeeze the blood out of my fingers for as long as he needed.

A few blocks ahead, the red brick building of the prestigious private school loomed, casting a shadow on the sidewalk below. I hoped Pippa had stayed put and holed up in a safe place. Knowing her, I was sure that she had. She was the sharpest seventeen-year-old I'd ever met, with a tongue to match, and she hadn't let the inconvenience of an accidental pregnancy stop her from getting an education. On the contrary, she'd written such a stunning personal statement on the judgement she received as a pregnant teenager that she had already been shortlisted for interviews at Columbia, Brown, and Dartmouth. She would have her pick of universities.

Unexpectedly, Jacob yanked me off the sidewalk and forced me down behind a stack of aluminum trash bins. I flatted out my left hand to steady myself, and the metal splint on my pinky finger scraped across the asphalt.

"What?" I demanded. Saint Mark's was so close. All I wanted to do was get inside the safety of the wrought-iron gates.

Jacob hushed me. A gaggle of voices floated through the air.

"Hey, pretty lady. Where you goin'?"

"Where's your mama?"

"You out here all alone?"

Three men. Maybe more if the others weren't as vocal. And someone else. Someone smaller and much more vulnerable.

"No." The reply was high-pitched but firm. A little girl's. "My big brother's around the corner."

"Really? Your big brother?" the first voice said. "I don't see him. What about you, boys? See a big brother anywhere?"

"Nope."

"No, big brothers here."

"You know, pretty lady," the first voice went on, "it's not polite to lie. Why don't you come with us? We'll get you home to your mama."

"Don't touch me!"

I rose from my crouch, my hand on the pistol at my waistband.

6

"*W*hat the hell are you doing?" Jacob growled.

I ignored him, emerging from our hiding place behind the trash cans. I kept the pistol behind my back as I approached the gaggle of men. There were three of them, each in their thirties or forties, and the girl at the center of their party could not have been older than twelve. She shook like a leaf as they advanced on her, eyes darting in every direction as she looked for an escape. Quick as lightning, she nailed one guy in the crotch and tried to sprint past him as he doubled over, but one of the others took hold of her arm and held her in place.

"I don't think so, girly," the man said. From the looks of it, he was the group's ringleader, though he was shorter and stockier than the men who flanked either side of him. "We're going to teach you a lesson."

"Let her go."

Three pairs of eyes, each more malicious than the last, turned to look at me. I squared my shoulders. The gun trembled in my fingers. Jacob drew level with me, drawing a small burst of confidence from beneath my anxiety. Jacob could be a threatening presence when he wanted to be. Even so, it was three against two.

The ringleader chuckled, tossing the girl away from him. She tripped and stumbled to the ground but automatically scrambled back to her feet. "Nothing to see here, folks," the ringleader said, blocking the girl's escape again. "You should be on your way."

"I said let her go," I repeated.

"She's my little sister," the man said, smirking.

"No, I'm not!" the girl shrieked, kicking out at the man's shins. The other, who had recovered from her crotch shot, wrapped her up in a bear hug.

Jacob stepped forward, closing the distance between us and the trio. "I would do what my fiancée asks of you."

The ringleader stepped forward too. "Or what? It's three against one, buddy. You really think you can take all of us?"

He planted his hands against Jacob's chest, but before he could shove him away, Jacob trapped the man's hands against his body and yanked him forward, pulling him off of his feet. It triggered an immediate response from the other two, who sprang into action. They jumped Jacob in a flurry of fists. I drew the gun. I aimed at the sky. I fired a shot.

There was a beat of silence before screams echoed from around the block. The men disengaged from Jacob, pulling each other out of the fight. They stumbled backward, eyeing the gun in my hand.

"Take it easy, lady!" the ringleader called. "We're leaving, all right? Take the brat. I don't give a shit."

"Let's go, man. She's nuts!"

The trio ran off, leaping over cars and trash until they disappeared down a side street. I lowered the gun and tucked it out of sight then ran over to Jacob, who was doubled over on the ground.

"Are you okay?" I asked, running my hands over his arms and

chest to check for injuries. The fight had lasted for less than fifteen seconds, but the men had had enough time to paint a black eye on Jacob's usually flawless face. "Jacob?"

"I'm fine," he gasped, catching his breath. "Where did you get a gun?"

"At the station," I admitted. "It's a long story."

"You're full of surprises, Georgie."

"Yeah, but that's why you love me, right?"

He didn't reply. His eye was beginning to swell shut. As I helped him to his feet, I noticed that the little girl watched us closely. Once Jacob was standing, I went over to her and knelt down to be on her level.

"What's your name?"

She eyed me warily but held her ground. "Ivy."

"Nice to meet you, Ivy. I'm Georgie. Did those men hurt you?"

"No."

Slowly, I reached out to give her shoulder a reassuring squeeze. "You were really brave to stand up to them."

A dark shadow crossed Ivy's expression. "They're not the worst I've had to deal with."

"During the blackout?"

"Ever."

I frowned, resisting the urge to hug the little girl. She was well-spoken and unusually self-aware for her age, a personality fit for someone who was forced to grow up faster than she should have. "Listen, Ivy. Those jerks won't be the only people looking for trouble out here. You should go home where it's safe."

Ivy looked down at her shoes. The white sneakers were gray with grime, and they appeared to be too small for her feet. A long, ropey scar stretched across her forehead. "I can't go home. Not yet."

"Why not?" I asked her quietly.

Her muddy brown eyes lifted to meet mine. She studied my face as if gauging whether or not to trust me. "Can you help me find something?"

I glanced over my shoulder at Jacob. He shook his head.

"What do you need us to find?" I asked Ivy. Behind me, Jacob let out a gusty sigh.

"A bottle of alcohol. It can be anything," she added hastily after reading my alarmed expression. "Rum, tequila, vodka. I can't go home without something."

"Ivy, why do you need alcohol?"

"It's for my dad."

"He sent you out to find booze?" I asked her, incredulous. "In this? Does he know how unsafe it is out here?"

She lifted her shoulders. "I'd rather be out here than with him. If I don't find something to bring back, he'll start throwing things at me again."

"Okay, you know what?" I stood up and took Ivy's hand in mine. To my surprise, she didn't resist. Her cold fingers curled around the back of my hand as if she had been starved of affection for years. "You're coming with us."

"Georgie, are you serious?" Jacob asked. Though he kept his voice to a whisper, Ivy looked up between us. "We can't take her with us. We have enough on our plates already."

"I can't leave her behind," I told him. "Don't try to argue with me."

He gaped, looking between me and Ivy, then threw his hands up in the air as he walked away. "This is fucking ridiculous."

I let him widen the gap between us then followed along with Ivy for the remaining blocks to the school.

"Is he mad?" Ivy whispered up to me.

"Yeah, but it's not your fault," I assured her.

Up ahead, Jacob had stopped short of the school's gates, waiting behind a parked delivery van. Ivy and I met him there.

"What's up?" I whispered, peeking out from behind the van.

"Looters."

The wrought-iron gates of Saint Mark's were chained and locked shut, but that hadn't dissuaded a mob of frenzied people from trying to get into the school. The reasoning was sound. Saint Mark's was a large Christian private school. They fed several hundred students each day, which meant that they probably had a ton of food in storage. In addition, the school would be a relatively safe space to buckle down as long as everybody agreed to cooperate with each other, but by the the looks of the mob outside, no one wanted to share.

"At least we know Pippa's probably safe," I muttered, watching as one of the looters attempted to climb the iron gate only to fall into the crowd below. "No one's getting through that padlock."

Jacob banged his fist on the side of the van in a perfect imitation of his father. "Goddamn it! What the hell are we supposed to do?"

"You need to get into the school?" Ivy piped up.

Jacob looked down at the little girl. "Yes. My sister's inside."

"Then let's go."

Ivy marched off, leaving Jacob and me to stare blankly at each other. Then we rushed after the preteen. Thankfully, she wasn't joining the throng at the gates. Instead, she led us away from the chaos, slipping into a skinny alley that led us toward the back of the school.

"Um, Ivy?" I asked, squeezing between the brick buildings. "What exactly are we doing?"

"You said you had to get inside," Ivy called over her shoulder. "Obviously, we're not going through the front gates, so we're going to find another way in. Here."

She pointed to the iron rods driven into the red brick base that encircled the entire campus. One of the rods was missing, leaving an opening in the gate just large enough for a full-grown person to squeeze through. From here, we could enter the back door of the school.

"Did you already know that was there?" I asked her.

"Nope. I'm just good at looking for details." She slipped through the space and stepped onto the perfect green grass of Saint Mark's lawn. "You guys coming?"

I maneuvered myself through the gap and turned to help Jacob. His broad shoulders almost didn't clear the space, and the iron rods on either side scraped against his sweatshirt, but he managed to worm his way through. Together, the three of us sprinted across the lawns toward the school. I tugged on the handle of the back door.

"It's locked," I said, planting my hands on my knees and panting.

"Should we knock?" Ivy suggested, not out of breath at all.

"There's no point," Jacob said. "The school's on lockdown for a reason. No one in or out. It's a safety measure. We're screwed."

"There's an open window down there," Ivy said.

We all looked. Sure enough, one of the basement windows, level with the ground, was propped open.

"It's too small," I said. "I won't be able to fit through there."

Ivy sat on the ground and dangled her feet through the window. "I can definitely fit through. Wait here. I'll go around and open the door."

"Ivy, no—"

But she slipped out of sight, landing with a soft thud in the school's basement. "Be right back!" she called through the window before the pitter-patter of her sneakers faded out of earshot.

"I guess we should go wait by the door then," I said to Jacob. He turned without a word and leaned by the back door, his arms crossed over his chest. I took a deep breath. "Is this how it's going to be? Are you going to huff and puff because I wouldn't leave a little girl all alone out there? She's already been a huge help, Jacob."

"It's not just the kid, Georgie," he replied.

"Then what is it?"

"You put yourself in danger to rescue a complete stranger," Jacob said. "Now we have one more person to look after. You won't tell me where we're going. I'm supposed to convince my parents to leave their apartment and head to some no-name cabin in the woods because you say so."

"I thought we were over this—"

"And you have a gun!" he went on. "The cherry on top. Not once have you ever mentioned to me that you knew how to shoot a gun. Not once! It's like I don't even know you, Georgie!"

"Someone's going to hear you if you don't quiet down."

He glared at me, and for once, his eyes did not exude their usual coffee-like warmth. They were cold and hard like a polluted river. "Tell me one true thing about yourself, Georgie."

"Jacob, this is stupid."

"Just one thing. Tell me what your parents' names are." When I didn't reply immediately, he shook his head in disappointment. "I don't know if I can do this. I don't know if I can marry someone who won't share the basic details of her life with me."

"Amos and Amelia."

"What?"

"Those are my parents' names," I clarified, unable to look him in the eye. "My mother died when I was ten. She was stabbed. One night, I wanted to make cookies, but we didn't have any eggs, so she went to the corner store to go buy a carton. While she was there, someone came in and told the cashier to give him all of the money in the register. My mother tried to reason with him. He had a knife. You don't reason with someone who has a knife and a purpose."

Tears threatened to fall over my eyelashes, but I refused to let them. Jacob watched me in stunned silence as I spoke, the pity obvious in the sad angle of his lips. I went on. If he wanted to know about my parents, then I would finally tell him.

"Her death ruined my father," I said. "He pulled me out of school, stopped talking to our family, to her family. We moved out to the middle of nowhere, some piece of land that he'd inherited from his grandfather. He built a house for us. He refused to go anywhere, not even the grocery store. He knew how to hunt and fish and pickle vegetables. He learned how to reduce the amount of waste we produced. He wired a satellite dish for an Internet connection and homeschooled me himself. I didn't see anything but the fifteen acres of our property for almost eight years. Never met anyone new either."

"Georgie—"

"The trauma of my mother's death made him agoraphobic, and I was too young to realize that he needed help," I said, speaking over him. If I didn't get this out now, it would get bottled up again. "When I told him I wanted to go to college in the city, he looked at me like I was crazy. Said he wouldn't let me go, that it wasn't safe. By that time, he had built a bunker underneath our house for who knows what reason. I didn't listen. I had to get out of there, so when I was eighteen, I snuck out in the middle of the night and made a break for the city. I've been here ever since, making my own way. I haven't spoken to my father in nine years."

Silence fell. The wind whispered through the blades of grass. Jacob's breath whooshed in and out of his lungs.

"Georgie," he said quietly. "I had no idea."

I was saved from having to answer when the door to the school wobbled and Ivy pushed it open from the inside.

"Come on," she whispered, waving us in.

The three of us crept inside. I had never seen the interior of a private school before, but the cold, stuffy design made me glad that I hadn't attended one. Aluminum lockers lined the hallways, creating the illusion of rows of tiny jail cells. The marble floor picked up every single sound and bounced it up to the high ceilings. No matter how lightly I stepped, the squeak of my boots across the floor echoed from the rafters like a bird's morning call. The only light came from the stained-glass windows set high above us. We moved cautiously through a kaleidoscope of colors as the saints watched us from their glass thrones.

"There's no one around," Jacob muttered.

"Or they're hiding," Ivy whispered back.

It seemed inappropriate to speak above a certain volume. The school mimicked the holy mustiness of a church. The air was thick and smelled faintly of incense. In the darkened corridors, I half expected the ghosts of past students to float in from the open doors of the adjoining classrooms.

"Let's just try to find Pippa and get out of here as quickly as possible," I said. Chills erupted on the back of my neck as we passed a dark science lab with glowing specimens in glass jars. "This place is giving me the creeps."

It was easier said than done. The school was huge. The hallways branched off in a confusing maze, which meant that we couldn't split up to hurry along the process. Jacob was the only person who knew his way around since he had also attended Saint Mark's in his younger years, so the three of us stuck together as he led the way. We checked each classroom, squinting through the gloom for any signs of life. We crept through the library, where the scent of old pages made camp in my lungs and the stacks of books seemed to watch us from their lofty shelves. We even checked the chapel in the hopes that someone might be attempting to pray away the chaos that had rained down on us in the last day.

"Nothing," Jacob said. He balled his hands into shaking fists as though trying to stop himself from punching a hole in the wall. I had never seen him like this before, so full of raw anger. He was usually so passive and unresponsive, quick to pacify or placate for the sake of staving off an argument.

I took one of his hands, rolled out his clenched fingers, and massaged the knots of tension in his palm. "Hey, look at me. We're going to find her, okay?" Jacob's eyes shone in the warped light of a glass window. "Let's think about this. The blast hit in the evening, around seven or seven-thirty, right?" Jacob and Ivy both nodded. "That's way past regular school hours. Did Pippa have a reason to stay here that late? Did she have something to do after class, any extracurricular activities?"

"I don't know." Jacob blotted his eyes with the sleeve of his shirt. He never cried in front of me, and he was furiously trying to stop himself from doing so now. "She used to play field hockey, but obviously she doesn't anymore."

"What days does the team practice?" I asked him. "She might still go to them just for the sake of it."

"I don't know," Jacob said again, his voice ricocheting off the stone walls and echoing back to us like a ghostly choir. He tore his fingers from mine to run them through his hair instead. For once, he had not had the time to tame it with gel or mousse, but the man in front of me with the tousled locks, red-rimmed eyes, and a shadowy jawline was not the same one that I woke up to every morning. "I don't know, I don't know! I see her once a week, Georgie. I should know this stuff!"

At a loss for what to do, I went with instinct and pinned Jacob to the wall, forcing his hands to his sides. Our chests pressed together, my heart thumping against his. His entire body tensed, and I thought he might throw me off, but I took his face between my hands and brought our foreheads together to touch. Right away, he slackened beneath me.

"You can't do this," I murmured. His breath tickled my lips. He smelled like peppermint, as if he had managed to sneak away to the bathroom and brush his teeth in between breakfast and heading out for the school. "You can't panic for nothing."

"It's not nothing. Pippa—"

"We don't know what happened to Pippa yet," I said,

squeezing his cheeks to make him listen to me. "That doesn't mean she's hurt. Calm yourself down. Look at this rationally. We'll do another sweep of the school, and if we still haven't found her, then we'll walk along her route home and search there. But you can't freak out like this. It's only going to cause us trouble."

"I'm sorry."

"You don't have to apologize," I told him. "I understand. You're not used to this kind of thing, but listen to me. The sooner you start letting the panic take over, the sooner we lose an advantage over everyone else. We have to stay grounded and be practical, especially under pressure. Do you understand me?"

Jacob nodded, the rough stubble of his cheeks scratching against my palms. I pressed my lips to his, and he kissed back before drawing away and opening his eyes. He looked up and down the hallway. "Where's the kid?"

Ivy was gone. There was no sign of her in either direction.

"Ivy?" I called. No answer. "What the hell? She was just here."

We prowled along the corridor, peeking into classrooms for a glimpse of the little girl. Around the corner, near the school's massive entry hall, I noticed a door to a supply closet was ajar. I inched toward it and nudged it open. A shaft of light illuminated a collection of cleaning supplies, brooms, buckets, and mops. Behind a big floor polisher, I caught a glimpse of a keen brown eye.

"Ivy, what are you doing in here?" I asked, kneeling down to get a better look at the girl. "Why did you run away?"

She hugged her knees into her chest, shaking like a leaf, but she wouldn't look at me. She kept her eyes trained on something behind me, and I glanced over my shoulder to see Jacob standing in the door of the closet too.

"Babe, could you wait in the hallway?" I asked him. "If you hear something or someone, let me know."

"Sure." Jacob retreated, leaving me alone with Ivy.

I edged farther into the closet, closer to the little girl. "Does Jacob scare you?"

Another tremble rocked her small frame. She nodded.

"Because he reminds you of your dad?"

Another nod.

"He won't hurt you," I told her, moving a mop that blocked my path to her. "He's not your dad. You're catching him on a bad day too. He isn't usually like this, all loud and grumpy." I shifted aside a bucket and took another step toward her. "He's sad because he can't find his sister, but he's not mad at you. He's actually really grateful that you've been such a big help to us so far." I squeezed past the handle of the floor polisher, finally within reach of Ivy. "I promise he won't hurt you. No one will. Not while you're with us."

I offered her my hand. She stared at it for a few moments.

"I don't want to go back to my dad," she whispered.

"You don't have to," I said. "You can stay with us."

She placed her hand in mine, and I pulled her to her feet. Together, we made our way out of the supply closet, where Jacob waited for us in the hallway.

"Hey, kiddo," he said to Ivy. "I didn't mean to scare you. I'm really sorry."

Ivy sniffed and wiped her nose on the ratty sleeve of her sweater. "It's okay. Georgie told me that you're sad about your sister. Don't worry. We haven't checked the whole building yet."

Jacob knelt down to look Ivy in the eye. "Where would you hide if you got stuck in here during the blackout?"

"The cafeteria," she said without hesitation. "We passed by it earlier. It's in the middle of the building, so it's safest, and there's bound to be food and water in there."

"Let's go then," Jacob said.

Ivy led the way, spurred on by Jacob's confidence in her. He occasionally gave her directions to keep her on course as we jogged through the hallways.

"You're good with kids," I said to him, our elbows bumping together. "I didn't know that."

"I used to babysit Pippa when she was little," he replied. "My mom and dad thought it was weird. They didn't get why a fifteen-year-old boy wanted to look after his four-year-old sister. They wanted to hire a sitter, but I didn't mind. I loved playing with her. Kids are just—I don't know—so naive and unaffected. They don't have to think about all the terrible things yet. I think talking and interacting with them resets your perspective. It definitely helps me see things in a more positive light. Left up here, Ivy."

"So does that mean you want to have kids?" I asked as we followed Ivy around the corner.

"Yes. Don't you?"

These were things we probably should have talked about before we got engaged. Children had never been on my to-do list. While I had no qualms with other people's kids and even enjoyed their presence, I had no desire to produce any of my own. It had taken me years to shake off the feeling of dread that rode along on my back when I'd left my father's property, to stop myself from thinking that every person in the pharmacy had a hidden agenda, to keep the loud, intrusive thoughts at bay. Those habits and emotions had been hammered into me by my own father. It wasn't his fault—he was sick and confused—but the last thing I wanted was to accidentally pass on my own shortcomings to some poor undeserving baby.

"I haven't really thought about it," I told Jacob.

"We should talk about it." He skidded across a slippery part of the marble floor, nearly slipped, and flailed his arms to right himself. "And we should talk about what you told me outside."

My lungs, already working hard to keep pace with Ivy's light-speed pace, tightened up. "We should talk about it, but let's find Pippa first. Besides, we might not have a future at all."

Jacob stumbled. "What do you mean?"

"Not because of us," I clarified quickly. "We might not make it out of this blackout alive."

"Don't say that."

"I'm being realistic."

We jogged through the main entryway of the school, where an elegant staircase with a balustrade carved out of rich dark wood led to the second floor. Ivy raced past the three sets of elevators on the far side of the room and disappeared into a dark hallway. As Jacob and I caught up with her, she emerged out of the gloom and ran smack into us.

"Whoa!" Jacob steadied the girl. "What's wrong? The cafeteria's that way."

She panted hard, scanning the massive entryway from the oak front doors to the enormous staircase. "I heard something."

"In the hallway?"

"No, out here."

"What did you hear?" I asked her.

"I'm not sure. Shh."

Jacob and I fell silent as Ivy roved the room. I strained to hear something other than Jacob's deep breathing and Ivy's gentle footsteps. Faintly, the clamor of the crowd at the gate made its way into the space beneath the illustrious domed ceiling, but other than that, I wasn't sure what Ivy was listening to. She continued to trace the outline of the entryway, taking her time as she moved along with her ear pressed to the walls.

"What are the odds we picked up some crazy little kid who hears voices?" Jacob muttered to me under his breath.

"Even if she does, I'm inclined to trust her," I whispered back. "She got us in here, remember?"

Ivy moved to the opposite wall toward the line of elevators, peering up at the needle above each lift that indicated which floor it had stopped at. The one in the middle was stuck between the one and the two. Ivy leaned against the door.

"Here!" she exclaimed, waving us over. "There's someone in the elevator!"

Jacob and I sprinted across the entryway to join Ivy. Jacob pounded on the elevator door.

"Hello!" he shouted. "Is there anybody up there?"

"Jacob?" a voice replied faintly. "Is that you?"

"Pippa!"

7

"*P*ippa!" Jacob thundered on the door of the elevator. "Are you okay?"

"No, I'm not okay!" she yelled back, her frustration dampened by the metal doors. Other voices overlapped with hers. She wasn't alone in the elevator. "We've been trapped in here for hours! I haven't had anything to eat or drink, it's absolutely freezing, my ankles are the size of bowling balls, and I can't even tell you how desperately I have to pee!"

"Pippa, try to stay calm," I called up. "We're going to get you out of there."

"Is that Georgie?"

"Yeah, it's me."

"Thank God," Pippa said. "If there's anyone who can pop open a rogue elevator door, it's you."

I grinned at the unusual compliment. "I appreciate that, but unfortunately we don't have anything to pop it open with at the moment. I'll have to go find a crowbar or something. Who else is up there with you?"

"Jaime and Emma," Pippa answered. "Girls from my field hockey team."

"Seriously, Pip," another voice said. "How relieved are you that you're in here with us instead of Sebastian?"

"Emma, I really don't want to think about my ex-boyfriend right now."

"Sorry."

I rolled my eyes. "Girls, is anyone injured?"

"Nope," Pippa answered. "Just pissed."

"What about Jaime?" I asked. "I haven't heard from her."

"She's paper-bagging it."

"She's what?"

"She's claustrophobic," Pippa clarified. "We've been trying to keep her from having a full-blown panic attack, so she's breathing in and out of a paper bag. What the hell is going on out there? We yelled for help for hours. Why didn't someone come earlier?"

"The whole city is out of power," Jacob said. "Something fried the grid. Georgie thinks it was an EMP blast. Phones and cars are out too. The cops haven't been able to get anywhere because of the road blockages."

"Great," Pippa said. "We're stuck in an elevator, and it's straight up postapocalyptic out there. I can't wait to get out of here. How are we coming on that rescue mission, guys?"

"Working on it," I called. I turned to Jacob and Ivy. "You stay here and keep them calm. Don't let Jaime freak out any more than she already has. I'm going to go try to find something to pry open the doors with."

"Can you find us some snacks too?" Pippa called down. "I'm famished. Seriously, I'm about to pass out."

"I'll do my best," I told her. Then I kissed Jacob's cheek, patted Ivy's shoulder, and went on my way, heading down the dark hallway to the cafeteria.

The cafeteria itself was dark and creepy. The long tables had been folded up at the end of the school day yesterday and stacked against the wall. The tall figures cast strange, ominous shadows across the floor. My boots clicked against the tile as I headed for the serving counter. The food trays were clean and empty. The trash had been taken out. The kitchen staff had prepared the cafeteria for breakfast the next day. Nothing looked out of the ordinary. The school could open Monday without a hitch if the power behaved.

I jumped over the serving counter, sending a loud thud through the room, and knelt down to shuffle through the boxes beneath the counter. They were full of plastic utensils, packages of condiments, and spare lunch trays. No juice boxes or snacks. I moved on to the actual kitchen. There were no windows at all, so I lingered in the doorway to let my eyes adjust. Like the serving counter, the kitchen had been cleaned and readied for the next school day. I rummaged through a collection of industrial utensils, wondering if the metal tongs for flipping burgers would hold long enough to pry open the elevator door. I tested them against the floor, stepping on one end and pulling the other up against the sole of my boot. They bent easily in half. With a sigh, I threw them in the garbage.

Two doors led off from the kitchen. One was simply marked with a brass plaque that read Storage. The other was made of shiny thick metal, so I assumed it led to the walk-in freezer. I picked the storage room, hoping to find some nonperishable food items to bring back to Pippa and her friends.

"Jackpot," I whispered to myself as I entered the storeroom. The shelves were lined with boxes and boxes of snack bags, juice pouches, packaged peanut butter and jelly sandwiches, and canned vegetables. I reached into the one closest to me, and a ruler smacked across the back of my hand. "Ow, shit!"

A figure stepped out of the shadows, a spindly woman taller than me with black-framed glasses and a round narrow face like a barn owl's. She held the ruler at the ready. "That, young lady, does not belong to you."

"Let me guess," I said, nursing the sting on the back of my head. "You're the lunch lady."

The woman's thin shoulders broadened, and her chest puffed out as though I had ruffled her feathers. "I am Mrs. Valachovic, the headmistress of this school, and you are trespassing on private property. How did you get in here anyway? We locked the gates and barred the front doors."

"You forgot the back," I said wryly. "And there's a gap in the gate. Listen, lady, I'm not looking for trouble—"

Someone else emerged from behind the shelves, a squat man whose multiple chins spilled over the collar of his starched button-up shirt. "You heard the headmistress," he said. "You don't belong here. Get out."

"Seriously, my boyfriend—"

But the longer I protested, the more people emerged from the shadows, faculty and staff that had been stuck in the school since yesterday's blast, about ten or twelve individuals collectively. They advanced like the front line of an army, forcing me out of the storeroom and pressing me against the serving counter in the cafeteria. When my back hit the counter and I had nowhere else to go, I held my hands up in surrender. I didn't imagine this was how it would go down, at the mercy of several educators, each demanding answers from me.

"Who else did you let in?"

"What did you take?"

"What do you want?"

"Help! I want help!" I finally shouted, shoving one of the teachers away and rolling backward over the counter. I slid under the warming lights and across the empty trays to land on the other side. The teachers rushed to find the opening at the end of the counter rather than jumping across it, which gave me time to catch my breath. "Please listen! I didn't come here to rob the storeroom. My boyfriend's sister goes to school here. Her name is Pippa Mason." Jacob's last name was the secret password. The teachers stilled their advances at once. The Masons had donated several thousand dollars to the school. Everyone here knew Jacob, Pippa, and their parents. "She's stuck in the elevator with two of her friends," I rushed on, taking advantage of the opening. "We just need help to get them out, and then we'll be out of your hair. I swear."

"Who are you again?" Mrs. Valachovic asked, squinting to see me in the dim light.

"Georgie Fitz," I replied. "I'm dating—I'm engaged to Jacob Mason."

"I've seen you before," she said. "At Pippa's field hockey games."

"Yeah, I've been to one or two," I confirmed. "Please, they've been stuck in the elevator since yesterday, and Pippa's pregnant—"

Mrs. Valachovic snapped her fingers, and the gaggle of teachers perked up. "We have a situation," she announced. "Does anyone here have the skills to free a trio of students from the elevator?"

A hand rose near the back of the group, and a man stepped forward. He wore pressed black pants and a white collared shirt with the Saint Mark's logo embroidered on the pocket. Unlike the other teachers, he sported work boots rather than heels or sensible loafers.

"I can go," he offered. "I'm the one who services the elevators anyway."

"Excellent," Mrs. Valachovic said, urging the man forward. "Miss Fitz, this is Jorge, one of our custodians. He would be happy to help you. Please let us know if Pippa needs medical attention. We have the school nurse here as well."

"She's hungry," I replied. "And you have more than enough food here for the lot of you. I know the Masons would appreciate it if you could put together a box of nonperishable things for Pippa. Sandwiches and snacks. Things like that."

"Of course," Mrs. Valachovic said. Now that she knew who she was catering to, she was more than compliant. "We'll have it ready for you by the time you finish with Jorge. Here, take some water with you."

Someone passed up a few miniature bottles from the store room. I juggled them in one hand and waved. "Thanks. Come on, Jorge. We shouldn't leave them for long."

We made our way back toward the main hall. This time, I didn't bother to stifle my footsteps against the marble. The teachers had held down Saint Mark's better than a small army. It was safe inside the school, at least for now.

"I need to stop by my office," Jorge said, veering left down a hallway. "My things are there."

"No problem," I replied. "So how long have you been working at Saint Mark's?"

"Since I was eighteen," he answered, coming to a door set well away from the other classrooms. He fit a key into the lock and went inside. The office was too small. The desk alone took up most of the floor space, but by the looks of the mountain of paperwork sitting atop it, Jorge didn't bother to sit down often.

"Do you ever get tired of it?" I asked him as Jorge disappeared behind the desk.

"I don't mind it." He came up holding a crowbar. "It pays the bills. Gets the kids to school."

"Oh, do they go here?"

Jorge chuckled as he shouldered the crowbar and led me out of the office. "No, sweetie. We can't afford it. They go to public school. Let's see what we can do for your fiancé's sister, okay?"

Jorge led me back to the main hall with such certainty that I was sure he could traverse Saint Mark's in his sleep. The thought comforted me. Hopefully, he had been servicing the elevators for as long as he had been working here.

"Finally!" Jacob said when we arrived. "What took you so

long? Jaime's hyperventilating, and Pippa's threatened to kill me eight times already."

"Nine," Ivy said.

"Thanks a lot, kid."

I called up to the elevator. "Pippa, is Jaime okay?"

"She's losing it, Georgie." Pippa's voice was strained, as if she was in pain and trying to hide it. "We need to get her out of here."

"What about you?" I asked. "How are you holding up?"

"I don't know," she said, short of breath. "The baby's moving a lot. The stress maybe—"

"Okay, try taking deep breaths," I told her. "I have Jorge with me. He's the one who keeps the elevators running. He's going to try to get you out, okay?"

"I love Jorge!"

I drew Jacob and Ivy away from the elevator so that Jorge could do his job. He fit one end of the crowbar into the seam between the doors and pried them apart with a grunt. The doors inched open until the gap was wide enough for Jorge to fit his hands through. As he tugged the doors open the rest of the way, I noticed a problem. The lift itself was stuck between the first and second floors. The girls had managed to get the inside set of doors open themselves, but only eighteen inches or so of the actual lift had made it anywhere near the first floor. The girls were stuck at the top of the opening.

Pippa stuck her face into the gap. "Oh my God, fresh air."

Jorge moved away, carefully avoiding the drop to the basement floor below, and looked up at the lift. "I can't pull it down," he said. "I don't have the tools to do it. They'll have to squeeze through the opening."

Pippa drew back. "Jaime, you go first."

"But—"

"Don't argue with me. I'm fine. Get out of here."

Jacob moved closer to the elevator. "Jaime, I'll be right here to catch you."

A pair of saddle shoes appeared in the gap as Jaime wiggled herself through the opening. Jacob leaned forward, dangerously close to the open shaft. As the high schooler slipped out, he caught her around the waist and set her down gently on the firm floor. Jaime wobbled as Jacob returned his attention to the elevator, but before I could help her, Ivy swooped in to let Jaime use her as an armrest.

"I got you," Ivy said, helping Jaime, whose face was bright red, sit down on the intricate staircase.

"Here, Ivy," I said, tossing her a bottle of water. "Get her to drink something. They're probably dehydrated."

At the elevator, Jacob and Jorge helped Emma down. She squeezed through the gap without issue, waved off my offer of water, and looked back up into the lift. "Pippa, come on! It's your turn."

Pippa had moved away from the opening, invisible to us. "I can't fit."

"Yes, you can," Emma urged. "Just try."

"I already know I can't fit!"

Jacob balanced on his toes in an attempt to find his sister again, but he was too short to see to the top of the elevator. "Pippa, you have to try."

"Stupid blackout," she muttered from out of sight. "Stupid baby. Stupid boyfriend!"

"Pippa! Get down here!"

"Shut up, Jacob!"

"Okay, just stop," I said, pushing Jacob away from the open shaft. "Yelling at her isn't going to help this go any faster. She's probably right. Jaime and Emma barely made it through that gap, and they're not pregnant. Let's not make things worse by making her force her way through. It could hurt the baby."

Jacob couldn't tear his gaze away from the doors. "What do you suggest then? We can't leave her there!"

"No, of course not." I turned to the custodian. "Jorge, can you open the doors on the second floor?"

"Certainly."

"Excellent. Please go do that for me." As Jorge jogged up the staircase, I turned back to Jacob. "I need you to give me a boost."

"What?"

"Lift me up so I can get into the elevator."

He raised an eyebrow. "You want to get *inside* the elevator?"

"Someone has to keep Pippa calm and help her get out," I said. "There's no way you're fitting through that gap, so it has to be me. Now give me a boost."

Grudgingly, Jacob knelt by the open door and cupped his hands together in a makeshift step. "Be careful. I don't want to have to go down to the basement and fish your body out of the shaft."

"It's not that far," I said, but I gulped as I looked into the darkness below. The drop was about ten feet, but the last time I'd been this high above the ground, I'd fallen off a roller coaster and broken my finger. I shook off the thought and placed my boot in Jacob's hand. "Pippa? I'm coming up."

Jacob lifted me upward, and I caught the floor of the elevator, flinching when my head bumped against the top of the door frame. Pippa sat in the far corner of the elevator, curled in on herself. Her face was red and puffy, though I wasn't sure if it was from the cold or her emotions. I lifted myself through the gap as Jacob pushed me up from below until I was all the way in. The elevator smelled faintly of body odor, but the fruity perfume of teenaged girls overpowered it.

"Georgie, what are you doing?"

"Helping." I slid over to Pippa and pulled her to rest against me. The tip of her nose touched my neck, and I tried not to grimace. She was freezing. I wormed out of my sweater and maneuvered it over her head instead. It didn't quite cover her baby bump, which had grown tremendously since I'd last seen her, but at the very least, it provided another layer over top of her thin school uniform.

"You're going to freeze," she mumbled, plucking at the thin cotton of my shirt.

"I'll be okay," I told her. "It's you I'm worried about. Let's get out of here, yeah? Your parents are waiting for you back home."

"Girls?" Jorge's voice floated through the closed doors on the second floor. "I'm getting started, okay?"

"Okay!" I called back.

A clang echoed through the shaft as Jorge fit the crowbar between the doors and levered them open. Suddenly, the elevator jerked, and Pippa shrieked as it dropped an inch.

"Pippa!" Jacob reach into the shaft from below as if he could catch the elevator should it drop the rest of the way.

"Move, Jacob!" I clutched Pippa tighter to me. Jorge had gotten the doors to open about two feet. "Jorge, is that as wide as they'll go?"

"I'm afraid the elevator might drop even more if I try again, miss," he replied. "I think it's best if you try to get out now."

Heart pounding, I unfurled Pippa's fingers from my shirt. "Pippa? Listen, we've got to try and get out of here, okay? I'm going to give you a boost up to Jorge, and he's going to pull you out."

Pippa shook her head furiously. "If we move, this whole thing's going down."

"No, it isn't," I assured her, though I had no idea whether I was telling her the truth or not. "Even if it was, we can't not try. We need to get you somewhere safe."

"I'm not moving."

"What did she say?" Jacob shouted up. "Pippa, what's the problem?"

Pippa's eyes flashed to the first floor at the sound of her

brother's voice, but I took her face in between my hands and made her look at me.

"Ignore him," I told her. "Look at me. I'm in here with you, okay? You have me. We can't stay here forever though. You have to take the boost."

Her lip trembled as she held back tears. "I'm scared."

"I know," I said. "But you're also incredibly brave. You know how I know that? Because no other seventeen-year-old would go through with an unplanned pregnancy with the same amount of finesse that you have. This is no different from you walking down the halls in maternity wear, Pip. You can do this."

She tucked her head into my chest. "I don't want to."

"You have to," I muttered into her hair. "For your baby."

She sniffed once and nodded. I stood up before she could change her mind, trying to keep my feet as level as possible. The elevator swayed but held firm. I had no idea what might've caused it to drop, but I wasn't keen on repeating the experience. I doubted two and a half floors was tall enough to pick up a dangerous speed before we hit the basement, but any kind of big jolt would be bad news for Pippa and the baby. My goal was to keep Pippa's baby inside her for as long as possible. This wasn't a world for a newborn.

"Up you get," I said to Pippa, lifting her from underneath her arms. When she was standing, I interlinked my fingers to make a step as Jacob had earlier. "All right, let's go. I'll lift you up."

She steadied herself against the wall of the elevator, one hand cradling her belly, and looked up to Jorge. "You're going to get me up there, right? It's been a while since I've done a pull-up."

Jorge smiled down at her. "I have a daughter your age. I will treat you as if you were my own."

"Wait!" Jacob called. "I should do it. I should be the one to pull her out."

"We don't have time, Jacob," I said. "Stay down there in case this goes wrong. Pippa, let's go."

"Georgie—"

"Quiet, Jacob!"

Pippa braced herself on my shoulder, planted her white Oxford shoe in my hand, and stepped up. I bent my knees and tightened my core as she wobbled unevenly, trying not to let out a strained grunt as I heaved her up toward Jorge. Even with the baby, Pippa didn't look like she could possibly weigh as much as she did. Then I remembered that prior to her pregnancy, she had been a prominent player for the field hockey team. The girl was all muscle. That was a good thing. Her back and shoulders flexed as she gripped the floor above and hauled herself up into Jorge's grasp. He wrapped his arms around her and pulled her to safety on the second floor.

"Is she good?" Jacob asked. "Is Pippa safe?"

"She's fine," I started, leaning down to peek at Jacob through the gap. "Get back so I can slide out—"

I didn't slide out or finish my sentence because the hydraulics gave up entirely and the elevator plunged into darkness.

Jacob's horrified yell followed me down. The elevator whizzed past the first floor and headed for the basement. Time seemed to slow down and speed up all at once. I had no chance to react or access the part of my brain that might have stored away the information regarding the best way to minimize injury in a scenario like this. Was it to jump the second before the elevator hit the ground? Or were you supposed to lie flat on your back to allow the impact to spread across your entire body rather than one localized point? I remembered that a woman named Betty Lou Oliver held the Guinness World Record for the longest fall survived in an elevator. She fell seventy-five stories through the Empire State Building when some idiot flew a plane into it. If she could make it, so could I. There was nothing else to do but prepare myself for the crash, so I held onto the support rails on the sides of the elevator for dear life and lowered myself so that only my heels were touching the floor. Then I squeezed my eyes shut and waited for the boom.

It came with an atrocious earsplitting crunch of metal on concrete, ripping my grip from the elevator. The impact traveled through the soles of my boots and rattled upward until it felt as if my head might shake clean off my body. The cheap ceiling tiles rained down from above, showering me with stucco and plaster. Then everything settled. That was it. My heart pounded and my head ached, but I was otherwise no worse for wear.

Jacob's terrified shouts echoed from above, but the ringing in my ears made it difficult to hear his words. I slumped to the ruined floor, letting the surge of adrenaline run its course. It was my second freefall experience in as many days. At this rate, I was going to develop an extreme fear of heights in no time.

Minutes later, while I was checking my feet and legs for fractures, the crowbar found its way between the doors leading to the basement, and someone ripped them apart so quickly that it left a dent in the metal. I squinted into the murky darkness, the only light filtering in from the shaft above. Jacob stood there, chest heaving, crowbar in hand. There was a look on his face that I couldn't quite figure out. It was two different emotions, as if hope and despair warred with each other to gain control over his eyes and mouth. Then I understood. He'd hoped I was alive, but he expected me to be dead.

"It was only two floors," I said.

"Georgie!" He rushed in and practically collapsed to pull me against him. I pressed my face to his neck and took a deep breath. His spicy sweet cinnamon scent had a tang of nervous sweat to it now. "Oh my God, you're alive."

"Careful." I winced as he rocked me back and forth. Something in my neck twinged. The collision had wreaked havoc on my alignment. "My whole body hurts. Is everybody okay?"

He drew away and tucked a strand of hair behind my ear.

"Yeah, everybody's fine, thanks to you. God, I thought I was going to go home with Pippa and not you."

"We're both going home," I told him. "And then we're all leaving town." I tried to get my feet under me, but my legs were shaking so much that I couldn't control them.

Jacob ducked his head under my arm and lifted me to stand. "Be careful. The basement's a mess. It looks like no one's been down here in ages."

"Maybe it's haunted," I said as he led me out of the elevator. Storage boxes lined the underground room, piled in high, precarious columns.

"Don't joke," Jacob said. "When I went to Saint Mark's, they sent kids who misbehaved down here to watch old sex ed tapes. It was torture."

"Had a lot of detention, did you?"

"No. Maybe."

"Jacob Mason, you are not who I thought you were," I joked as he carried me into the concrete stairwell.

"Neither are you."

8

$\mathscr{I}$n the main entryway, after everyone was done expressing their awe at my lack of injury, we planned our escape route from the school. One look through a gap in the boards on the windows showed us that the looters had yet to give up. A few of them had almost made it to the top of the gate a couple of times. Once someone finally produced a ladder, it would be easy to find a way into the school.

"It's not safe to stay here," I told Jorge when he returned from the kitchen with a care package that the other teachers had put together for us. "You can't defend the entire school. That mob outside is going to get in, and when they do, they won't care about what happens to this place or the people inside it. They'll hurt you and the others to get to that storeroom. It'll be a madhouse."

"I wasn't planning on staying anyway," Jorge replied. "I have a family to get back to."

I hugged him. "Thank you for everything, and be careful out there."

"You too," he said. "And stay out of trouble. You seem like the type of girl that goes looking for it."

"I don't," I told him as I drew away, aware of Jacob's eyes on the back of my head. "Trouble tends to find me."

"Even so," Jorge said, his voice fading as he moved toward the kitchen. "You stay safe."

I sighed as he left and turned to the rest of our party. "We shouldn't go around the front. With this many people, someone's bound to notice us, and we have a giant box full of food that screams trouble."

Emma, Pippa's friend, pointed toward the rear of the school. "I'm heading that way anyway. Don't worry about me."

"Me either," Jaime said. Now that she was free of the confines of the elevator, she appeared more sure of herself. "I live over there too."

"The two of you shouldn't go alone," I said.

Emma slung an arm across Jaime's shoulder. "We won't be. We'll have each other."

"You know what she meant," Jacob said. "I don't feel comfortable sending the two of you home alone. Why don't you come with us?"

I suppressed a ripple of agitation. We couldn't take care of everyone that Jacob or Pippa knew. Ivy was one thing—she didn't have the means to take care of herself—but Emma and Jaime had families of their own.

"I can't," Jaime said. "My parents are out of town, which means my little brother is all alone at our house. I got to go find him."

"And my parents are probably apoplectic over the fact that I haven't made it home yet," Emma added. "We'll be fine. We'll stick to the back roads. And if anyone messes with us"—she banged open one of the lockers, pulled out a field hockey stick, and brandished it about—"they'll be damn sorry about it."

"She's not kidding." Jaime smirked. "I saw her clock a guy in the shins after a game once just because he tried to hit on her."

"That pickup line was terrible," Emma said.

Jacob stepped between the two of them. "Listen, girls. Don't linger out there. Go straight home. Don't talk to anyone. Don't go into any of the stores—"

Emma saluted him. "Yes, sir, Big Brother."

Jaime threw her arms around Pippa. "I wouldn't want to be trapped in an elevator for fifteen hours with anyone but you. Be careful, okay?"

Emma joined in on the hug, and Pippa squeezed her friends tightly. "You guys be careful too. Don't hesitate to use that hockey stick on anyone."

Emma grinned savagely and swung the stick through the air with a menacing whoosh. "Oh, don't you worry."

"You're giving her too much power," Jaime muttered as she straightened out the collar of Pippa's shirt beneath my sweater.

"Let's go, Jaime!" Emma hollered, already on her way toward the rear hallway. "I'm ready to bash some heads in."

Pippa rolled her eyes and kissed Jaime on the cheek. "Go. I'll see you later."

"Hopefully."

And then Emma and Jaime were off, the heels of their shoes clicking against the marble floors as they jogged toward home.

"Pippa, do you have a nail file?" I asked her.

"Sure." She dug through her backpack, stamped with the Saint Mark's crest, and produced a metal file. "What do you need it for?"

I wiggled the file into the seam of the closest locker and popped the lock out of place. "Your friends gave me an idea."

"Stealing?" Jacob asked, his tone dry. "That's your idea?"

The locker swung open, revealing several textbooks, general trash, and a Saint Mark's peacoat. I drew open the coat and flapped it open. It was tiny, so I handed it to Ivy, who promptly drew it on over her ratty sweatshirt. I moved on to the next locker, where an extra-large coat had been crammed inside.

"Here," I said, helping Pippa into the sleeves. It swamped her, hanging almost to her knees, but at least she would be warm. "Do you still disapprove, Jacob, or would you like your sister and her baby to freeze to death out there?"

Jacob was smart enough not to answer as I perused the row of lockers for anything else we could use. I found another coat for myself and a couple of apples that I shoved in the box of food that Jacob was carrying. Then I waved our group toward the exit.

We left the school the same way we came in. We locked the doors behind us, and Ivy pulled the basement window shut, just to buy the teachers inside a little more time when the mob at the front gates finally found a way through. After filing through the gap in the iron bars, we turned right toward the road behind the school rather than left toward the havoc. Pippa and I leaned heavily on one another, supporting each other's weight. Ivy led the way as Jacob brought up the rear. She had been quiet since our talk at the school. I couldn't help but wonder what she was thinking about. Out of all of us, she was probably the second most prepared for this sort of thing after me. If I knew anything about the lives of abused, half-homeless children, it was that they harbored a resilience like no other. Was Ivy's silence a coping mechanism, or had the events of the day begun to wear her out already?

I didn't have time to ask her. We turned down a dark alley, trying to find an alternate way to the street that would lead us back to the Masons' apartment building, and a shambling shadow appeared at the opposite end. Ivy froze in place, causing our party to come to an abrupt halt behind the little girl. The shadow paused and half turned toward us. It was tall and thin, with angled limbs that seemed to jut out at unnatural angles.

"Oh no," Ivy whispered.

The shadow lurched toward us, and as it drew closer, the clumsy but quick limbs rearranged themselves to form a man. He was not much of a human. His eyes sank deep into his skull, and his cheeks looked as though the skin had been pasted directly to the bone beneath. He reeked of booze, body odor, and vomit.

Jacob took hold of his sister and piloted her around the corner, away from the monstrous man. Without thinking, I stepped in front of Ivy, who appeared rooted to the asphalt below her feet, until the man was nearly upon us.

"*Ivy!*"

He spat her name out like a dirty word. I pushed Ivy back, concealing her completely behind the thick wool layer of my Saint Mark's coat.

"I don't know who you're talking about," I said, forcing myself to speak calmly. "My little sister's name is Amelia."

"Bullshit," the man growled. "You think I don't recognize my own daughter when I see her?"

"Judging by the alcohol on your breath and your state of being, it wouldn't exactly surprise me," I replied, taking another step toward the mouth of the alley. His stench made my eyes water. It was no wonder Ivy had chosen to roam the dangerous streets instead of returning to whatever place she called home.

"Get out of the way," he snarled, but he didn't give me the chance to respond. Without warning, he pushed me over.

I tripped over Ivy, toppling us both, and landed on top of her. My muscles seized, fresh off the trauma of the elevator crash. Ivy scrambled to get away from her father as he loomed over us, her feet kicking mercilessly at my back to dislodge me. Once she was free, she sprang to her feet, but her father was quicker. He leapt over me and caught hold of Ivy by her coat, ripping the collar. He jerked her against him, leaned down, and tipped her head back so that she was forced to listen as he whispered in her ear.

"One bottle." Spittle ran down the man's chin. "That's all I asked of you. You've been gone for hours, and all I wanted was one bottle."

"I couldn't find anything!" Ivy whimpered.

"You found yourself a new mommy, apparently," her father replied. "You found a pretty new coat." He toyed with the torn collar. "Is this the life you wanted, you little brat? Pretty parents and a private school?"

When he twisted Ivy's neck at a dangerous angle, red-hot hatred coursed through my veins. I flipped over, ignoring the all-over pain, and drew the handgun once more. As the man tilted Ivy's head even further, drawing a yelp of pain from the girl, I fired once. Into his leg.

He dropped Ivy at once, screaming as he collapsed on the asphalt. Like before, a wave of noise washed through the blocks around us. Anyone within earshot had panicked at the sound of the gunshot, including Jacob and Pippa, who had peered around the corner to see what had happened. Blood spurted from between the man's fingers as he applied pressure to a spot above his knee.

"You bitch!" His eyes bulged out of his head as he screamed at me. "I'll kill you! I'll kill her!"

The narrow alleyway amplified the shrill threats. The man's fit would attract attention, and if anyone found us next to him, me with a gun in hand, it would raise questions and trouble. I pushed myself to my feet and grabbed Ivy's hand, but she was stunned into silence, staring at her father as he bled out on the ground.

"Let's go," Jacob shouted from the end of the alley.

"I'm trying!" I called back.

Ivy wouldn't budge. "Is he going to die?"

There was no point in lying. Her father's screams had already lost their intensity as the blood pooled around him. "Probably," I admitted. "There's a big artery in the leg there. He's losing a lot of blood, and no one's going to come and take him to a hospital."

Ivy turned her face to look up at me. "It's that easy?"

The question and the glimmer of wonder and freedom in her

117

eyes made my stomach turn. "No, Ivy. This wasn't easy. Not for you and not for me." The man gurgled on the pavement, slumping over his ruined leg. I tugged on Ivy's hand again. "We have to go now."

"In a second." She pulled out of my grasp to lean over her father. For once, she loomed over him instead of the other way around. She pulled the collar of his shirt up so that he had to look her in the eye. "I hate you. That's all."

For a brief second before his daughter allowed him to fall again, a spark of something—remorse or realization maybe— flashed across the man's face. Ivy didn't look back as she fit her hand in mine and ran toward the mouth of the alley.

"Oh my God," Jacob said as he and Pippa followed after us. We slowed down once we cleared the alley since Pippa wasn't in the best shape to run. "Oh my God, Georgie."

"Stop saying that," I snapped.

"You killed him."

"He was going to kill Ivy."

"You don't know that!"

"You didn't see him!" I fired back, marching along the sidewalk without looking at him. "He was about to break her neck clean off! What would you have done?"

"She's his daughter," Jacob replied. "It's none of my business."

A bitter taste flowed across my tongue. "If you really mean that, then you're a heartless asshole who only cares about the people who are closest to him."

"No, I just don't want the people closest to me to get arrested for murder!" he said. "Especially not my fiancée!"

I whirled to a stop outside the shattered windows of a pharmacy. "Look around you, Jacob! Do you see any cops? Do you? No, because guess what! They're all doing the same thing that I'm trying to do, which is protect the people around them. I made a decision to protect Ivy. It was either her or her piece-of-shit father who can't stay sober long enough to take care of his own daughter."

"You shot him, Georgie," Jacob snapped. "He's going to die because of you. You can't do that. Not everyone has daddy issues like you do."

The remark was like a crisp slap to the face. "I can't believe you just said that to me."

"Yeah, well—"

"No," I said. "You don't get to use my vulnerabilities against me, especially not now. I told you about my dad because you practically begged me to. It took me a lot of time to get over what happened to my parents, and I won't let you treat me like a joke you tell to your gym buddies just to get a laugh out of them."

I walked off with Ivy.

"Where are you going?" he called after me.

"Back to your fucking parents' house!" I replied. "You may be a jerk, but that doesn't change what we have to do."

"Georgie—"

Pippa interrupted him. "Jacob, just stop. Shut up. You're making it worse."

I picked up the pace, leaving their squabbling behind. Ivy squeezed my fingers.

"Are you okay?" she asked quietly.

"No."

"For what it's worth, I'm glad you shot him."

I blew out a sigh big enough to puff out my cheeks and ruffled Ivy's oily hair. "I know that, kid, but it doesn't change what I did."

Ivy scrunched up her nose. "Why do you like Jacob?"

I checked behind me to make sure that Jacob and Pippa were still out of earshot. They were buried in discussion with each other, and by the looks of it, Pippa was reaming him out for what he said.

"It's a long story," I told Ivy. "When I met Jacob, he had everything I wanted. A place in the city, a sense of purpose, and a normal family. Everything seemed so easy for him. His life was set up for him at birth. Graduate college, work for his dad, get married. That's what normal people do, right? I wanted that. I wanted something normal."

"Normal is so boring though," Ivy said.

"Fine. I wanted something steady then," I clarified. "Something that I could count on so that I wouldn't have to keep thinking about what I left behind."

"What did you leave behind?"

"I'm probably going to find out in a couple of days—"

"Ivy!"

A middle-aged woman emerged from the remains of a walk-in clinic as we passed by, her gaze trained on the twelve-year-old at my side. I reached for the gun again but stopped myself. This woman was not like Ivy's father. She was well put together, wearing sensible boots, jeans, and several layers of sweaters. She was clean and smelled of fresh linens. A small boy peeked out from behind her waist.

"Miss Williams!" Ivy tore her hand free to sling her arms around the woman, who lifted her into the air and twirled her around before setting her down again. Ivy hugged the little boy next. "Leon, I missed you."

"We heard a gunshot," Miss Williams said. "Are you all right?"

"It's my dad," Ivy replied stoically. "He's dead."

"Oh dear." Though she tried her best, there was absolutely no remorse in Miss Williams's tone. She held her hand out to me. "And who do we have here?"

"Georgie," I answered, shaking hands. "I was looking after Ivy."

Miss Williams planted a kiss on top of Ivy's head. "Thank you so much. She's safe now."

The little boy, Leon, ducked under Ivy's Saint Mark's coat

and started laughing, his little giggles muffled by the thick wool fabric. She buttoned the front, trapping him inside with her.

"You're going to look after her?" I asked Miss Williams, watching as the two kids stumbled aimlessly around. "I didn't know—"

"That she had anyone else?" Miss Williams finished. "She doesn't. She and her father lived in our building until they were evicted. She came to our unit when he got too violent. I called the cops multiple times."

"So you know her pretty well?"

"I practically raised her," she said. "I even asked for child services to release her into my custody a few times. I guess now we've got a better shot."

A lump rose in my throat. Despite the fact that I'd known Ivy for less than half a day, the thought of parting with her unnerved me. "You should leave the city. It's not safe here."

"I know, dear," Miss Williams said. She reached out and stroked my cheek. "Look at those lines on your face already, baby. You're an old soul, aren't you?"

The unexpected affection had an immediate effect. The tears that had been waiting to fall finally made their appearance, and Miss Williams produced a pocket-sized package of tissues. As I dabbed at my face, she squeezed my shoulders.

"You hang in there," she ordered. "You're a good person. You brought Ivy home when I've been the only one on her side for years. Don't you forget that."

"Are you leaving?" Ivy asked, having finally freed Leon from the confines of her new coat.

"Yeah," I said, sniffling. "You want to stay here with Miss Williams, right?"

Ivy beamed proudly. "Yes. She's better than a mom."

"She is," I agreed, kneeling down to give Ivy a hug. "You behave, okay? Stay safe. Maybe when all of this is over, we can find each other again."

ALEXANDRIA CLARKE

"I'd like that," she replied. "And you shouldn't let anyone boss you around. No one can make you feel inferior without your consent."

I laughed and straightened up. "How does someone so young know a quote from Eleanor Roosevelt?"

"Miss Williams taught it to me."

"Smart lady."

Miss Williams ushered the children back inside the walk-in clinic, waved goodbye to me, and disappeared into the gloom. Ivy was gone, and hopefully, with Miss Williams's skills, she would be able to ride out the other effects of the EMP blast.

"Who was that?" Pippa asked.

"The woman who looks after Ivy," I told her, wiping the last bit of moisture from my cheeks. "She's going to take care of her."

"That's good, right? That means we don't have to take her with us," Jacob said. Pippa elbowed him in the ribs. "Ow!"

"Yeah, it's good," I said. "It's one less person to feed and worry about. Let's get back to the condo. This is starting to feel like the longest day of my life, and we haven't even tried to get out of the city yet."

We trudged on, sticking to the less populated side roads rather than walking up the main stretch. I wished I had my bike. It was slow going with Pippa. Though she was in good shape, she was unaccustomed to speed-walking with the weight of the baby. We had to stop a few times to let her catch her breath.

"Almost there," Jacob said, using the sleeve of his shirt to wipe sweat from his sister's forehead. "Another block maybe."

The Masons' building was visible, and the sun had climbed high enough to beat down on us again. I shrugged free of my borrowed coat and draped it over my shoulder in case I needed it for later.

"I don't know how the two of you think you're going to get me out of the city," Pippa said. "This is taking way too long."

"We do have a wagon," I offered.

122

"Which is currently loaded with water bottles," Jacob reminded me. "Maybe we can find a stroller. We could tie it to the back of someone else's bike. That'd be fun. Right, Pip?"

She glared at him as she got back to her feet. "Try and put me in a baby stroller, Jacob. See if you survive the experience."

"Don't your parents own a tandem bike?" I asked. "Pippa can ride on the back of that. No stroller or wagon necessary."

"See?" Pippa said to Jacob. "At least Georgie offers a real solution to the problem. Let's keep moving. I'm fine now, and I bet Mom and Dad made breakfast."

Pippa strode ahead, leaving Jacob and me to deal with the thick, palpable tension in the air between us. Our hands bumped together. I shoved mine into my pocket.

"Georgie, listen—"

"We can't keep doing this," I said, strolling after Pippa. Jacob hurried to catch up. "We can't argue over stupid shit. It's not going to turn out well for us."

"Then let's talk about it." Jacob threaded his arm through mine in an attempt to get me to slow down and walk evenly with him. "Hmm?"

His grip felt too tight. I shrugged out of it. "I tried to talk to you about it. I told you about my parents like you wanted me to, and not an hour later, you threw it back in my face like it was something I had to be ashamed about."

"I didn't mean it."

I whirled around to face him, forcing him to stop walking. "Yeah, but you did it. You took something that you knew would bother me and used it against me because you were mad in the moment and wanted to hurt me. That's not right."

"Fine, you're right."

"Don't just say that because you're trying to make this go away."

"I'm not!" His hot reply startled a flock of birds from a nearby telephone wire. Jacob took a deep breath and tried again.

"What I said was stupid, and I'm sorry, okay? But I just watched my fiancée, who I've known as a specific type of person since we met in college, shoot a man in the leg and leave him to bleed out and die. Georgie, every time we found a spider in the apartment, you made me trap it in a cup and carry it outside. Now, all of a sudden, you're GI Jane."

I scuffed the toe of my boot against the sidewalk, mindlessly filling in a crack with the dirt from an ant pile. "What you don't understand is that I've always been that person. The GI Jane one that knows how to shoot at a moving target and pick locks and steal without remorse. All these years, she's been right there, just below the surface, but I never needed her until now." Jacob stared at where my boot worked against the ground. I lifted his chin, his whiskers rough against the pads of my fingers. "You need her too. You need *me* to get out of this mess alive, and the faster you accept that terrible things are going to happen to us, the easier this is going to be. Can you understand that?"

"I'm trying to."

The sun turned his brown irises gold. He was doing his best. That was true. I could see that in the puffy bags under his eyes and the lines around his mouth that seemed to have deepened since last night's blast. Jacob was a trust-fund kid who'd been thrown into the deep end without a floatie. He wasn't used to death and gore unless he was watching it in high definition on a gigantic television. That would all change soon. Clouds drifted across the sun, casting a chilling shadow.

Jacob pressed his forehead against mine, looking for my lips, but I drew away before he could find them. He wanted something normal to rely on, but I couldn't give it to him. The truth, rather than the blackout, had made room for something darker to lie between us.

9

I found Pippa on the third-floor landing of the stairwell in her family's apartment building. She had stopped to catch her breath, holding the support railing with one hand and cradling her belly with the other.

"You know, I used to be in great shape," she said when she noticed me plodding up the stairs. "I was captain of the field hockey team. I ran a five-minute mile. Now a few flights of stairs have me completely whipped. It's ridiculous."

I forced a grim smile. "Don't worry. I'm sure you'll go right back to your five-minute mile after you deliver the baby."

She looped her arm around my shoulders when I offered. "Did you talk to Jacob? Where is he?"

"He gave me a head start."

"So you didn't talk."

"We did," I replied as we started up the steps to the next floor. "The problem is that we can't really do anything about the things we talked about right now."

Pippa flipped her curly blond hair, the same color as Jacob's, over her shoulder to see the stairs better. "Because of the blackout?"

"Partially."

"You have to give me more than that, or I can't help you." She tugged on my bright purple locks. "I hate to break it to you, but you've always been cryptic. It's no wonder Jacob has a difficult time communicating with you. That boy is dense, like most men, but he does try."

"I know he does—"

"All I'm saying is that some guys don't try." She drew open the lapels of her coat to reveal her belly again. "*This* is a perfect example. When I told Sebastian that I was going to have the baby, he switched schools to get away from me."

"Why did you?" I asked her. "Decide to have the baby, I mean."

She shrugged. "I don't know. It was such a shit show when I found out about it. Part of me wanted to own up to the responsibility of it. I made a mistake. I screwed up, so now I have to deal with the consequences." We lugged ourselves up another flight of stairs. "Then another part of me wanted to piss everyone off. Jacob got into all kinds of trouble when he went to Saint Mark's, but he played on the football team, and he was a straight-A student, and he was a boy, so it didn't matter if he acted up. My parents went ballistic when I told them about this. They even said I'd have to get rid of it."

"I thought your parents were super Christian."

Pippa rolled her eyes. "It turns out that having a pregnant teenage daughter wasn't their idea of how Christianity is supposed to go. They were more concerned about our family's reputation than what God might think of me."

"That's shitty."

"Yup," Pippa agreed. As we rounded the seventh floor, her feet began to drag, so I propped more of her weight over my shoulder. "Anyway, I figured I'd have the baby and give her up for adoption. Let some couple who actually wants her get a beautiful newborn."

"You're not keeping her?" I asked. Jacob hadn't mentioned that Pippa was considering adoption.

"No way," she replied. "I'm seventeen. I don't want a kid, not right now, at least. I want to go to school and study abroad and have a life. Could I do that with a baby on my hip?"

"Probably."

Pippa nodded appreciatively. "That's true, but I don't want to. This little girl deserves more than constantly being reminded that she was a mistake. I don't want that for her."

"You put a lot of thought into this, haven't you?"

Her expression sobered, her mouth setting itself in a determined pout. "When I'm not studying, it's literally all I think about."

She missed a step and tripped. I caught her around the waist before she could tumble down the flight of stairs, and set her gently on her feet. She grabbed my wrist, her pulse hammering against mine.

"Georgie?" Her voice was suddenly small and timid, a vast distance from her usual tone of showy confidence. "What do you think is going to happen?"

"With your baby?"

"With the world."

I considered my answer, wondering if I should tell Pippa something to make her feel better or give her my genuine opinion. She wasn't the same as Jacob, who loved tradition and normality so much that he couldn't wrap his mind around the situation at hand. She was strong and practical, and she deserved an honest answer.

"I don't know," I answered truthfully. "It depends on the scope of this thing. First off, who did it? My best guess is that the blast was an act of terrorism to send the United States back to the dark ages, and it worked. A lot of people are going to die in the next few weeks, Pippa."

"The hospitals aren't running either, are they?"

"No," I said. "No, they're not."

She looked down at her stomach, running a hand over the swell. "It might be you and me after all, little one."

Floors below us, a door slammed shut, echoing up the stairwell. Jacob was on his way up. The Mason family reunion was imminent, and the four of them together was like watching an avalanche in slow motion. Someone always got buried.

"Come on," I said. "It's going to be a long day. You should rest while you can."

When we finally made it to the apartment, we found Nita wrapping gauze around Jove's finger at the dining room table while Penny attempted to wrap the leftovers from breakfast in individual aluminum foil packets. Penny dropped a sausage and ran to her daughter.

"Pippa!" She hugged her tightly from the side so as to avoid Pippa's extra passenger. "What took you so long to get home?"

"I was stuck in the elevator at school."

Penny sniffed the air around Pippa's hair. "Is that why you smell funny?"

"I don't smell funny."

I left the mother-and-daughter duo to chat about the limited bathing options and walked over to Nita and Jove, eyeing Jove's injury. "What happened?"

"He burned himself on the grill," Nita said with a quirk of her eyebrow that boasted disapproval. "He was trying to fry up more bacon after Leti left. I told him that the heat was too high."

"I damn well know how to cook bacon," Jove grumbled, swiping his hand away from Nita as she finished tucking the gauze against itself.

"If you'd listened—"

"This is my house."

"So you keep reminding me," Nita said as she stacked the rest of the first aid materials back into the box. "But ignorance lives in even the grandest of dwellings, Mr. Mason. Excuse me."

I wiped the indulgent grin off my face at Jove's dumbstruck expression and followed Nita out of the dining room and into Jacob's, which Nita had claimed as her own for the time being. "I can't believe you just said that to him."

"Why not?" she asked, adding the first aid kit to a spare pocket in her backpack. "I'm not his daughter-in-law. You are."

"Not yet."

"Whatever," she said. "I figured since you couldn't set him straight without Jacob getting on your case, then I would have to do it for you. How's Pippa? Did I hear she got stuck in an elevator? Is the baby okay?"

"The baby's fine, and so is she," I answered. "For right now, at least. Who knows what's going to happen once we get on the road. How's it going here? Did you get Jove and Penny to pack a bag for themselves?"

"The bacon incident derailed things," Nita admitted. "On the upside, I convinced them to go, but Penny can't seem to grasp the concept that we can't carry things like a foot bath or a heating pad with us."

"There's no power," I said. "Where does she think she's going to plug those things in?"

Nita picked nervously at a hangnail on her thumb. "I have no idea. Are you sure you don't want to hit the road just the two of us? We might have a better chance of making it out alive."

I shot her a look. "Don't think I didn't consider leaving Jacob's parents behind."

"But that would probably cast a pall over the wedding plans," Nita added. "I get it."

I sank into Jacob's rolling chair and rested my head against his desk. Someone—an adolescent Jacob or one of his immature friends—had carved a lovely anatomically correct cartoon into a less visible section of the polished wood.

"They're going to be a pain in the ass," I warned Nita, curling my arms around my head to block out the world around me.

"Jacob and I are already at odds with each other, and Jove is going to drive me up a wall. He's going to make mistakes, dangerous ones—"

Nita forced me over so that she could share the chair with me. "I'll be your buffer. I'll deal with the Masons. You focus on getting us out of Denver. Okay?"

I peeked out at her from beneath my arm fort. "Have I ever told you how glad I am that you exist?"

She flipped her dark hair over her shoulder in a show of faux superiority. "Oh, honey. You didn't have to."

I shoved her off the chair.

BY THE TIME we returned to the main living area, Jacob had arrived and already started an argument with Jove about his injury. Pippa lay on the perfectly white sofa, her back turned to her mother, who was attempting to wipe her daughter's forehead with a warm compress. A half-packed suitcase lay open in the middle of the floor, filled with things like battery-operated razors, cell phone chargers, and electric toothbrushes. The constant chatter roared in my ears like some extra-terrible form of tinnitus, cutting off any rational thought.

"You should have waited," Jacob scolded.

"I was still hungry!" Jove replied.

"Come on, honey, just let me take care of you," Penny pleaded.

"Mom, seriously, go away," Pippa ordered.

"Can everyone just shut up for a minute?"

Everyone turned to face me, surprised by my outburst. I usually excused myself when the Masons got too loud for me to handle, choosing to step out onto the balcony instead of riding out the thunderstorm. Other than Jacob, they hadn't heard me raise my voice before.

I pointed to the suitcase. "This isn't going to work. First off, we can't carry it. Everyone needs to find or rig a backpack. Second"—I reached down to toss the toothbrush, charger, and razor out of the bag—"anything that needs a battery or an outlet is useless. Use your freaking brains, people. Pack all-weather clothing and shoes, nonperishable food, camping supplies, that kind of thing. We're not going to an all-inclusive resort. We're heading up to the woods where—guess what—you're going to have to shit in a latrine. Then at some point you're going to have to clean the latrine. Do you get my gist?"

It was clear that the Masons did not. Jove let out a dismissive grunt, though I assumed it was because someone other than him dared to say "shit" in his house. Penny looked horrified at the thought of cleaning up after her own waste. Jacob sank his face into his hands in an attempt to hide his mortification. Only Pippa seemed quiet and listening, though I suspected she had fallen asleep on the sofa. Nita, on the other hand, tried to reel in a satisfied smirk.

Now that I had the floor, I lowered my voice. "If you don't listen to me, you will not survive. Is that clear?"

Jacob was the first to reply. "Yes. Right, Dad? Mom?"

"It's clear," Penny said.

"Uh-huh," Jove added gruffly. "I still don't know what you expect us to do. Jacob told us you want to ride bikes out of the city? How are we supposed to get up the mountains on bikes?"

"We could hike," I suggested, "but I realize that's a bit of a stretch. Hiking doesn't seem like an activity the four of you ever engaged in, and it would be especially difficult for Pippa."

"Hiking sounds terrible," Pippa agreed, not asleep after all.

"We need a plan," I announced. "Here's the thing. When Jacob and I were leaving the theme park last night, we noticed that some cars were still working. They were all older models, which means that they probably didn't have electrical components. They weren't affected by the blast. Jove, don't you show a few cars at an antique show every year?"

"Yes," Jove replied. "Where is this going?"

"We're going to drive up into the mountains," I told him. "We just need a working car that's big enough to fit all of us."

"Well, it won't be one of the Spiders," Jove declared. "They took me years to rebuild, and they're worth a lot of money."

"Dad, the Spiders only seat two people apiece," Jacob said dryly. "They're out of the question anyway."

I leaned against the dining room table next to Jove. For once, we were speaking the same language. "Do you have anything bigger? Something that could make it up the inclines?"

"I have an original Humvee."

"You do?"

Jove proudly puffed his chest out. "Yes, ma'am. We'd have to go get it. It's in storage."

My shoulders dropped. "In storage where?"

"I keep it in a warehouse by the airport."

Jacob picked up Pippa's feet, sat beneath them, and began massaging her ankles. "That's thirty miles from here. It'll take us three hours to get there on bikes, and it's in the complete opposite direction of where we're heading."

"It's our best shot," I said. "We can ditch the bikes once we get the car, and we'll get up to my dad's property in no time. It'll be safer too."

"What about the roads?" Penny handed the warm compress to Jacob, who leaned over Pippa and pressed it to her forehead. "Aren't they all blocked by the cars?"

"If we have a Humvee, it won't be a problem," I pointed out. "Have you seen the tires on those things? We wouldn't be confined to pavement."

"How about gas?" Jove said. "That thing eats it up, and the pumps won't be working for us to refill."

"I can siphon gas from other cars," I told him. "If you want, I can teach you how to do it. We'll bring extra containers and fill up as many as we can."

Jove looked impressed by my knowledge of car tricks. "All right then."

"So we have a plan?" Jacob asked.

"We have a plan."

WE SPENT another hour and a half preparing for the trip. Nita managed to separate Penny from Pippa. I took Penny and Jove into their room to pick out more sensible clothing for the journey, while Nita briefed Pippa on how she should take care of herself on the road. Jacob searched the apartment for anything we might be able to use, coming up with a few ancient oil lanterns, a box of barbeque matches, and a four-man tent that the Masons had purchased ten years ago but never used. It was still in the box.

"My dad has a cabin," I reminded him when he showed me the tent. "But you should bring it anyway in case we don't make it there. Do you have sleeping bags?"

"Just Pippa's old princess one," he said, adding the tent box to the growing pile by the door. "I'll see if I can find a few blankets to bunch up."

Jacob, Nita, and I toted the Masons' bike collection down the stairs and into the lobby. Jove and Penny usually shared the tandem bike, but we decided that I would ride it with Pippa instead. That left Penny with my road cruiser and Jove with Jacob's old mountain bike. The lobby was empty. Frank was gone. He had either gone to some other floor to help another resident or finally given up on the extravagant high-rise and gone home to his family. I hoped it was the latter. Either way, we lugged the rest of our things from out of the storage room without his supervision. It was all there, including the water, though one of the packages was missing a single bottle.

"Frank got thirsty, I guess," Jacob said, tugging the wagon out from behind the counter. He set to arranging the things he had found upstairs around the water like a reality-based game of Tetris.

Jove and Penny emerged from the stairwell, flanking Pippa on either side. For once, she wasn't fighting off her parents. There was already a sheen of sweat across her forehead. My stomach plummeted. Maybe transporting Pippa wasn't the best idea. She had already been through enough in the past twenty-four hours.

"Are you all right?" I asked her once her parents had joined Jacob in his quest to strap everything to a backpack, bike, or wagon.

She waved me off. "I'm totally fine."

"Really? Because you don't look fine."

"Stop worrying, Georgie."

"I can't," I told her. "So you need to keep me updated. We have Nita with us for a reason. Mostly because she provides much-needed comic relief, but also because she's a med student. If you feel like something's going wrong, tell me. And don't pedal, okay? I'll do it."

"You sound like my mother."

"Pippa, just promise me you'll listen to me."

"Fine, I promise."

Ten minutes later, we were finally on our way. Jacob took the lead, followed by Jove, Penny, Pippa and me, and finally Nita. We looked like a line of misshapen tortoises, each of us forced to slump over the handlebars due to the weight of our backpack. Pippa, of course, was excused from carrying her own bag. I had tied it between her knees instead, out of the way of the pedals. If she wanted, she could rest her feet on the bag rather than trying to keep up with my pace. Very briefly, as Pippa dozed off against my back, I wished that I were the pregnant one. I quickly banished the thought. For now, Pippa had it easy, but it wouldn't be that way in another few weeks.

There were several challenges in riding with the Masons.

One, Jacob and Jove argued constantly about the best route to the airport. Twice, they led us down the wrong road and we had to turn around. Two, Jove was horridly out of shape. His girth spilled over the skinny bike seat, and the gears groaned beneath him. After a few miles, he began to pant like an overheated dog until we had to stop long enough for him to chug a few sips of water. Three, Penny's shrill voice reached an octave that echoed throughout the entire city, which I feared would draw too much attention to us. We had already been the subject of several suspicious looks from the other people on the streets, but I kept the handgun strapped visibly against my thigh. Once everyone noticed it was there, they turned their heads away from our party.

Eventually, we made it to the interstate, which was more of a mess than I expected. Though the blast had hit after rush hour, there had been enough people traveling at high enough speeds to create enormous pileups. Without anyone to tend to the injured, both sides of the road looked like a battlefield. No one said anything. There was nothing to say.

"Pippa, are you awake?" I murmured.

"Yeah."

"Close your eyes."

"It's too late."

The stench was the worst part. The bodies had begun to decompose, and a number of hungry critters arrived to clean up the aftermath. They were also a convenience. Death drove people away. Other than the six of us, the interstate was free and clear of the living. We rode along the shoulder, which was relatively passable, and tried not to look at the horrors beside us.

The storage warehouse was off an exit ramp, so we didn't actually have to ride all the way to the airport. Even so, it took us over two hours to get to it. My stomach grumbled in protest. I hadn't eaten since abandoning my breakfast at the Masons' earlier. The sun sank below the tree line, leaving us in the brisk purple dusk. The wind dried out my lips, so I drew the collar of my sweater up over my mouth and nose. If I was struggling, my companions were too, though it shocked me that none of them had voiced their complaints aloud yet.

"How much farther, Dad?" Jacob asked, the wind carrying his voice back. He sounded hoarse, as if he was watching a cold.

"It's just over the hill," Jove answered.

I pushed ahead, pumping my legs vigorously to get Pippa and me over the crest. When we reached the top, we nearly ran into the wagon tied behind Jacob's bike. He had stopped there to stare down at the warehouse, his expression knitting together in a frown.

I looked too. Down below, outside the warehouse door, a few fires blazed in big metal trash cans. People huddled around them, men mostly, warming their hands or frying hot dogs and beans for dinner. If that were all, it wouldn't have worried me so much, but a line of rifles decorated the side of the warehouse. This was not a group of people that I wanted to mess with.

"Who are they, do you think?" Jacob muttered.

"No one good," I said back.

"I know them," Nita chimed in, having made it up the hill after Jove and Penny. "See that mark?" She pointed to a crude crest that had been spray-painted on the side of the warehouse above the row of guns. "It's a gang. They call themselves the Silencers."

"Great," Jacob said. "I don't suppose the Silencers will let us go get the Humvee out of storage, will they?"

"I doubt it," Nita replied. "From what I've heard, they make most of their money out of chop shops. It's probably why they decided to post up here. They've got a whole warehouse full of expensive car parts."

"Parts that don't belong to them," Jacob growled. "I'm going down there."

I grabbed the back of his jacket to keep him from rolling down the hill. "No, you're not. You want to get killed?"

"I want to get out of here," he replied sharply. "What do you suggest?"

I monitored the gang's movements for another minute. There were about twenty guys down there, but they were all centered at the front door. No one moved around the back of the warehouse. "I'll go down. There's got to be a back door, right? I'll slip in unnoticed."

"And what happens when you try to drive a Humvee out of there?" Jacob challenged. "That's not exactly discreet, and I bet the Silencers would love an excuse to use those rifles."

"It's an armored car, Jacob. I'll figure it out." I swung my leg off the bike as Pippa balanced herself. "Nita, can you switch with me?"

"Sure." She set down her own bike and grabbed the tandem instead. "What are you going to do?"

I shrugged off the borrowed Saint Mark's coat and traded it for a plain black jacket that I'd packed in my bag. I zipped it up over my red sweater, covering the brighter color, and drew the hood up. "I'm going to sneak in. If I'm not out in an hour or if they start firing, assume I got caught and get the hell out of here, okay?"

Jacob flicked the hood off of my head. "I don't like this, Georgie. I should go down there. Not you."

I shook him off and pulled the hood up again. "Jacob, face facts, will you? I'm a woman, okay? A decent-looking one—"

"Girl power," Nita interjected.

"—which means that the guys down there are going to be way less willing to shoot at me than another strange man," I finished. "That's how society works. I have a better chance at surviving this than you do, so shut up, stay here, and make sure your family is safe. Got it?"

Jacob grabbed hold of my jacket and yanked me toward him.

"I never knew that I could love and hate someone so much at the same time."

"You'll thank me when we turn the heat on in the Humvee," I returned.

He crushed his lips against mine, curling his arms around me.

"Enough already," Pippa said. "I'm going to be sick."

I drew away from Jacob. "Go a little ways down the hill," I told Nita and the Masons. "If they look up here, they'll see you right away. I'll be back as soon as possible."

Without waiting for an answer, I darted away from the group and into the trees that bordered the road, letting gravity's momentum draw me closer to the Silencers.

$\mathcal{T}$he trees gave me the cover I needed to get close enough to scope out the Silencers' camp. I slid to a stop behind the wide trunk of an old oak, knelt down, and peeked out from behind it. First, I checked the hill. Thankfully, the Masons had taken my advice. The fading sky lit the terrain like the backdrop of a school play. Had they not moved, their silhouettes would have been plainly visible to the gang below. I shifted my gaze to the warehouse itself.

"Listen to me, George," my father's voice rang in my head. "Those men are here for you. They want to take you away from me because you're not going to school. They'll take you back to the city, and you know what that means, right?"

I was thirteen. "I'm dead."

"That's right," my father replied. "You make a sound, you're dead. You hear me?"

"Yes, sir."

The bright beam of a searchlight permeated the curtains that hung on the windows of our cabin. My father forced my head down below the sill but not before I'd caught a glimpse of the police officers outside.

"They're going to come inside," he whispered. "We need to get to the safe house. Remember, George, if you make a sound—"

"I'm dead."

That was the mantra. It always ended the same way. No matter what the situation. No matter who the person outside the cabin was. Run to the safe house. The bunker. Lock yourself underground. Stay quiet. Don't make contact.

As I studied the Silencers' camp, I half wished that I had yelled out to those cops when I was thirteen. It would've saved me a whole lot of childhood trauma. Then again, if I had done that, I would've been way less prepared for this moment. All those years of creeping around had paid off. If I wanted to make it somewhere silently, I could do it.

So when the Silencers burst into laughter simultaneously, I used the racket as cover and darted across the open space between my hiding spot and the dark side of the warehouse. I pressed myself against the cold metal wall, steadying my breath. The gang members went on with their storytelling and gesticulating. None of them had noticed the breach in their poor security measures.

"So then I said to him," a buff man with a black bandana around his neck went on with a chuckle, "'Hand over the cans, or I'll shove one up your ass.'"

The group guffawed, and I rolled my eyes at the lack of innovative threats. It was a gift to move away from them, toward the rear of the warehouse. I went slowly, rolling through each step from the heel of my boots to the toe. My father had taught me that it was the smoothest, quietest way to walk since it stopped you from stomping around like an elephant. Apparently, he had learned the skill from when he was in his college marching band, though I'd never seen him play an instrument in his life.

The Silencers' festivities took place outside the warehouse's big rolling garage doors, but I knew there had to be a few other entrances. Getting inside wasn't going to be the problem. Getting out was going to be a lot trickier. I found a side door around the back, jimmied the cheap lock, and cracked it open. After peeking inside to make sure none of the gang members was taking refuge from the wind, I snuck into the warehouse.

It was pitch black. The first thing I did was accidentally slam the top of my head against a mirror protruding from the side of an enormous pickup truck because I didn't allow for my eyes to adjust before popping out of my low crouch. I rubbed at the new lump as my eyes watered. The warehouse coalesced into a collection of shadows. It wasn't the average storage facility full of old people's junk or random odds and ends. This was a garage belonging to the wealthy. It was full of expensive vehicles from end to end, many of them priceless antiques or shiny foreign sports cars that were not meant to be driven through the thick snow that would find its way to the city in the next few months. There were Ferraris and Lamborghinis. Bugattis and Maseratis. And a line of original combat vehicles all parked next to one another.

I approached the row of Humvees from behind. Apparently Jove wasn't the only man in Denver that had an interest in collecting them. What could a person possibly need with this many old military vehicles? It wasn't as though you could drive them comfortably around town. Hell, you couldn't drive them comfortably at all. Lack of luxury aside, I couldn't help but appreciate Jove's unbridled fascination with the Humvees. When he wasn't arguing with his son, he and I had talked about certain aspects of the vehicle. He knew all about them, which was actually helpful in the grand scheme of things.

I reached a Humvee with a Saint Mark's Student of the Month bumper sticker plastered to the back window and clambered up into the driver's seat. Jove had upgraded the interior with leather accents, a new radio, and several speakers, but the upgrades didn't hide the practicalities that made the vehicle what it was. The bad news was that there was way less room in it than I thought there would be. There were only four seats, and the rest of the cabin space was taken up by a massive center console. Thankfully, the interior opened up to the trunk space in the back. Two of us would have to ride along there. It would be uncomfortable, but we would at least make it out of the city in one piece.

Jove had handed over the key before we'd left the apartment building. I fit it into the ignition and braced myself. If the Silencers heard the engine turn over, they would be inside in a heartbeat. As soon as I turned the truck on, I'd only have a few minutes to get out of Dodge. With a deep breath, I turned the key. Nothing happened. The engine sputtered and whined. The Humvee was out of gas.

"Are you freaking kidding me?" I muttered, banging on the steering wheel. I hopped out of the Humvee and looked around. There were a ton of cars to steal gas from, but I actually needed something to siphon with.

In the bed of the same truck that had nearly given me a concussion on the way in, I found a garden hose. I pulled a knife out of the inside pocket of my jacket and flicked it open then set to work on trimming the hose to an appropriate length. The knife was yet another thing that Jacob didn't know I owned. It was the same knife I'd learned to do everything with as a kid, from gutting a fish to skinning a rabbit. I tugged the shortened length of hose free from the bed, popped open the truck's gas tank, and got to work. There were empty gas jugs lined up against the warehouse wall. I positioned one of them where I needed it, fed one end of the hose into the truck's tank, and put the other end in my mouth. Then, trying to ignore the tangy metallic taste of the garden accessory, I sucked the gas into the hose. When I felt it surge toward my mouth, I quickly fit the hose into the jug and watched in satisfaction as the gas splattered into the plastic jug. Once it was full, I ditched the hose and hauled the jug back to the Humvee, where I dumped the stolen gas into the armored car's tank instead.

"Eat up," I muttered, patting the side of the Humvee. "Great, I'm talking to a truck."

Outside, another roar of laughter went up from the Silencers. I hoped they were drunk enough to stay put for another couple of minutes. Maybe their inebriated shenanigans would buy me more time to get out of here. I hopped up into the driver's seat again and tried the key for the second time. The Humvee engine roared to life, sending a rumbling echo through the warehouse.

"Hey!" someone shouted from outside.

"Here we go," I said. I threw the vehicle in drive and pulled it out of its tight parking space. Across the warehouse, someone rolled up the giant garage door. "Well, that was convenient."

Before the Silencers had the time to react, before any one of them even had the chance to pick up one of the rifles that rested against the warehouse, I pressed the Humvee's gas pedal to the floor and gunned it for the exit. The Silencers dove like Olympic swimmers to get out of the way. None of them were stupid enough to stand in front of the Humvee's massive grill once it was clear that I had no intention of stopping. I crashed through two of the trash can barbeques, sending sparks and hot dogs flying. As the Humvee careened up the hill, the Silencers finally sprang into action. I ducked as the quick pitter-patter of a firing rifle rang through the air. A few rounds hit the rear end of the Humvee, and I gritted my teeth at the harsh sound of metal against metal. I swerved closer to the woods, taking out the lowest level of tree branches. Night had fallen completely now, and the shadows made it difficult for the gang members to get off a clear shot. Bullets whizzed over the roof of the Humvee until I was out of range. I glanced in the mirror to check the situation behind me. The Silencers were already working on righting the barbecues and had not bothered to hop in another working vehicle to chase me. It was the smart thing to do. One stolen Humvee wouldn't put enough of a dent in their illegally appropriated inventory to warrant wasting resources on recovering it. Still, I wasn't going to take any chances by slowing down.

I revved the engine as the Humvee made it over the hill and skidded to stop beside the Masons and Nita. Each of them wore a stunned expression as I unlocked the doors and rolled down the window.

"What are you all waiting for?" I asked. "Get in before they decide to follow us. Move!"

As Nita helped Pippa and Penny into the backseat, Jacob loaded the bags into the rear of the vehicle. Jove, of course, climbed into the passenger's seat and looked over at me.

"Sure you don't want me to drive?" he asked.

"I got it, Jove."

Jacob appeared at my window. "What do we do with the bikes?"

"Leave them," I told him. "We don't have the room to bring them with us."

He rolled the bicycles into the woods, hiding them amongst the trees. Then he and Nita climbed in to sit between the bags in the trunk.

"Everyone ready?" I asked, checking to make sure everyone that had a seat belt was strapped in. "Here we go."

The Humvee lurched forward as I hit the gas, and everyone braced themselves. It was a rough ride, especially since we were driving on the shoulder to avoid the stagnant cars that littered the road. There was no use in returning to the interstate. It would be practically impassable in the Humvee.

"Uh, Georgie?" Jacob said, looking out of the Humvee's rear window. "We got trouble."

Two trucks rumbled into view behind us, close enough for me to catch a glimpse of the Silencers driving them.

"Damn it. I didn't think they would be stupid enough to follow us."

"Well, you did ruin their barbecue," Nita pointed out.

"Hold on, everyone." I raced up the hill as the trucks followed after us, aiming for the ramp that led to the interstate.

"What are you doing?" Jove demanded. "We're going to get stuck up there, and then they'll definitely catch us!"

"Shut up, Jove," I growled.

He reached for the steering wheel. "I won't let you drive my family straight into a situation that we won't be able to get out of."

I pulled the gun from the strap around my thigh and pointed it at Jove. Penny screamed, Pippa gasped, and Jacob yelled, "Georgie, what the hell are you doing?"

"Don't touch me," I said calmly to Jove. I had no intention of shooting him. The safety was still on, but he didn't need to know that. He raised his hands above his head and shrank into his seat. When I was satisfied with his submission, I returned my attention to the road, roaring up toward the interstate. The Silencers' trucks followed close behind.

I weaved in and out of the ruined cars, carving a quick path along the road. Occasionally, the Humvee clipped another vehicle, sending us all bumping up toward the ceiling. Jacob's head crashed against the hard top before he took a cue from Nita and lay flat against the padding of our baggage. The Humvee's tires stuck firmly to the pavement, no matter how hard I jerked the steering wheel around. The Silencers, on the other hand, hadn't picked the best vehicles to chase after us in. They had to follow each other in single file, driving over the debris that the Humvee left in its wake. As I wove around the tail end of an eighteen-wheeler, the first truck lost control and ran into another sedan. The second one narrowly avoided his buddy and, in a lucky coincidence, found enough room on the road to pull up next to the Humvee.

"Georgie, the guy riding shotgun is holding a freaking shotgun!" Pippa yelled.

"Everybody duck!" I ordered.

My passengers obeyed just in time as bullets rained through the windows. Shattering glass and horrified screams split the air. Up ahead, a school bus had turned and tipped over, blocking the road. I braked hard, screaming to a stop, but the Silencers noticed the obstruction too late. The brake lights of the truck flashed red as it smashed into the underside of the school bus. I didn't pause to take in the wreck, instead taking the nearest exit ramp to get off the interstate, then corrected my course toward the mountains, ignoring the pavement and driving across the curbs and sidewalks instead.

"Are you insane?" Jove thundered. "We could've died up there!"

"It was the best way to lose them," I shot back. "We got out, didn't we? Is everyone okay? Is anyone shot?"

"No," Pippa replied, "but Mom has a giant piece of glass in her leg."

I briefly looked behind me to check it out. Penny stared silently at her thigh, where a sharp pizza-shaped slice of the broken window had imbedded itself in the muscle. She didn't yell or cry or express any sort of emotion at all.

"Jesus, Penny!" Jove released his belt to reach over the back of his seat.

"Don't touch it!" Nita ordered, slapping Jove's hand away. "As soon as you pull that thing out, she's going to start bleeding like crazy. I'll take care of it."

Jove hesitated but took Nita's advice. He tapped Penny's uninjured knee. "Penny? Penny, look at me."

But his wife continued staring at the glass. Nita worked her way up to sit on the center console, the first aid kit in her lap.

"What's wrong with her?" Jove asked.

"She's in shock," I said. "It's a reaction to the adrenaline. It'll pass. Let Nita focus."

To my utmost surprise, Jove actually listened to me and turned around in his seat to face the front again. "So where exactly are we going?"

I reached into the pocket of my jacket again. Next to the knife, there was a folded-up picture. I drew it out and handed it to Jove, who unfolded it to look at it. I had the photo committed to memory. I had taken it nine years ago before I'd left for the city. It was a picture of my father's homestead. It looked quite nice. Peaceful, even. It had been a pretty day. The sunset painted streaks of orange and pink in the sky. The neon colors reflected off a thin layer of white snow. Smoke puffed from the chimney of the cabin. A man in a red flannel coat who had broad shoulders and long legs was frozen in the action of gathering an armful of chopped firewood from our stockpile. He faced away from the camera, but the figure was unmistakable. Two seconds after I'd clicked the picture, he'd turned to face me. *George, put that damn thing away.*

"It's not far," I told Jove as he studied the picture. "A few hours up the mountain. It's self-sustaining, and no one else but me knows where it is. We'll be safe there."

Jove's fat finger tapped the red flannel. "Who's this man?"

"That's my father."

"And is he going to be okay with all of us just showing up like this?"

The answer, without a doubt, was no. "I'll talk to him."

Jove sensed that that was the end of the discussion. He handed me the photo so that I could tuck it away again. "Let me know if you get too tired to drive."

A few hours later, when we had cleared the city and the moon had risen high into the sky, I took him up on his offer. He took the front seat, Nita took the passenger seat, and I joined Jacob to lie down in the back. Pippa and Penny dozed in the middle. Nita had wrapped Penny's leg tightly enough to stop most of the bleeding, but the wound needed stitches, which we wouldn't be able to tend to until we came to flat ground. Nita and Jove discussed Penny's wound care up front, giving me and Jacob the illusion of privacy in the trunk.

He lay flat on his back, his knees pressed against the wall of the Humvee as he stared at the ceiling.

I nudged his shoulder. "What are you thinking about?"

"You, mostly."

"Nice things about me, I hope."

"You left your engagement ring in the apartment."

I wiggled my barren ring finger, jostling the splint on my pinky. The tape around the splint was beginning to peel off, gray with the dirt that had stuck to the underside. It was hard to believe that the moment of forgetfulness had happened just that morning. It felt as if years had passed since then.

"I didn't mean to leave it," I told Jacob quietly. "Nita said my finger would swell—"

"You could've put on a necklace," he interrupted. "Worn it that way."

Anger and annoyance nibbled at my conscience. "Sorry, I was a little preoccupied trying to pack up our stuff for the American apocalypse."

"It was expensive."

"Is that all you care about?" I demanded. Pippa stirred in her seat. I lowered my voice. "You're worried about the price of a damn diamond right now? It's not going to matter in a couple of months, Jacob. No one's going to be bargaining over gold and jewelry. We're going to be fighting for food and water."

"It's not just the ring," he whispered back, finally rolling over to look at me. "It's everything you've ever hidden from me. What happened to your mom, the way your father raised you. I can't believe you didn't tell me any of that."

"I didn't need to," I argued.

"It's your life, Georgie!" he said. "We were engaged! I'm supposed to know these things about you."

"Were?" I repeated. "What's with the past tense?"

Jacob's Adam's apple bobbed as he swallowed anxiously. "Nothing. It seems unlikely that we're going to get married now. Kinda feels like a big white wedding isn't flush with the whole end-of-the-world thing."

"That's not it, is it?" I'd known Jacob long enough to figure out when he was using half-truths to cover up what he really meant. "If you really wanted, we could march up the mountain, exchange rings that we weaved out of friggin' grass, and say our vows, but you don't want that, do you?"

"That's not a real wedding."

"It would be real enough for me," I declared.

He covered his face with his hands and groaned. "I can't do this right now."

"This is the only time we have to do this—"

"No, I meant *this*." He gestured to the space between the two of us, his expression hardening into something cold and empty.

The Humvee rolled over a ditch, and something sharp from one of the packs dug into my lower back. "You don't want to do what?"

Jacob met my eyes. "I don't know you, Georgie. I thought I did, but I watched you shoot that guy. Cold-blooded. No hesitation. There was something dark in your eyes, like you enjoyed it—"

"That's fucking ridiculous, and you know it."

"I saw it, Georgie!"

"So while I was putting myself in harm's way to save the life of an innocent little girl, you were watching and judging me," I hissed. "I did what I had to do in that moment. What would you have done? Let her go back to an abusive father?"

"Maybe. I don't know."

"It would have been a death sentence," I snapped.

"I'm not doubting your reasoning," he argued, glancing toward the others. Penny and Pippa were still asleep, while Jove and Nita continued their discussion unhindered. "I'm saying that I didn't know you had that in you."

"A will to survive?" I challenged.

"The ability to kill."

"You're oversimplifying things."

He didn't reply and returned to staring at the ceiling of the truck.

"So that's it?" I asked him. "You said you can't do this anymore. What does that mean?"

"I think you know what it means, Georgie."

I stared at him in disbelief. "You're breaking up with me. Now? While I'm taking your entire family to safety with me? I could've gone alone, Jacob, or just brought Nita. Do you realize that?"

He inhaled deeply and blew out the breath in a hot sigh. "I'm not saying we have to figure it out right now—"

"No, it's fine," I said. "You want to be done? We're done. It's as easy as that. Sorry about your ring. I can't promise it'll be there when you get back."

He turned toward me. "Georgie—"

I rolled over so that the only view he had of me was my back. I was too angry to cry, but my face burned with pent-up emotions that I couldn't express in the confines of the back of the Humvee. It had been so quick. One challenging day had driven a wedge between him and me. If we couldn't get through one day, how were we supposed to get through the rest of our lives? I wanted to hit something, to feel some kind of release. Instead, I balled up my hands and tucked them under my arms, hugging myself together.

AT SOME POINT in the journey, I must have fallen asleep, because the next thing I remembered was Nita nudging me awake. The Humvee had come to a stop in the middle of the woods, angled upward on a steep incline.

"Georgie?" Nita mumbled. "Jove needs you to give him directions. You should take my seat."

I slipped out of the trunk. Jacob was either asleep or pretending to be asleep in order to avoid talking to me. Either way, I felt a pang of longing and resentment in my chest as the collar of the coat he was using as a blanket shifted to cover his face. Nita took my place, and I joined Jove up front with a yawn.

"Still good to drive?" I asked him as we trundled upward.

"I'm wired," he replied. The Humvee's lights illuminated the road that weaved through the mountains. "I couldn't sleep if I wanted to."

"Good, because we're about to go off-road," I told him. I pointed to a gap in the trees. If you didn't know it was there, you wouldn't have seen it. "Make a left up there."

As I directed Jove in relative silence, the rough terrain woke up the others. Bleary-eyed, we watched the trees scratch what was left of the Humvee's windows, occasionally dodging wayward shards of grass. Pippa held her mother's hand over the center console. In the far back, Nita and Jacob lay on their stomachs and looked ahead. I caught Jacob's eye in the mirror and quickly looked away.

"We should be close," I said to Jove as we rolled up another incline. "It should be right over this hill—"

Without warning, blinding floodlights illuminated the cabin of the Humvee. I squinted through the windshield. There, where my father's property was supposed to be, was a sky-high fence with an electrified gate, flanked by a crank-up, generator-powered stadium light on either side. Behind the gate, I could make out several tents set up in neat rows, more light fixtures, and a collection of outhouses on the far side of the campground.

The whole place buzzed with the rumble of several working generators.

Four burly men dressed in boots, neon vests, and ski masks stood at the gate. Each of them held a military-grade rifle, though none raised a gun to the Humvee. Instead, the tallest man stepped up to the driver's side window and peered inside.

"Evening, folks," he said, pulling the ski mask down to speak clearly. "What can we help you with?"

I leaned across Jove before he could answer. "What the hell is this place? Where's my father?"

"I don't know who you are, ma'am," the man said as he spread his arms out to indicate the land behind him, "but this is Camp Haven."

he growl of the Humvee's powerful engine loosened rabbits and raccoons from beneath thick bushes and sent them scurrying for quieter hiding places. Headlights pointed straight ahead, toward a twenty-foot gate reinforced with steel and barbed wire. The window buzzed down. A big man with a bigger gun approached the driver's side. His gaze ran the length of the Humvee before scanning the inside. Inquisitive gray eyes scrutinized our faces. Six people packed into one truck with all of the supplies that we could carry. The overweight driver in an extra-large Ralph Lauren sweater with a supercilious sneer. The half-conscious trophy wife, her thigh wrapped in bloodstained gauze. The pregnant seventeen-year-old who was so far along that she couldn't see her own feet. The petite medical student whose pretty, angled cheekbones were more suited for a runway than an operating room. The wannabe photojournalist—my fiancé or ex-fiancé, depending on how recently you asked him—with soft brown eyes who spent too much time in the gym and not enough seeking the work he claimed to be so committed to. And me. The nobody. Who was I really? A radio persona. A talk show host. A voice without a face.

The only person in the Humvee with any inclination as to what we were up against.

The man tugged his ski mask off, resting his rifle across his chest. "Evening, folks. What can we help you with?"

"What the hell is this place?" I asked. "Where's my father?"

"I don't know who you are, ma'am, but this is Camp Haven."

The first light of the morning peeked over the horizon and crept through the trees, reaching its long arms across the stretch of land confined within the towering fence line. Nine years ago, I'd left this exact spot without looking back. I'd hiked hours across the Rockies until I made it to Denver. The busy roads and bustling coffee shops and the sheer amount of people were a far cry from the home I'd left behind, but Camp Haven wasn't home. Home was one log cabin and an underground bunker and acres upon acres of undisturbed property. Home was a fire in the hearth and wild game on the table. Home was my father without his wife, me without my mother, doing our damnedest to make the world mean something again. It was the place that I counted on to be there, no matter what befell the rest of society.

"You don't understand." I peered up at the sign above the gate. Someone had shaped thick wire into the title of the homestead, spray-painted it red, and mounted it to the top of the wall that enclosed the camp's perimeter. "This is my father's property. My property. This is my home."

The large man ducked his head to get a better look at me through the driver's window. "Camp Haven's been here for a good six or seven years, ma'am. You must be confused. Tough times like these will do that to you."

"I'm not confused!"

The man's fingers tightened on his rifle as the volume and tenacity of my voice stirred a sparrow from the nearby trees. Our driver, Jove, pushed me off of his armrest. A mere hour ago, he was my soon-to-be father-in-law. Now he was just a wealthy man with a working vehicle and a poor attitude toward me.

"Sorry about Georgie," Jove said. "She's been on edge since the blast. We're looking for a place to stay."

"Can't stay here," the man said.

"This is *my* land—" I started.

"Do you know what's going on out there?" Jove jabbed his thumb behind us, toward the city that we had left in ruins. "Do you know what Denver looks like right now?"

The man hefted his rifle to rest on his hip. "I can imagine. Most people don't know their ass from a hole in the ground. Can't fathom what an EMP bomb did to them."

"So you know," I said, nudging Jove aside. "You know what Denver—and the rest of the United States—is going through right now."

"Of course we know," the man replied. "It's our job to know. That's why we're still standing, miss. Camp Haven doesn't rely on electricity or technology. We're off the grid."

Less than thirty-six hours ago, life as we knew it had ended. Someone—terrorists, North Korea, Russia, whatever—had detonated an atmospheric bomb over the United States. The resulting electromagnetic pulse had knocked out anything that ran on electricity, circuit boards, or batteries. The only reason our Humvee worked was because it was a military original. It didn't rely on any electronic components to run. It was by the miracle of my unusual upbringing that I'd managed to get those closest to me out of the war zone that Denver had morphed into. People were dying in droves. Emergency services either ignored or couldn't reach those who needed help. The streets were rife with looters and violence. The mountains, where people were few and far between, were safer.

The man outside the window extended his hand toward Jove. When they connected, it was like fusing the same end of two D batteries to each other. They were of the same make—each of substantial height and weight—but while Jove's girth boasted excess and gluttony, the other man's spoke of strength out of necessity.

"Let me introduce myself," the man said, pumping Jove's hand. They each squeezed so hard that the skin around their fingers turned white. "Name's Ludo. I'm the head of security here at Camp Haven. My main goal is to keep this place running as smoothly as possible, which sometimes means making difficult decisions. This is one of them. I can't let you in."

"Listen to me," I said, annoyed that this Ludo fellow was determined to speak with Jove instead of me. I was the one who'd gotten us this far. "My name is Georgiana Fitz. My father is Amos Fitz. This is his land. He built that cabin—" I pointed through a gap in the reinforced fence, where smoke plumed from the chimney of my old home "—with his bare hands. I helped him do it."

"Don't know anyone by the name of Fitz," Ludo said. "A brave man by the name of Sylvester built Camp Haven from the ground up."

"Sylvester who?"

"No matter. Can't let you in."

The trunk of the Humvee popped open, and Jacob—non-fiancé, ex-boyfriend, whatever he was now—slid out from between the duffel bags and backpacks full of our supplies. Ludo raised his gun and took a step back from the truck. Three other men were stationed at the gates to Camp Haven, and each of them lifted their rifles as Jacob rounded the Humvee. He lifted his hands to eye level and stopped several feet from Ludo's barrel.

"My name is Jacob Mason," he said. "This is my father, Jove, and my fianceé, Georgie. My mother, Penny, is sitting in the backseat. A shard of glass went through her thigh. She needs stitches. My sister, Pippa, is eight months pregnant. She needs somewhere warm and dry to recuperate. We already have a medic, Nita, and our own supplies. All we need is a safe place to crash."

Ludo lowered his rifle a bit. "A medic, you say?"

"A med student," Nita muttered from the open trunk. I shushed her.

"I'll make you a deal," Ludo said. "Camp Haven relies on the skills and prowess of its members to stay up and running. We do everything ourselves. Cook, clean, build, hunt, et cetera. Everyone pulls their weight. If you can prove to me that each of you has something to bring to the table, I'll let you in. The medic's valuable enough, so she's good to go. Who else you got?"

"You guys got communications?" I asked at once. "Looks like a big ass camp. Five hundred acres or so, right? I imagine you need handheld radios to get messages from one end to the other."

Ludo lifted his broad shoulders. "No radios, no tower. It's old-fashioned smoke signals and bird calls here at Camp Haven."

"I could build one for you," I offered. "A tower, I mean. Radios too. It would do you a lot of good in case of emergencies. Or you can keep whistling at each other. Your choice."

Ludo considered my proposition. "Fine. Miss Fitz is in. Who's next?"

"I can do manual labor," Jacob said. I swallowed a sharp scoff. Jacob Mason, who had never lifted anything other than a weight plate at the gym in his entire life, was offering himself up for manual labor? "You said you build everything yourselves. I can help with that and whatever else you need. I'm young, fit, and strong. Put me anywhere."

"Mason Junior's in," Ludo barked. He leaned against the window of the Humvee. "What about Mason Senior?"

Jove eyed Ludo's thick forearm. "I brought the truck. I imagine it'll do you some good."

Ludo thumped his fist against the door panel of the Humvee. "Until it runs out of gas. No good. What else you got?"

Pippa, who had been quiet until now, unbuckled her seatbelt from her wide belly and popped up between the two front seats. "Excuse me, Mister Ludo—"

"Just Ludo, kid."

"Right," she said. "Ludo, I've been sitting in this terrible truck for several hours and I was stuck in an elevator overnight before that. Long story short, I really have to pee. Think of this Humvee as the Titanic. Would you deny a pregnant teenager a lifeboat? Women and children and all that, right?"

Ludo's bushy white beard, which spilled over the collar of his thick Kevlar jacket, bristled as he tried to keep from smiling. "Smart one, aren't you? Fine. You're in. Next?"

"What about Penny?" I asked. Jacob's mother was as white as a clean sheet in the backseat. She had lost a lot of blood, and if we didn't get her leg stitched up soon, I feared she might not recover from the wound.

Ludo squinted into the backseat. "She's not looking good. My bet is she'd be a waste of resources."

"A waste of resources?" Jacob stepped toward Ludo, who automatically raised his weapon again. "That's my mother you're talking about."

Ludo nudged Jacob with the butt of his gun. "Step back, son. I'm just doing my job. Without proper medical attention, your mother's going to be on her way out real soon. Like I said, no point in wasting the bandages and ointment on her."

Jacob turned red. Sensing danger, I kicked open the passenger door of the Humvee to join the party outside Camp Haven's gates and put myself between Jacob and Ludo's gun. "We brought our own first aid supplies. We won't use any of your resources to tend to Penny. All she needs is a bed in your med bay."

Ludo studied me from head to toe, taking in everything from my violet-dyed hair to my camouflage snow jacket to my all-weather boots. "You ain't one of them."

"Sorry?"

He stepped on the toe of my boot. I didn't wince. "You're dressed sensibly and affordably. Got boots that'll keep your toes warm during a long hike. Navigated a Humvee up the Rockies. You're the sore thumb, aren't you? So why didn't you just make it up here on your own?"

"This is my family. I couldn't leave them behind."

He chewed on his tongue, reviewing the occupants of the Humvee once more. "I like you," he said to me. "Fiery. Quick. Loyal. You'll be a good asset to Camp Haven. We value loyalty."

I waited on his final decision, folding my arms across his chest.

"Fine." Ludo waved to the three men who guarded the gate. They slung their rifles across their backs and went to work pulling the gate open. "You can all come in, but we have conditions. Number one, like I said before, everyone works. As soon as you're up to it, you'll get assigned a position. Number two, you will consent to an obligatory medical screening at the med bay before advancing to any other part of the camp. We do this for our own protection. Can't have outsiders bringing in bacteria or viruses into camp. Do you agree to participate?"

"Yes, sir," I said, answering for the group.

Ludo tapped the side of the Humvee to get Jove's attention. "Pull through the gates and park on the left next to our vehicles. We'll unload the truck for you, categorize your inventory, and add it to our own."

"Hold on a minute," Jove said, the brake lights of the Humvee flashing red. "I brought these things here. They belong to me. You won't go giving my clothes and shoes to people I don't know."

"That's the deal here," Ludo replied. "We share everything. You want in, you agree to our conditions. Otherwise, I'm sure you can find your way back to Denver on your own."

"What's stopping me from driving straight through your men

and into your pretty camp however I want?" Jove challenged, revving the engine.

Ludo patted his gun. "I highly suggest you do not attempt to do so, or I can assure you that will not survive this gorgeous morning."

"Enough pissing, Jove," I said. "Do what the man asks of you so we can get your wife and daughter somewhere safe."

Jove glared at me but drove through the gates without further argument. Jacob and I followed Ludo on foot.

"Change of guard will be here to relieve you soon, fellas," Ludo announced to the other men who patrolled the fence. Then he leaned closer to one of them, and I tilted my head to catch the muttered conversation. "Keep an eye on the big man. He's going to cause trouble."

"Yes, sir."

The gate rattled shut behind us, and we were officially inside Camp Haven. The sight made my jaw drop. My father's land, once just a cabin in the middle of nowhere, was now a square of organized civilization. Most of the trees had been cleared for simple block buildings, log cabins, and platform tents. In the distance, a water wheel turned over the part of the river that my father and I used to fish in. People bustled about, fulfilling early morning duties. Some mopped out the row of outhouses that bordered the far end of the camp. Others carried canvas sacks of potatoes and dried meat toward a long, low building with the laughable label *Bistro* painted in white over the doorway. Still others transported water, or lugged shovels and trowels, or shouldered compound bows as they headed toward the gate. The EMP blast had not so much as tickled the residents of Camp Haven. They went about their lives as if it were any other day.

"Unbelievable, isn't it?" Ludo said, noticing my open-mouthed stare. "Completely self-sustaining. It's amazing what we've done in a short amount of time. Even got a sewage system. It ain't pretty, but it works."

"But why?" I asked. Those who passed by observed us without shame. Camp Haven must not have seen newcomers in a while. "Why work so hard to build this place? It's not like we're living in the age of the Roman Empire."

"Aren't we though?" Ludo replied. "Look what happened to the rest of the United States in just a few short hours, Miss Fitz. Most people go crazy if they can't charge their phones or flip on a light switch. They rely too much on modern day accommodations. They don't think about the future. It's privilege, plain and simple, and privilege will get you killed. *That's* why we built this place. To disconnect from the noise down there. We're always safe here at Camp Haven, always prepared. Life might be simpler, but we're alive and well, and that's all that matters."

Jove put the Humvee into park and switched off the engine. It turned out that Camp Haven owned a few similar vehicles, but from the layer of dirt and grime on the hoods, it looked like the other trucks hadn't been in operation for quite some time. However, a collection of man-powered surrey bikes, each built with a convenient platform for hauling goods, appeared well-worn.

"Keys?" Ludo asked.

Jove tossed them over with a grimace. "Don't scratch my truck. It's a collectible."

"That's the least of your worries, Mason Senior." Ludo stopped one of the men passing by. "Eirian, do me a favor, won't you? Inventory our guests' supplies."

"Sure thing, boss."

I caught the man's—Eirian—eye as he brushed past me to get started on Ludo's request. They were bright green, the color I imagined a dragon's scales to be. He flashed me a grin, rolled up his sleeves, and got to work, the lines of his back moving fluidly as he unloaded baggage from the Humvee.

Nita helped Pippa out of the truck, while Jacob did the same for Penny. His mother hung onto consciousness by a thread. Her pants were soaked through with blood. It dripped into the dirt as Jacob lifted Penny into his arms.

"Med bay," Ludo ordered, pointing toward one of the block buildings at the center of camp, this one with a bright blue cross painted on the front. "Everyone. Let's go."

The medical bay was small but practical, more like a walk-in clinic than a hospital. It had room for ten patients at the most, a bed for each of them lined up against the concrete wall. Only two of them were occupied, one by a small boy with a plaster cast around his elevated foot and another by an elderly woman with a hacking cough. Jove directed Jacob to one of the free cots, where he lay Penny down and propped several pillows under her bleeding thigh. Pippa sank down on the bed next to her with a deep sigh.

Two women emerged from the med bay's office. The first was shorter than Nita, five feet tall at the most, but she exercised the energy of a lioness as she stalked toward us. The second was younger, in her early thirties maybe. She wrung her hands nervously as she trailed behind her superior.

"What have we got?" the first woman barked.

"Visitors," Jove answered. He pointed to Penny. "This one needs your immediate attention, Jax. As for everyone else, I need screenings." He turned to our group. "This is Jax, our head of medical, and Maddy, her assistant. No one leaves here until you've been cleared by one of them. Understood?"

Jax didn't bother to wait for our assent. She hip-checked Jacob to get him out of the way and unwrapped the gauze on Penny's leg, wrinkling her nose as she checked the wound. "That's a deep cut. It's going to need to be flushed out and stitched up. Decent job on the wrappings though. Who did that?"

Nita raised her hand. "That would be me?"

Jax trained her laser-like gaze on Nita. "Are you an EMT or something?"

"I'm a medical student," Nita said. "General surgery."

Jax turned to Jove. "She's mine. Don't assign her anywhere else."

"I already assumed as much, darling," Jove replied.

"You," Jax said, pointing at Nita. "Wash your hands and help me out. You—" She jabbed a finger at Maddy "—start the work-ups for everyone else. Let's get through this as quickly as possible. I have other patients to tend to today."

Maddy clapped her hands together. "Not to worry, everyone. Our medical screenings are pretty routine. Any volunteers to go first?"

I stepped forward.

I HADN'T BEEN to the doctor in years. I avoided sterile offices unless it was absolutely necessary. My father's descent into paranoia encompassed every facet of his life, including his opinion of the medical profession.

"Quacks!" he barked at ten-year-old me. "They're all quacks!"

We had taken care of ourselves so well on the homestead that doctor's visits became obsolete. Things changed when I left that life behind and moved to Denver. That first winter, I fought through a raging sinus infection, refusing to go to the doctor until my lungs filled with so much fluid that bronchitis and pneumonia set in. Antibiotics were a beautiful thing. I wondered how Camp Haven managed in that respect.

Maddy examined me in a private room, going through all the motions. She listened to my heart, took my pulse, and measured my blood pressure. Then she shined a light into the back of my throat, my nose, and my ears, all while firing rapid questions at me.

"Have you had any sort of infection in the last ten weeks?"

"No."

"Are you taking any medications?"

"No."

"Do you have a history of diabetes, cancer, or heart disease in your family?"

"Not that I'm aware of."

"Are you allergic to anything?"

"Stupidity, mostly."

"Are you sexually active?"

"Yes."

On and on it went, until Maddy knew more about me and my personal history than Jacob did. Then she administered a "general" vaccine that was supposedly required to remain a resident of the camp, drew several vials of blood from a vein in my arm, and finished up by taping a piece of cotton to the pinprick on the inside of my elbow.

"There you go," she said, patting my shoulder. "Make sure you drink plenty of water today. You'll need it to help replenish the lost blood."

"Can I ask you a question?" I flexed my arm experimentally, trapping the dollop of cotton in the crook of my elbow. "What's all of this for? Is it really necessary?"

Maddy taped labels to the vials of blood and stacked them neatly in a handy holder. "We screen every single person who comes into Camp Haven. We can't risk spreading bacteria or viruses through the camp. We live in tight quarters. If one person gets sick, we all get sick. Then no one's healthy enough to get the work done, and the whole camp suffers. It's a vicious circle that we'd all like to avoid."

"Sounds like you learned this from experience."

She grimaced as she tossed the used needle in a bin marked with the biohazard symbol. "A few years ago, when we were less lax, someone returned from a trip into the city with a stomach flu. We figured it was food poisoning and let it go. A few days later, the whole camp was puking their guts up. You can't imagine the smell."

I wrinkled my nose. "Oh, I can."

"Now we quarantine the sick until they're no longer contagious," Maddy explained. "It's safer and more comfortable for all us."

"Should I bother to ask what's in that vaccine?"

"No."

"Noted."

"Can I give you some advice?" Maddy asked, wiping the counter and the exam table with rubbing alcohol. "Keep your head down and do your work. Camp Haven functions best when no one stands out or makes trouble. From your haircut, I assume you like to stand out."

I rubbed the shaved portion of my head. "It's more freedom of self-expression in my opinion."

"We forego a lot of freedoms here to keep this place running smoothly." She caught sight of my tight-lipped expression and gave a wry smile. "You'll get used to it. You should consider yourself lucky. You were the first to find us after the blast. Chances are Ludo won't be so kind to the next group of people that wants in. How'd you do it anyway?"

"Do what?"

"Find us," she clarified. "We're not exactly on the map, you know?"

"I used to live here," I told her. "You built your little prepper camp on my father's land."

Ludo knocked on the door to the exam room before she could process my answer. "Everybody decent?" he called.

"Yes, sir," Maddy replied.

Ludo came in. "Has she been cleared?"

"She checks off."

"Good." He took my camo jacket from where it hung over the

back of an extra chair and handed it to me. "Hop to it, Miss Fitz. It's time for a tour of the compound."

I slipped my arms into the jacket and zipped it up. "What about my family?"

"Jax and your medic friend are finishing up Mrs. Mason's leg," Ludo reported. "Maddy needs to examine the rest of them. I'll have someone show them around the camp once they're cleared, but for now, I'd like to talk to you about the way we run this place."

Maddy shot me a look. So much for flying under the radar. For whatever reason, Ludo had already singled me out. I hopped off the exam table. "All right. At your leisure."

Jove led me through a rear exit of the med bay so that we didn't pass by the Masons again. Part of me was grateful. I had no desire to sit by Penny's side, or help Pippa to the bathroom, or listen to Jacob babble on about the fissures in our relationship. I wanted to know more about Camp Haven and how it had come to be. Ludo's tour was the first step in acquiring that information, though his skills as a guide lacked eloquence.

"Mess hall," he announced, pointing to the low building that I'd clocked on our way in. "Meals are served three times a day. Snacks are portioned out appropriately." His finger drifted to the next structure over. "Community hall, which everyone calls DotCom."

I shot him a look.

"Bad joke, I know," he admitted. "Anyway, that's where we hold any camp-wide meetings or events when it's too cold to do it outside. You already know the med bay. Over there's the school—"

"Do you have a lot of kids in the camp?" I asked him as we passed the one-room building that served as Camp Haven's educational services.

"Nine," he answered. "Ten, once your little sister delivers. We have rules concerning intercourse, but we'll get to that later."

"Rules—?"

"Those are the dorms," Ludo went on, gesturing toward two block buildings separated by a simple courtyard. "One for women and one for men. We have family units and single units as well for special circumstances, but they're hard to come by. Hope you don't mind sharing."

"It's not me you'll hear complaints from," I said, thinking of Jove and Jacob.

"I get complaints every day," Ludo said. "Ain't nothing new. Anyway, there's a reason I wanted to talk to you, Miss Fitz."

"Please, it's just Georgie."

"Georgie then," he said. "I got a good feeling about you. Honestly, the only reason I let your folks into camp was because you were with them. You know things about this place, don't you? About the things we do here?"

"I grew up like this," I told him.

"And you mentioned your father earlier."

A gust of wind bit at my cheeks. It was colder here than in the city below. "This is his land. That's his cabin. When I left this place nine years ago, there was nothing here but that cabin and my father. Now it's—"

"An entire community," Ludo finished.

"What happened to him?" I asked. "You have to know. You said Camp Haven's been around for six or seven years. Someone has to know how it started."

Ludo led me toward the Bistro, where the residents of Camp Haven were lining up to be served breakfast. "Everyone knows how Camp Haven started. We tell the story to the kids during campfires."

"Well, fry me up a s'more, Ludo, and clue me in."

Ludo chuckled deep in his belly as he held open the door to the Bistro for me. We filed in after everyone else. The hall reminded me of the cafeteria at the sleepaway camp I'd attended a year or so before my mom died. The long tables and benches had been hand-crafted from felled trees. Oil lamps lined the wall at evenly spaced intervals to light the interior. A serving counter stretched from one end of the room to the other, laden with fresh and dried meats, drop biscuits, fruits and vegetables, and even pancakes. Ludo grabbed two metal trays from a stack near the door and we joined the line to be served.

"A long time ago, a lone hiker decided to take on the Rockies by himself," Ludo said. "The story goes that he was on a quest to find the soul that the noise of the world had robbed him of."

"A soul searcher, eh?" I muttered.

"He left everything and everyone behind," Ludo continued as we shuffled forward. "Packed up only what he needed to survive in the wilderness and headed into the hills without so much as a backwards glance. Didn't even say goodbye to his family or friends."

"So he was a selfish loner," I interjected. "No wonder."

"He was on a mission to cleanse himself."

"Because that always ends well."

"The point," Ludo pressed on, "is that he went. He left society behind to start anew, but he soon realized that this was harder than he anticipated."

"Color me flabbergasted."

"An unexpected blizzard hit the Rockies," Ludo said, now ignoring me completely. "It was early in the season. There shouldn't have been snow like that at all. The man was buried in an avalanche. For three days, he burrowed in the snow. Didn't know which way was up. He thought he was going to die there." All around us, the other people in line listened in to Ludo's story, as if they hadn't heard it enough times already. "But on the fourth day, the man heard a woman calling his name. He followed her voice, digging through the snow until he burst through the surface. The woman was nowhere in sight, but he emerged right below the cabin on the hill. The cabin was unoccupied, but there was food in the cupboard and a fire in the hearth. To this day, the man claims that the woman was a spirit sent to save his life. He decided to do the same for anyone who chose the path that he did, and so Camp Haven was born."

"So he's still here then?" I asked Ludo.

"He lives in the cabin on the hill," Ludo confirmed. "Camp Haven's director. His name is—"

"Sylvester."

*L*udo and I ate breakfast inside the Bistro, joining a group of other Camp Haven residents at one of the wooden tables. They watched me eat like kittens around a lion. Apparently, Camp Haven wasn't used to visitors. I stared at my plate, shoveling eggs and bacon into my mouth without looking up. The food felt wonderful in my stomach, even if it was a bit bland. According to Ludo, spices were hard to come by, but they did grow and dry herbs to season their meals. I caught the eye of the teenaged boy sitting next to me as I ripped a piece of bacon apart. When I grinned, he tore his gaze away and scampered off with his tray.

"Is this how it's going to be?" I asked Ludo. "Is everyone going to treat us like we're interlopers?"

"Gotta look at it from their perspective." He dusted biscuit crumbs from his beard. "These people have only known each other for the last seven years. They know every single face in the compound by heart. Now, all of a sudden, there's six new ones. How would you feel?"

"So you never took in anyone new?" I said. "How'd they all get here then?"

"Sylvester brought them in," he explained. "I thought you'd already gotten the gist of this."

"I don't understand how this many people up and moved out of their heated houses to live up in the mountains with no electricity." I stacked bacon and eggs inside a biscuit like a sandwich. "Why'd you do it, Ludo? How did you end up here?"

He licked grease from his fingers and wiped them on a cloth napkin. "Funny story actually. Five and a half years ago, I was hunting with a few friends nearby. We were being stupid. Brought a shitload of beer with us, and I got drunk enough to shoot myself through the foot. My buddies thought it was hilarious, but I was bleeding out pretty bad."

"Your friends sound swell."

"They weren't the best group of guys," Ludo agreed. "So when a beautiful woman came out of the woods and told them very eloquently to fuck off, they took her word to heart."

"Another spiritual guide?" I asked.

"No, ma'am," he said. "It was Jax. She got me to camp and patched me right up. I knew as soon as she pulled that bullet out of my foot with her bare hands that she was the one for me."

"You and Jax?" I smothered a snicker. "Really?"

"You can laugh, but she's a tough cookie," Ludo went on. "Never met a stronger woman. She convinced me to stay at Camp Haven. I used to be a cop, see, and the camp needed someone to take charge of security."

"So they picked an inebriated cop who shot himself in the foot?"

Ludo tossed a grape across the table. It bounced off my tray and into my lap. "You got a mouth on you. Enough about me though. Tell me about yourself. How'd you end up here?"

"I told you," I said, popping the wayward grape into my mouth and enjoying the burst of fresh juice across my tongue. "The EMP blast knocked out all the power in Denver. Staying in the city with everyone else would've been certain death. I knew getting up here was our best bet at surviving, but I wasn't planning on all of you being here."

"I didn't mean today," Ludo said. "I meant when you were a kid. You claim that your father built that cabin, that you lived out here off the grid, but you keep asking me why anyone would give up all that noise to come out here. Something doesn't mesh."

I spat out the grape seed. "The abridged version is that I had a traumatic childhood, and instead of facing our problems head on, my father ran from them. If you don't mind, I'd rather not sink my teeth into the details."

"I suppose that's your prerogative."

"Speaking of my father," I said, "I came up here with the intention of locating him. Do you have any idea how I can find out what happened to him?"

"You can check the archives." Ludo folded a large strip of bacon in half and consumed it in one bite. "They're kept in DotCom. Got the names and signatures of everyone who ever set foot inside Camp Haven, starting with Sylvester."

"Yeah, Sylvester," I mused. "I'm quite interested in him."

"We all are," Ludo said. "He's a great man."

"When can I go to my cabin?" I asked. "I need to see if my dad left anything behind for me and—"

Ludo coughed into his cup of black coffee. "Steady there, Georgie. Ain't no one going up to the cabin."

I stared him down. "Why not? It's my cabin."

"Not anymore, ma'am," Ludo replied. "The cabin belongs to Sylvester. No one goes in without express permission."

I thunked my fork on the table. A few heads turned in our direction. "That cabin belongs to me."

Ludo weaseled the fork out from beneath my fingers. "If your story's true, I believe that nine years ago, this land and that house were yours. Times change, my dear. This is present day, and you're a guest in our home. You can either accept that and take advantage of our hospitality, or you can continue traipsing around here with your grand declarations and high-and-mighty attitude. I can tell you right now which one's going to get you further though."

Before I could answer, the doors to the Bistro opened, spilling sunshine into the dimly lit. Jacob, Jove, Nita, and Penny traipsed inside, escorted by Maddy, and stamped their boots on the rug. As Maddy guided them into the breakfast line, Ludo watched me watch them.

"That's not usually the face someone makes when they see that their family is safe and sound after a cataclysmic disaster," Ludo said, innocently spearing another grape with his fork and popping it into his mouth.

"You don't know my face." I looked away from Jacob's broad shoulders, back to Ludo. "What about Sylvester? He was the first one to arrive here, which means he most likely met my father. Can I talk to him?"

He chuckled deep in his belly. "No one talks to Sylvester."

"Does this guy even exist?" I demanded. "Because everything you've told me leads up him being a fake figurehead holed up in a cabin that no one sees or talks to. Sounds like a load of shit to me."

"He exists. I've spoken to him."

"You just said—"

"No one talks to Sylvester without good reason," he rectified. "He's the director of Camp Haven for a reason. Most days, we get along fine within the system that he built and laid out for us. Every once in a while, something goes wrong, as things are prone to do. That's when we go to Sylvester, when we don't know how to solve a problem on our own. He always has the answer. He also does weddings."

My coffee slipped, and I pushed away from the table to avoid a stain on my pants. "He does what now?"

"Weddings," Ludo said again. "No preacher men up here at

Camp Haven. We have a chapel and all, but it's more of a spiritual thing. If a couple wants to get married, they have to appeal to Sylvester. He reviews the case, decides whether or not the couple is fit for each other, and marries them in the cabin."

"Please tell me you realize how absurd that is," I said. Jacob's golden hair shone under the warm lights of the oil lamps as he shuffled through the line with his tray. "Who is this guy to decide whether or not two people are right for each other?"

"You don't understand how Camp Haven works yet," Ludo replied. "We don't have time for messy relationships, drama, or fights within the community. Everything, including personal relationships, must benefit the camp." He looked over his shoulder to where Jacob tried to stop Jove from arguing with the woman serving the food for another scoop of scrambled eggs. "I'd keep that in mind if I were you, and I say that for your sake, not the camp's."

"I didn't ask for your impression of my relationship, and I sure as hell won't ask this Sylvester guy for his blessing—"

A metal tray piled high with sausage and bacon and not much else plunked to the table as someone sat down next to me. It was the guy from earlier, with bright green eyes and wavy black hair in need of a trim that curled around his ears. He commanded the attention of the room with his height. Even sitting down, his wiry figure towered over me. When he noticed my stare, he flashed me a blinding smile equivalent to the one he'd displayed earlier.

"Morning, Ludo," he said brightly. "I see you've welcomed one of our guests already. I'm Eirian, by the way."

His grip warmed my cold fingers as we shook hands. "Eirian. Is that…Welsh?"

Eirian nodded. "Impressive deduction skills, Holmes."

"It's Georgie, actually."

Specks of molten gold flickered in Eirian's eyes when the light hit his irises just so. "Georgie. I like that."

"Did you finish unloading that caravan?" Ludo asked him, sweeping crumbs off the table and dusting his hands off over his tray.

Eirian dug into his breakfast. "Yes, sir. I inventoried everything myself and put it all away. Quite a haul you had there."

"Thanks," I bit back, unable to keep the edge out of my voice.

"Don't worry," Eirian said. "We're pretty well in stock for right now. Chances are, the stock workers will assign those clothes right back to you." He turned to Ludo again. "There was a bunch of equipment in there that I wasn't sure what to do with. Circuit boards and other little pieces. What should I—?"

I pinned Eirian's hand to the table before he could lift his fork again. "What did you do with them?"

"Excuse me?"

"The radio parts," I said. "That's what that equipment was. I nearly got shot getting that stuff, so I swear if you tell me—"

"I put it all in a storage room in DotCom," Eirian interrupted, lifting his hand free of mine. Though the movement was gentle, his forearm flexed, lifting veins from his skin. "Can't inventory things if I don't know what they are, right? Are we keeping that stuff, Ludo, or should I pitch it?"

Ludo must've seen the steam coming out of my ears because he answered quickly. "Keeping it. Georgie here has previous radio knowledge. She's going to build a communications system for the camp."

"Wow," Eirian said. "That's new for us. Are we sure that's something we want to start relying on?"

"I'm willing to risk it," Ludo replied. "I doubt another EMP blast is coming our way. What would be the point? The U.S. is already down for the count. We might as well take advantage of Georgie's knowledge. Radios could save lives if we have an emergency."

"Agreed," Eirian said. "Georgie, do you really have the knowledge to build an entire camp-wide communications system?

"The knowledge, yes," I said. "But I'll need to borrow some manpower. The first order of business will be to build a signal tower for the camp, and I can't do all the heavy lifting by myself."

"I volunteer." Eirian raised his hand, realized he had a sausage in it, and lowered his appendage to finish the meat. "I've never seen anything like that before. I'd love to learn more about it. If you're willing to teach me, of course."

"You've never seen a radio?" I asked, skeptical.

"Eirian was born on a homestead," Ludo explained. "This is all he knows. That's why we keep him around. Best resource we got."

Eirian winked. "Ludo, you flatter me."

"Shut up, kid."

Genuine interest lifted one side of Eirian's lips into a crooked but annoyingly attractive smile. "So what do you say, teach? Can I crash your radio party?"

"Fine," I said. "You can help."

"Help with what?" Jacob stood over Eirian's shoulder, holding a tray full of food. He looked down expectantly at Eirian's seat. "You're sitting next to my fianceé."

Eirian beamed up at Jacob, oblivious to the implication of Jacob's statement. "Congratulations! Did *you* know that she can build radios out of nothing?"

"Yes," Jacob said, straight-faced.

Eirian cleared his throat, picking up on the rough vibes. He picked up his tray and stood up. "All righty, then. I've got things to do. Georgie, let me know when you need me."

"It'll be a while," Ludo told him. "We've got to get our newcomers settled in first."

"Whenever," Eirian said, taking his startling smile out once again. He watched as Jacob took his seat and slid so close to me that our elbows knocked together. "I'll be here."

As Eirian walked away, I shoved Jacob across the bench to free up some space between us. He'd broken up with me. There was no excuse for him to behave so possessively. Pippa, Jove, and Nita joined us at the table before he could protest. Jove and Pippa dove headfirst into their breakfasts—it had been hours since we'd last eaten a hot meal—but Nita was more interested in Ludo than her food.

"So what's next?" she asked him. "Now that we've all been inoculated for your survival camp, where do we go from here?"

Ludo stretched, belched, and excused himself. "The first order of business will be assigning each of you to a bunk. As I was telling Georgie, we have women and men's dormitories. It's a bit like college—"

"Hold on a minute," Jacob said. "You expect me to split up from my family and sleep with a bunch of strangers? We just met you people."

Ludo regarded Jacob over the lip of his coffee mug. "We don't do preferential treatment here, sir."

"My sister is pregnant, and my mother has twenty stitches in her leg," Jacob argued. "I'm not going to let them sleep in a room full of other people."

"I'm fine with it," Nita piped in. "Put me in a dorm."

"Easy," Ludo said, grinning at Nita. "I like you."

"I agree with my son," Jove said, his mouth so full of roasted potatoes that I strained to make out his words. "My family requires separate housing."

Ludo looked at Pippa, who leaned over the table at an extreme angle to compensate for her enormous belly. "I'll see if I can pull a few strings for your sister and your mother. Just for the first few weeks though, until you adjust to the way we do things here. After that, you give up the room to the next person who needs it, understood?"

"What about us?" Jacob asked, dropping his fork to clutch my hand. "Please, sir, we're engaged. We haven't slept apart in the last five years."

Ludo stood up, scraped his food scraps into a nearby

compost bin, and stacked the tray on top for the kitchen staff to collect. "Engaged, are you? Where's the ring?"

"She lost it coming here," Jacob said.

Ludo looked down at me. I avoided his gaze. "All right, fine. I'll get you a room with two double beds."

"There's five of us," Jacob said. "We'll need an extra."

"Your mother's staying in the med bay actually," Nita said. "That gash in her leg is too big to move her right now."

"Two double beds," Ludo repeated. He zipped up his thick winter jacket and pulled on a fleece hat. "If you'll excuse me, I'm off to meet with the department heads to see who needs bodies. Meet me at DotCom after you finish your breakfast. We can talk about how each of you intends to contribute to Camp Haven."

As he walked off, Jove slid into his empty seat for no other reason than to mark his territory. "Righteous prick, isn't he?"

"I kinda like him," Nita said. "He seems like a no-nonsense kind of guy, but he also cares about everyone in the camp."

Pippa missed her mouth, and a burnt potato landed on her stomach. "I don't know. I get weird vibes from everyone here."

As they continued to discuss Ludo's character, I pushed my empty tray away and nudged Jacob. "What the hell was that all about? With the ring?"

He wiped up bacon grease and oatmeal from his tray with a clean biscuit. "What are you talking about?"

"Telling Ludo that we're engaged," I said. "You broke up with me, Jacob, or did you forget?"

"Gee, I'm sorry," he replied, sounding not sorry at all. "I figured I was saving you from sleeping in a dorm full of fifty other people, but if you want to bunk with the masses, go right ahead."

"Maybe I will!"

He slammed his spoon against the tray, sending a spoonful of oatmeal flying. "Damn it, Georgie! Why can't you do things my way for once in your life? I'm trying to keep all of us together, for shit's sake."

Nita leaned over the table. "Guys, you're causing a scene."

Sure enough, heads turned in the Bistro. The camp residents clocked the spilled oatmeal on the table, as if they couldn't believe Jacob had wasted food for his temper tantrum.

I swallowed the frustration that rose in my throat and climbed out of the trap of the cafeteria table. With my tray in hand, I leaned over Jacob's shoulder. "I'll go along with this until we get our feet under us here, but make no mistake. We're not together anymore. I'm sleeping with Pippa. You can share a bed with Jove."

I didn't wait for him to reply. Instead, I followed Ludo's lead and cleaned off my tray before stomping out into the cold again. The sun had risen high enough to peek over the trees. The sky was clear blue for miles. The air smelled crisp and clean. Snow would be on its way soon. I turned toward the cabin on the hill, made a frame with my index fingers and thumbs, and boxed the little house in my fake viewfinder. For a moment, I was twelve years old again. Dad had just put the finishing touches on the cabin, and we lit a fire in the new hearth to celebrate. At the age, I didn't know what I was missing yet. It seemed like a gift, just the two of spending time together, but the reality was that my father, mentally ill, had hidden us away from the rest of the world.

"Nice, isn't it?" Eirian's deep voice was soothing, even if it was interrupting my recollection. He had stripped off his thick jacket, leaving him in a tight-fitted white thermal that accentuated the lines of his torso. "I could stare at that view all day."

I dropped my hands to gaze up at the Rockies as they overlooked the camp. "Really? It doesn't get old after a while? Don't you ever wonder what's on the other side?"

Sweat beaded at his temples as he hefted part of a huge tree trunk over his shoulder. "Not really."

"What's the tree for?"

"Firewood," he said. "We go through a ton of it here."

"Right." I smacked my head. "Duh."

His laugh resonated like a low note on a perfectly tuned timpani. "Don't worry about it. You're probably exhausted. I can't imagine what the ride was like out of the city. Smart thinking, by the way, finding a truck without electrical components to get up here. Was that your idea?"

"Yeah."

"And you have working radio parts," he observed. "Sounds like you know a little bit more about this kind of thing that you let on."

"You could say that."

A couple workers passed by, carrying armloads of wood. Eirian fell into step behind them. "Well, I can't wait to get started on the radios," he called to me. "Make sure you tell Ludo to sign me up for that. Don't let anyone take my job."

"I won't!" I shouted back to him. Another grin, and he vanished amongst the other campers to continue his job. A smile tugged at my lips. Eirian was so light-hearted and carefree. It was a welcome break from the tension between me and the Masons.

An enormous fire pit, which had been lit while we were eating breakfast, sat in the center of the main square of buildings, surrounded by a wide circle of hand-carved benches similar to the ones in the Bistro. Girl Scouts would jump for joy at the set up. It was perfect for roasting s'mores and telling ghost stories, though I doubted Camp Haven used the sitting area for such purposes. I settled down on one of the benches to wait for the Masons to finish their breakfast, kicking the toe of my boot into the hard dirt. The ground would freeze soon, and I wondered how Camp Haven stockpiled for the harsh winters in the mountains.

Nita found me first, dusting biscuit crumbs off her fingers

before winding a scarf around her neck and joining me at the fire pit. Her thigh pressed warmly against mine, her breath condensing in the chilly wind. "How are you holding up?"

"As well as I can, I guess. You?"

"Fine," she said. "I don't mind all of this. I grew up with eight brothers and sisters, so sharing everything I own isn't anything new to me."

"I wouldn't mind sleeping in the dorms either," I told her. "It would be a relief, but Jacob—"

"Yeah, I kind of sensed that the two of you were on the rocks," she said. "Anything I can do to help?"

I squeezed her hand. "Just keep being my friend."

"I can do that." She tucked our conjoined hands into her coat pocket. "You and me are lucky though. We're pretty much guaranteed to get jobs that we like. You have your radio stuff, and I'm a shoo-in for the med bay. Jax even let me suture Penny's leg. I've never done anything like that before in my life. I have a feeling I'm going to get more experience here than I would at any hospital. Did you know that they *make* their own Penicillin here? It's crazy!"

Her enthusiasm brought a grin to my face. "I'm glad you're fitting in."

"Me too," she said. "I worry about the Masons though."

"Wait until Jove realizes that he has to pull his own weight," I told her. "That's going to be something to see."

As if on cue, the Masons burst forth from the Bistro doors and made a beeline for the fire pit. Jove's stomach pressed against the buttons of his coat. Apparently, he'd gotten enough scrambled eggs to expand his waistline.

"What now?" he thundered, guiding Pippa to sit down beside us. Jacob remained standing, folding his arms across his chest and tucking his chin into his collar to fend off the wind. "Are we supposed to just sit out here in the damn cold?"

"It's not so bad by the fire, Mister Mason," Nita said. "You should get off your feet and warm up."

"What I'd like is to find a damn room," Jove rumbled. "Where is that giant buffoon that pretends he's in charge? I've got a bone to pick with him."

"Right here."

Jove jumped, his great belly jiggling, as Ludo turned up right behind him. His bushy mustache did not entirely hide his smirk at Jove's antics.

"I've spoken to the head of residency," Ludo went on. "And I have your room assignments. Nita, you'll be in bunk thirty-nine in the women's dorm. It's pretty easy to find. They're all numbered. If you drop by DotCom, someone there will give you what we call a bug bag. It's a big canvas tote that can hold all of your belongings in case we need to evacuate the camp. Pick yours up and get comfortable in your bunk. Feel free to take a nap. I assume you guys didn't sleep a wink in that truck last night. When you're ready, report to med bay. Jax and Maddy are eager to get your training started. Clear?"

"Yes, sir." Nita saluted him then kissed my cheek. "Hang in there, buddy. I'll check on you later."

If there was anything I envied about Nita in that moment, it was her ability to separate herself from our group and blend in effortlessly with the other campers. On the other hand, I was stuck with the Masons, who drew attention to themselves like strippers at a black tie affair.

"As for the rest of you," Ludo continued, "I had a few of our boys drop your bug bags off in your room. We're heading there now. It's a bit removed from the rest of the living space. For privacy and all that. You ready?"

"As I'll ever be," Jove grumbled.

We fell in step behind Ludo as he led us past the main square of the compound and the dormitories. Out here, there were smaller cottages and tents, built between fields for growing crops. Most of the dirt was barren, but a few late-blooming patches of winter squash decorated the area with vibrant oranges and yellows. As we walked, Ludo talked.

"Out here's where most of our agriculture workers live," he said, pointing to the small cottages. "They're up earliest and they work the hardest, so they get the benefit of living close to their work instead of traipsing all the way out here from the dorms every morning. Do not bother them. Do not complain when they wake before dawn and make noise outside. If you do, I won't hesitate to revoke the privileges of a private cottage." He rifled inside the pocket of his coat and drew out a stack of laminated, color-coded squares. "These are your identification cards. They state your name, your immunization record, your job title, and your demerits. Demerits are given out if you do not perform your duties as asked or cause trouble within the camp. If you get three demerits within the timespan of a month, you will be asked to sit in front of a tribunal of five camp superiors who will then decide on an appropriate course of retributive action. Believe me, you do not want to deal with the tribunal, so take my advice and keep your noses clean. Here." He passed out our identification cards. "I spoke to my department heads, and you have been assigned job titles according to our current needs."

Jove stared at his brown card. "Sanitation? What the hell does that mean?"

Ludo shielded his eyes and pointed to a series of massive tanks far outside the fence line of Camp Haven. "See those beautiful pieces of machinery out there? They filter our waste. Your job is to transport waste from the outhouses to the tanks. They run on manpower, sir, so we need plenty of strong men like yourself out there to keep them operating."

"You want me to shovel shit?" Jove shoved the identification card into Ludo's chest. "Go to hell."

"Someone's gotta do it," Ludo replied. "If you think the work's beneath you, then feel free to see yourself out of the compound." When Jove stood his ground, Ludo tucked the identification card into the pocket of Jove's coat. "Glad to hear you're on board. You start this afternoon. Any other questions?"

"Miscellaneous crew," Jacob read off his red card. "What's that?"

"You basically do whatever we need you to do," Ludo explained. "Hauling, building, planting, wherever we need a hand."

"Why can't I do that?" Jove demanded. "Or run security?"

"Don't worry, the crew pulls sanitation duties sometimes too," Ludo said. "And our security officers have to pass a rigorous physical test before they're approved for duty." He looked Jove's massive figure up and down. "You think you got that in you?"

An embarrassed blush crept across Jove's face.

"Didn't think so," Ludo went on before turning to Jacob again. "Eirian works miscellaneous as well, son. He'll teach you the ropes. Most of the boys enjoy it. You get to do something new every day."

"If you say so," Jacob replied.

"I have a question," Pippa said, holding a card that was half-blue and half-pink. "What's a maternity specialist? I haven't given birth yet, and I am far from specializing in anything concerning babies."

"Which is exactly why you've been assigned to that position," Ludo said. "All of our new mothers are temporarily re-routed as maternity specialists. They take care of the kids in the compound. You'll learn everything you need to know about raising a child."

"How very patriarchal of you," Pippa said dryly.

"On the contrary," Ludo said, "half of our maternity specialists are men. We think it's important to teach both boys and girls the value of good parenting."

"Ninnies," Jove muttered under his breath.

"What was that?"

"Nothing."

"As for you, Georgie," Ludo said, pointing to my bright purple card. "We had to fly by the seat of our pants. We created a position for you."

I glanced down at the card. "Communications manager? That's a promotion, I suppose."

"Matched the color of the card to your hair," Ludo said with a grin. "Anyone who gets assigned to Communications will get a purple card too. You're in charge though. I'm trusting you to build up the department. Feel free to recruit a few people to help you out. Interview some of the other campers. Let me know who your choices are. Once you get a radio tower up and running, it will be up to you to operate and maintain it. Sound good?"

"Sounds great," I said. "You guys like morning talk shows?"

"Can't say we've ever had one," Ludo replied. "But we could all do for some entertainment. Here we are."

Ludo stepped up to the porch of one of the block cabins. It was smaller than the rest, set deep in the recesses of the compound. It was a good thirty minute walk back to the start of the camp. Ludo gestured us inside. The one-room building was just large enough for two double beds to fit against the walls. It was barren of decoration or adornment. There was one window. On the upside, it smelled like mountain air and cinnamon sticks.

"Home sweet home," said Ludo.

13

$\mathcal{I}$ could practically taste Jove's disgust. It filled the tiny room with a bitter bite to match a look of distaste that he didn't bother to disguise. I helped Pippa sit on one of the beds. The blankets were stiff but clean. Woven from sheep's wool, they carried a distinct must that Pippa wrinkled her nose at.

"This is it?" Jove thundered. "This is your grand family suite? This is ridiculous!"

"This is not a five star hotel," Ludo replied. "I'm sorry if you were ever under the impression that it was. We do what we can here. If you think you would all be more comfortable in the dormitories, then I would be happy to escort you there."

"No," Jove said, shucking off his coat. He pointed to an archaic iron furnace in the middle of the room. "How do we turn this thing on?"

"Light a fire," Ludo said, "to heat the coals."

Jove stared at him.

"Don't tell me you don't know how to start a damn fire," Ludo said.

"I can do it." I patted Ludo on the shoulder. "Thanks for

186

everything, Ludo. I know that this has been a major imposition on you." Jove scoffed, but I pretended not to hear him. "I'll take it from here."

"Mm-hmm," Ludo said, stepping toward the porch. "Let me know if you need anything. Lunch is at noon. Take the morning to rest and get used to the place. I'd like to introduce you to your positions in the afternoon."

After he left, I sank onto the bed next to Pippa, who cast a glance between me and Jacob but was wise enough not to comment.

"How the hell are we supposed to know when noon is?" Jove grumbled as he opened the grate to the furnace and poked around in the cold coals. "There are no damn clocks."

I kicked off my boots and massaged my feet through my thick socks. They were sore and numb from walking and running for a solid forty-eight hours. At this point, I was happy to wiggle my toes free of their prison despite the cold air.

"They probably use the sun," I said. "Here, get out of the way."

Camp Haven had left a fire starter kit next to the furnace, which my father had taught me how to use way back then. I struck the pieces together, which sparked and flashed until the kindling caught fire. I closed the grate and looked up to find all three of the Masons staring at me.

"What?"

"How do you know how to do all of this again?" Pippa asked.

The bug bags were under the beds. I pulled one out and unzipped it. "Pippa, it looks like this one's yours."

"Oh, thank God," she said as I tossed it up on the bed. "I'm dying for a change of clothes."

"Listen, we don't know how laundry works around here yet, so don't get too overzealous," I told her. I unzipped the second bug bag and tossed it to Jacob. The third one was mine. Thankfully, the camp had been kind enough to give most of my things back to me. I was only missing a few pairs of socks. That made sense. I imagine people wore them out pretty quickly working out here in the woods. I pulled a comfortable sweater over my head and burrowed under the covers beside Pippa.

"What are you doing?" Jacob asked. Jove had already sat down on their bed to unlace his own boots.

"I'm taking a nap," I told him, plumping the rough pillow beneath my head. The coals in the furnace had started to heat up, and I reveled in the relative warmth and comfort of the bed. "You should too. We've been awake for way too long, and they're expecting us to work this afternoon."

Jacob knelt by the bed and lowered his voice. "Don't you think we should talk?"

I opened one eye. Jacob's expression was unreadable. Did he actually want to talk or did he simply want me to give him an excuse not to? "Jacob, I'm tired."

I rolled over, toward Pippa, which put an abrupt end to the conversation. I stared through the window. From the low angle, all I could see were the peaks of higher mountains around the camp. Was my father up there somewhere? Or was he traipsing around the land that was once our home, blending in with the residents of Camp Haven, hauling water and filtering waste? He couldn't be. He hated people. Or if he didn't hate them, he mistrusted them. My entire childhood had been built upon that mistrust. It took years to overcome it, but now here I was again, dredging up old memories to make sure that we survived.

I woke up when the sun rose high enough to strike the warped glass of the window and fill the inside of my eyelids with a blinding red. The Masons were all asleep, including Jove, who must have been too exhausted to complain about the low thread count of Camp Haven's sheets. I slipped outside, where the rest of the camp continued their daily activities. The agricultural specialists picked the late-blooming winter squash, while others escorted bundled-up children of all ages on some kind of field trip through the camp. I smiled when a toddler wrapped up in an impossibly large parka tripped over the hem of the coat and bounced to the ground. The adult in charge didn't react immediately. Instead, she let the child pick himself up and dust himself off. In the world outside this one, a parent would have overreacted about the child's fall, but at Camp Haven, children apparently learned to care for themselves at an early age. The door to the cabin opened and closed, and Jacob sat on the porch step next to me.

"Why did you do that?" I asked him.

"Do what?"

"You told Ludo that we were together," I clarified, squinting into the sun rather than looking at Jacob. "We're not anymore. Are we?"

"Georgie, what I said to you last night was rash and hasty," he said, "but it doesn't mean that it wasn't true. I don't really know you."

"It's a simple yes or no question, Jacob," I said. "Are we together or not?"

He pondered the question for a long moment, gazing toward the main part of the camp. In the far off distance, the red cross above the med bay stood out like a beacon. "No."

I wasn't sure what answer I had expected, but I definitely hadn't anticipated the intense rush of relief that flooded my chest and let me take my first deep breath of fresh mountain air. If there was one good thing about tragedy, it was that it made you realize certain things about yourself. Jacob and I had never been well-matched for each other. I had gone after him because he had the things that I'd always wanted. He had grown up in the city with other people and learned how to socialize and be loved by others, whereas I struggled to connect with my peers after years of only knowing my father. No matter how much I tried, I was always going to be the survival-based introvert, and being with Jacob wasn't going to change that.

"Okay," I said.

"That's it?" he asked. "That's all you're going to say after five years together?"

"I'll tell Ludo," I said, pushing myself up from the porch and dusting my hands off. "He'll want to assign me to the dorms."

"Whoa, wait a minute." Jacob leaned forward and took my hand before I could get any farther. "You don't have to do that. I meant what I said this morning. You don't have to sleep with a bunch of other people. The rest of the camp doesn't have to know we're not together anymore."

"That sounds like a recipe for disaster," I told him.

"It doesn't have to be," he said. "We've known each other for a long time, Georgie. Just because we're not getting married anymore doesn't mean we have to be strangers. For one thing, this place is not very big, and it's going to be impossible not to run into each other. We may as well be cordial."

"I wasn't planning on anything else."

"Stay here," he said, pouting with his big brown eyes like a sad puppy. "Please. We need you. Pippa loves you too, and she's going to need a friend here until she settles in."

"What about your dad?" I asked.

"What about him?" Jacob said. "He's going to have to deal with it. Whatever it is."

He still had my hand. I reclaimed it as my own. "Fine. I'll stay for now, but if things get weird or Jove is insufferable, I'm going to Ludo. Understand?"

"Yes, ma'am."

AFTER LUNCH, Ludo dropped us off to the heads of our departments, which meant that Jove, Jacob, and Pippa all had someone new to report to. I, on the other hand, worked alone for the present, so Ludo became my temporary Communications Assistant. The camp had set aside all of the radio parts that I'd brought with me. It wasn't much, but it would at least get us started. Ludo helped me inventory what I had then asked me what materials I would need to get started on building a free-standing radio tower. For each item I listed, he asked me for the purpose and for potential substitutes in case we couldn't find what we needed. It was engaging, creative work that challenged me to think outside of the box. Ludo didn't know much about radios to begin with, and I surprised myself with how much I enjoyed teaching him about it. We worked through the entire afternoon and into the evening, until a bell rang to signal that dinner was served at the Bistro.

"That's the day," Ludo said, clapping me on the back. "You made it through. How ya feeling?"

"Safe," I replied as we packed up our notes. We'd been working in Ludo and Jax's shared space, which was even smaller than ours. "That's all that matters."

"That's a great attitude to have," Ludo said. "I hope the rest of your family sees it the same way."

"Me too," I muttered.

"Before we head over to the Bistro, I have one more thing to show you," Ludo said, leading me out of the tiny apartment. His place, along with a few other rooms meant for married couple, occupied a building adjacent to the dormitories. DotCom was just across the way. He led me to the community building, through the empty main hall, and into a private hallway in the back. From there, rooms branched off in every direction, labeled for use. Most of them were storage, but we finally reached a door that did not have a plaque on it.

"Here we are," Ludo said, unlocking the room. "Have a look."

I peeked inside. Like the others, it was small, but instead of being full of extra food or supplies, this one was empty except for a desk.

"It looks like an office," I said. "What do you use it for?"

"We don't use it," Ludo replied. "We keep a few rooms empty in case something like this pops up. I thought you could use it as your office. If you get your tower up and running, you can broadcast to the camp from here."

"Really?" I walked into the office, running my fingers over the layer of dust on the desk. "It's going to take some time before I get everything up and running."

"Understandable."

"And we probably don't have everything on hand to do what I really want to do," I went on."

"We usually send crews into the city when we desperately need something," Ludo explained. "I was planning on sending a salvage crew in anyway, what with all the insanity. We need to take action before this goes further south, get what we can while it's still available. That includes whatever you need to get this communications system up and running, so it's very important that you don't hold back. Just remember the foundations of what this camp was built on. No electricity here."

"How do you feel about batteries?"

"They run out of juice eventually."

"Good point," I said. "No worries. I can make do."

"That's what I like to hear," Ludo replied. "Come on. Let's go eat. By the way, did I mention that tonight is open mic night?"

It turned out that Camp Haven wasn't all work. After dinner each night, the camp held a variety of community activities like open mic night, talent shows, s'mores nights, and ghost stories. Most days, the entire camp gathered in the center square around the massive bonfire to be with each other. If it was too cold, they relocated to DotCom. I learned quickly that "cold" to us was not "cold" to Camp Haven. They were used to the extreme mountain temperatures. When it dipped into the thirties, I expected the open mic night to be inside, but we gathered around the fire instead.

The fire had been stoked to roar higher than the tallest resident of Camp Haven. From a general guess at the number of heads, about a hundred people lived here. They all turned out for the after-dinner event, and the bonfire seemed to warm all of them. I stayed close to the roaring flame, but not so close for it to lick the seams of my winter coat. A few members of the camp had been assigned to douse the fire if it got too out of control. Camp Haven had safety precautions for everything. On one hand, it seemed like paranoia. On the other hand, they had survived out here for this long according to those precautions.

Jacob spent the first hour of the event attempting to convince everyone in the vicinity of our mutual love. He was trying too hard, holding my hand, kissing my cheek every few minutes or so. After a while, I told him that I was going to help distribute the hot cocoa, slipped away, and lost him in the crowd. I bypassed the ladies serving the cocoa, disappearing into the cold, dark night.

A few minutes later, I found myself at the base of the hill atop which my father's cabin sat. A small plume of smoke puffed out of the chimney. Someone was inside my home—Sylvester, supposedly—cooking or sleeping or whatever.

"Don't do it," a voice whispered.

I whirled around, flicking open the switchblade that I kept on my person at all times, and found myself face-to-face with Eirian, who raised his hands above his head when my knife neared his throat.

"Whoa, easy there!"

"Shit, I'm sorry." I quickly folded the blade again and stored it in the pocket of my coat. "I get anxious. New place, people I don't know. You know how it is."

"Not really, but I can take a guess," Eirian said. "Does Ludo know you have that?"

I stayed quiet.

"Thought so," he said, chuckling. "We don't allow residents to keep weapons in the camp. If someone wants to duke it out, they have to do it with their fists. Less casualties that way."

"Does that happen often?"

"Not at all," Eirian answered. "We know what we have to lose here. We need everyone in the best shape so that no one slacks on their job. Fighting is stupid. It only causes problems. I'm surprised they didn't find that knife on you when you checked in. Where did you hide it?"

Again, I didn't answer, although I did let a smug smile tug at my lips.

"Never mind," he said, catching the grin. "I don't want to know. I do, however, have to ask why you slipped away from a perfectly in-tune rendition of Britney's Toxic to come stare at Sylvester's cabin."

"How do you even know Britney?" I asked him. "If you've been living on homesteads for your whole life?"

"Top Forty haunts us all," he replied. "Although I've only heard covers, never the original. I answered your question. You answer mine. What gives?"

I sighed, looking up at the cabin again. "I used to live there."

"In the cabin?"

"My father built it," I said, wondering how many times I would have to explain this. "I helped him. I came out here to look for him and found Camp Haven instead."

"Huh."

"What?"

"It makes sense this way," Eirian said, brushing his wavy dark hair out of his eyes. "I never bought that whole 'Sylvester found an angel' story. It's more likely that he got lucky, found the cabin, and then started Camp Haven."

"That doesn't explain what happened to my dad," I told him.

"When was the last time you saw him?"

"Nine years ago."

"Wow," Eirian said. "That's a long time. How do you figure he didn't just move on from here and go somewhere else?"

"He was agoraphobic," I explained. "He would've never left this place willingly. It was perfectly set up for what he wanted. Complete seclusion."

"Maybe he's still here then."

I shook my head. "No, there are too many people here. My dad was a loner. But I would like to check to make sure. Ludo mentioned earlier that Camp Haven keeps archives of every resident in DotCom. Do you know where they are?"

"Sure."

"Do you think you could show me?" I asked him, batting my eyelashes.

He covered my eyes with one gloved hand for a brief moment. "You don't have to do that. I don't need convincing. Do you want to go now?"

Fighting off a flush of heat, I nodded. Thank goodness it was dark and cold outside. Otherwise I would have died of embarrassment. I wasn't used to guys who didn't require persuasion. Then again, I wasn't used to guys who had never been exposed to the toxic masculinity of regular society. Eirian, raised as he had been, was a rarity.

"Follow me," he said.

He seemed to automatically understand that I needed to be alone, so we skirted the main square where the event was still in high swing. Someone belted Aretha Franklin from the podium, accompanied by an acoustic guitar that did not fit the genre at all. Eirian hummed along as he led me behind the main the buildings until we reached the rear door of DotCom.

"I heard Ludo got you an office," he said, lighting a lamp in the hallway with a metal Zippo. There was something carved into the side of the lighter, but he tucked it into his pocket before I could get a better look. "Which one is yours?"

I pointed to the door. "That one. It's not much right now."

He looked through the window. "I'm sure you'll fix it up. Come on. The archives are this way."

We turned the corner and reached another door, which Eirian unlocked with his own set of keys.

"Does everyone get keys?" I asked him as we went inside.

"Nope," he replied. "High-ranking individuals only."

"I thought this camp was built on a trust system."

"It is," he confirmed. "But you can only trust people so much before they want more for themselves. It's human nature."

I thought of Jove. "You're telling me."

The archives room was no grander than any other part of the camp. It was full of repurposed cardboard or metal boxes stacked on simple handmade shelves. Each one held stacks and stacks of paper. The room was organized alphabetically by subject.

"Where do you get the paper?" I asked.

"We used to buy or steal it from the city," Eirian answered. "Now we make it ourselves. We recycle everything here to make sure there's as little waste as possible."

I looked through a nearby box, kneading the strangely textured paper between my finger and thumb. "That's amazing. You guys have really thought of everything, haven't you?"

"I like to think so." He pointed to a shelf near the rear of the room. "I believe the archives start over there. The names aren't alphabetical. The signatures will be organized according to the earliest date. When do you think your dad might have been here?"

I maneuvered through the shelves and peered up at the faded labels on the boxes. "Right at the beginning, I'd guess. Those are from 2008 and 2009. That'd be it, right?"

Eirian stood on his toes and stretched up to get the box. His many layers rode up, and his undershirt untucked itself from his waistband, revealing the line of one muscled hip. I quickly cleared my throat and looked away.

"Here we go," he said, bringing the box down to the floor and popping the lid off. "What name are we looking for?"

"Amos Fitz."

He handed me a stack of papers to look through. The pages were crisp and fragile, torn out of old school notebooks or journals. Each one boasted at least twenty signatures of those who had come to Camp Haven in the last decade.

"I didn't expect the archives to be this extensive," I muttered, scanning the signatures for a glimpse of my father's name. "There aren't that many people here."

"We made a lot of mistakes in the beginning," Eirian said. "We recruited too many people. Advertised to campers and hikers. They didn't understand what we really wanted to do here. A lot of them showed up, stayed for a week or so, realized that this wasn't what they wanted, and went back to the city. It wreaked havoc on our system. We were wasting supplies, and our visitors were treating the compound like some kind of vacation retreat. They wouldn't pull their weight, and they complained about everything."

"So you stopped advertising," I said.

"Pretty much," Eirian replied. "We had enough people to keep the place running. We became our own community. We had plans to expand before the EMP hit. We were thinking about letting a few more couples have children—"

"Doesn't that sound absurd to you?" I asked him. "Controlling childbirth?"

"We don't have a choice," he replied. "Think about it. It's the middle of the woods. No pharmacy, no birth control. We have to manage our population wisely."

"There's no way everyone here is abstaining."

Eirian grinned. "Of course not. We're human after all. We take a lot of precautions, but we do get the occasional accidental pregnancy."

"How many demerits is an accidental pregnancy worth?"

He shot me a confused look. "We don't shame women for the natural state of things. If someone gets pregnant, it's not the end of the world. They have their baby, and everyone moves on. No big deal."

I continued scanning the papers for my father's name.

"Are you worried about your fiancé's sister?" Eirian asked. "I noticed how young she was."

"Pippa can take care of herself," I assured him. "I guess I'm just not used to how things are done around here."

"Feel free to ask me anything," he said. "I'm a wealth of knowledge when it comes to Camp Haven. I was actually in the first group of people to move here. Does this look like Fitz to you?"

I squinted at the cramped handwriting. "No, that says Fisk. My dad wrote in all caps no matter what."

"Gotcha."

"So you've never lived off a homestead?" I asked him, intrigued. "How is that even possible in this day and age?"

Eirian lowered himself out of his squat to sit on the floor with a groan of relief and continued to look through his batch of signatures. "It's a long story. My real parents abandoned me when I was born. I have no idea who they were. They dumped me somewhere in the hills of Southern California. I guess they figured I'd die out there, and they wouldn't have anything to worry about anymore."

"And I thought my childhood was messed up."

He laughed, a sound that I decided I liked quite a bit. "It's not as dramatic as it sounds. I don't remember it at all. Anyway, a group of women found me up there. They called themselves the Sisters of the Wind. The Sisters grew out of the idea that we owed something to nature in return for taking care of us. That's why they lived as simply as they did. They took me in and raised me."

"What happened to them?"

"A few died," he admitted. "There were only ten of them to begin with, and some of them were already quite old. A few others assimilated into other homesteads in order to survive. That's how I ended up here. I went from the Sisters to a campground in Idaho to here in the Rockies. Wynonna, the Sister who I always regarded as a mother, actually made it here with me. She's a maternity specialist now. Fitz!"

I dropped to my knees at his exclamation, accidentally tipping over the box and scattering papers everywhere. "That's him! Amos Fitz. He was here!" I ran the pad of my finger over the capital letters, a declaration of my father's existence. "What now? That means he's here in the camp, right? I can't believe it." A muscle in Eirian's jaw twitched, and I understood that my enthusiasm was premature. "What is it?"

"I know everyone in this camp," he said. "If there was an Amos Fitz here, I'd know him."

"Then where did he go?"

"I'm not sure," Eirian replied. "There's no sign-out here, which means that if he left the compound, there's no record of it. There is one other list we can check, but…"

"But what?"

He stacked the papers neatly, put the lid back on, and returned the box to the proper shelf. "We keep a book of everyone who's passed away at Camp Haven. I'm not saying that he's on it, but if he is, it might give you the closure that you're looking for."

Somehow, it had never occurred to me that my father might actually be dead. After all, he did live in the middle of nowhere. If an emergency situation arose, he had no way of calling someone for help. For all I knew, he was dead.

"Do you want to check?" Eirian asked. "We don't have to."

"No, we should," I said. "I want to know."

He approached a different shelf and took down a different

box. "Death certificates are in alphabetical order, no matter the year. Here's the F's."

We sat on the floor again, leaned in at the same time, and bumped shoulders. Eirian didn't pull away, ensconced in the search for my father's name in the death box. I stayed put too, savoring the warmth that we shared in that small space.

"Finigan, Fisher, Fitch," Eirian muttered, licking his finger to separate the certificates. "And then Flagler. No Amos Fitz. He's not in here."

"This doesn't make any sense," I said, slamming the lid onto the box. It was made of recycled aluminum and clanged loudly. "I know this says that he was here during Camp Haven's inauguration, but he never would have let so many people onto his land."

"Maybe he was having trouble surviving on his own," Eirian suggested. "He thought he might benefit from Camp Haven's existence."

"You don't know my father," I said. "He would rather suffer and die than trust someone else. I don't get it."

I rubbed my temples. A headache grew in the space between them, from dehydration or stress or lack of sleep. Eirian reached into his pocket and produced a small tube.

"Here," he said, tipping the tube on its side. A few drops of liquid, smelling strongly of candy canes, plopped onto his finger, which he dabbed against my temples. "It's peppermint oil. Natural headache relief."

The oil chilled my skin, but the crisp scent cleared my mind. "Thanks."

"Of course," he said, capping the tube. "Is there anything else I can do that might set your mind at ease about your father?"

"I suppose not," I said, shoulders slumping in disappointment. "Unless you have another suggestion."

"None that I can think of at the moment. Come here." He stood up and offered his hands. I took them, and he gently pulled me to my feet. "What do you say we go back outside and enjoy the rest of open mic night? It's actually quite fun, and it'll give you a chance to meet some of the others. Plus, I'm sure your fiancé is missing you."

"He's not—"

Once again, I thanked the low lighting, which covered my slip-up. I yearned to talk about my broken engagement with anyone other than Jacob. I needed that release, to work out what had gone wrong with someone other than my own self. Eirian, however, didn't seem like the best choice. For one thing, I hardly knew him, and for another, Jacob's behavior at the Bistro during breakfast implied that he already harbored a disliking for the Camp Haven native.

When we returned to the square, some of the event's energy had died off. The kids had gone to bed, and the older residents of Camp Haven had retired too. The music turned to soft folk and blues rather than pop and rock songs. Jacob had, in fact, taken the podium to sing an old Lou Reed song.

"I'll let you listen," Eirian said, squeezing my shoulder in farewell. "Have a good night, Georgie. I'll see you tomorrow for my first shift."

He saluted me with two fingers before disappearing into the crowd to join a few of his friends for a drink. Nita, who'd been sitting on one of the benches around the fire to listen to Jacob, waved me over.

"What was that all about?" she asked, her eyes lingering on Eirian's statuesque figure.

"He was helping me figure out what happened to my father," I told her. Jacob plucked dutifully at a borrowed guitar, his voice velvety and soft in the cold night. "We looked through the archives."

"Did you find anything?"

I leaned my head on Nita's shoulder. "No."

She perched her chin on top of my head. "Is everything okay?"

Jacob finished his song. The last chord lingered in the air. Then the crowd clapped politely as Jacob handed the guitar off to the next open mic participant.

"I don't know," I said.

14

_____

$\mathcal{B}$efore I knew it, two weeks had passed at Camp Haven. I fell into step with the rest of the compound quickly. The schedule and work was familiar once I remembered how to do it. This was the way I had grown up, with candles and well water rather than a monthly electricity bill and working toilets. To me, it felt natural, so I assimilated within a few days, eliciting a number of questions from the other members of Camp Haven. After the third or fourth unprompted interview, I stopped mentioning that Sylvester's cabin used to be mine. No one was inclined to believe me, though they nodded politely to placate me. I did, however, ask every single person that I talked to about my father in the hopes that someone might recognize his name. No such luck. They all claimed ignorance about Amos Fitz, leaving me to continue to wonder about my father's fate.

The radio tower went up in about a week and half. It would have been sooner, but the camp didn't have all of the construction materials that I needed to make it work, which meant that Eirian and a few other men had to venture closer to the city to scalp industrial yards for parts. They left in makeshift combat armor, carrying rifles across their backs. To someone naive, their vehemence may have come across as paranoia, but I understood the precautions. As the days passed us by, Camp Haven went on unhindered. The people lived as they had always lived, off of the land and off of the grid. I knew that the regular population of Denver, and the rest of the United States for that matter, would not fare the same. By now, if I was right about the level of destruction, thousands of people had died from lack of care, no access to medications, violence in the streets, and general idiocy. When Eirian and his friends returned, they confirmed my assumptions. Denver was in ruins, taken over by gangs and other crime circles. Though the camp's scavengers had not ventured far enough into the city to get into trouble, Eirian had seen enough to hollow out his eyes. As he hauled parts for the tower to the location I'd requested for it, the usual gleam of his green irises was absent.

"Are you okay?" I had asked, pulling on a pair of thick workman's gloves, the fingers of which were too long, and lifting the other end of the steel support that he'd been dragging through the compound.

"I don't want to think about it," he replied. "Let's just work."

So we did. It was the first time I'd ever been in charge of such a process. I drew up rough blueprints of what I needed from the crew, picked a place for the radio tower that was central for the entire camp in order to get the best range possible, and asked Ludo for a small team of workers that could get the tower up and running as quickly as possible. From there on out, I spent the days in a hardhat and steel-toed boots, helping as well as instructing. Eirian's desire to work suddenly made sense. The more I threw myself into the tower's construction, the less I thought about the destruction on the other side of Camp Haven's walls. It was a relief to sweat and ache from a physical standpoint rather than a mental one. Each night, exhausted as I was from the day's work, I fell asleep moments after my head hit the pillow.

The rest of our group varied in the success of their adaptations to Camp Haven. Nita did well. She was in awe of Jax's work in the med bay. Apparently, the camp had never had medical students before, and Jax was eager to teach Nita what it was like to treat patients in the middle of the wilderness without the advances of medical technology. Every time I ran into Nita, whether at the Bistro or DotCom for community events, she was always studying something. She read books on natural remedies, identifying useful herbs in nature, concocting medications in a low-level laboratory, and other curious subjects that would have never crossed her path during standard medical school.

"Did you know Jax used to be a trauma surgeon at a level one trauma center?" she babbled one night, her nose buried in yet another textbook that she had borrowed from the med bay. "And then one night, they had a giant pile up come into the emergency room, and she just couldn't take it anymore. Can you imagine? She gave up her entire career to live in the woods. Brutal, right?"

The only thing Nita every complained about at Camp Haven was the cold. As a native of Spain, Colorado wasn't her ideal place of residence, but it was easier to ignore the harsh winters in the heated comfort of an apartment. As November wore on, the degrees dropped off one by one, until the first of many snow flurries fell upon the compound. For the residents of Camp Haven, the snow brought more work. When I wasn't setting up our communications system, I helped out in other areas. I dried and stored food, sewed wool lining into jackets for added insulation, and prepped the radio tower for harder weather.

Others did not take so well to the work and the cold. Jacob's feet were freezing no matter how many layers of socks he wore. I was grateful that he and I no longer shared a bed. I certainly didn't miss his frigid toes seeking the warmth of my calves in the middle of the night. The wind whipped at his sensitive skin, leaving his cheeks red and dry. His lips peeled from the exposure no matter how much soothing balm he smoothed over them. I did not miss kissing him either. He suffered from other complaints too. Despite his eager declaration to ensure his entrance to Camp Haven, manual labor did not sit well with Jacob. Hours upon hours at the gym, benching and squatting away in an air-conditioned room, had not prepared him for lugging wood, constructing buildings, and mucking bathroom stalls. His palms bled from the wear and tear before calluses hardened the skin. He often lay awake in bed, rolling from one side to the other in order to find a position that didn't compromise his sore muscles. He found no energy to complain, but rather moped in dejected silence about his new way of life.

Penny, Jacob's mother, had yet to recover from the open wound in her leg. No one said it out loud, but the signs were bad. She suffered from weakness and general fatigue, unable to stand for more than a few minutes at a time. The wound itself failed to close, which was a sign of infection. Jax administered small doses of the camp's antibiotics, but supplies were limited and Penny wasn't responsive to the drugs. She was the only permanent resident of the med bay, and I could tell by the whispered conversations that this was an unusual circumstance. Nevertheless, Penny remained there, existing without full awareness of her circumstances.

Pippa, weeks away from her delivery, had rejoined her mother in the med bay after Jax assigned her to bed rest. I visited her every once in a while. She resented being stuck inside on a cot all day, but I did well to remind her that at least she was out of the cold and free of the labors that the rest of the camp pushed through. At this point, her belly had grown to such proportions that I feared she might burst like an overfilled balloon. She perched books and plates on top of it as she lay in bed as if it were a convenient table to use at her disposal. Other that her restless boredom and impending epidural-free delivery, the only thing Pippa worried about was the state of her friends back home. And the fact that Camp Haven had no access to nail polish.

"What do you think happened to them?" she asked me one morning when I delivered her breakfast to the med bay. She picked crumbs from the extra muffin I'd swiped for her. "My friends. They probably found somewhere safe, right? I'll see them when all of this blows over."

I sat down on the edge of the small cot. "Maybe one day. Sure."

Her big brown eyes were doleful. "You think they're dead, don't you?"

"No, of course not."

"I've known you long enough to tell when you're lying," she said. "It's how I know that you and Jacob aren't together anymore."

I looked down at my ring finger. A few weeks ago, Jacob and I had been fighting over my lack of dedication to the diamond engagement band. Now, we were nothing but a pair of pretenders, taking advantage of our previous relationship to pull one over the heads of Camp Haven.

"Why bother faking it?" Pippa asked. "Who cares?"

"Your brother does."

"Jacob's an idiot."

"I'm trying to make this as easy on everyone as possible," I told her. "If he wants to pretend that we're still together so he can sleep in his own room, then that's fine with me. I don't mind."

The door to the med bay opened, and a gust of wind rushed in as Eirian entered the room.

"Hi," he said, his cheeks pink from the cold and his dark hair tousled. "How ya doing, Pippa?"

"I'm fat, Eirian. What else is new?"

"That's the spirit." He stomped snow off of his boots on the mat near the door before plopping down on the cot next to Pippa's. "I have to get back to work soon, but I just wanted to know what time you needed me for Communications today, Georgie."

I checked my watch, one that I'd managed to procure from the extra storage room at DotCom. "How's four o'clock sound? Meet me at my office?"

"Four o'clock sounds great," Eirian said, cupping his hands around his nose to warm the pink tip of it. "Can't wait. Hang in there, Pippa."

"Oh, I'm hanging."

He patted her knee, smiled at me, and left the med bay.

Pippa nudged my thigh with the toe of her foot. "Well, I know one person who might mind that you and Jacob are only pretending to be engaged."

"Shut up. Eirian and I are just friends."

As soon as I said it, the phrase felt like a lie. Pippa wasn't entirely wrong. There was a natural ease between me and Eirian that had always been missing with Jacob. We could talk, really talk, about the matters at hand. We didn't bicker or moan at each other. He had a steady hand and a steady attitude. Not to mention, he'd grown up like I had. We bonded over our similar childhoods, though I had yet to mention how mine had come about. It was easier this way, for now at least, that it had always just been me and my dad on the homestead, father and daughter learning to make it on their own. The messy details could run dry for a while.

Pippa pinched my cheek. "Just friends. Sure."

"I have things to do," I told her, stealing the uneaten muffin from atop her belly. "And I'm taking this back. Think of it as a tax for teasing me."

"Rude."

I left the med bay, muffin in mouth, thinking that I might work a few hours in the Communications office until it was time for Eirian to meet me. What with the snowfall, we had put aside assembling radios to focus on more important things, but the kitchen staff had released me of my duties that day. I figured I could at least start gathering the pieces that I needed, but that plan was derailed when a shouting match reached my ears. I gritted my teeth together as I recognized one of the voices. Jove. I veered off course from DotCom, following the argument toward the outhouses.

"I won't do it!" Jove yelled to another man. He was, like the other sanitation workers, dressed in a gray jumpsuit that protected his clothes from the hazardous waste in the outhouses. He threw a shovel to the ground. "I'm sick of shoveling shit. Do you know who I am? Do you know how much money I have? I could *pay* someone to do this disgusting work for me."

The other man, Jimmy, was the burly head of sanitation. A layer of blubber sat upon his entire body, hiding the muscle beneath. The result was a large man with a larger presence who spent every day knee deep in human waste. I couldn't imagine the kind of patience a man like that preserved, but I was certainly smarter than Jove not to test it.

"Of course I know who you are. You won't stop reminding all of us." Jimmy waddled around and waved his arms in a strikingly accurate imitation of Jove. "I'm Jove Mason! CEO of Mason Property Management! I own half of Denver! Well, guess what, Mr. Mason? You ain't in Denver anymore, and here at Camp Haven, what I say goes, so pick up your damn shovel and get back to work."

Out of all the members of the group that I'd arrived at Camp Haven with, Jove was the most problematic. This wasn't the first time he'd gotten into an argument with the superior officers in the sanitation department. Not only did he fail to perform his job assignments efficiently or effectively, he also complained about everything. The food served at the Bistro was bland. The mattress in the cottage was too small for both him and Jacob, as well as far too lumpy. The events at DotCom were crass and boring. No matter how little an inconvenience, Jove made sure to let everyone within a fifty-foot proximity know that he was dissatisfied with the way the camp ran things. So it wasn't a huge surprise when he kicked the shovel with such force that it skidded across the frozen ground and bumped up against the heel of Jimmy's boot.

"I sure as hell won't," Jove declared.

Jimmy, who had already turned his back on Jove's petulant temper tantrum, looked down at the shovel. "Mr. Mason, I would like to remind you that your identification badge already bears two demerits. One for failing to show up to work on time for more than three days in a row and one for failing to complete your sanitation duties. If you do not retrieve this shovel and follow the rest of the boys out to the filtration systems, I'm afraid I'll have to add a third demerit to your collection. Do you know what that means?"

"I don't give a damn what it means."

"It means you'll sit for the tribunal," Jimmy said. "And you won't like what they have to say."

Jove closed the gap between he and Jimmy, stepping on the wooden handle of the shovel and cracking it in half, until his nose was a mere inch from the other man's. "Give me the demerit, asshole."

Jimmy looked more amused than intimidated by Jove's ridiculous show of arrogance. They were matched in height and girth, but the laugh etched on Jimmy's face gave him an edge. It infuriated Jove that he couldn't rile up his opponent and act on the resulting emotions.

"Hand over your badge," Jimmy said.

Jove pulled the tiny card out of his pocket and flicked it at

Jimmy. It bounced off Jimmy's cheekbone, close to his eye, but Jimmy refused to flinch. Instead, he stepped on top of the badge and ground it into the dirt.

"There's your third demerit," he told Jove. "See you when the tribunal gathers."

Jove waited until Jimmy was out of sight before he picked up the badge, dusted it off, and tucked it away again. He spotted me watching him.

"What?" he demanded.

"What is your problem?" I asked him. "These people didn't have to let us live here. They could have closed off the gates when we showed up here and sent us back to the city to die. The least we can do is help them to accommodate us and everyone else here."

"Do I look like a sewage worker to you?"

"Yes, actually. The jumpsuit works wonders for your complexion."

He furiously unzipped the suit, stepped out of it, and kicked it aside. "Goddamn it. I'm—"

"Jove Mason," I finished for him. I picked up the jumpsuit, flapped it around to dislodge most of the dirt and snow, then folded it neatly. "Yeah, we know, but here's a concept that you appear unable to grasp. Nobody here gives a damn about Jove Mason. You don't matter. Your money doesn't matter. All that matters is the two good hands that you aren't putting to use." I drove the point home by shoving the folded jumpsuit into his chest, nearly knocking him off balance. "So put them to use, Jove."

"This place has made you bold, hasn't it?" he asked, his voice low and dangerous. "You think you're hot shit because you don't have to clean toilets or shuck corn or whatever the hell else the people here do. You just sit in that little office of yours. Tell me, Georgie, what exactly did you do to win all of these idiots over so quickly?"

"I help out wherever I'm needed," I told him. "I don't turn my nose up at jobs that I think are beneath me. I get my shit done correctly and on time. That's how I won them over. You could take a couple pointers from me."

Jove scoffed and turned away, slinging the jumpsuit over his shoulder. "Pointers from you. That would be the day."

"You should be careful," I warned him as I turned back toward DotCom. "I hear the tribunal is strict. You might want to reassess how you behave here, or you might find yourself on the other side of that wall."

"Tribunal, my ass."

The comment wavered a little at the end, the only hint that Jove preferred the inside of Camp Haven to the outside. I let him stew in his own guilt. It wasn't my job to keep Jove in line. That fell to Jacob, yet another thing that we argued about whenever we had the cottage alone together. I refused to take responsibility for Jacob's father. If Jove wanted to gamble his place at Camp Haven away, then that was his choice, but I wouldn't go down for his mistakes.

DotCom, which usually bustled with winter preparation activity, was slow that day. The community center—the big shared room with the low ceiling in the center of the building— was currently home to several children and their teachers. The school was in the process of being renovated ever since the leaking roof had caved in due to a snowfall. I smiled as I watched the toddlers shove handmade baby toys into their mouths while the older kids completed lessons on reusable chalkboards. The orange glow of the oil lamps staved off the wintry gray light that filtered in from outside, and the center smelled like hot tea leaves. While Jove and Jacob craved a higher level of comfort, the warmth and coziness of the community center was more than enough to relax me.

The Communications office in DotCom had become a safe haven of sorts. It was quiet, set away from the rest of the camp, and there were only three people who had the key. Me, Ludo, and Eirian. No one bothered me there as I tinkered with parts, trying to build working walkie talkies and radios with rechargeable batteries. The problem was finding an energy source to charge the batteries. The closest I'd gotten to a breakthrough was when Eirian brought me a broken solar panel from one of their salvage missions. I fixed the panel and managed to get it working, but I couldn't figure out the wiring to get it hooked up to the battery chargers. Despite the lack of development, the radios, like the labor, took my mind off of everything else going on, so I spent as much time in the Communications office as possible. When Eirian came in hours later, I was immersed with the solar panel, the battery chargers, and several half-built radios.

"How's it going?" he asked, closing the door behind him and flicking open his lighter to light a second lamp. "You shouldn't work in the dark. You'll ruin your eyesight."

My eyes watered at the sudden illumination as I hunched over my work. "Sorry, I got a little carried away."

"A little?" Eirian said. "How long have you been doing that?"

"About an hour."

His hand covered mine. "Okay, take a break."

I sat back and rubbed my eyes. They felt stiff in their sockets, like I'd forgotten to blink while I was focusing on the solar panel. Eirian moved my work to clear a space for himself to sit on the desk, something that would've driven me nuts if Jacob had done it. However, Eirian handled the solar panel and spare parts with such obvious care that I couldn't get mad at him.

"What's wrong?" he asked.

"What makes you think anything's wrong?"

"Because you're holed up here in the dark with bloodshot eyes and a knife," he reminded me. "No one's that determined to get an old broken solar panel to work, Georgie. You're clearly worried about something."

"Ugh," I groaned, slumping in the chair and covering my eyes. "What am I not worried about? Penny's infection is getting worse, Pippa's about to burst, Jove just got himself a meeting with the tribunal, and Jacob hasn't looked me in the eye for two weeks. Meanwhile, my dad's still missing, and I can't even go look for him because I'm stuck waiting out this post-apocalypse bullshit—"

"Hold on," Eirian said, his expression solemn. "Did you just say that Jove is going up against the tribunal?"

"Yeah," I sighed. "He got his third demerit from Jimmy today because he's an idiot and an asshole. Honestly, it's not my problem. Jove won't change his attitude about this place, and I'm done trying to change it for him."

"It's going to be your problem," Eirian said. "Camp Haven doesn't take a tribunal meeting lightly, Georgie. It's a community event. Everyone turns up to vote on the outcome, but the tribunal gets the final say. From the way Jove behaves around camp, he definitely won't have it easy."

"So let them smack him down a little bit," I said with a shrug. "That's what he needs anyway."

"I don't disagree," he replied. "But I'm afraid the camp has stricter rules than that. They could kick Jove out of Camp Haven, and then you'll have even more things to fight about with Jacob."

I straightened up. "Wait, they would actually kick him out? I threatened him earlier about that—told him that they would—but I figured it was just a white lie to get him to fall in line."

"They've done it before," Eirian said. "If someone's a danger or a detriment to the camp, they can't be allowed to live here. It's as simple as that."

"Yeah, but there was no EMP blast before," I argued. "Whoever got kicked out could run back to the city or find another homestead if they really wanted to. Jove doesn't have that option."

"He probably should have thought about that before he went and landed himself three demerits." He picked up the solar cell that I'd been working on to examine it. "This is going to be a mess. Tribunal meetings are crazy. They get the whole camp riled up."

"Why?"

"Why did people use to attend hangings in the town squares as if they were parties back in the old days?" he said. "It's entertainment, which, in Camp Haven, is pretty thin on the ground. People pick sides, gamble under the table, pick fights. It's nuts. We don't need that right now. We should be focused on gathering extra supplies to get us through the darker months and fortifying the camp against attacks."

"Attacks?" I repeated. "Who's attacking us?"

"No one yet," Eirian said. "But I overheard Ludo and the other security officers talking last night. Apparently, another survival camp has gone up a few miles south of here. They're not like us—they're terribly prepared and totally clueless— which means one thing. They're going to take what they can't find or make for themselves, and Camp Haven is the closest target."

He was worried about it. I could see that in the way his dark brow knitted together, casting a scrunched shadow on the rest of his face as he fiddled with the solar panel with the exact same amount of focus that I'd employed before. I wasn't the only person trying to get stuff off my mind. Eirian needed the Communications office as meditation space just as much as I did.

"Do they know we're here?" I asked him.

"Not yet, I don't think," he said. "But they'll figure it out eventually. Ludo's already on top of it. He's sending scouts to check it out tonight. I might volunteer to go, see if it's worth the fuss that security is making."

"Is that safe?" I confiscated the solar panel from him as he started bending it experimentally. "You just said yourself that the people there might be dangerous."

"From what I gathered, it's a stealth mission," Eirian explained. "We won't be making contact. We just want to see what kind of setup they have going on. But if there's a tribunal, we might not have time for that kind of thing." He dropped his head into his hands. "Ugh, this is going to be a total disaster."

Instinctively, I rubbed his back through the thick fabric of his sweater. "How bad can it be? Look on the bright side. The other camp doesn't know we're here yet. That means we can buy some time. I'm sure Ludo is already working on a plan to beef up the security around Camp Haven. Don't worry."

For a minute or so, we sat like that, flames flickering in the lamps as I massaged the tension out of Eirian's shoulders and neck. Eventually, he ducked out from under my touch.

"You okay?" I asked as he slid off the desk, increasing the distance between us, and fiddled with the bag he'd brought with him.

"Yeah, I think I just figured you out."

"What's that supposed to mean?"

He pulled a steel water canteen from his bag and handed it to me. "You're the type of person that worries about everybody else so that you don't have to worry about yourself."

I refused the canteen. "I have no idea what you're talking about."

"It's not a bad thing." He pried open my fingers and placed the canteen in my palm. "On one hand, it shows that you're self-less and you care deeply about the people around you. On the other hand, it means that you're avoiding your own problems by focusing on everyone else's."

"Tell me, on which homestead did you take Psychology 101?" I asked him, finally taking a sip from the canteen. "Was it here at Camp Haven?"

He gave a wry smile. "When you live as simply as we do,

there are less distractions. It makes observing other people that much more interesting. You can learn a lot just by watching and listening."

"So you're a stalker."

"I pay attention," he rectified. "Like with Ludo earlier."

"When you were eavesdropping on a private conversation?"

"Listening," he corrected. "And you're deflecting. I get it, but let me tell you something. As noble as it is to put everyone else before yourself, it's no good if you're neglecting your own care. Self-care isn't selfish, Georgie. I get the feeling someone taught you differently when you were growing up."

I opened my mouth to answer, but Eirian stopped me.

"You don't have to explain," he said. "I just wanted you to know that it's okay to need a break from taking care of everyone else. You're allowed to focus on you every once in a while. Should we get to work?"

As simple as that, he changed the subject, turning away from me to focus his attention on the solar panel and the rough models of walkie talkies that I'd made. I watched as he studied my handwritten notes on what I could remember about wiring electronics, his nose wrinkling in concentration.

"It was my dad."

"Hmm?"

"My dad was the one who taught me that self-care was selfish," I clarified, glad that Eirian kept his eyes on his work rather than turning to face me. "Not directly. I'm sure he didn't mean it. After my mom died, he was a complete mess. He was paranoid about everything, and it caused him to have crazy mood swings. The entire world scared him. That's why we came out here."

Eirian continued playing with the solar cells and spare bits of wiring, but the pair of pliers that he'd picked up weren't moving between his fingers. He was listening to me speak but respecting the fact that I wasn't used to sharing this information with other people.

"It was just the two of us," I went on. "I was the only one who *could* take care of him, so that's what I did. He thought it was the other way around. I guess we took care of each other. He kept me alive, and I kept him sane. Or at least I did my best to keep him sane. Not sure that worked out so well."

"It sounds stressful," Eirian said. "Looking after your father at such a young age."

"It was," I agreed. "Ultimately, that's why I left. Those mood swings were bleeding into me. I'd get angry at the smallest inconvenience or cry if someone went wrong. If a tree branch tapped on the window, I had a moment when I was convinced he was right, that someone had finally come to kill us."

"God, I'm sorry." Eirian finally turned around to face me, and I wiped a few stray tears from my cheeks so that he wouldn't see them.

"It doesn't matter," I said. "That's why I got out. That's why I left him here and went into the city. It scared the shit out of me to be around that many people at first, but I did it."

"If you don't mind me asking," he said, "why is it that important for you to find your father if he treated you so poorly in the past?"

"Because I know my dad," I said, wiping my nose on the sleeve of my shirt. "And he's probably terrified."

15

I lay in bed in the cottage before dinner, savoring the rare moment of alone time. Jacob was still at work and Jove was off somewhere else, no doubt causing more trouble for the camp. The sun had set already. Leftover light glinted off a fresh snow flurry as it settled on the ground. As always, I studied the view from the window. The Rockies stared back, looming over Camp Haven. Some saw their towering grace as protection. The mountains shielded us from the horrors below in the city. Sometimes, I felt the same, cocooned between the walls of rock and snow. Other times, the mountains were dark and daunting, daring me to leave Camp Haven to trek through their obstinate passes. My father's voice woke me in the middle of the night, calling to me, pleading for me to come find him. It was a haunting lullaby that I wished I could forget.

Jacob burst in, ruining my attempt at a nap. As usual, he was sweating through the layers of sweaters and jackets that he wore, having just come off a shift with the Miscellaneous crew.

"I hate this place," he groaned, shedding his outermost coat, which was covered with oil smears. "Do you know what we had to do today?"

"Something terrible, no doubt," I replied.

"We had to turn animal fat into lamp oil." He fell onto the bed opposite mine, and the metal frame creaked with his weight. "Hours of chopping up fat. I never want to see another deer in my life."

I turned over, away from Jacob, and pressed a pillow over my ears. "That's how things are done here."

"I know," he snapped. "You don't have to remind me."

"Then stop bitching about it."

"What's your problem?"

I pulled the blanket over my head. "Five minutes, Jacob. I wanted five minutes of peace and quiet before the dinner bell rang, and here you are."

"I live here too, you know."

"Then live here quietly."

The mattress groaned as he rolled over with a scoff. His frustration radiated off of him like a heat wave, spreading across the small room to fill me with annoyance. This was what it had come to. Jacob's mere presence irked me. Sharing a room with him and Jove painted a target on my back. Most of the compound respected me, but they had reservations about my relationship with the Masons, especially since they all still thought that Jacob and I were engaged.

Just as my eyes started to drift shut again, a roar of noise echoed into the cottage from outside. The thwack of a fist meeting a face tore me out of bed. I ignored the boots and stormed outside. Jacob followed, a little slower on the uptake, and we found Jove going head to head with one of the other sanitation workers. The two men were locked together in a vicious fistfight. The other guy, a younger man in his thirties, proved to have the upper hand. He gripped Jove around the neck with one arm and used the other to punch Jacob's father repeatedly in the face. A crowd had gathered around them, but it was mostly women and children who didn't want to intervene.

"Stop, stop, stop!" I ordered, pushing through the circle of spectators and catching hold of the other man's arm before he could land yet another punch to Jove's demolished nose. "You're going to kill him!"

The man's temper faded as soon as I interrupted his barrage of attacks. He dropped Jove in the dirt and tried to step away, but Jacob took him up by the coat collar. The other man, who was taller than Jacob, automatically lashed out. Jacob ducked, tackled the man around the midriff, and they both sprawled to the ground.

"Jacob, don't!" I said, unable to break up the new fight while Jove lay unconscious on the ground. His nose was beyond help, and his airways were filling up with blood. "We need to get Jove to the med bay. He can't breathe."

Within minutes, someone produced the sheet off their bed, which we rolled Jove into. Jacob released Jove's opponent to help carry his father across the compound to the med bay. To my surprise, the man Jove had been fighting helped too. One of his eyes bore a hefty bruise.

"What's your name?" I asked him.

"Mitchell."

"He hit you first, didn't he?" I said. Jacob's shoulders rose toward his ears. He was listening in.

"Yup," Mitchell said. "I'm sorry about all of this. I totally lost it. This guy's been a pain in my ass ever since he got assigned to Sanitation. Won't do the work. Thinks he's all high and mighty. He slows the rest of us down. A few nights ago, I missed dinner because I had to fix this jerk's mistake. I had enough. I said something nasty to him, and he snapped. That's when the first hit landed."

"I've been on the other end of Jove's comments," I assured Mitchell. "I can understand wanting to punch the guy."

"That's my father you're talking about," Jacob said over his shoulder as we continued lugging Jove toward the med bay. He stirred in the sheet, mumbling incoherently. Blood gurgled at the corner of his lips.

"It's no secret that your father's an ass," I reminded him. "Do you remember what he said when we told him that we were engaged?"

"No."

"He looked at me from head to toe and then turned to you and asked you if you'd found me on the discount rack," I said, gritting my teeth at the memory. "I'll never forget that."

"Wow," Mitchell said as we approached the med bay.

Jacob declined to comment and kicked open the door of the bay. As we maneuvered Jove inside and rested him gently on one of the cots, Pippa looked on in a mixture of horror and astonishment.

"What did he do this time?" she asked.

"Punched me in the face," Mitchell answered, pointing to his black eye.

"Damn it, is anyone here?" Jacob jogged to the end of the med bay and pounded on the door of Jax's office. "Hello! We need help!"

Nita emerged from one of the exam rooms, textbook in hand. "Jacob. Hey, what's going on? Holy shit, what happened to Jove?"

He took her by the arm and led her to Jove's bedside. "Please, I don't think he can breathe. You have to do something."

Nita jumped into action, tipping Jove's head back to assess the damage. She produced a strange instrument from a nearby drawer and bent over Jacob's father. "Of course this happens as soon as Jax takes a break. Christ."

Jacob and Nita crowded Jove, so I stepped away to give them space. Mitchell ran his fingers through his long dusty hair, pacing from cot to cot. When his repetitions made me dizzy, I caught him by the shoulder and sat him down.

"What if he dies?" he asked me. "What if I punched him so

hard that he dies? They're going to kick me out of the camp! I don't want to leave. This is my home."

"He's not going to die," I assured him. "He's got a broken nose, and at worse, a concussion. Once Nita clears his airways and resets his nose, he'll be fine."

"That doesn't mean I won't get a demerit for this," Mitchell said. "Oh, man, is this bad enough to call a tribunal for?"

I offered Mitchell my water canteen. "I have news for you. Jove is already waiting on a meeting with the tribunal. He's in deep shit for all the trouble he's caused in the past few weeks. I highly doubt they'll even bother with you."

Mitchell relaxed as he sipped from the canteen. "A tribunal's already been called? Wow, we haven't had one in years."

"Dad's in trouble?" Pippa chimed in from the next bed over. "What's going to happen to him?"

"We don't know yet," I told her. "Don't worry about it right now."

Nita and Jacob continued working on Jove. Nita had managed to clear the blood from his throat. He was breathing on his own again. As he slowly regained consciousness, the pain became harder for him to ignore. He let out a noise somewhere between a moan and a yell.

"Jove," Nita said, steadying the big man's shoulders against the hospital bed. "Your nose is pretty badly broken. I'm going to have to reset it, and it's going to hurt like hell."

"Painkillers," Jove begged, his voice garbled. His fingers twisted in the bed sheets. "Please, Nita."

"I can't give you anything," she told him as he whimpered. "We have a limited supply of painkillers, and I'm on strict orders not to give them out unless completely necessary. Get ready, Jove. Here we go."

Jacob held Jove against the mattress as Nita took Jove's nose between her hands. With a disgusting crunch, she moved the bone back into place. Jove howled in pain, bucking against Jacob's hold.

"That's it!" Nita said. "You're done. All I have to do now is tape it up. All you have to do is take care of it and not cause any more trouble. Do you think you can manage that?"

"Doubtful," I muttered, but Jove nodded.

Nita left Jove's bedside to fetch the things she needed to splint his nose, but she paused before passing me. "Listen, Georgie. I'm obligated to record everything that happens in the med bay so that we can inventory supplies. That means I have to report this to Jax."

"Go ahead," I told her.

She looked over at Jacob and Jove. "It's not looking good for Jove, and I'm not talking about his face. The whole camp hates him."

"I'm aware."

"I've already heard rumors that they're going to kick him out," she said, keeping her voice low.

"I'm not sure those are just rumors anymore," I told her.

"Aren't you worried?" she asked. "About what this could do to Penny, Pippa, and Jacob?"

My stomach rolled over, either out of hunger or increasing vexation. "I told Jacob. I told him over and over that Jove needed to toe the line. It's all we've been arguing about for the past few weeks. I did what I could. The rest is up to Jove and the tribunal."

I stormed out of the med bay, leaving Nita to patch up Jove with the company of Jacob and Mitchell. The fight had made us miss the dinner bell. The Bistro teemed with campers enjoying a hot stew and fresh bread rolls. The delicious scent of marinated meat and broth tickled my nose, but as much as I wanted a hot meal, the last thing I wanted was to be around that many people. I settled for lurking around the Bistro's back door, the one that led to the kitchen, and hoping that someone would magically emerge with a bowl of stew to offer. The chances were thin. No one ate out here in the snow and the cold. Except Eirian apparently.

He shouldered the door open, still wrapped up in his big coat and scarf. The fluffy neck piece was bright purple, which brought out the pretty pale tones of his skin.

"That's a good color on you," I said.

He started, surprised to see me loitering in the bushes, but regained his composure in a flash. "I'll have you know that purple is the color of royalty among other things."

"I wasn't kidding," I said, bumping his shoulder. "It brings out your eyes."

"Why, thank you." He looked around at the empty campground then back at me. "What are you doing out here alone? Where's Jacob?"

"In the med bay."

Eirian's eyes widened. "What happened to him? Is he okay?"

I waved away his concerns, eyeing the bowl of soup that he balanced between his gloved palms. "He's fine. It's Jove. He picked a fight with someone and got his nose broken."

"This is going to keep escalating, isn't it?" Eirian sighed. He noticed my laser sharp focus and lifted the bowl of stew. "You want to share this? You look like you could use a pick me up."

"No, thanks. I'm fine."

He sat down on the top of the compost lid and patted the space next to him. "Remember what I said earlier about not taking care of yourself? Refusing to eat definitely falls into that category. Come on, they served me way too much anyway."

He waved the spoon at me until I snatched it out of his hand and took a bite of stew. It warmed me all the way down, and I moaned in relief.

"Hold this," he said, offering me the bowl as he dug in his coat pocket. "I have something else for you."

I lifted the bowl, letting the steam warm my frozen nose. "Honestly, I don't need much else."

A metal flask glinted in the moonlight. I traded Eirian the bowl for the flask, uncapped it, and took a whiff.

"Is this moonshine?"

Eirian beamed proudly. "My own recipe. That's the last of it though. We won't have any more maize or barley until the spring."

"I can't believe Camp Haven allows that," I said. "Doesn't seem like something they would want in the compound."

"They don't," Eirian said. "But it's also unrealistic to keep the camp totally dry."

"Does Ludo know you make that?"

"He buys it from me."

"No kidding!"

"Have a sip," he offered. "It's a decent remedy for a cold night. Keeps you warm."

I tipped the flask to my lips. The smell alone was sharp, but the taste was even more potent. I coughed as the homemade whiskey burned my throat but relished the flood of warmth through my bones.

"Thanks," I said. "I needed that. The stew too."

"I figured." He finished off what was left of the meal, tipping the bowl to drink the leftover broth. "Listen, I've been thinking about your father. You still want to find him, right?"

"Of course I do."

"It's kind of a long shot, but there is one person who might know something about where he went," Eirian said.

"Who?"

"Sylvester."

I slumped against the wall of the Bistro. "It's no good. I asked Ludo about Sylvester weeks ago. He told me that no one gets to talk to Sylvester face-to-face."

"That's mostly true," Eirian said. "Actually, I don't think

anyone has ever seen him in person, but you can request a meeting in the cabin with him. It's a long list. Plenty of people want his advice, and most of them get denied the privilege, but you could at least try."

"How do I request a meeting?"

"There's a box in one of the offices at DotCom," he replied. "Just write your name down and put it in the box."

"Really? It's that simple?"

"Like I said, it's a long shot," he said. "We could go now if you want."

I hopped off my seat on the compost bin, took one more sip from the flask, and handed the moonshine back to him. "I'm down."

I waited for Eirian to return the bowl to the Bistro, then the two of us headed into DotCom. The night's event, a trivia contest, hadn't started yet. Everyone was still eating dinner. We found the office with Sylvester's box. It was nondescript, an old ammunitions tin with a slot drilled in the side. I'd seen in a few times without knowing what it was. Now, I jotted my name down on a small slip of paper, folded it in half, and jimmied it through the opening in the box.

"That's that," I said. Outside the office, DotCom began to fill up with those who wanted to participate in the trivia contest. "What now?"

"Now we wait to see if your request gets approved," Eirian said. "In the meantime, what do you say to a round of trivia? We could team up. I'm hopeless at pop culture."

"Whoa, I can't have an amateur dragging me down," I joked, leading him out of the office and down the hall toward the main room.

"Excuse me, but there is an entire category on scat, and I don't know if you know this, but I am the master of—"

"Shit?" I finished for him. "You're the master of shit. Yeah, you're really selling me on this whole trivia partner thing."

"You know what?" He dove forward, tickling me around the waist. I laughed and tried to bat him away. "That's what you get. Who's the trivia master now? Huh?"

"Still me!" I gasped, grinning from ear to ear. "You're forgetting that I grew up in the woods too."

Eirian's fingers danced playfully at my sides. "You've wounded my ego. I can't go on like this."

"Oh, shut up!"

Someone cleared their throat, and we both looked up from our playful tussle to see Jacob standing in the doorway to the main hall. At once, Eirian dropped his hands from my waist and took a step away. I straightened the hem of my sweater and smoothed out my ruffled hair.

"I just came to tell you that Dad's doing better," Jacob said, though his eyes remained on Eirian. All of his muscles were pulled taut, the tendons in his neck standing out against the skin. "Nita splinted his nose, and he's sleeping now. Jax checked on him too. She said he got lucky. No concussion."

"I should let the two of you talk," Eirian said, trying to pass Jacob in the doorway. "I'm glad your dad's all right, Jacob."

Jacob didn't move, blocking Eirian's exit. He stared up into the taller man's face. "Are you?"

Eirian, confused, replied, "Of course."

"Let him go," I told Jacob. "He's supposed to be helping with the trivia contest."

Jacob finally stepped aside to let Eirian pass, but Eirian lingered a moment longer before exiting to the main hall.

"Let me know if you need anything," he told me, glancing at Jacob with a worried tilt to his lips.

"I will."

When Eirian left, Jacob folded his arms across his chest and stared at me from across the hall. "The two of you seem awfully friendly."

"Yeah, because we're *friends*," I said coolly. "Am I not allowed to make any at Camp Haven?"

"Like you've had any trouble in that department," he returned. "Do you ever get tired of pandering to these weirdos? The only reason they've survived this long is because they're just like your father. Paranoid and probably a little sick in the head."

"I'm not pandering to them." My hands began to shake, not from the cold, so I balled them up and shoved them into my pockets. "And you have no right to talk about my father."

"Why not?" Jacob challenged. "You talk about mine."

"Yours is *here*," I told him. "And he's causing trouble. If Jove calmed down and started acting like a civilized human being, I wouldn't have to talk about him."

Before Jacob could reply, the door opened again, and Ludo butted into the hallway. "Hey, folks. Eirian said you were back here. Aren't you coming to play trivia?"

Jacob rolled his eyes. "Oh, *Eirian* sent you back to check on us, huh? No, I don't want to play any damn trivia—"

"I do," I said, raising my hand. "Want to be partners, Ludo? I bet we could kick some ass together."

"Sure thing, sweetheart," Ludo said, "but before we head out there, I wanted to clue the two of you in. Jax reported your father's fight, Jacob. Originally, we were going to call the tribunal next week since this camp a few miles over looks like they might be on the hunt for supplies soon, but we can't ignore your father's behavior. The situation has escalated too far. He's causing harm to himself and others, and that's one thing that Camp Haven does not condone. We moved the tribunal meeting up."

"For when?" Jacob asked.

"Tomorrow."

.   .   .

THE WORD of Jove's tribunal meeting spread like wildfire through the camp. People talked about it all day long, discussing Jove's misgivings at length while they worked around the compound. Storytime was cancelled that evening in order to leave DotCom free for the event. Children were not allowed to attend. Apparently, the camp had witnessed some pretty violent reactions to the tribunal's orders in the past. The tribunal itself was a bit of a mystery. Ludo admitted that he had used to have a seat in the panel, but after a particular grueling meeting, he gave it up to another high-ranking member of the camp. After working with several different department heads within Camp Haven, I could guess which ones were involved with the tribunal, but I would have to wait until the actual event to see if I was right.

I tried to avoid Jacob as much as possible during the day. Ludo had excused him from his miscellaneous duties to sit with Jove in the med bay and prepare his father for what might happen during the tribunal meeting. I wasn't sure what Ludo expected Jacob to do. He didn't have any knowledge of the camp's judicial system either. No matter what, I had no plans to join them. At this point, the entire Mason family was holed up in the med bay, and playing pretend engagement with Jacob was getting tiring, but of course, while I was working at the Bistro, the servers asked me to bring lunch trays to the med bay.

"Food," I announced to the Mason family as I entered the room with a stack of trays. "Where do you want it?"

"I'm not hungry," Jove said. His face looked nasty. His nose had swollen to the size of a tomato, and Nita's splint looked ineffective compared to the damage. "Can barely eat anyway with this damn thing on my face."

Jacob relieved me of the trays and placed one each on Jove, Penny, and Pippa's beds. "You need to eat, Dad. We don't know what's going to happen tonight."

"Bah!" Jove knocked the lid off of a steel camping bowl. "Stew again! God, do these people know how to make anything else?"

"It's leftovers from last night," I told him. "No waste, remember?"

"It's garbage," Jove spat. "Leftovers are for rats and homeless people."

"And on that note, I'm out of here," I announced. I stopped by Pippa's bed. She, unlike Jove, did not complain about the food that was delivered to her. "How are you doing, kid?"

"As good as I can, I guess," she said, slurping broth off of her spoon. "Have you heard anything?"

"About your dad? Not really?"

"What about Mom?" Pippa looked over at Penny, who was asleep once again. I couldn't remember the last time I'd seen her awake and alert. Penny's lunch tray lay untouched at the foot of her cot. "She's barely coherent, Georgie. Nita won't tell me anything. I know that's not good."

"I'll ask Nita about it when I get the chance," I promised her. "For right now, you should focus on yourself. Keep your stress levels down. That baby's coming soon."

"Thirty-eight weeks," she grumbled. "I wish he would move it along. I'm beyond uncomfortable, and this place is boring as hell. At this point, I'd rather clean the toilets than spend another hour in the med bay."

I grinned and patted her shoulder. "Be glad you're assigned to work with the kids. You don't want to know what your dad smelled like when he got out of work each day."

I SPENT the rest of the day toying with the solar panels and walkie talkies. Eirian was busy setting up DotCom for the tribunal meeting, so he couldn't make it to Communications for his usual lesson in handmade, solar-powered electronics. I fell asleep on the desk, my cheek pressed to a coil of copper wire. When I woke up, night had fallen, and a cyclical imprint decorated my cheek like a poorly cut doily pattern. As I rubbed my face to restart the circulation, voices carried down the hall from the main room. I stood up, grabbing my coat on the way out.

"What's going on?" I asked when I found Eirian, Ludo, and a few other camp members talking animatedly in DotCom's vast meeting room. "Has something happened?"

"The tribunal wants to meet outside," Eirian announced. "By the bonfire."

"It's freezing outside," I said. "Why did they move it?"

"They're anticipating trouble," Ludo explained. "They're expecting the whole camp to turn up. If Mason gets too belligerent, it could encourage unfavorable behavior. The tribunal figures that if we hold it outside, the cold will subdue some of the campers. Less people will show up."

"Camp Haven has its shit together in every area," I said. "You're telling me it turns into a riot as soon as someone sits in front of the tribunal?"

"It's the nature of the event," Eirian replied. "That's just the way it is."

I sighed and threaded my arms through the sleeves of my coat. "Outside it is. What time are we starting? Do you need help?"

"It starts in ten minutes," Eirian said. "And you can carry one of these warmers out to the square for me if you don't mind."

I accepted the free-standing warming lamp from Eirian's grasp. They were an invention of the camp's, made to burn coals at about shoulder height to heat the air around us. Together, Ludo, Eirian, and I lugged a few of them to the square. The bonfire had already been lit, and a crowd gathered, craning their necks for a look at the small group of people hidden behind a room divider in the corner of the main square. Six chairs had been placed on the stage that the camp usually used for outdoor events. Five of them were arranged in a semicircle, facing the sixth. The sixth was alone.

We stationed the warming lamps and got them lit. I shivered

in the moonlight anyway, though I think the chill was more from anticipation than the biting mountain air. Eirian rubbed my shoulders to warm me up.

"Need a shot of moonshine?" he asked in a low, teasing voice.

"More like five," I replied.

A roar went up from the crowd as the tribunal emerged from behind the room divider, stepped onto the stage, and took their seats in the five chairs. I had worked in so many departments of the camp that I recognized each member of the panel. Jax sat on the far left. Next to her was Helen, the strong-armed woman who ran the kitchens. In the middle sat Randall, Ludo's second-in-command for security. To his right were Todd and Terri, who were brother and sister. They were amongst the oldest living members of Camp Haven, and so were considered the wisest.

Jax stood and the crowd cheered again. She waved at them to be quiet and cleared her throat. "This tribunal has been called together to question the behavior and intent of one Jove Mason. Bring him out, please!"

The doors to the med bay opened and two of Ludo's men escorted Jove to the stage. The crowd jeered as he passed by, making faces and calling names. I spotted Mitchell, the man that Jove had punched yesterday, standing quietly away from the others. Jove yelled back at the crowd, spittle flying from his lips as his face turned bright red. Little did he know that he was giving the crowd the exact scene that they wanted. Jacob followed behind his father, his head bowed to avoid the glares of the campers. Pippa, blessedly, remained inside.

"This is barbaric," I muttered to Eirian as we watched Ludo's men heave Jove into the final seat on the stage.

"I agree," he said. "If it were me, these tribunal meetings would be held in private, but they allow the campers to vote on the outcome."

"The campers decide what happens?" I asked him.

"In a way," Eirian explained. "The tribunal takes their concerns into account, but Sylvester has the final say."

"Jove Mason," Jax said, facing Jove from her chair. "You have been called here today because your integrity has been challenged. Randall will read you the list of complaints set against you. Randall?"

Randall cleared his throat and unfurled a short piece of paper to read off of. "Mr. Mason has been accused of the following: failure to arrive to work in a timely manner, failure to complete obligatory tasks assigned to him, failure to comply with Camp Haven's regulated safety standards, failure to resolve personal disagreements without physically harming the other party, and failure to respect those who make Camp Haven's mission possible. Mr. Mason, do you admit guilt to these accusations?"

"Go to hell," Jove snarled.

"We'll take that as a yes," Randall said. "Now we'll hear from members of the camp on their opinion of Mr. Mason. We have Jacob Mason to speak for his father and a number of campers to speak against him. Let's get started."

The proceedings were lengthy. There was a long line of people who wished to express complaints about Jove's behavior. Each of them was allowed two minutes to make their case, during which the tribunal took notes. In a manner of weeks, Jove had managed to offend nearly a fourth of the entire camp, and they had not taken kindly to his attacks. Jacob was the last to speak. When he did so, his voice wavered as the night swallowed it.

"I know that my father has not been the most helpful addition to Camp Haven," he began, immediately eliciting boos and hisses from the crowd. He ignored them, focusing on the tribunal instead. "I implore you to remember that we come from a different world than this one. It's been difficult for my father to adjust, but I think we can come to a compromise that would be agreeable to everyone."

"What kind of compromise?" Jax asked.

"Move my father out of the sanitation department," Jacob suggested, and once more, the crowd roared with displeasure. Jacob raised his voice. "He can work elsewhere. Anywhere."

"Mr. Mason Junior," Jax said, peering over the top of her glasses at Jacob. "If we allowed every person to switch jobs simply because they didn't like it, we would have chaos on our hands."

"I understand that—"

"Do you have anything to say about your father's character?" Jax asked him. "Have you discussed possible solutions to these issues?"

"He's a good man," Jacob said. "He's spent the last thirty years contributing to society. He should have a chance."

"Unfortunately, we're not concerned with any society outside this one," Jax replied, "to which your father has refused to contribute, I might add. That's two minutes. Please step down from the stage."

"But—"

Jacob was interrupted as Ludo's security men took him by either arm and attempted to lead him away from Jove's chair. He shook them off and stepped off the stage himself.

"Mr. Mason," Jax said, raising her voice as she addressed Jove. "You now have two minutes to defend yourself. Is there anything you wish to say? Please keep in mind that derogatory remarks and defamation will immediately serve as reason to strip you of the privilege of these two minutes."

"Privilege?" Jove snorted like an angry bull. "You call two minutes privilege? This whole thing—this tribunal—is a farce. What could you do to me, eh? What's the punishment? Muck more toilets? Clean more shit? I will not stand for this treatment. Just wait until I can get in contact with my lawyer…"

On and on he went for the allotted time. The tribunal let him speak, watching him with amused smirks as the crowd egged on

Jove's temper. Two minutes felt like two hours, until Jax finally held up a hand to stop Jove from talking.

"That will be all," she said over him as he continued on about his lawyer in Denver. "Ladies and gentlemen, you have heard both sides of the argument. It's now time to vote. The matter at hand stands as follows: Jove Mason has proven himself a detriment to this compound. Your decision is this. Shall we allow Mr. Mason to remain here as a member of Camp Haven under the assumption that he will work to change his ways or shall we expel Mr. Mason from the security of our compound in order to protect the people within it?"

Jacob's face fell. This was it. Either Jove stayed or went, and I had a feeling I knew which way the crowd was leaning.

"All in favor of giving Mr. Mason another chance?" Jax called. A few scattered hands went up. "All opposed?"

A sea of fingers reached toward the sky, accompanied by another roar of noise. For the first time, Jove looked worried. Sweat beaded on his red forehead and dripped down his temple as he looked out at the crowd as they condemned him.

"The tribunal will confer," Jax announced.

The five members on stage put their heads together. For the longest minute of my life, they murmured their opinions to one another. The crowd was dead silent, as if hoping that the tribunal's voices might carry on the wind. There was no need. Jax stood up once again.

"Unless Sylvester decides otherwise," she began, "Jove Mason is no longer a member of this compound. He shall be banished from the premises as soon as we see fit."

The crowd cheered with mass approval, but when I saw the look of horror on Jacob's face, I wondered if I had given the people of Camp Haven too much credit before. Before the EMP blast, Jove would have considered being expelled from the compound a blessing. He would have fired up his Humvee and driven it down the mountain back into the city without a glance over his shoulder at what he'd left behind. Things were different now. There was nothing to go back to in Denver except for disastrous trouble. Jove had never been camping a day in his life. I doubted he even knew how to get a fire started without a blow torch, let alone set up a shelter for himself or find food. The animals were starting to burrow away in preparation for the incoming snow storms. It was rare to find one out and about these days, but if a rabbit did stick its head out of its cubby hole, Jove wasn't keen enough to catch it. Camp Haven had all but condemned Jove to death.

"No," Jacob shouted over the crowd. Ludo's security guards kept the onlookers from climbing the stage. Jove, whose hands were bound to the chair, rocked to and fro in an attempt to free himself from the restraints. "You can't do this!"

"Silence!" Jax said, and the crowd fell quiet. "The decision will be taken to Sylvester for the final review. In the meantime, I cannot condone this behavior while we wait for his confirmation. Please disperse. Return to your dormitories."

The people of Camp Haven erupted into loud complaints. This was the event of the season, and Jax was cutting it short. I was grateful. The jeering crowd was making all of this worse. Jacob grew more tense with every shout. The whites of Jove's eyes shone in the dark night as he yelled at the tribunal to cut the ropes around his hands. Jax put two fingers in her mouth and let out an earsplitting whistle.

"This camp will come to order!" she boomed. "Now! Unless you all want a demerit?"

The residents of the compound recognized that she was not bluffing, and the throng finally began to disperse. I slipped in with a group of people heading back to the dormitories, but Jacob leapt off the stage, bullied his way through, and caught me by my coat.

"What are you doing?" I asked, tugging free.

"Me?" he said. "What about you? You brought us here, Georgie! To keep us safe, you claimed. Did you hear what they said? They're kicking him out. He won't survive out there. He doesn't know how."

"I don't know what you expect me to do about it," I told him.

"You have pull with people here," Jacob said, pleading with his eyes. "Everyone likes you. You could talk to Ludo or Jax. Tell them that he didn't mean it. Tell them that we'll make sure he toes the line from now on."

Behind Jacob, Jove argued with the tribunal from his chair. Jax and Helen attempted to reason with him, but the other three members of the panel pointedly ignored him. The full extent of what expulsion meant to Jove was finally setting in. There was a note of panic in his deep voice, which carried to where Jacob and I were standing.

"This is all just a terrible mistake," he was saying. I recognized that oily tone. It was the one he used when he was trying to close a business deal. "It's the stress, you see? Once I become accustomed to the camp's ways, I'll be better. I swear."

"You've had weeks to assimilate, Mr. Mason," Jax said wryly. "And you failed to make that argument moments ago when we asked you to defend your place here in the compound."

"I can't lie to them," I told Jacob. "I know your father, Jacob. If he gets a second chance, he'll use it to weasel his way in and take advantage of every person here."

Jacob fixed me with a withering stare. "He's going to die out there, Georgie."

"He should have thought of that before he decided to be an ass." I tried to walk away, but Jacob seized me again and pulled me into the shadows between the Bistro and DotCom.

"This is what it's come to?" he asked, whirling me around so that we were face to face. I hadn't been this close to him in weeks, close enough to see the sparkling embers of anger in his light brown eyes. "Are you that angry at me for breaking up with you? Because this is really petty, Georgie, even for you."

"Are you serious right now?" All of my frustration with Jacob that I'd kept inside during the five years of our relationship began bubbling to the surface. "That's what you think this is about?"

"It's the only thing I can think of," Jacob shot back. "You won't help him. You're forcing him out of the compound."

"*I'm* not doing anything," I said loudly, catching the attention of a few passers-by. "Don't you dare try to make this my fault. Jove made his own bed. His behavior is his own responsibility. Besides, I have problems of my own."

"Oh, problems of your own?" Jacob challenged, throwing his hands up. "What could those possibly be?" He leveled up the pitch of his voice to mock mine. "Learn how to pluck a chicken, build working radios with golden boy Eirian?"

"Eirian does whatever he has to in order to keep this place running." My face grew warm as I defended the other man, and I hoped that the lamps around the bonfire weren't bright enough for Jacob to see the red in my cheeks. "And for your information, I do have other problems. My father—"

"Not this again," he said. "Your father isn't here, Georgie. That means one of two things. One, he left because he figured you would never come back to him, or two, he's dead. I'm betting on the latter, if the things you told me about your father are true."

The anger boiled over. I shoved Jacob backward, and he stumbled over the uneven ground. He caught himself against the wall of DotCom, but it took him a second longer to rearrange his countenance. He stared at me, mouth open in shock that I'd laid hands on him.

"How dare you?" I whispered, advancing toward him like a tiger stalking its prey. "I brought you here to keep you safe, even when I knew that you and I were never going to work. Your mother and sister are alive because of me, but *my* family is gone, Jacob. I'm not a part of yours, remember? The thought of my father is the only thing I have left, and I will not let you take that from me."

Jacob didn't back down. "Be realistic," he said. "It's been weeks since we got to Camp Haven, and there's been no sign of your father. No one's heard of him, Georgie. You need to face facts. He's gone."

"You don't know that," I said, "and I won't stop looking for him until I've exhausted every single possibility."

"What other possibilities are there?"

"Sylvester."

For the first time since the argument began, Jacob paused to consider my reply before jumping in with a hurtful comeback. "Sylvester? What are you talking about?"

"I applied for a meeting with him," I told him, more to prove that he was wrong about my father. Jacob didn't need to know how slim my chances were of actually procuring the meeting. "If anyone knows what happened to my father, it's him."

"This is perfect." He half-smiled as he turned around to check on Jove, who was still making a case for himself on stage with the tribunal. Jacob laughed, picked me up, and swung me around.

I thumped on his shoulder. "Put me down!"

He obliged, setting me on my feet. "Georgie, why didn't you say something before? This is amazing. You can ask Sylvester to give my dad another chance."

A coldness swept through my body, one that didn't have anything to do with the chilly nighttime air. "Jacob, I'm not asking Sylvester about Jove."

The happiness slid off of Jacob's face in less than a second. "What are you talking about? Why not?"

"The tribunal already decided," I reminded him. "Jove's out. I need to find out about my father, and I'm not going to waste time fighting a losing battle."

"Damn it, Georgie! You are so selfish!"

Eirian appeared behind Jacob, towering over my ex-fiancé. "Everything okay over here?"

Jacob started and whirled around to face the other man. "None of your damn business. Jesus, you're everywhere, aren't you? I'm starting to think you have a thing for my fianceé."

"I'm not your—" I began.

"I just came over to tell you that the tribunal heard back from Sylvester," Eirian said, holding his hands up in a gesture of innocence. "You seemed too busy arguing with Georgie to notice that they're taking your father to the gates."

Jacob spun around toward the stage. The tribunal and Jove were gone, and other members of the camp lugged the six chairs off the lifted platform to put them away. Jacob scanned the campground. Ludo's security team dragged Jove, hands still tied behind his back, toward the massive gates that kept the riffraff out of Camp Haven. Jacob sprinted toward them, and I followed after him.

"It's no use," Eirian said to me. His legs were so long that he took one stride for every two of mine. "Once Sylvester decides that someone's out, they're out for good. Georgie." He took my hand before I could catch up with Jacob fully, pulling me to a stop. "Listen to me. Defending Jove isn't going to help anyone. If anything, it's just going to ruin the positive relationships that you've worked so hard to build here."

Ludo's men worked together to operate the massive locking mechanism that kept the steel gates sealed. All the while, Jacob pleaded with them to stop. Jove had given up. His enormous form slumped over, his knees resting against the dirt, head bowed to his chest. For once, I actually pitied him.

"Can you talk to them?" I asked Eirian, clutching the front of his coat. "Please? I don't give a damn about Jove, but he has a wife and a daughter here, both of whom are stuck in the med bay. I really don't want to be the one that has to tell them that he's been kicked out."

"I already tried talking to Ludo and Jax."

"You did?"

He unfurled my fingers from his coat collar and covered them with his gloved hands. "Of course I did. I know what kind of trouble this is going to cause between you and Jacob's family. I did my best, Georgie, but once the tribunal gets confirmation from Sylvester, the decision is set in stone. I'm so sorry."

Without thinking, I threw my arms around him, burying my face in the warmth of his coat. After a moment's hesitation, he returned the gesture, resting his chin on the top of my head. I watched the gates from the circle of Eirian's arms. The security team had pulled them open just enough for Jove to fit through, but they couldn't get the man off the ground. Jacob knelt beside his father, hands clasped together, begging the other men to let

Jove stay. Two of Ludo's team dragged Jacob roughly away from Jove. Tears streamed down Jacob's face, but Jove remained impassive, as if his expulsion had numbed all emotion. It took three additional men to lift Jove far enough from the ground to haul him across the camp's border. Once he was outside the gate, they cut his hands free from the ropes. Jacob ripped free of his handlers and made a break for the doorway, but it was too late. The enormous gate slammed shut, and the team moved the locking mechanism back into place. Jove was officially no longer a member of Camp Haven.

The security team dispersed, leaving Jacob at the gates. He yanked at the mechanism, but it took more than one man to move it out of place. Fruitlessly, Jacob pounded on the gate. There was no answer from the other side.

"Should I—" I began, pulling slightly away from Eirian.

"It's probably better not to."

He was right. After several minutes, Jacob finally gave up. He straightened his coat, wiped his eyes, and turned from the gate. I drew away from Eirian, but not before Jacob spotted our embrace. When he stopped in front of me, his nose inches from mine, Eirian shifted his stance into a more defensive one, but Jacob only had a message for me.

"I'll never forgive you for this."

THE NEXT SEVERAL days were torture. I slept on the floor of my office in DotCom, unbeknownst to Ludo or any of the other campers. I couldn't stand the thought of sharing that tiny cottage with Jacob, not after everything that had happened. He ignored me entirely. If we passed each other at the Bistro, he pretended not to see me. If that was my only punishment for not coming to Jove's defense, I would have been able to handle it. Unfortunately, Penny and Pippa had heard word of my actions. Pippa had asked that I stay away from the med bay, as she no longer had any desire to see my face. Penny, during her limited waking hours, sobbed into her pillow. If I had to drop off supplies to the med bay or run an errand for Jax, I did not go inside. Nita met me around back and finished off the errands for me. Even my friend was being short with me. She had only gotten one side of the story, the side that made me look like the villain.

Alternately, the rest of the camp was displeased with me simply because I was related to the Masons. No matter what department I worked with, I couldn't escape judgmental stares and whispered accusations. It was easier when Jove was around for me to publicly denounce his poor behavior. Now that he was gone, people seemed to forget that I'd never been a huge fan of his in the first place. I stopped asking where I was needed. I stopped offering to lend a hand to different departments. Instead, I holed up in my office and worked on my equipment for hours on end, emerging only for meals and to update Ludo on my process.

Eirian was one of the few campers that still spoke to me as if I wasn't a leper. The more I kept to myself, the more he made himself available to work in Communications. He brought food from the Bistro and moonshine from his personal stash, and we hunkered down to get the radios and solar panel working. Occasionally, the moonshine was too effective as a remedy. More than once, we found ourselves tipsy and laughing over some inane joke rather than working. It was a good thing that Eirian was so well thought of in Camp Haven. Otherwise, I'm sure we would have received a demerit each for wasting time in the communications office.

A week after Jove's expulsion, Ludo found the two of us at DotCom. Thankfully, we were actually working rather than shooting moonshine.

"Bad news, Georgie," he said, examining the bits and bobs on the desk that were supposed to make working radios.

"Ludo, I'm not sure I can take any more bad news," I replied, accidentally clipping a piece of wire too short. "What is it this time?"

"Your request to meet Sylvester has been denied."

I dropped my wire cutters. "Why?"

"He doesn't give a reason," Eirian explained. "He doesn't need to."

"I want a reason!" I said hotly.

Ludo rested a heavy hand on my shoulder, preventing me from rising out of my seat. "If he denied your meeting, chances are that he doesn't have anything to say on the subject. I'm sorry, Georgie."

"It's fine," I said, though clearly it was not fine. I picked up the wire cutters again and went to work on a new strand. "I have work to do, Ludo, if you don't mind."

THAT NIGHT, I lay on the floor of my office wrapped in the blankets from the cottage, staring up at the ceiling. The rest of the camp had gone to sleep hours ago, but I was wide awake. I heard every rustle of the breeze through the crunchy leaves outside, every scrape of trees' dead branches against the roof. An owl hooted into the lonely night, calling out with its melancholy voice. I rolled over, squeezing my eyes shut in an attempt to trick myself into slumber, but it was no use.

Who was this Sylvester anyway? The origin of Camp Haven felt little beyond magical realism. There had to be a different truth to the camp's birth, to the real identity of the man who supposedly founded it. Why was he such a recluse anyway? Why isolate himself from the people who claimed to have been saved by him? It was high time to find out. I kicked aside the blankets and slid my feet into my boots, then pulled on my coat and hat. If Sylvester refused to take a meeting with me, I would make one myself. Quietly, though DotCom was devoid of other campers at this hour, I snuck into the hallway and out of the building.

It was colder than the deck of the Titanic on that fateful night. A pristine inch of snow covered everything like a white cotton blanket. The crunch of my boot tread sounded impossibly loud as I crept into the dark. The lamps were extinguished, so as to not waste oil, and I traversed the camp by the light of the full moon. It sparkled off the snow, beautiful in all its silvery shades. I wished I could appreciate it more, but the shadow of the cabin looming on the hill drew my attention from everything else.

The outside of my childhood home had not changed, I realized as I started up the hill. The log structure had remained firm, though a few patches indicated spots where repairs had been made. The curtains in the window, red with white flowers, were the ones that my father had brought from the house that we had lived in before my mother died. I wondered if the inside had remained as unchanged, if Sylvester slept in my father's bed, if he cooked in my kitchen, if he sat on the armchair with the claw marks from our old cat. The closer I got, the faster my heart pounded. I peered into the front window, reaching for the door handle.

"Georgie."

I spun around, my hand to my chest to stop my heart from leaping out of its rightful place. Eirian stood below the hill, looking up at me, his pretty green eyes reflecting the moonlight.

"God, you scared me," I whispered.

"What are you doing up there?"

"I need to talk to Sylvester."

He waved me down with a gloved hand. "That won't work. Do you want to get kicked out of camp too?"

I hesitated, contemplating my options. I was a step away from meeting Sylvester in person. All I had to do was open the door and walk inside the cabin. It was my home in the first place. I had a right to return to it. However, Eirian had a point. This was no longer the place where I had grown up with my father. It belonged to other people with different rules, people who were not fond of those who refused to follow the rules. I drifted away from the front door of the cabin, staring wistfully at the threshold.

"That's it," Eirian encouraged. "Come here."

At the bottom of the hill, he collected me in a one-armed hug, leaving enough space between us to make clear a lack of romantic interest. It had been like this ever since Jacob had seen us hugging at the campfire. Though Eirian's unfailing positivity had not wavered and our camaraderie went on uninterrupted, he made a point to keep a fair amount of distance between us.

"Let's get you back to your room." He tugged me in the direction of the cottage where Jacob slept, but I planted my feet. "What's wrong?"

"I've been sleeping at the office," I admitted, dipping my head to avoid Eirian's eyes.

"Why?"

"You heard Jacob," I said. "He won't forgive me for the part I played in Jove's expulsion. He hates me."

Eirian instinctively squeezed me tighter. "I'm sure he doesn't hate you."

"Believe me, he does."

He sighed and switched direction, leading us toward DotCom instead. "I'm so sorry, Georgie. Maybe if you talk to him—Move!"

The command was issued in a hushed urgent whisper as Eirian practically lifted me from the ground, rushed us into the shadows of DotCom, and pressed me up against the wall. His body enveloped mine, and heat rushed through me from my head to my toes, but when a set of footsteps that did not belong to either one of us turned the corner, my skin went cold again. Eirian dipped his head and pressed his lips to the pulse pounding in my neck. My eyes fluttered shut, getting lost momentarily in his touch until I realized what he was doing. A lamp light flickered on.

"Having fun?" a low voice drawled.

Eirian sprang away, shielding his eyes against the light, and the cold rushed in to meet my body again. Ludo smirked from behind the lamp.

"Boss!" Eirian said with feigned surprise. "What are you doing out here?"

"Funny," Ludo replied. "I could ask the two of you the same thing."

"We were just—" I started.

"Taking a walk," Eirian finished.

Ludo raised an eyebrow. "I see that. Eirian, you should know better. Curfew is ten o'clock. I could give you both a demerit for this. We have these rules for your safety."

Eirian stepped in front of me. "Please, sir, don't blame Georgie. This was all my idea. It's just that—well, you know, it's been rough between her and Jacob—and we couldn't—we haven't—If you have to give out a demerit, it should be to me."

"Eirian, no," I whispered, trying to shove him aside so that I could speak to Ludo truthfully.

"Slow down, kid," Ludo said. "I get it. Things change. But you know how we do things around here. No drama. Solve your problems. Get back to your bunk, the ones that were *assigned* to you. And Georgie?"

"Yes, sir?"

"We'll talk about the cottage tomorrow," he said. "Other families need the space. You and Jacob will need to bunk somewhere else."

"Of course, sir."

"All right," Ludo said, fixing us with one more warning look like a principal scolding misbehaved students. "Get out of there."

"Thank you, sir," Eirian said, taking my hand and leading me around the other side of DotCom. Once we were out of Ludo's earshot, he abruptly let go. "I am so sorry. That was a complete invasion of your privacy, but Ludo is ridiculously strict about curfew. The only thing that softens him up is a good romantic subplot."

"It's fine," I said, trying not to shiver as I remembered the feeling of Eirian's firm body against mine. "But I can't go back to the cottage."

"I have a single," Eirian offered. "You can take the bed. I'll sleep on the floor."

"And what happens when the whole camp sees us come out of the same room in the morning?" I asked him.

"Right."

"I just want to go back to the office," I told him. "It's warm there, and I can work if I can't sleep."

"You've been working through the night?" he asked. "No wonder you've looked so tired these days. Come on. Let's get you back."

He peeked around the corner of the building to make sure that Ludo had gone on his way. Then we snuck into DotCom and returned to the communications office. Eirian looked at the pile of blankets on the floor.

"This isn't right," he said. "You should have a real bed."

"It's fine. Besides, I'm talking to Ludo about it tomorrow, remember?"

"You better," he replied. "Otherwise, we're switching rooms."

I shook off my coat and shoes. "Hit the lights on your way out, will you?"

The joke was a feeble one, but it still made him chuckle. "Good night, Georgie."

"Night, Eirian."

THE NEXT DAY was a rough one. I woke with a kink in my neck

due to the distinct lack of pillows in the communications office. I was late to breakfast, which meant that I had missed out on the eggs and bacon and got stuck with cold oatmeal. To make matters worse, Ludo cornered me in the Bistro with Jacob at his side. He pulled us both into his office at DotCom to talk to us about the sleeping situation.

"As I'm sure you're both aware, the camp's bed numbers are limited," Ludo began as Jacob and I stood awkwardly shoulder-to-shoulder in the cramped office. "The cottage you're currently staying at is needed for a couple with a newborn. As such, we plan to reassign both of you to different bunks. For now, you'll each have a bed in the dormitories, but you can apply for a private room together." His gaze drifted toward me, but I kept my eyes on the floor. "Would you like me to put your names on the waiting list?"

"That won't be necessary," Jacob said. "Georgie and I are no longer engaged."

A mixture of shock and relief flooded through me. He'd said it out loud. We were broken up. There was no "we" anymore. I was Georgie Fitz, and he was Jacob Mason, and we were entirely separate entities.

"I'm sorry to hear that," Ludo said. "Will there be any problems regarding this split or was it amicable?"

"I wouldn't say it was amicable," Jacob replied.

"But we won't cause any issues for you or the camp," I added quickly. "If you don't mind, I'm running behind on my work, Ludo. Can we move this along?"

"Sure thing," he said. "Georgie, you've been assigned bunk twenty-five in the women's dorms. Jacob, you have bunk nineteen in the men's. Please move your stuff from the cottage to your new lodgings by the end of the day."

We left Ludo's office, standing in the hallway of DotCom.

"What now?" I said.

"Nothing," he replied, buttoning up his coat in an indifferent manner. "I'll see you around, Georgie."

When he had gone, I stood for a moment longer in the hallway, wondering if I should feel something deeper than I actually did. The only thing that was lost to me was the idea of normalcy that I'd been nursing since I was nineteen, but the EMP blast had destroyed that long before Jacob and I arrived at Camp Haven. Things would be better this way. There was no more pretending, no more walking on eggshells to keep secrets that didn't seem to matter anyway.

I found Eirian in the Communications office, already tinkering with radio parts. He had folded my blankets into neat squares and stacked them out of the way.

"Good morning," he said, glancing up before returning to the gadget in his hand. "Is everything okay?"

"Let's just get to work."

The communications office was starting to feel like a joke. The radio tower stood in the middle of camp like a giant symbol of my failure to build a working radio. For some reason, I just couldn't figure out how to wire one with the components that were available to me, no matter how many hours I spent hunched over the desk. Eirian's patience was helpful and irritating at the same time. He continued to show up and listen to me babble about the history of radio while we worked. I was letting him down, along with the rest of the camp. I'd promised them camp-wide communications, the possibility of reaching out to other survivors, and a morning talk show. So far, I'd failed to deliver on all three.

That day, though, something was different. My mind felt clearer than it had since the EMP blast went off. The radios were a puzzle that I had always loved. I started fresh, fitting together the pieces one by one. At some point, Eirian stopped his own work to watch me. He didn't interrupt or ask questions. He simply studied my hands as they wrapped wire and connected pieces together until I had completed an entire unit. Then I hooked up the solar panel to the battery charger in a new pattern.

"Moment of truth," I said. "Let's go outside and see if it works."

We stood behind DotCom with the radio and panel in hand, waiting for the sun to hit the panel at the right angle. Eirian blew air into his hands to warm them up as I fiddled with the panel. The light on the battery charger turned on, flashing red to indicate that the batteries were almost dead.

"Panel's good," I said, trying to contain the excitement building in my chest. The working charger meant nothing if the radios themselves didn't work. I popped the battery out of the charger and into the radio, then turned the dial. The rugged piece of technology sprang to life, sputtering static from the salvaged speaker.

"Is that—?" Eirian began.

"It works!" I said.

I leapt into Eirian's arms, and we both laughed as he swung me around. The static of the radio buzzed in my ear like a happy bumblebee. When Eirian set me down again, grinning widely, I stretched up on the tips of my toes and kissed him. He kissed back, his lips warm against mine, before pulling away.

"I'm sorry," he said, breathless.

"What are you apologizing for?"

"You're engaged," he said. "We shouldn't be doing this. Last night—"

"We broke up," I told him. "Eirian, we've been broken up for a while. We just thought it would be easier to stick together for a while, but everyone knows now. Ludo assigned us to the dormitories. We're not together anymore."

"You're not?"

"No."

His smile returned, and he pressed his lips to mine eagerly, the radio trapped between our chests. "Whoops," he said, pulling away as it crackled. "We should be careful with that."

"Let's see if we can hook up a microphone and get it broad-casting," I said, trying to catch my breath. Between finally making a breakthrough and the energy between me and Eirian, I felt more motivated that I had in weeks.

17

---

*W*e were so excited to have discovered a working prototype for the radios that we stayed in the Communications office most of the day to build as many as we possibly could with the limited parts that we had. We left the building twice, once to get food from the Bistro and once to stand on opposite sides of Camp Haven to test out the range of our brand new walkie talkies. They stood up rather well to the camp's broad area. Finally, the radio tower that had been standing for weeks without purpose was actually good for something. We made plans to distribute radios and walkies to the heads of each department, then spoke about the possibility of salvaging more equipment from the city. We worked well into the night tinkering with our new toys until we both fell asleep on the floor of the office, curled up around each other like nestling birds. Unfortunately, the satisfaction of the day's triumphs and our dreamless sleep didn't last long.

I stirred beside Eirian. He slept peacefully, stretched out from one end of the office to the other, oblivious to whatever had woken me. I sat up, careful not to uncover him from the blankets, and listened. Silence. I rubbed my tired eyes. Whatever

254

I had heard in my slumber was probably just the wind outside. I lay beside Eirian again.

A door slammed. Eirian jolted upward, ready and alert, and noticed that I was already awake. He pressed a finger to his lips.

"Who could that be?" I whispered.

"It's probably Ludo," he whispered back. "He's the only one that trolls the camp at night. If he finds us out of the dorms again, he'll definitely give us demerits."

I captured his lips with mine. "Then be quiet."

We kissed silently for a minute, smiling against each other's mouths, but broke apart when a much closer door opened and shut. Footsteps scuttled down the hall, toward the communications office.

"That's more than one set of footsteps," I muttered, disentangling myself from the blankets and creeping over to the door.

"Georgie, get down," Eirian said as I inched toward the window.

I peeked into the hallway. It was pitch black. None of the hanging lamps were lit, nor did anyone carry a handheld oil lantern. And then the bright white beam of an LED flashlight, something that Camp Haven certainly did not keep on hand, illuminated the small window in the door of the communications office.

"Shit!" I ducked down as the beam haphazardly shone in and out of the room. "Eirian, those are not campers."

Keeping low, he crept across the floor and joined me at the door. When the beam passed again, he chanced a look outside.

"Damn it," he growled, his expression darkening.

"Who is it?"

"Camp Havoc."

"What?"

He lowered himself to the floor again, and we both pressed our backs to the door, as if barricading it might keep the intruders from searching the office.

"That's what we've been calling the other camp," Eirian said. "Shit, I knew this was going to happen!"

"Shh! They'll hear us."

"We should have taken more security precautions," he went on in a hushed voice. "I told Ludo! I told him that they would find us and try to get in. Damn!"

He slammed his fist against the floor. I pinned it down. "Eirian, stop. Calm down. Everything's going to be okay. We'll just hole up in here until they leave."

"They're here for our supplies," he said. "We have a limited amount of things to get us through the winter. If they take even a fraction of it, it will put the rest of us in danger. We can't let them steal from us."

He surged to his feet. When he stepped into his boots, I had no choice but to mimic his actions, but when he pulled a handgun out of the pocket of his jacket and loaded it, I stopped in my tracks.

"You have a gun?"

"It's officially issued," he said. "Don't tell anyone. I carry it for everyone's protection, not just mine. It's moments like this that justify it." He paused to consider the weapon in his grip. "Does it scare you?"

"No. Actually, I came into the camp with one before they confiscated it. I wish I had it back. My dad taught me how to shoot."

"Are you any good?"

"I don't like to brag."

Eirian grinned. "I knew I liked you from the second I met you."

Together, we looked through the window, Eirian's chin stacked on top of my head so that we both had a decent view. From what I could see, there were two intruders in DotCom. They wore all black, their faces covered with ski masks. They prowled the hallway, checking each door to see which ones were unlocked. Thankfully, Ludo was thorough when it came to the camp's internal security. The only supplies they found at their disposal were the extra cloth napkins and dishware from the Bistro.

"They're armed," Eirian muttered. "Or at least the point man is. Right coat pocket hanging low."

I squinted into the dark hallway, marveling at Eirian's keen eyesight. Sure enough, there was an outline of a pistol pressed against the coat of the figure closest to us in the hallway.

"What's the plan?" I asked as they moved closer to the communications office.

"You stay here—"

"Oh, please."

"It was worth a shot," Eirian said. "But I have a better idea."

He whispered his plan into my ear, all while the flashlights swept closer and closer to our hiding spot. I nodded to Eirian, mouthing a silent affirmation. Then Eirian pressed himself against the wall behind the door. The intruders were nearly level with the communications office. With a deep breath, I unlocked the door then joined Eirian against the wall.

A flashlight beam shone directly into the window, illuminating the radios, walkie talkies, and spare parts strewn across the desk. I held my breath and grasped Eirian's hand. He squeezed tightly.

"Hey, boss," a deep voice mumbled outside the door. "I think we got something in here."

A second flashlight joined the first, dangerously close to sweeping across the shadows where me and Eirian hid.

"Looks like solar-powered radios or something," a second voice said. "We could use those, especially when we run out of battery power."

"Try the door."

The handle jiggled and turned, setting my heart racing.

"Get ready," Eirian whispered.

"It's open," the first voice said.

"Let's check it out."

The intruders entered slowly, so focused on the radios that they failed to notice us standing stock still behind the door. Each of them carried a duffel bag, presumably full of whatever supplies they had stolen from Camp Haven. They moved farther into the room, their backs to us as they examined the parts on the desk.

"Jackpot," the second man muttered, rifling through my things.

"Hey, boss," said the first man, nudging the blankets on the floor with his boot. "I don't think we're alone."

"Now!" Eirian said.

We leapt into action, attacking the two men from behind. I aimed a swift kick at the back of the first man's knee, which buckled quickly. He dropped his flashlight as he sank to his knees with a yelp, and I moved into position quickly, locking his head at an uncomfortable angle in the crook of my arm. Eirian disabled the other man just as effectively. He reached into the man's pocket, drew out the pistol, unloaded it, and threw it across the small room. Then he put his own gun to the man's head.

"Don't shoot! Don't shoot!" he pleaded, his hands raised in the air.

"How the hell did you get in here?" Eirian snarled, twisting the man's arm behind his back. "We have security posted at every entrance."

"Your security team isn't very bright," the man said. "We set a fire a mile or so away from your front gate, and all but one of them set off to check it out. We snuck past the last guy."

"You couldn't have opened the gate on your own," Eirian replied.

"We didn't. We went over it."

"How many of there are you?"

"Just the two of us, I swear!"

"Don't move." With the gun still aimed at the second man's head, Eirian rifled through the duffel bags that the intruders had brought with them. He found a length of rope in each and tossed it to the men. "Tie yourselves to those chairs."

"Look, we aren't trying to cause trouble—" the leader started.

"Shut up!" Eirian ordered, brandishing the gun. "Tie yourselves up!"

"Okay, okay!"

The leader slowly reached for the rope, sat in the chair, and began looping the rope around his ankles. I slammed the other man into the opposite chair, twisted his hands behind his back, and started binding him up as well.

"Check the first one," Eirian told me. "We can't let them go."

As expected, the leader had left the ropes loose around his wrists so that he could escape as soon as we left the room. I fastened them securely with a tricky knot that I'd learned from my father years ago. Then I picked up the pistol that the leader had brought with him and reloaded it.

"What now?" I asked Eirian.

"I don't believe for a second that the two of them are alone," he replied. "We've been watching Camp Havoc for weeks. They've been planning this raid for a while. There have to be more of them."

"Look, man," the leader said. "I don't know what you're talking about. There's no one else here. Just let us go. We'll give you your stuff back. No harm, no foul."

"Nice try," I said, kicking the leader's shins.

"Let's find Ludo," Eirian suggested. "He can alert the rest of the security team. They'll sweep the camp for anyone else that doesn't belong here."

"And these two?" I asked.

Eirian dangled his key to the communications office. "We'll

lock them in. Then the tribunal and Sylvester can decide what to do with them."

We took their flashlights, then left the intruders in the office, locked up, and crept down the hallway toward the main room of DotCom. The building was empty.

"Still think they were lying?" I muttered to Eirian, shining the blinding white light around the eerie community room. I had become so accustomed to the soft yellow lights of the camp's lanterns that the flashlight's beams made my eyes water.

"Yes," he replied. "Keep your eyes peeled for movement. Let's get to Ludo's."

Ludo and Jax shared a room in another resident building near the dormitories. We turned off the flashlights as we crossed the camp, lest we draw unwanted attention, and knocked softly on the door to Ludo's room. He answered with bleary eyes and rumpled hair.

"Didn't I warn the two of you not to get caught outside your bunks after curfew again?" he growled.

"There's been a security breach, sir," Eirian reported in a low whisper.

"Yeah, you two," Ludo shot back. "I'm off duty. Talk to Peters. If Jax wakes up—"

"Camp Havoc is already inside, sir," Eirian pressed. "They tricked the security team out front, including Peters. We caught two of their men in DotCom, scouring for supplies."

Ludo slammed the door shut in Eirian's face. We looked at each other in consternation, but the door opened again to reveal Ludo in boots and a fleece jacket to cover his thermal pajamas. He carried a shotgun in hand.

"Let's go," he ordered, joining us in the hallway. "Where are the intruders now?"

"We locked them in the communications office," I told him as the three of us headed back outside. "They said they were the only ones here."

"What a crock of shit," Ludo said, visually combing the camp.

"That's what I said," Eirian agreed.

"Let's get to the front gate." Ludo broke into a light jog. "We need to find Peters and assemble the rest of the security team to sweep the camp. When do you plan on distributing those radios, Georgie? They would have come in handy tonight."

"We just got them working yesterday, sir," I told him. "We planned on distributing them to security and the department heads this morning."

Ludo shook his head. "Figures."

I pulled ahead of Ludo and Eirian, lighter and faster on my feet, but as we passed through the main square of the camp, Ludo yanked on the hood of my jacket and tugged me to a stop.

"Wait!" he hissed, breathing hard. He jerked the muzzle of the shotgun toward the med bay. "You two see what I see?"

I watched the building closely. There, in the windows of the left side of the building where the medical supplies were kept in the offices, were a series of silhouettes.

"They're robbing first aid," Eirian muttered.

"Pippa's still in there," I breathed. "And so is Penny. If they hurt them—"

"Let's move," Ludo said.

"Shouldn't we get the rest of the security team?" I asked him. "We don't know how many there are."

"There's no time," Eirian said as we fell into a triangle formation behind Ludo. "The camp has lockdown procedures, but we can't start them without alerting the intruders to our presence. They'd be out of here with our stash before we even had a chance of assembling a team."

"Here's the plan," Ludo said. "Eirian, you take the back door. Georgie, you're with me in the front. We'll corner them in Jax's office. Don't let any of them leave, understand?"

We nodded. As we approached the building, Eirian turned to split off from me and Ludo. I grabbed his hand before he could roam too far. Our eyes met. A few weeks, a month maybe, I'd known him, and yet the thought of losing him was far too painful to consider.

"I'll be careful," he promised, giving me a quick kiss.

We parted, and he disappeared into the night. I fell into step behind Ludo, and we entered the med bay through the main doors. Immediately, the sounds of the intruders rummaging through the supplies in the back room reached my ears. Pippa was wide awake, her back turned to the offices, the blankets pulled up over her head as if she were pretending to be asleep. The whites of her eyes gleamed in the darkness. When she saw me, she mouthed my name, but I pressed a finger to my lips to keep her quiet. We inched by. A few beds down, Pippa and Jacob's mother lay still and oblivious, asleep or unconscious.

In the hallway to the offices, LED lights flashed against the walls. There were way more than two intruders in the med bay. Camp Havoc was obviously more interested in our medical supplies than the random assortment of things we kept in DotCom.

"Five or six of them, I'd guess," Ludo whispered to me, his shotgun wedged against his shoulder, aimed outward, as we crept closer. "We're outnumbered. Try to keep them in the office. Eirian will catch any that get out the back."

I raised my borrowed weapon. "Yes, sir."

The plan was shot to hell before we could begin to enact it. Without warning, one of the intruders stepped out of the office and into the hallway, shining his light directly into our faces. As my eyes watered, Ludo backed up, stepping on the toe of my boot and causing us both to trip. I lost my grip on the pistol, and it clattered across the floor out of my reach, rupturing the thick silence inside the med bay.

"We got company!" the intruder roared, and he lifted a rifle.

Ludo and I dove in opposite directions. He took cover in one of the exam rooms while I hid behind a wall as bullets ripped by and ricocheted off of the metal bed frames in the bay. Pippa shrieked and rolled out of bed. With adrenaline-infused strength, she flipped the metal cot on its side and used it as cover from the rain of gunfire. Penny, on the other hand, was completely exposed, unable to move herself to safety. We had to force the intruders back somehow.

When the intruder stopped firing to reload, Ludo and I both took advantage. I slid across the floor and grabbed the pistol. Ludo leaned out of the doorway and fired the shotgun. The blast sent the intruder flying backward through the rear exit door of the med bay. Eirian stared at the bloody body then leapt over it to make his way inside. At the same time, Ludo and I converged on the intruders who remained in the office, but we weren't fast enough. Five more men emerged from the office, each carrying a bag full of medical supplies. Two of them were armed with guns while the others carried hunting knives. They opened fire, once again sending Ludo and I running for cover, and sprinted out through the back exit. One of them fired a handgun at Eirian's leg, who immediately dropped to the ground and covered his head with his hands. Then the five intruders sprinted out into the night, leaving the body of their comrade for us to deal with.

"Eirian!" I said, dropping beside him. Blood darkened the leg of his jeans.

"Go after them!" He shoved me away, encouraging me to follow Ludo as he charged behind the intruders. "Georgie, go!"

I surged to my feet, grabbed the rifle off of the intruder's dead body, and ran after Ludo. Lamps and lanterns flickered on as I sprinted through camp. The gunfire had woken many of the residents, and they emerged from the dormitories to see what was happening. Some of the off-duty guys who ran security joined the race once they saw Ludo running by with his gun.

"What's happening?" one of them, Kirsch, shouted as he fell in step beside me.

"Camp Havoc!" I answered. "They stole our medical supplies!"

Gunfire echoed ahead, near the perimeter of the camp. I slowed down as we drew closer. Other men in black had joined the group from the med bay until there were roughly twenty intruders charging toward the wall that was supposed to keep Camp Haven safe from this exact scenario. Ludo had taken cover behind a nearby building. He fired shot after shot, but it was no use against so many trespassers. But why weren't the intruders running toward the front gate?

"Stop!" I yelled, digging my heels in the dirt and flinging my arms out to either side to prevent Camp Haven's off-duty security team from getting any closer to the trespassers. "Don't go any closer!"

As the command left my mouth, a section of the camp wall exploded. The intruders waited just long enough for some of the debris to clear, then escaped through the massive hole. Within seconds, all twenty of them were gone, invisible beneath the shadows of the trees, leaving the rest of us to stare open-mouthed at the wreckage.

"THEY COMPLETELY CLEANED us out of antibiotics," Nita reported. She and I had been assigned to assess the damage the intruders had done in the med bay. I tried not to look at the streaks of blood in the hallway. The body had been disposed of, but the remnants of the event remained. "No bandages or wraps. Nothing topical. They took everything. Jesus, there's nothing left!"

"Try to calm down," I said, despite my own panicked pulse. "Some of the campers were wounded in the blast, and we have to find a way to treat them. Let's think outside the box. What else can we use to wrap injuries?"

Camp Haven had never faced this kind of disaster before.

According to Ludo, the worst challenge they had ever encountered was a particularly nasty winter a few years ago. They had run out of food, and the campers were close to starving. Then, Ludo had been able to send a team into the city to shop for groceries as a last resort. We weren't so lucky now.

"I don't know," Nita said, slamming a cabinet door shut with unnecessary force. She kicked over a trash can. "I don't know!"

"What about the extra cloth napkins that we keep in DotCom?" I asked her. "They're clean. They should work, right?"

She combed her fingers through her hair. "Yeah. Yes, that should work. I'll go get them. Tell Jax I'll be right back."

When she left, I headed back into the bay. There were bullet holes in the concrete block walls. I kicked aside some of the shell casings that littered the floor. A few more beds in the bay were occupied now. Eirian lay in one, Ludo in another. Three of the security guys had caught some shrapnel in the blast, but thankfully we were far enough away from the explosion that their wounds were superficial. Ludo wasn't so lucky. A bullet had gone right through his shoulder. Nevertheless, he was still giving orders.

"I want a twenty-four watch on that hole in the wall," he was yelling to Peters as Jax did her best to stem the flow of blood from his arm with a sheet from one of the empty beds. "Get the miscellaneous crew out there too. We need to rebuild as quickly as possible or we risk them coming back for more." He spotted me walking toward him. "Georgie! Tell me something good."

"Sorry, Ludo," I said. "It's bad news. Camp Havoc completely screwed us over. No meds. The Bistro got hit too. They cleaned out the dried meats."

Ludo swore, and a fresh wave of blood gushed from the hole in his arm.

"Lie still," Jax snapped at her husband, forcing him against the pillow. "Unless you want to die of blood loss." She tied a makeshift tourniquet around Ludo's arm as she addressed me.

"Would you check on the others? This one came out of it with the worst, and he won't be happy when I pluck this bullet out of his arm without any painkillers."

I wandered away from Ludo's bed to do as asked, stopping by Eirian's cot next. He was propped up against the pillows, his leg elevated on a cardboard box. The thigh had been crudely covered with a cotton pad that the camp usually kept on hand for menstruating women. He frowned as he surveyed the ruined bay.

"How are you holding up?" I asked him, lifting the napkin to check the wound. Thankfully, the bullet had grazed the skin rather than going through his leg. It would scab over in a few days, and Eirian would be no worse for wear. Even so, he needed better bandaging if he was going to avoid infection.

"I hate this," he said, teeth clenched. "I want to help, but Jax won't let me get up. There's still blood in the damn hallway! It needs to be sanitized. What did they do with the body? What about the two intruders that we locked in the communications office? Who's out there watching the wall—?"

"Eirian, relax," I said, resting my palm against his chest. "We're taking care of it. The security team moved the trespassers to a different room in DotCom until we figure out what to do with them, and Ludo's assigning the miscellaneous crew to watch and rebuild the wall."

"I can help—"

"Not right now," I told him. "You need to stay here until we can flush that wound out and bandage it properly."

He let out a sigh and rubbed his eyes. "They took everything, didn't they?"

"Yeah. The medical stuff at least. And some food."

"This is bad," he muttered. "This is really bad. I don't know how we're supposed to make it through the rest of the season."

I smoothed his sweaty curls away from his forehead. "I'm

sure the department heads are coming up with a solid plan as we speak."

"Hey!"

I jerked my hand away from Eirian as Jacob's voice echoed through the med bay. He marched through the door, bee lining for us, but his step faltered when he noticed the bloodied security boys.

"You should be at the wall," Ludo barked at him from his bed. "Miscellaneous crew members—"

"My sister and my mother are here," Jacob said. "And no one bothered to tell me that the freaking med bay got shot up. What the hell, Georgie? I heard you were here when it happened. You couldn't take five seconds to come get me?"

"I've been a little busy," I snapped.

"Yeah, playing house with your boyfriend," he replied, sneering at Eirian. "Meanwhile, my family—"

"Your family is safe," Eirian told him. "The first thing Georgie did was make sure that your mother and sister were okay."

"They're asleep now," I said, pointing to where we had moved Pippa and Penny out of the way of those who needed immediate treatment. "You can wake them if you want, but I wouldn't suggest it. Pippa was pretty stressed out. She needs the rest, especially now that her baby's overdue."

Jacob's temper flared out as he watched his little sister's baby bump rise and fall with the sound of her breath. "What about Mom?"

"No change," I told him. "She's been in and out of consciousness."

"That's bad, isn't it?"

"It's not good."

As he studied his family, I noticed how much of him had changed in the weeks that we'd spent at Camp Haven. The designer clothes were gone, replaced with practical flannel and fleece layers. He'd grown out his beard rather than learn how to shave with a straight razor. He was skinnier now, having lost some of the muscle tone that came from lifting heavy at the gym. Now his physical was honed to complete whatever jobs that Ludo needed done. He looked like a completely different man than the one I had met in college all those years ago.

"I should go," he said. "You heard Ludo. I should be at the wall." He backed away from Pippa's bed and bumped into another cot behind him. "Can you let me know if anything changes, Georgie?"

"Of course."

"Thanks."

As Jacob left, Eirian patted my hand. "You really care about him, don't you?"

"We were together for five years," I said. "He took care of me, and vice versa. You don't just forget about that."

"I understand."

"Besides, his mom and his sister were always good to me," I added. "They deserve my care and attention."

"Fitz!" Jax said from Ludo's bed. "I thought I asked you to check on *all* of the patients."

"Yes, ma'am," I said, drawing away from Eirian. "Right away."

I moved to the other beds, picking shrapnel and debris out of skin with a pair of tweezers sanitized with moonshine. When Nita returned with the napkins from Dotcom, we worked together to rinse and bandage wounds. After we had finished, Nita turned to me.

"Did you know that there's a massive gash above your eye?" she asked.

I reached up and prodded my forehead. Sure enough, the skin was tender, covered in a layer of crunchy dried blood. "I didn't even notice."

"I figured as much." Nita took my hand and made me sit down on an empty cot. "Let me clean it out for you."

She went to work, scrubbing off the blood that had dried to

my forehead and cheek. I couldn't remember what had happened to cause the wound, but I imagined that it had happened during the blast. Nita flushed it out with water so cold that it made me shiver.

"Sorry," she said, catching the rivulets that ran down my neck with a towel.

"It's fine."

She examined the divot in my skin. "Looks like you caught a rock or some debris to the face. It's not too deep. Shouldn't leave a scar or anything."

"I'm not really worried about a tiny scar on my face." I looked up at her. Her mouth was set in a worried frown. "What's wrong?"

"I'm sorry," she said.

"You already said that."

"No, not for the water," she replied. "I've been avoiding you lately because of what happened to Jove, and for the way I thought you were treating Jacob. I picked sides, and I shouldn't have."

Suddenly, exhaustion swamped me, as if the adrenaline from the night's events had finally worn off. "It's okay, Nita."

"No, it's not." She mixed up an herbal paste and applied it to the cut. "I should have known that there were two sides to the story. This whole invasion has made me realize what an idiot I've been. We need to support each other. We're all each other has."

"I'm glad you feel that way."

We smiled at each other in a rare moment of peace as she rinsed her hands of the herbal mixture.

Kirsch, who lay in the next bed over, leaned toward us. "Excuse me, ladies? That woman in the corner looks far too pale for comfort."

We looked to where he was pointing. Penny's hand had slipped over the edge of her mattress, limp and lifeless. Her face was completely white with a purplish tint. I leapt off the bed, knocking the herbal paste to the floor, where the ceramic bowl shattered, and ran to Penny's side. I pressed my fingers against her neck.

"She doesn't have a pulse!"

I flattened Penny out against the mattress, pressed my hands against her chest, and began pumping her heart, but Nita and Jax soon pushed me out of the way to tend to her themselves. I looked on, pacing back and forth in front of Penny's bed. Pippa slept through the resuscitation attempt.

"She can't die," I said. "Please, she can't die. Jacob and Pippa will be devastated."

"It's no good," Nita said.

"Move!" Jax ordered.

Nita cleared the way. Jax lifted her fist into the air and slammed it down on Penny's chest, directly over her heart. Then she checked her pulse again.

"We got her back," she said. "It's weak, but she's here."

Relief surged through me. "That actually *worked*?"

"Don't get too excited," Jax said, rearranging Penny's limbs in a more comfortable position. She unwrapped the bandage around Penny's leg.

"Oh God." I covered up my nose with the hem of my shirt. "What the hell is that awful stench?"

"It's her leg," Jax replied, peeling the bandage back to show me the damage. The skin was a disgusting blend of sickly green and purple, and the wound leaked yellow pus. "We never got rid of the infection. It's killing her."

18

*P*enny was running out of time. She had been ever since that glass shard had pierced her leg on our way to Camp Haven. We were too blind to pay attention to her injuries. I had been so desperate to cater to Ludo, Jax, and the other department heads that I neglected to check in on Penny as much as I should have, but when I expressed this thought to Eirian, he didn't agree.

"You can't place the blame for this on yourself," he said. Jax discharged him from the med bay as soon as Nita had managed to wrap his leg securely. "There were a lot of people involved in this. Jax was the one that decided our antibiotics wouldn't be able to keep the infection at bay. To use them would have been a waste of our resources."

"Don't tell that to Jacob," I said, helping Eirian test his weight on his leg so that we could leave the med bay. Nita had sent someone to bring Jacob to his mother, and I didn't want to be here when he returned. "He won't understand why we didn't exhaust every possibility to save her."

"Sometimes, you have to make sacrifices for the good of the

many." Eirian's leg held firm. There was no damage to the muscle. "That's how it works here."

"You forget that not everyone was raised like this," I reminded him. "That idea is relatively foreign to somehow who grew up having everything."

"I guess he's going to learn the hard way then."

"I guess. We should go."

As we were leaving, I spotted Jacob hurrying toward the med bay. I ducked behind a row of bushes, tugging Eirian down too. We watched as Jacob, already covered in dirt and sweat from working at the wall, rushed into the building.

Eirian poked the worry lines around my mouth. "You're going to have to face him eventually."

"His mother is dying," I said, pulling Eirian out of the bushes. "He needs some time to himself."

An anguished yell echoed from the med bay. Jacob. My throat closed up at the thought of him in there with Pippa, both of them crying over their mother, unable to help her.

"Go," Eirian said, nudging me toward the front door. "You should be with them."

"I should get you to your room first."

He waved off my offer. "My leg is fine, see?" He bounced up and down a couple of times. "Besides, I'm not going to my room. I'm going to see what I can do to help the camp regroup."

"You should rest," I scolded him, cringing as another cry went up from the med bay. "You're no use to us if you get sick too."

"I'll take it easy," he promised. "Go inside. I'll check on you in an hour or so."

He waved and, limping slightly, headed for the breach in the wall. The thought of returning to the med bay haunted me. I could just as easily leave Jacob and Pippa to their mourning and return to the communications office. The radios and walkie talkies were waiting to be assigned to department heads for a trial run. I could bury myself in work and avoid facing the people that, not long ago, were meant to become my family.

I went to the communications office and sat in relative silence, staring at the units that Eirian and I had assembled together. After several minutes of contemplation, I pulled one of the radios toward me, turned it on, and started broadcasting as far as the signal would reach.

"This is Georgie Fitz," I began. I had no idea who might be listening, but I hoped that someone else in the area would have the information that I wanted. "I'm currently located in the Rocky Mountains, northwest of Denver, Colorado. We have an emergency situation that requires a high dosage of antibiotics. I repeat, we have an emergency situation that requires a high dosage of antibiotics. If anyone's listening, we need help."

I waited for a reply, any reply, but none came. I fiddled with the dials on the radio and tried again. For over an hour, I repeated the same message until my throat was dry. I slouched over the desk and rested my head between the walkie talkies. The crude devices mocked me from either side, reveling in my failure.

And then my radio crackled to life.

"Miss Fitz?"

I snatched the radio up. "Hello? Yes, this is Georgie Fitz."

"If you're looking for antibiotics, there's a hospital at the edge of the city that wasn't hit as hard as the rest," the voice, female and tired, said. "We stocked up there just last week. Be careful though. It's dangerous out there. Lots of gang members and addicts in the area."

"Thank you so much," I said

"No problem. Over and out."

The static returned as the anonymous caller disappeared. I took a few seconds to collect myself, reining in a sob of relief, then left the office to return to the med bay. I found Jacob and Pippa asleep there. Jacob had dragged Pippa's bed next to their mother's so that it formed one big queen bed instead. Jacob sat on the floor next to his mother, her limp hand clutched in his. His cheek pressed against the quilt, and his mouth was slightly open. I gently shook his shoulder.

"Jacob, wake up."

He came to, blinking languidly. He lifted his head from the quilt, wiped a droplet of drool from his chin, and looked around. His lips quivered when his gaze landed on his unconscious mother and sleeping sister.

"I almost forgot," he said. "For a second, I thought we were back home in the apartment, and everything was okay." He squeezed his mother's hand. "But it's not, is it?"

"Jacob, there's a hospital at the edge of the city that might still have enough medication to save Penny," I told him. "We can send a salvage team in to get it."

Jax, who was sitting with Ludo a few beds over, perked up. "Excuse me? What did you just say?"

"We could get antibiotics from the city," I repeated, announcing it to the rest of the patients and workers in the med bay. "That way, we can treat everyone and save Penny."

The bay broke out in excited murmurs, but Jax planted her hands on her hips. "Who exactly do you think you are, Miss Fitz?"

"Sorry?"

"You are not a department head," Jax continued as the room fell silent to allow her to speak.

Ludo took his wife's hand. "Honey—"

"You have no power to authorize a salvage trip into dangerous territory," Jax said. "Therefore, you have no right to instill false hope in our patients."

I stood from Jacob's side. "Are you kidding me? Penny is dying! She needs treatment. Why wouldn't we take this opportunity?"

"How do you figure that any hospital within walking distance is still stocked with medication?" she challenged.

"I called on the radio," I said. "Someone answered. They told me—"

"Whoever it was isn't a reliable source," Jax said. "Besides, most liquid antibiotics have to be refrigerated."

"It's the only chance we have," I argued.

"It's not worth putting our salvage team at risk," she fired back.

"Fine, then I'll go!"

Stunned, Jax finally backed off. "You want to trek into the city by yourself to look for medication that might not even be there for a woman that will most likely be dead by the time you return?"

"Yes."

Jacob got to his feet. "She won't be by herself. I'll go with her."

"Jacob, no," I said.

"Yes," he replied firmly. "I won't let you go into the city alone. You need at least one other person to back you. Besides, it's my mother we're talking about here."

"You should stay here, Jacob," another voice said. It was Eirian, who had appeared in the med bay from the hallway that led to the offices. He'd been listening in to the entire conversation without me realizing it. "You should be with your family in case something happens. I'll go with Georgie."

The fact that I didn't immediately feel the need to tell Eirian that he should stay in Camp Haven made me realize that I didn't *want* to go into the city alone. I wanted someone to come with me, someone who knew the mountains, could hold his own during the trip, and could keep a level head if things took a turn for the worst. Eirian was the best fit for the job, but it still wasn't his responsibility to take care of the Masons.

"Eirian—"

"Don't argue with me, Georgie," he said. "If Jax doesn't want to send a salvage team, and you're determined to go, then I'm going with you. My leg is fine, and you know that I'm the best person to have with you. No offense, Jacob."

"None taken," Jacob said. "Georgie, listen to him. I think he's right. I've seen the two of you work together. If anyone can get to the hospital and back in one piece, it's you and him."

Jax cleared her throat and crossed her arms. "You still need approval from a department head to leave the camp, which you'll find difficult to acquire considering this harebrained scheme."

"I approve," Ludo chimed in. His wife leveled him with a withering stare, but he held firm. "Face facts, Jax. We're heading into winter with no medication and no first aid kits. If it stays like that, I can guarantee that more people will die. We have two options. First, send a team to Camp Havoc to regain what was taken from us, which would result in casualties on both sides. Second, send Georgie and Eirian into the city to salvage what they can. That's the safer route."

"And what if there's nothing to salvage?" Jax challenged.

Ludo looked at me and Eirian. "Then we go to plan B."

THERE WAS no time to waste. Penny was deteriorating by the minute. Eirian and I prepared for our trip in little under an hour. We packed hiking bags, layered up in clothes and boots that would protect us from whatever harsh weather we might encounter, and gathered supplies that would help us survive in the woods. Then Ludo's second in command assigned us each a rifle to take with us in case things got nasty. I hoped I would never have to use it.

Jacob took a break from watching over his mother to see me and Eirian off into the woods. As the security team went to work opening the gates, he adjusted the straps on my backpack so that it rested more securely on my shoulders. Eirian pretended to help open the gate so that we could have a moment alone.

"You don't have to do this," Jacob said. "It's my mother. I should be the one to put myself in danger to save her. You don't owe us anything."

"Jacob, if the situation were reversed, would you sit around and do nothing when you had the opportunity to help?"

"No, of course not."

"Then it's settled," I said. "Stay with Penny and Pippa. They need you now more than ever. I'll be back as soon as possible."

I kissed Jacob's cheek and joined Eirian at the gate. The locking mechanism squeaked as the men pulled the massive door open. Outside Camp Haven, the mountain woods stretched on and on unbroken. I took a deep breath and squeezed Eirian's hand. Together, we stepped beyond the wall.

"That wasn't so bad," I said, advancing into the woods.

The gate behind us slammed shut. We were officially locked out until we returned from the city. Doubt in my own survival abilities rose in the back of my throat like stomach bile. I swallowed it down. Eirian looked equally spooked.

"Are you okay?" I asked him.

"For now," he replied. We walked down the mountain, following the guidance of a handheld compass. "I've been outside Camp Haven a number of times since we arrived here. Sometimes, the miscellaneous crew gets assigned to salvage. This is different though. It's one thing to comb through a couple of warehouses that fell out of use. It's a whole different story walking into a city of dead people. The last time—"

Eirian had been out to Denver with the salvage team shortly after the EMP blast, when they combed the calmer parts of the city for materials to build the radio tower. That alone had scared him, but it would be even worse now that weeks had passed. I wondered how many people had actually survived in the city.

"We'll be okay," I assured him. "Let's just get in and out as quickly as possible."

It would take us roughly a day and a half to reach the city on foot. We jogged lightly most of the way, trying to shave a few minutes off the total time, but when twilight fell, we had not even reached the bottom of the mountain. We stopped to camp for the night, eating a dinner of beef jerky and lighting a fire to keep warm. The city was visible from our campsite, but instead of the usual bright lights and bustling automobiles, the buildings were all dark and brooding.

"Tell me something," Eirian said as he stretched out in his sleeping bag and chomped on another strip of jerky. "Why go this far to help Jacob's mom? It's one thing to comfort Jacob and Pippa like I suggested, but you didn't have to risk your life for hers. You and Jacob aren't engaged anymore, so technically you don't even have ties to Penny."

"That may be true," I agreed, "but if I let Penny die without trying to do anything about it, that means losing a part of my humanity that I'm not ready to let go of yet. This whole EMP blast has been terrible, but if we forget who we are, it could be a lot worse. We got lucky at Camp Haven. It's a group of people who already understood how to work together to survive before it became a necessity instead of an option. Sure, I could just say fuck it and leave Jacob to deal with his mother's death on his own, but what kind of person would I be if I did?"

"You're very moral."

"It's common decency," I said. "Besides, the camp needs these supplies anyway."

"Jax would've eventually realized that when people started getting sick," Eirian said, finishing off his jerky and rolling onto his back to gaze up at the stars through the trees. "She would have sent a salvage team them."

"How long would that have taken though?" I asked. "It could have been weeks or months, by which time the hospital might very well have been ransacked. As it is, we don't actually know if it has the supplies we need now."

"We'll find them," Eirian promised, his eyelids drifting shut. "Get some sleep. We'll need our strength for tomorrow."

AT DAWN, we were woken by a terrible inhuman scream. The birds that had yet to migrate south took flight from the trees, scared out of the branches. The sun was blood red on the horizon, like an omen of impending doom. The screams continued, one after the next in terrifying succession. Eirian and I tore through the forest, trying our best to follow the yells as they bounced off the trees from every direction. I slipped down a patch of icy dirt and fell, bruising my tailbone, but the pain was nothing in comparison to whatever excruciating torture elicited the screams of terror. Eirian helped me to my feet, and we skidded to a stop at the edge of a small clearing to find a bloody scene. A gray wolf had its muzzle buried deep in the abdomen of a large man.

"Oh my god," I said. "It's Jove."

Eirian fired his rifle into the air above the wolf's head. The animal, unconcerned, withdrew from Jove's mauled stomach, its gray fur stained red, and stalked toward us. Eirian fired again, this time clipping the wolf's pelt. It yelped and bolted away, and I rushed to Jove's side. He'd stopped screaming at long last. Shock had set in.

"Jove," I said, lightly smacking the man's cheek. "Hey, look at me. It's Georgie."

Eirian knelt beside me, examining Jove's injuries. The wolf had done too much damage. Jove's intestines were spilling out of his torso. Blood seeped into the damp cold ground at an alarming rate.

"He's as good as dead," Eirian muttered close to my ear so that Jove wouldn't hear. I had a feeling it wouldn't matter anyway. Jove was hardly present with us. His eyes darted back and forth, never focusing on anything.

"I'm surprised he made it this long," I said.

"Georgie!" Jove gasped suddenly. He seized the front of my coat and pulled me closer. Warm blood dripped onto my hands. "Georgie."

"Yes, Mr. Mason. It's me."

"Jacob." Blood bubbled at the corners of his mouth. "Pippa."

"They're okay," I replied, wanting more than anything for him to let go of me. "They're safe at Camp Haven."

"Penny?"

I hesitated, looking across at Eirian. He shook his head. "She's fine too, Jove. Your family is safe. It's okay."

His grip on my coat loosened until his hands fell limply to his sides. "Thank you."

Then his mouth went slack, and his head lolled back on his neck. He was dead. I scrambled away from the fresh corpse, scrubbing the blood off my hands with the hem of my shirt. It was everywhere, on the ground, on my shirt, on my hands.

"Hey," Eirian said, as I rubbed my hands until the skin was red and raw. "Georgie, stop."

"He's dead," I muttered, unable to tear my gaze from Jove's ruined body. "He's dead. Oh God, he's dead."

"Hey!" Eirian snapped his fingers in front of my nose, redirecting my attention to him. "Look at me. Listen to me. We can't let this slow us down. I know that sounds crass, but it's the truth. Jacob's dad is dead. We need to make sure that his mother doesn't meet the same fate. At least not anytime soon."

His level-headed speech permeated my panic, filling my brain with practical plans instead. I closed my eyes, trying to expel the image of Jove's ruined body from my memory. "You're right. Let's go. We need to go."

Eirian turned me around by the shoulders before I opened my eyes again, and we left the bloody clearing behind us to return to our camp. It occurred to me that we should have given Jove some sort of send-off. We should have said something nice or crossed his arms over his chest or laid flowers for him. But all the flowers were dead, and I couldn't form words to say much at all.

We picked up our belongings at camp, scattered the ashes of the campfire, and proceeded along our route in silence. The trees began to clear as we neared the bottom of the mountain, where the roads were asphalt instead of dirt. It was quieter closer to the city. No birds chirped. No wind blew. No dogs barked. The absence of sound played with my voice of reason.

"There's the hospital," Eirian said, pointing. The building rose from the wreckage of the city, a few miles away from our lookout spot. A section of it had been burned down, but the rest remained standing.

"Let's go."

We held our rifles at the ready as we emerged from the woods and onto the roads of the city. Denver was deserted, or so it seemed. It was a dead city, full of dead bodies and dead hopes. The stench of rotting corpses had yet to clear. I doubted it would take several months or years before I forgot that smell completely. It was the scent of despair and grief. It was the end of the modern world as we knew it.

A loud crash startled us both as we crept through an alleyway near the hospital, looking for the safest way in. We both swung around, aiming the nose of our rifles toward the noise, but it was only a tin trash can that had fallen over. It rolled across the alley, spewing putrid garbage across the street. I lifted my sweater to cover my nose and looked up to the burned side of the hospital, which was the obvious way in.

"Too dangerous," Eirian muttered, reading my thoughts. This section of the building was a maze of demolished hallways. "The floor's probably unstable. Let's keep looking."

We circled around, keeping our eyes peeled for an alternate

entrance as well as for anyone else in the vicinity. We made our way to the back side of the hospital, where the road opened up to let the ambulances drive in and out as quickly as possible. Giant sliding doors led from the dock to the emergency room, but they were automated. No good without electricity.

"Maybe we can push them open," Eirian suggested. We each took hold of a door and tried to force them apart to no avail. Eirian wiped his forehead. "Damn it."

"Got a window over here," I said, wandering farther away from the ER bay. I peered inside. "Looks like some kind of office. The door's open to the hallway. Looks like this is our way in."

I slammed the butt of the rifle against the window. The glass cracked. I hit it again, and the window shattered. Eirian used one of his thick gloves to clear the rest of the jagged pieces from the opening.

"Ladies first," he said.

I maneuvered the gun through the window first then climbed in after it, careful not to cut myself on any of the glass shards. Eirian followed suit. We brushed glass from our coats, regripped the rifles, and left the small office.

"What exactly are we looking for?" Eirian asked as we crept through the first floor hallways."

"Storage rooms, nurse's carts, that sort of thing," I replied. "Cabinets or refrigerators that might have medication in them."

He nudged open a door to a room marked Hospital Staff Open and peered inside. "Here's storage. Looks like this place has already been hit though."

I took a look. The room had been ransacked. There was nothing left, other than a few bedpans and a couple trampled boxes of safety gloves. We moved on, sweeping the entire floor for anything that we could use.

"Damn it!" Eirian turned over yet another empty rolling cart in the emergency room. "Still nothing. Georgie, what if this trip is a total bust?"

"Relax, Eirian." I found an unopened package of gauze and shoved it into my bag. "We're only on the first floor."

We moved upstairs, searching level after level. Here and there, I found something useful like unsoiled blankets or whole-sale boxes of Band-Aids. I even found topical antibiotics for small cuts and bruises.

"Too bad we can't smear this all over Penny's leg," I said, holding up the little yellow tube for Eirian to see.

"If only it were that easy."

In the operating rooms, we stole scalpels and clamps and other medical instruments that we didn't know the names of. Jax could no doubt make use of them. In the patients' rooms—some of which still housed those who were unable to move themselves from the hospital when the EMP blast went off—we collected clean sheets, blankets, clothes, and simple medications like ibuprofen and acetaminophen. Still, there were no signs of anything that could help save Penny. We had one more floor to search. Then we had to face facts and return to Camp Haven with what little we had. We took the stairway up to the top floor, but Eirian, who had taken point, stopped short when he looked through the window into the last hallway.

"What is it?" I whispered, my pulse quickening.

"People."

"Survivors?"

"Of sorts. Addicts."

"How can you tell?"

"Because they're all hanging out near a drug cart," he said in a hushed voice, eyes fixed on the hallway. "And they've got track marks on their arms."

"How many are there?"

"Three by my count."

I climbed the last few steps and joined him at the door. Sure enough, a trio of two men and one woman loitered in the hall-way, slumped against the wall. The only reason I could tell that they weren't already dead was because their chests rose and fell with their breath.

"I think we have a pretty good shot of sneaking past them," I said. "Let's go."

We inched open the door and snuck into the hallway. The trio did not stir, even when our boots squeaked across the linoleum flooring.

"Must be good, whatever they're on," Eirian muttered as he stepped over one of the men's legs.

"Let's see if we can find some of it," I said, opening the door to the drug cart. It was by far the fullest stocked one we had found so far. I pulled out vials of morphine, epinephrine, atropine, and a few others with names that I didn't recognize. I carefully loaded it all into my bag.

"There's a fridge in here," Eirian announced, sliding into one of the rooms that branched off of the main hallway. I followed him in, where he opened the fridge and extracted a vial. "Peni-cillin. That's what we need, right?"

"Yes!" I took the bottle from him, studied the label, then pumped my fist in triumph. "Oh, thank goodness."

"Don't drop it," Eirian warned, rifling through the rest of the fridge. "That's all there is."

"It'll be enough."

"Who the hell are you?"

We whirled around to face the owner of the slurred speech and found ourselves face to face with one of the men who had been sleeping in the hallway. He had yellow teeth and drooping eyelids, and he held a standard-issued Glock that didn't match his wayward, careless appearance, as if he'd stolen the weapon from an unlucky police officer. I tucked the vial of antibiotics safely into my pocket then lifted my rifle toward the man.

"Easy," Eirian warned, aiming his own gun. "We're not here to hurt anyone."

The man's sleepy eyes flickered to our loaded bags. "You took all the drugs, didn't you? The morphine? I need that, man!"

"No, you don't," Eirian replied. "You just think you do."

"Don't mess with me, man." He stumbled forward, and the Glock flopped wildly in his grip. Eirian and I both stepped away from each other. The man looked from me to him and back again. "There's two of you?"

"Sheesh," Eirian muttered under his breath. "He can't even see straight. Let's get past him and get out of here."

"Easier said than done," I replied. "An addict with a gun is even less predictable than a cop with one."

"Are you talking about me?" the man sputtered. "I don't appreciate that. Give me the morphine, or I'll shoot!"

He didn't give us a chance to consider his ultimatum. Without preamble, he fired the Glock. The bullet whizzed so close to my ear that I heard it go by. I reacted instinctively and pulled the trigger of the rifle. The gun hammered against my shoulder. The man with the Glock fell to the floor. I stopped firing and stared at the man, the rifle drifting out of position to hang loosely at my side.

"Georgie?" Eirian said.

I checked my pocket to make sure that the penicillin had survived the ambush. "I can't think about it, Eirian. Let's go."

We stepped over the body to leave the room. I refused to look down, but it was impossible not to catch sight of the man riddled through with bullet holes in my peripheral vision. I had killed him. It was the second time that someone had died at my hands for the sake of my own survival. I knew I'd never get used to the feeling of emptiness that taking someone else's life left in my soul.

"Are you okay?" Eirian asked as we headed down the stairs to the main floor. "You had to do that, Georgie. He was aiming for your head, but I know it's hard—"

"You're not scared of me?"

Confused, he looked back at me. "Why would I be scared of you?"

"I just killed someone."

He stopped on the next landing and took my hands in his. "This isn't real life, Georgie. This isn't how things are supposed to go. That means we have to do a lot of things that we wouldn't normally do. It was either him or you. I'm glad it was him."

We spoke nothing more of it, but I was grateful that Eirian reacted rationally. It helped clear my mind. We made it out of the hospital without meeting anyone else, and when we left the city and climbed back into the mountains, the trees welcomed us back into the relative safety of their shadows. We trekked upward in silence, heavier than we had been on the way down, both in physicality and in spirits. When the sun sank below the horizon and the moon lifted itself into the sky, Eirian turned back to make sure I was still following him.

"Should we stop for the night?" he asked.

"Do you mind if we keep going?" I said. "I know I won't be able to sleep if we stop, and I figure we might as well get back to the camp as soon as possible."

So on we went through the night. We arrived at Camp Haven hours later, shoulders slumped and feet aching. The night watch security team was thin. A few of them had been reassigned to the breach in the wall. One of them, Peters, held up a lantern to illuminate our faces.

"You made it back," he said, not bothering to hide his note of surprise.

"Sure did," Eirian said. "Can you open the gate?"

"You got it," Peters replied, using hand gestures to communicate the order to his troops. "Did you find what you needed?"

"Yeah."

"Glad to hear it," Peters said. "It's only getting worse. You two haven't heard, have you?"

"Heard what?" I asked him.

"The Masons' daughter. What's her name? She went into labor a few hours ago."

19

***

*W*e ran to the med bay despite our aching feet, but Pippa, Jacob, and Penny were nowhere to be seen. Most of the guys who had been hit by the explosion near the wall were gone, having recovered from their injuries enough to get back to work. Kirsch was the only one left. He lay upside down on his cot, his feet propped up against the wall as he tossed a rubber band ball into the air and caught it again.

"Kirsch!" I said, snatching the ball out of the air to get his attention. "Where's Pippa and Penny?"

He pointed down the hallway to the exam rooms. At the same time, someone let loose a shrill scream.

"Stay here," I told Eirian. I wrestled the penicillin from my bag and ran into the back. I found Jacob, Pippa, and Nita in the first exam room. Pippa squeezed Jacob's hand so tightly that his fingers were white and his eyes threatened to pop out of his skull.

"Another contraction," Nita said, wiping the sweat off Pippa's forehead with a damp rag. "You're doing great, sweetie."

"Don't tell me how I'm doing!"

Jacob caught sight of me in the doorway and pulled his hand

288

free of Pippa's to meet me. "You're back! Thank God." He threw his arms around me and hugged tightly. "Did you find the medication?"

I held up the vial.

His face fell. "Is that it?"

"It's better than nothing. Where's your mom?"

"In the next room over," he said. "Jax is trying to keep her alive. We've had to resuscitate her twice since you've been gone."

"And she's still hanging on?" I asked in disbelief.

"Go!" Jacob said. "We'll take care of Pippa."

I left Pippa's room and headed to the next one over. Penny already looked dead. Her skin was pale green and covered in sweat. Thankfully, the wound on her leg was covered, though the stench now permeated every corner of the room. Jax sat by the woman's side, her head in her hands, but she looked up when I entered.

"Did you get it?"

"Yes."

"And a syringe?"

I emptied my bag onto the counter, spilling medical supplies all over. "Take your pick."

Jax leapt into action, choosing her tools from the options on the counter. I handed her the vial of penicillin. She inserted the needle into the bottle and drew the antibiotic into the syringe. Then she turned to Penny, found a vein in her arm, and inserted the needle. As she pushed the plunger down and the medication entered Penny's bloodstream, I let out a sigh of relief.

"Nice job," Jax said, throwing the used syringe into the biohazard bin to be sterilized. "I didn't think you'd get back in time."

"Will she be okay now?" I asked her. There was no immediate change in Penny's state, though I wasn't sure why I had expected one. "She's going to make it through, right?"

"I don't know," Jax answered, observing her patient. "She's

got a major infection. She's probably septic. One dose of penicillin might not be enough to fight it all off. We'll watch her overnight, but if she doesn't improve, there isn't much else we can do about it."

A violent gurgle interrupted our conversation. Penny's eyes flew open. She clutched her throat, her back arching off the exam table.

"She can't breathe!"

"Damn it," Jax growled, returning to where my hospital haul was strewn across the counter. "She's allergic to penicillin. Please tell me you found some epinephrine in that godforsaken city."

"Yes, it's there somewhere!" I held down Penny's hands and looked into her wild eyes. "Penny? Hey, it's me. It's Georgie. Just try to relax. We're going to fix this."

Jax prepared a second syringe and jabbed it into Penny's arm. A few seconds later, Penny's airways opened up, and she took a huge, gasping breath. A drop of water splattered against the exam table. I wiped my eyes. I hadn't realized I'd been crying. Penny's eyes fluttered shut again as she dropped back into unconsciousness, but at least she was still breathing.

"What happens now?" I asked.

"Now we wait."

THE HOURS PASSED IN AGONY. We sat and waited with Penny, hoping for some kind of visible improvement. Camp Haven had no heart rate monitors or other equipment that needed electricity to run, which meant we had to track Penny's status largely by guesswork. We took her pulse every few minutes, but there was nothing much else we could do but wait. The main problem was that Penny's body had rejected the penicillin, and I could tell by the look on Jax's face that she didn't expect Penny to make it through the night.

Sometimes later, Nita rushed in from the next room over. "Jax? Pippa's just about ready. I've never done this before. What do I do?"

"I'll help," Jax said. "You okay in here, Georgie?"

Though I didn't like the idea of being alone with a half-dead woman, I nodded. Pippa needed Jax more than I did. After all, she had a better chance of surviving than her mother. Jax and Nita left the exam room. Not long after, Jacob knocked quietly and entered.

"Hey," I said softly. "You're not staying with Pippa?"

"She kicked me out." He stared at his mother, who looked more zombie than human at this stage. "God, she looks awful. Did you give her the medication?"

"We did." I rubbed my eyes. When was the last time I'd slept? "But it turns out she's allergic to penicillin. Did you know that?"

Jacob began to shake his head before a look of realization crossed his features. "Yes, I did. She used to wear a medical bracelet for it."

"What happened to the bracelet?"

"She stopped wearing it because she thought it was ugly." He groaned, leaned against the wall, and sank to the floor. "Oh, God. I can't believe I forgot!"

"It's not your fault," I told him. "It's not like we thought we were going to facing this anytime soon."

"But I should have known—"

I knelt on the floor and took his hands away from his face. "Jacob, stop. If there's one thing I've learned since that damn EMP went off, it's that you can't keep blaming yourself for every single mistake you've ever made. Learn from the experience and move on. Better yourself. That's our only option."

We locked eyes. He leaned in, his lips nearing mine, but I bowed my head and pulled away.

"Sorry," I muttered.

He covered his eyes again. "No, no. You're not the one who

needs to apologize. I am. I shouldn't have done that. I'm sorry for putting you in that position. Old habits, you know? It just felt normal."

"I get it."

"You're with Eirian now. Aren't you?"

I sat next to him, wrapped my arms around my legs, and rested my chin on my knees. "We haven't talked about it in so many words yet."

"I've seen the two of you around camp," Jacob said, stretching out his legs along the floor. "You fit together so well. It pissed me off at first because you and I were never like that. It was never easy for us. I didn't realize that until now."

"I think we were both too busy convincing ourselves that our relationship would eventually work out," I said. "We weren't paying attention to the things that were keeping us apart."

"Yeah." Jacob sighed. "I just feel like we could have done better. Any word on your dad?"

"Not even a whisper," I replied. "I even tried to sneak into Sylvester's cabin."

"You did? What happened?"

"Ludo caught me," I told him. "I guess it's a good thing he did. Otherwise, I might have gone the same way as your—"

I cut myself off before I could finish the thought. I'd just remembered that Jacob had no idea that his father had died in the woods, mauled by a wild animal.

"Like my dad," he finished. He tipped his head back against the wall and blew his hair out of his eyes. "What do you think happened to him? Do you think he's still alive?"

I remained quiet, pretending to study my fingernails as I tried to think of something to say. Jacob nudged me.

"Georgie? Hello?" He waved in front of my face. "You still in there?"

"Jacob, listen," I said, deciding that Jacob and I had lied to each other enough for one lifetime. "We saw your father in the woods."

His expression brightened. "You did? How was he? What did he say?"

"No, you don't understand." I swallowed hard. "We found him—he was—"

"He was dead, wasn't he?" Jacob asked, his voice hollow.

"Not quite," I said. "He'd been attacked by a wolf. There was nothing we could do. If I could have saved him, I would have."

He tucked his head between his knees. "What did you do with him?"

"Sorry?"

"The body. What happened to him?"

"We had to leave him," I told him. "We didn't have a choice."

"Where?"

"Down the mountain a ways," I replied. "Looked like he might have been walking back toward the city."

"I'll have to find him," Jacob said. "He'll need some kind of proper burial."

"Jacob, there won't be much left to find."

"I don't care." He shot up from the floor, as if he suddenly couldn't stand being in such close proximity to me. "You don't get it. He was a Christian. This would have mattered to him."

Before I could argue further about the dangers of going into the woods alone just to give Jove a funeral, two things happened at once. First, Pippa screamed next door. It ripped through the walls and pierced my eardrums. Second, Penny's body began to seize uncontrollably on the exam table. Jacob caught her as she rolled toward the edge of the table, eyes rolling so far back in her head that I could only see the whites of her eyes.

"Help me!" he yelled, bracing his bucking mother against his torso.

I took hold of Penny's ankles, and we lowered her onto the floor. "Turn her on her side. Gently!"

Together, we rolled her over. Jacob pinned her arms to the ground, trying to quell her movements, but I swatted him away.

"Georgie!"

"You're not supposed to hold her down," I snapped, putting myself between Jacob and his mother. "You could hurt her even more."

The seizure subsided as quickly as it had come on, but another problem soon arose. I pressed two fingers to Penny's wrist, panic rising in my throat. Once again, she had no pulse. I started CPR.

"Get Jax!" I ordered Jacob.

He flew out of the room, but from the way Pippa was yelling, I had a feeling I knew which patient that Jax was going to prioritize. Seconds felt like hours as I pumped Penny's heart for her. My mind worked in layers. The first was focused on saving Penny's life. The second warred with the idea of losing yet another one of Jacob's family members. The third listened to the heated conversation that filtered into the exam room from next door.

"Jax, my mother's heart stopped again," Jacob was shouting over Pippa's anguished groans.

Jax's reply was muffled and agitated. "In case you haven't noticed, I kind of have my hands full at the moment. Push, girl!"

Pippa released another bloodcurdling scream.

"Please, Jax," Jacob begged. "She's dying."

Beneath my palms, Penny's heart did nothing to contradict Jacob's statement.

"Nita, go!" Jax ordered. "See what you can do for her."

Moments later, Nita and Jacob returned to help me. Nita rifled through the vials on the counter, filled a syringe, and dropped to her knees beside me and Penny.

"Keep going," she encouraged, pushing the needle into Penny's arm.

My arms were giving out, but I repeatedly pushed on Penny's

chest with the last of my strength. Nita held Penny's wrist with two fingers, searching for a pulse. Jacob paced from one end of the tiny exam room to the other, threading his fingers through his hair.

"God, not Mom too." He looked up the ceiling and pressed his hands together. "Please God, don't take her too. What am I supposed to tell Pippa?"

I had never heard him pray before. He was at the end of his line, but so was everybody else.

"One last big push!" Jax yelled next door. "Go, baby, go!"

Pippa screamed her loudest yet, a prolonged, determined yell that shook the walls of the med bay, followed promptly by an intense cry of relief. My arms buckled, the muscles no longer able to keep up the work. Nita took my place. As I backed away from Penny, I already knew that our efforts were pointless. Penny stared blankly at the ceiling with cold, empty eyes.

"Give me more epinephrine!" Nita shouted.

I moved toward the counter to obey, but someone grabbed me from behind. It was Jax, her hands wrapped in clean towels.

"Don't waste it," she said, looking down at Jacob's mother. "She's gone."

"No!" Jacob shoved me out of the way and scattered the vials across the counter. His eyes bulged as he studied each label for the right one. "No, we can't let her die. Nita, what are you doing?"

Nita had stopped pumping Penny's heart and sat back on her heels. She looked up at Jacob. Her long, dark hair was askew, and her pretty olive skin flushed red with stress and grief. "I'm sorry, Jacob."

"No, she can't be dead!"

Everyone in the room cringed as he swept the vials from the counter in a fit of rage. They scattered everywhere, bouncing off the floor and rolling away. One shattered, spraying some kind of drug across the walls of the exam room. Jax gripped Jacob under one arm, and with an astonishing show of strength for such a small woman, yanked him out into the hallway.

"Get yourself together," she ordered, pinning Jacob to the wall. "This is the end of our world, kid. Shit happens. People die. But my job is to make sure we prevent as many people from dying as possible, and I can't do that if you're throwing the only supplies we have all over my med bay."

Jacob struggled against her grip, his face growing redder as her fist pressed against his windpipe. He appeared deaf to her words. She smacked him hotly across the face. Nita and I both jumped at the sound of skin against skin, but Jacob's eyes cleared. He stared into Jax's face, and his chin began to tremble. Then he collapsed altogether.

"It's okay," Jax said, lowering Jacob gently to the floor as he sobbed in her arms. "Everything's going to be okay. Girls, get out of that room and shut the door. He doesn't need to see her."

I didn't need further coaxing. Nita and I hurried out, leaving Penny and the fallen medication. I didn't look back as I shut the door. It wasn't something I wanted to see either.

"Nita, can you check on Pippa and the baby?" Jax asked, still holding Jacob. "They were okay when I left them. Georgie, maybe you should come here."

I sat on the floor as Nita went into Pippa's room. Jacob was completely sprawled out. Jax wiggled out from underneath him, and I took her place. He rested his head in my lap, and I threaded my fingers through his hair, combing out the tangles. We stayed like that until he fell asleep, out of exhaustion or grief. Jax and Nita helped me get him into one of the cots. Afterward, I left the med bay, found a quiet spot away from everyone else, and cried. If I never had to see the inside of that exam room again, it would be fine with me.

WEEKS LATER, things began to go back to normal, or at least as normal as they could be in Camp Haven. Penny's body was cremated. There was no ceremony. Jacob went back to work, throwing himself into the efforts for rebuilding the camp's ruined wall. He worked dawn until dusk, drowning his grief in manual labor. I only ever saw him in the Bistro at mealtimes. Part of me was fine with that. His empty expressions were difficult to look at, and our limited conversation was falsely nonchalant. Pippa was finally able to leave the med bay for the first time in over a month. Her newborn, a little girl that she had yet to name, was doing well. The problem was with Pippa herself. Like Jacob, she had not taken the news of her parents' deaths well. On her first day out of the med bay, she left her baby with the other people who looked after the children and disappeared for hours on end. When night fell, Jax organized a search party to look for her with no luck. I finally found her holed up in a hollowed-out tree near the edge of camp. She didn't say a word, but merely picked up her baby and walked back to her bunk in silence. The situation repeated itself each day. She dropped off the newborn, vanished to a different hiding place, and reappeared in the evening to collect the child. After a while, we stopped looking for her. One day, I found Ludo and Jacob at odds with each other outside of the med bay. The baby lay swaddled in Jacob's arms, screaming as the two men yelled over her.

"This is more than postpartum depression, Mason!" Ludo was saying. "She hasn't been pulling her weight. You of all people should know what that means."

"You're seriously going to hold a tribunal for a seventeen-year-old girl?" Jacob challenged. "Our parents are dead, Ludo!"

"Okay," I said, ducking between the two to scoop the baby from Jacob's arms. "Have either of you noticed that this pretty little girl is upset?" I fixed the blanket around the newborn's face. "They're so noisy, aren't they, pretty?"

"He wants to kick Pippa out," Jacob said, fuming.

"I don't want to do anything," Ludo growled. "But she isn't giving us much of a choice."

"Ludo, is this really necessary?" I asked him, swaying back and forth in an attempt to soothe the squalling child. "Pippa's had it pretty rough. Like Jacob said, she just lost both of her parents. And she's taking care of a child that she never intended to keep to begin with."

"That's the problem though," Ludo replied. "She *isn't* taking care of her. She disappears all day. Doesn't help out in maternity. Doesn't help out anywhere else. I don't even see her at the Bistro. I mean, does she even eat these days?"

I decided not to mention that I had been bringing Pippa breakfast, lunch, and dinner each day. For now, I was the only one she allowed near her. Sometimes, she even hid out in the communications office with Eirian and me.

"She needs more time," Jacob argued. "She'll get better."

"Not unless she lets someone help her," Ludo said. "We have therapists here. There are people that she can talk to."

"She doesn't need a shrink," Jacob replied.

"Lucky for her, no one here ever got a degree in psychology," said Ludo. "Listen up, Mason. I'll give her another week to pull herself together. She needs to meet with our camp counselor. If she blows it off or she disappears again, that's it. I'm calling a tribunal to figure out what to do with her."

The week passed without change. Pippa continued her absent streak, except she stopped cluing me into her hiding places once I suggested that she should consider attending the meeting with the counselor. She seemed wholly unconcerned about the prospect of a tribunal, which made me worry for her even more. Clearly, the events of the recent past had had a traumatic effect on her. She wasn't thinking straight. It wasn't her fault, but the rest of the camp couldn't understand that. Ludo officially put in a request to gather the tribunal, but this wasn't the piece of news that really surprised me that day.

"I got a meeting with Sylvester," Jacob announced over lunch at the Bistro. It was a rare occasion that we sat together. Usually, he avoided me, but Eirian was working through lunch, and so I was much easier to approach.

"You did?" I missed my mouth, and a piece of beef plopped from my spoon back into the bowl of stew. It didn't entirely concern me. Food was thin on the ground, which meant that each meal grew more and more difficult to stomach. "You mean it was actually approved?"

Jacob nodded, powering through his own lunch without complaint. He tore a piece of bread in half and wiped broth from the edge of his bowl. "I'm going to ask him to get Ludo to drop the tribunal. The camp's rules should include a bylaw for mental illness in situations like this. It's not fair to Pippa. Don't you think?"

"I totally agree." I pushed the stew away in favor of my own roll of bread. It was easier to eat that than the tough meat in the bowl. "I find it hard to believe that no one at this camp has ever suffered from depression before. They're treating her like this is a choice."

"That's how it is though, isn't it?" Jacob asked. "It's an invisible disease. People would rather pretend like it doesn't exist."

"They don't get it," I added. "She needs time. I would love to help her. I actually think she would benefit from meeting with the camp counselor, but *she* has to be the one that decides that she wants to go. That's the hard part."

"She listens to you," Jacob said. "She likes your advice. Don't you remember? Before all of this, she used to call my phone and ask for you when she had trouble at school or whatever. Don't give up on her, Georgie. Please. I might be able to buy her a little more time, but I think you're the one who's eventually going to get through to her."

"Don't worry," I told him. "I'll do my best. When is your meeting with Sylvester?"

"Tomorrow."

"Well, good luck."

AFTER LUNCH, I picked up the baby from the childcare building and stopped by the breach in the wall to look for Eirian. Most days, he didn't have much time to spend working communications with me. I'd seen him less and less since Camp Havoc had broken in. I spent a lot of time by myself, but the sight of the new barrier the construction crews had erected to fill the gap in our defense helped to set my mind at ease.

Eirian was busy hammering together a new section of the barrier. When he bent down to find another nail, he caught sight of me lingering just outside of the construction zone and jogged over.

"Hey there," he said, grinning down at the baby tucked into the sling in the front of my coat. "I see you brought company."

"I thought she could use a little fresh air." I stood on my toes to kiss him, and a few of the other guys whistled and catcalled while they continued their work. "Oh, shut up!"

He took off his work gloves and tapped his fingers against the baby's lips. She hummed, spit bubbling as she gummed Eirian's fingers. "Any word on Mom?"

"Ludo wants to hold a tribunal for her," I reported. "Jacob's pissed. He has a meeting with Sylvester tomorrow to ask him to postpone it."

Eirian raised his eyebrows. "Really? That's surprising. Is he going to ask about your dad too?"

"I didn't ask him to," I replied, rocking the baby side to side. "It's too much. Besides, back when I requested a meeting with Sylvester, I flat out told Jacob that I wouldn't bother to mention Jove. Why should he go the extra mile for me?"

"A lot has happened since then," he said. "The two of you are in better spirits now."

"I guess."

The baby wrapped her tiny hands around one of Eirian's fingers, and he smiled widely. "She still doesn't have a name, huh?"

"Nope," I said. "Pippa hasn't picked one yet."

"Sounds like she's not going to," he said. "A pretty girl should have a pretty name."

"Or a badass name," I said. "After all, she was born into this insanity. She'll have to be a badass in order to survive it all."

"Like what?"

I pondered the question, looking down at the little girl in my arms. She would grow up in a completely different world than the one the rest of us had known. She would never know the United States as it was before the EMP blast. She would grow up similarly to Eirian, on a homestead, watching the country rebuild itself from the ground up.

"Athena," I decided.

"Goddess of wisdom and war," Eirian added, nodding in agreement. "Got a thing for the Greeks, I see." He smoothed out the tuft of hair on Athena's forehead. "It's perfect."

"It's temporary," I reminded him. "We can't really name Pippa's baby."

"Until then," he said, "she remains a tiny goddess."

"Eirian!" Ludo trotted across the construction site to catch up with us. "What are you doing right now?"

"Sorry, boss," Eirian replied. "Just saying hi to the kid."

Ludo waved away his excuse. "I'm not worried about that. I need to speak with you. I've been sending scouts out to Camp Havoc ever since the breach. So far, they haven't picked up any useful information."

"Okay. So?"

"Kirsch and Peters headed out last night," Ludo said. "They were supposed to return by lunchtime today, but no one's heard hide nor hair of them."

"Did they take a radio with them?" I asked.

"They did," Ludo replied. "But we can't reach them. Either the signal doesn't reach that far, or they aren't able to answer."

"So what happened to them?" Eirian said.

"I'm thinking that Camp Havoc got a hold of them." Ludo planted his hands on his hips with a grimace. "I want a second team out there ASAP to figure out what those idiots are planning."

20

here was nothing to do but watch as Ludo sent out a second group of scouts, heavily armed, to check if Camp Havoc had appropriated the first security team. The night was tense. A pall hung over the compound. Even the children were quiet. It was as if everyone knew that something wasn't quite right. Dinner at the Bistro, usually a chatty occasion, was a hushed affair, and the community event was canceled on account of lack of interest. We were all waiting to hear back from the scouts. When they didn't reappear by curfew, Ludo ordered the camp to bed, and we trudged to the dormitories on worried, wearied feet.

The morning brought no news, which in any other circumstance, I would have considered good news, but times were changing, and to hear nothing from our comrades was a sure sign of trouble. Ludo felt it too, but he hid it beneath his usual gruffness as he went about his scheduled business of assigning jobs for the day. It was a smart move on his part. If Ludo panicked, the whole camp would panic, and that was the last thing we needed. I went to the Communications office as usual to pass out radios and walkie talkies for the day. After that was through, I started scanning the waves for signs of other operators outside of Camp Haven.

At lunchtime, I took my stew, the portions of which seemed to be growing smaller with each passing day, and ate around the back side of Dotcom since the tension in the Bistro was so smothering. As I fished through the gravy for the vegetables, I caught sight of Jacob heading up the hill to Sylvester's cabin. His meeting about Pippa was today. I shifted sideways to get a better view as he approached the front door and knocked. When one of Ludo's security boys answered the door, I rolled my eyes. Of course Sylvester himself couldn't be bothered to receive guests at his own house.

It wasn't long—fifteen or twenty minutes—before Jacob reappeared. He waved in thanks to the security guard who saw him out then trotted down the hill. He was smiling. When he saw me sitting on the bins behind DotCom, he walked over.

"Looks like good news," I said.

"It is," he replied. "Pippa's tribunal is going to be put on hold indefinitely."

I set down the nearly empty bowl of stew to hug him. "Jacob, that's great! I'm so happy for you."

"Thanks," he said. "That Sylvester guy is a trip though."

"What do you mean?" I asked. "What was he like? Who is he really?"

"I never actually saw him." Jacob sat down on the bins next to me. "We spoke through the door of his bedroom."

"You're kidding."

Jacob shook his head. "His voice is weird too, like he's changing it to sound less like himself. I couldn't get a read on him at all. Kyle, the security guard up there, says that Sylvester's the most paranoid out of all the campers. That's why he quarantines himself."

"Sounds like my dad, but at least he went outside," I said. "So what happened then? You were only in there for a few minutes. I can't believe it was so easy for you to convince him."

"All I had to do was explain the situation." Jacob pulled his gloves from the pocket of his coat and put them on. "I told him everything. That we're new to the camp, that we lost both of our parents, that Pippa has been having a hard time adjusting. As soon as I mentioned that she was having trouble with depression, he agreed to postpone her tribunal right away."

"I'm so glad."

"Listen, while I was up there, I had the chance to look around a bit." Jacob unzipped his coat and reached into its inside pocket. "Georgie, it was like looking into your childhood photo albums. If I had to guess, Sylvester didn't touch anything in that cabin other than whatever's in the bedroom. It looks like a damn shrine."

My rib cage tightened around my lungs. Suddenly, the air felt too cold to breathe. As the months passed me by in Camp Haven, I had dwelt less and less about the time I'd spent on this land before the EMP blast went off. Now, it all came back in full force. This place was the home that my father had made for me. Why had he left it so suddenly?

"I found this," Jacob said. Something small and sparkly glinted in the palm of his hand. A gold wedding band. "Look familiar?"

Gingerly, I took it from him. "This was my mother's."

"I guess as much," he said. "I figured you should have it."

Once more, I linked my arms around Jacob's shoulders and pulled him close. "Thank you so much."

"Don't mention it."

Boots scuffled through the dirt and snow, and Eirian skidded around the corner of the building, heaving for breath. "Georgie!"

Jacob immediately released me. "It was just a hug, man. I swear."

"No, it's not that," Eirian said. "It's Camp Havoc. They're at the gates. Actually, they're all around. It's bad, guys. Really bad."

I caught Eirian's forearms and made him sit on the bins. "Slow down, Eirian. What are you talking about?"

"Ludo's scout team never came back," Eirian said, pushing his fingers through his curls in an effort to get them away from his eyes. "Not the first or the second. I was working security at the front gates just now. We saw them coming up the hill. There's hundreds of them, more than we could feed here at Camp Haven. And they're all armed. We couldn't have stopped them. We had to come inside."

"Holy shit," Jacob muttered. "They're storming the camp. What are we going to do?"

"There's nothing much we can do," Eirian said. "Other than buckle down and try to defend the place. Ludo wants the miscellaneous crew to meet in the square with the other security guards. He's redirecting anyone able to work with security. Are you two in?"

"Hell yes," I said. "There's no way I'm letting those idiots take down all of our hard work. Jacob?"

"I'm in too," he said. "Pippa's safe here. That's all that matters. Let's go."

But we didn't even make it around to the front of DotCom when a series of four explosions rocked the entire camp. They came from different directions, one from each corner of the camp.

"No," Eirian whispered.

There was one moment of silence. Then the camp exploded in chaos. Camp Havoc had blown the wall in four different places. Their people poured in from all sides, dressed in crude combat gear and armed with homemade weapons. They threw our campers to the ground, where they were trampled by more invaders or others trying to flee. The trespassers tossed fire-bombs into the windows of the buildings, where they exploded amidst screams of terror. Camp Havoc didn't just want our supplies. They wanted to bring the compound to the ground. Eirian dragged Jacob and me between DotCom and the Bistro, which the invaders had yet to discover.

"I have to get to Pippa!" Jacob yelled, his eyes bulging out of his skull. "I can't lose her! I can't!"

"She's at the med bay with the baby for a checkup," Eirian said. He grabbed Jacob's coat to keep him from running out of the alley. "I can get you to her, but you have to calm down and think rationally. Follow my lead. Don't get ahead of me. Do you understand?"

Jacob nodded furiously. Eirian pulled his gun from its hiding place and cocked it. I followed his lead. Ludo had assigned me a weapon once he considered me trustworthy enough to handle it. With Jacob between us, we dove into the melee.

The camp was already trashed. Fires burned in nearly every window. People ran to and fro. Some of them screamed for mercy. Others had found weapons of their own to fight back with. Gunfire and explosives filled the mountain air as our trio scuttled along the front of DotCom toward the med bay. Bullets from an automatic rifle lodged themselves in the concrete block of the building right above my head. I crouched lower, my thighs aching in protest, and darted after Eirian and Jacob. As we passed a fallen body, I grabbed the high caliber rifle from its still hands for my own use.

The med bay had barricaded its doors, following the lock-down procedures, so we climbed through a shattered window instead. On the other side, I coughed debris and dust from my lungs only to find Nita pointing a gun at me through the haze.

"Nita, it's me!" I said, putting my hands up.

"Georgie!" She lowered the gun and hugged me fiercely, then embraced Eirian and Jacob as well. "Thank God the three of you are all right."

"Where's Pippa?" Jacob demanded.

"In the back," Nita said, pointing toward the exam rooms.

"Room two. I told her to hide with the baby."

Jacob ran to find his sister, navigating through the devastated bay. The place was a disaster, but the patients from the last attack had finally healed, so the cots were empty. Nita had piled them up near both of the exit doors.

"How are you still alive?" Eirian asked, taking in the state of the bay.

"I heard the bastards coming." Nita wiped sweat from her brow. "So I barricaded the doors and took cover behind one of those cots. I shot at anyone who tried to come through the window."

"Thanks for hesitating when we came in," I said. "Where's Jax?"

"No idea. It was a slow morning, so she was running errands for Ludo."

I wandered over to one of the shattered windows and chanced a look outside. Bodies littered the ground, but plenty more were still actively tearing Camp Haven to shreds. "They're raiding the Bistro and DotCom. Why haven't they come here yet?"

"They probably think they nabbed all our medical supplies during the last visit," Eirian said. "Get away from the window, Georgie."

I joined them at the center of the room again. Jacob emerged from the back room with Pippa in tow. They had fashioned a baby harness out of a spare sheet so that Athena could rest safely against Pippa's chest while keeping Pippa's arms free. I hugged Pippa and kissed the top of her head.

"What do we do now?" Jacob asked, flinching when another bullet hit a window pane and sent glass flying everywhere.

"I say we hole up here," Nita offered. "Nowhere else is safe. They're destroying everything, but they've spared the med bay. Our best bet is to stay here and defend the place. It's worked for me so far."

Eirian stared out of the windows. "But everyone else—"

I took him aside, away from the others. "You want to go out there, don't you?"

"Ludo's out there," he said. "And so are a bunch of other guys that I know."

"Yeah, and they're most likely going to die," I replied. "Eirian, it's you against all of Camp Havoc, and in case you haven't noticed, there are a lot more of them than there are of us. If you go out there, you'll get hit in less than a minute."

"I can't let my people suffer without trying to help them."

"You won't be able to help them anyway if you're bleeding from multiple gunshot wounds," I said, smoothing down his wild hair. "I can't tell you to stay here. It's not my place. But I also can't bear to lose you. Please stay. Buckle down with us. When all of this is over, we can comb the camp for survivors. They'll need you, Eirian. I need you."

He rested his forehead against mine, breathing evenly in and out, but he winced when another explosion went off outside. "Okay. I'll stay."

"Get over here, you guys!" Nita shouted. She had tipped more cots on their sides, forming a square of relative safety in the rear corner of the med bay. Jacob was already crouched beside Pippa, his little sister and her baby safe within the circle of his arms. Eirian and I stepped over the cots to join them. We knelt next to Nita, who had her gun propped up on a metal leg of the bed, aimed at the window. As soon as I got comfortable, a man in dirty combat pants shoved his boot through the last remaining window and climbed into the med bay.

"Hey, we got live ones!" he shouted outside, setting eyes on our meager bunker. With a grin, he raised his gun, but he didn't get a chance to fire. Nita, Eirian, and I all pulled our triggers at the same time. The man fell to the ground, dead and gone.

"Call your shots," Eirian said. "So we don't waste ammo like that again."

Another man crawled through an open window.

"Mine," I said, and shot him through the leg.

We held our own for some time, but the battle outside didn't die down. The ground shook with new explosions as Camp Havoc wreaked destruction on years' worth of our campers' dedication and hard work. We popped each and every person that tried to enter the med bay, but I feared that we were the only people who had managed to set up a relative safe space to duck and cover. Who would be left after all of this was done?

"I'm running out of bullets," Eirian said, checking his pockets for spare ammunition.

"I'm already out," Nita replied as she lowered her rifle. "Shit."

Another trespasser barreled inside. I fired once. The bullet hit the man's arm. He dropped his gun and looked up from his wound to find all of us staring at him. He reached into the pocket of his jacket and pulled something out.

"It's a fucking grenade!" I yelled, pulling the trigger of my rifle. It clicked pointlessly. I was out of bullets too. The man pulled the pin on the grenade and tossed it mercilessly in our direction.

Suddenly, Jacob was at my side. "Georgie," he said, his eyes dark with an unreadable emotion. "Please. For me. Save Pippa." And then he leapt over the barrier of cots and flattened himself out over the live grenade.

"No!"

The grenade exploded. It took out half the med bay, showering us with debris. I ran to Pippa and covered both her and the baby with as much of my own body as I could. Tears threatened to fall over the edge of my lashes, but I kept them at bay. Jacob was gone, but there was no time to mourn the loss. The grenade had blown a hole in the side of the med bay, and some of the invaders had noticed our hiding place. We were exposed. We couldn't stay here anymore.

"Out the back!" Nita shouted, shoving aside the cots to make an escape route. "Go, go, go!"

I heaved Pippa up from the floor and shoved her in front of me. We ran single file down the hallway and through the back door. When we burst outside, I turned around to count heads. Eirian was directly behind us. Nita was missing.

"Nita," I gasped, still holding Pippa upright. "Where's Nita?"

Eirian shifted aside, clearing the view of the hallway behind him. Nita lay across the floor, open eyes staring blankly, her med coat perforated with bullet holes.

"We have to keep moving," Eirian said as the man who was responsible for Nita's death appeared in my line of sight. "Georgie, let's go."

I listened to him, but not before I picked a handgun off another body outside and fired at the man in the med bay. He dropped to the floor, cradling his throat as blood gushed out of his carotid artery. Eirian pushed me and Pippa through the camp, using his keen instinct to keep us out of the line of fire. We sprinted in short bursts toward the hole in the wall on the north side of camp, taking cover when we needed to. Once we cleared the rubble and escaped into the woods, the trees muffled the sounds of terror at Camp Haven. Eirian kept us moving, until the leaves overhead were so thick that the gray sky above was no longer visible. When we finally slowed, Pippa's legs gave out, and she began to fall over.

"Whoa," I said, catching the girl beneath her arms and lowering her slowly to lean against a tree trunk. I knelt in front of her, but she stared past me, unseeing. "Pippa? Hey, are you all right?"

"She's in shock," Eirian said, scouting the woods for signs of movement. "Check on Athena."

I pulled the makeshift sling aside to look at the baby. She slept peacefully against Pippa's chest, completely unaware of the mayhem that she had just survived.

"God, I wish I was that age again," I mumbled.

Eirian remained standing, facing Camp Haven. Smoke spiraled through the forest, while the orange glow of the fires burned on. Not many people would survive the raid.

"I can't believe it," Eirian said. "Dead. They're all going to be dead."

"And so are you."

We whirled around. An entire truckload of Camp Havoc members had snuck up on us. They were covered in mud and dirt. They must have been camouflaged on the ground, waiting for us to come closer. It was fifteen against three. We didn't stand a chance.

"Run!" Eirian shouted.

I heaved Pippa up and followed his lead, but Eirian's legs were longer than mine. I lost him in the trees as the invaders ran after me and Pippa. Half of the group split off to follow Eirian. Pippa tripped over a rock and tumbled toward the ground, tucking herself around Athena to protect her from harm. I skidded to a stop, turned back, and tried to pull her to her feet, but the Camp Havoc intruders had caught up with us. I fought them over Pippa, punching noses and pinching pressure points as hands closed in around us. I wrapped my fingers in Pippa's coat, but the intruders ripped us apart, the fabric tearing away as we were separated. I fought against my captors as they dragged me from Jacob's little sister.

"Stop!" I yelled, kicking my feet to get them off of me. Pippa was hardly visible through the trespassers who tried to subdue her. "She has a baby! Leave her alone!"

"Shut up!"

Someone aimed a kick to the side of my head. A boot connected with my temple, knocking the world out of place. My vision blacked out for a few seconds. The returning image was blurry and dense, as if I was staring at the scene from underwater. Eirian and Pippa were nowhere to be found. The woods were thick with the stench of Camp Havoc's men.

"What are you doing?" one of them asked. "Kill them."

"No," a second voice said. "I recognize this one from last time. She runs the radios. We could use her. And that other girl has a kid. We can't kill a baby."

"So kill the girl."

"And do what with the baby?"

"Good point. Did you find the guy?"

"Alan's got him," the second voice confirmed. "They're taking him back to camp. He's in good shape. We can use him for labor."

"Have you heard from anyone else?"

"Logan's just got here from the attack," the voice said. "We completely trampled the place. Barely any survivors. We got what we needed. Come on, let's get out of here. I'm starving."

Someone took hold of my coat and began dragging me across the ground. Sticks and rocks ripped through my clothes, scraping against my skin.

"Why?" I forced out.

"Hey, boss. She just said something."

One of the intruders leaned over me. A black scarf protected his nose and mouth from the cold, but his black eyes were shrewd and calculating. "What do you want?"

"Why?" I said again, the words rasping against my windpipe. "You have your own camp. Why would you trash ours?"

The man's scarf lifted upward, as if he were grinning beneath it. "I don't know what hippie dippie shit you were practicing at your little kumbaya compound back there, but I can assure you that it won't fly at Base One."

"Base One?"

"Yeah," he went on. "We got different rules, little girl. It's every man for himself out there, or in this case, every base for itself. We take what we need, and we don't feel guilty about it. Your camp was a threat to ours. You were using up the resources in the area. We have more people to take care of. We need those resources."

"You killed them all."

"Let bygones be bygones," he said. "Don't worry. We'll get you a cozy bed at Base One. I'm sure there's an old bunker we can lock you up in."

His buddies laughed and thumped him on the back as he stood up, but their camaraderie was short-lived. Out of nowhere, a crossbow bolt whizzed through the air and thunked straight into the heart of the raid party's leader. He looked down at the bolt sticking out of his chest.

"Shit," he said and fell to the ground.

The rest of them panicked. They cocked their guns, aiming wildly into the forest.

"What do we do? What do we do?"

"Where did it come from?"

Another bolt found its home, taking down another trespasser. There were three left.

"Run!"

The trio scattered, taking off in different directions. Only one of them was lucky enough to make it far enough to escape the bow's deadly force. The other two were hit in the back. When the forest was clear of enemies, I lay still, hoping that the owner of the bow was finished firing, or if he wasn't, that I looked dead enough not to be considered a threat. Footsteps neared my position. I felt them rather than heard them. These feet were trained not to make a noise in the woods. This person knew where to step to avoid cracking branches. An immense shadow came over me. I slowed my breathing. I was dead. Dead.

The person nudged my side. "Up you get, George. We got work to do."

My eyes flew open at the familiar voice, a voice that I had not heard in over nine years.

"Dad?"

stared at the dead man. Ten seconds ago, he was alive and well, ready to drag me all the way to his own survivalist camp, where the residents there would use my knowledge for their own needs. Now the man had a crossbow bolt through his eye. His legs had crumpled beneath him when the bolt punctured his brain. They lay folded beneath his limp body at sinister angles. His remaining eye was still open wide, as if his abrupt end was such a surprise that he carried the shock with him into the afterlife. The other men, or most of them anyway, were dead too. The ones that had gotten away from the crossbow's deadly fire didn't deserve it. They had taken my friends. Eirian, a man who meant more to me than most everyone else even though we'd only known each other a few short months, and Pippa, the seventeen-year-old sister of my now-dead ex-fiancé, were gone, and there was a damn good chance I was never going to see them again.

Another man stood above me, the crossbow resting over his shoulder. Layers of fur made him seem larger than he actually was, but underneath all the coats, I knew that his frame was lean and strong. His face had hardly changed over the last nine years.

He bore the same downward tilt to his lips, the same steely eyes with their steady gaze, and the same aura of a man who was not quite flush with the rest of humanity. Flat on my back in the snow, I gazed up at my father. Nine years. It had been nine years since I'd seen him last. I was at a loss for words. He, much to my surprise, was not.

"What the hell have you done to your hair?"

My hat had blown off in the fight. I brushed my fingers through my hair. I hadn't seen myself in a mirror in months, but there was no doubt I looked ridiculous. I could tell from my dry split ends that the violet dye had faded, leaving a blotchy lilac tint in its wake. The side shave grew out in uneven patches. Under my father's scrutiny, I suddenly felt unbalanced. I plucked my hat from the ground, brushed the snow off, and jammed it on over my cold ears.

"It was a dare for my radio show," I explained, ignoring his outstretched hand and pushing myself up from the damp, cold ground. The dead man's good eye watched me as I left him to rejoin the living.

"One hell of dare," my father—Amos—said.

"Are we really going to talk about my hair right now?" I asked, eager to put a few paces between me and the dead man. "You just took out half a platoon with a crossbow, my home is gone, and my friends have been captured by a rather shitty branch of the military. This doesn't seem the time to discuss my stylistic choices."

My boot slipped in the snow. Automatically, he reached out to steady me by the shoulders but left his hands there after I'd regained my balance. We were almost the same height now. Our eyelines were nearly level. The sad lines around his eyes and mouth trapped my attention. He *had* changed, but I couldn't put my finger on the difference between this man and the one that had raised me to fear everyone and everything. I had left him.

Nine years ago, I had left him alone in the woods because I thought I knew better. What did he think of me now?

He pulled me into a rough hug, my cheek against the soft furs of the hand-sewn coat over his shoulders. Raccoon pelts. The gray and black hairs tickled my nose, and I convinced myself that they were the reason for the moisture collecting at the corners of my eyes.

"I'm so damn glad to see you, George," my father said.

The tears leaked over and dropped onto his wild coat. "You too, Dad."

Our emotional reunion didn't last long. My father pushed me out of his embrace, grabbed the front of my winter jacket, and yanked me behind the wide berth of a nearby tree trunk.

"Get down on the ground," he hissed, peeking out from behind the tree to aim his crossbow again. From what I could see, it was the only weapon that he had on him.

A flurry of footsteps crunched through the snow, on our way toward us. More men from the camp that had destroyed mine. My father couldn't take all of them alone. I left my cover and darted across the snow.

"George!"

I pried the rifle from the dead man's stiffening fingers, stole the extra ammunition from his utility belt, and shoulder-rolled to the cover of a tree opposite my father's, where I gave him the thumbs-up. Not a moment later, the owners of the footsteps marched into view. There were five of them, all dressed in military grade tactical gear, each touting a slightly outdated weapon. They came from the direction of Camp Haven, the compound that I'd called home for the last few months before these men had set fire to it.

"Damn, that was too easy," one of them said. "I almost feel bad."

"Don't," said another. "Remember the motto. Base One

comes first. They were hoarding a ton of supplies. We had to do that in order to survive."

"I know, but—shit!"

The footsteps shuffled to an abrupt halt. I chanced a look around the tree. The men had discovered the bodies of their dead comrades.

The one who'd touted the motto used the barrel of his gun to nudge the dead man with the crossbow bolt through his eye. "It's Stiles."

"And Andrews," one of his comrades, tall and skinny with bright orange hair, added as he eyed another body. "And Hogan and Klein and Killips. Holy shit, this guy with the crossbow nailed everyone. We shouldn't have split up. Buddy's going to be pissed."

The motto man grabbed his friend by the straps of his body armor and pulled him down to his own height. "Listen up, Kalupa. When we get back to Base One, you don't say a damn word to Buddy about this. We never saw these guys out here, understand?"

Kalupa shook free of the other man's grasp. "He's gonna find out, Wood. He takes attendance before and after every raid, remember?"

"And when Stiles and Andrews and the rest of these guys don't answer, you're going to keep your mouth shut," Wood replied. He looked around at the other three men in their group. "Here's the story, boys. We got separated from the rest of the unit during the raid and stayed behind at Camp Crap to make sure that everything was taken care of. We figured we'd meet up with everyone else back at Base One. We had no idea that they were killed in the woods. If any of you so much as lets slip the fact that we purposely fell behind, I'll make sure Buddy has your guts for garters."

"It was your idea," Kalupa muttered.

Quick as a flash, Wood jammed his rifle up under Kalupa's jaw and clicked off the safety. "Say again, Private?"

My father stepped out from behind his tree and fired the crossbow. The bolt landed at the base of Wood's skull before he could even hope to pull his trigger on Kalupa. As he dropped to the ground, joining those amongst the afterlife, the four other men panicked. Three of them raised their weapons as they spotted us behind the trees, firing at random. A bullet ripped through the sleeve of my coat, and the cold seeped in. I switched shoulders, looked out from the opposite side of the tree, and picked off a guy at the kneecaps. My father didn't play by mercy rules. The other two soldiers went down like the first, each with a bolt in the brain. Kalupa was the only one left, cowering behind a dead bush, his rifle slung pointlessly over his shoulder. He watched as my father and I emerged from our cover, hands lifted over his head.

"Please," he said, lips trembling. "I have a little brother. Our parents both died in the blast. I'm all he has left now."

"You killed my people," my father said.

"I didn't," Kalupa replied. "I swear I didn't. I don't have it in me. You can check my gun. I haven't fired it once."

My father's crossbow remained prepared to fire. His finger neared the trigger.

"Dad, don't shoot."

"George, now is not the time for pity."

"He's telling the truth," I said, lowering my rifle as I watched Kalupa shiver in the snow. "And I know how he feels. Most of the people that I care about are dead too. You do what you have to do in order to keep the rest of them alive. In his case, it's marching around with these idiots. Am I right?"

Kalupa nodded furiously.

"Go," I told him. "Don't tell anyone else that you saw us out here, but you damn well better remember my face. I saved your life today. If there comes a time when mine needs saving, I expect you to pull through, no matter the consequences."

"Yes, ma'am." Kalupa scrambled up and stumbled away from us. "I promise. Thank you so much."

He disappeared through the dry, dormant trees, his clumsy, panicked footsteps fading as the snow swallowed his noisy retreat. Dad finally shouldered his crossbow.

"You can't do that, George," he said. He lowered himself to a crouch and patted the pockets of the nearest dead private. "You can't feel bad for the enemy just because he's got a sob story. Everyone's got a sob story."

"If I killed everyone on sight, I would be a shell of a human being," I told him. "Besides, that's not the only reason I kept him alive. I needed someone to track back to Camp Havoc—Base One—whatever they call it."

Dad paused in his search of the dead man. "Excuse me?"

"They took my friends," I said, taking stock of my current state. My head throbbed from the blow I'd received when one of the soldiers had attacked me. My camo winter coat, the one that I'd had ever since an ill-fated ski trip with my ex-fiancé's family, was torn to shreds. Getting dragged across rough terrain was the easiest way to wear out a good coat. "The man and the girl that I was with before you found me. Those assholes took them back to their camp. I have to find them." I shook off my ruined outer layer, then peeled the tactical coat off of the man with the bolt through his eye, rolling him over to his arms from the sleeves. "Sorry, buddy. This belongs to me now."

My father pocketed a few packets of freeze-dried snacks that he'd found on one of the bodies. "You can't be serious."

"Don't tell me you're opposed to stealing from a dead man," I said, sweeping my long hair out from under the collar of my new jacket. The sleeves were slightly too long, but the heavy-duty Kevlar patches on the front and back would do me some good if I got into a spot of trouble. For good measure, I took

another man's balaclava—one that wasn't stained with blood—
and wormed it on over my head.

"Not the jacket," Dad clarified. "I can't let you go to Base
One."

I paused in swapping the empty magazine in my new rifle for
a full one. "Excuse me?"

"George, I just got you back," he said, finally abandoning his
search of the fight's casualties. "Base One isn't some little camp
that you can sneak into in the middle of the night to rescue your
friends. If you try, you will die."

"They're the only people I have left," I told him. "I can't leave
them there."

"Yes, you can."

"Jesus, you haven't changed, have you?" In the silence of the
woods, my voice was louder than I meant it to be. I took a deep
breath and tried again. "Ever since that fucking explosion went
off, I have been trying my hardest to keep the people I love safe.
Most of them are dead now. Only two are left, three if you count
a baby that deserves to grow up in a world that's better than this
one. Now I didn't ask you to come with me. You have no obliga-
tion to me. You haven't for a long time. You can go back to
whatever hole you've been hiding in, scared shitless, for the last
decade, but I refuse to let those assholes get the better of me. I'm
going to Base One whether you like it or not."

I zipped up the tactical jacket, swung the rifle over my shoulder, and headed in the same direction as Kalupa's footprints.

"Is that what you think of me?" my father called. "That I don't
care about anyone but myself? That I'm still holding on to the
fear that your mother's death instilled in me? Camp Haven is
gone, George. Gone! And I feel the loss of every single one of
those people as if they were my own family. I can't lose you too."

I paused and turned around. "What do you know about
Camp Haven?"

"What do you mean?"

I marched across the snow toward him. "I mean that I've been looking for you for months. No one at Camp Haven knows who you are. No one knows you even exist. I thought you were dead or, at best, long gone from the Rockies, so what the hell do you know about Camp Haven?"

"George," he said softly. "I built Camp Haven."

"What?"

He sighed and gestured for me to follow him. I trailed after him out of sheer curiosity. We could always come back to the bodies and Kalupa's trail to Base One later.

"Did they ever tell you the story of how Camp Haven came to be?" Dad asked, clearing aside dead branches as the trees gathered closer together.

"Yeah, they fed me some bullshit about a guy named Sylvester," I said. "According to Ludo—he's dead too by the way—Sylvester got caught in a snowstorm and almost died. Then a woman, an angel or whatever, came to him in his dreams and led him to our cabin. He built Camp Haven from there."

"That's bullshit."

"Well, I called that from the start."

The ground sloped upward, and my father easily lifted himself onto a rock ledge carved into the side of the mountain. He grabbed my hand and hauled me up after him. Then we continued on our way. Where we were going, other than up, I had no idea.

"Here's the truth," he said, his breath puffing out in clouds of condensation. "After you left, I was crushed. Don't give me that face. I understand why you did it. Back then, I tried to convince myself that you had gotten lost in the woods. I spent weeks combing the mountains for you, ignoring the signs that you'd gone to the city. I thought about going after you. I even got halfway to Denver a few times before turning back. Every time I got close enough to see the lights in the city, anxiety took over me. I couldn't do it. I couldn't go back there, not after what happened to your mother in that terrible place."

"Dad—"

"No, let me finish." He climbed on, never looking back to check if I was following. "I hated myself for never going to rescue you, but after a few years, I had to accept that you had either made it to the city safely or you had died trying. Either way, it was enough of an excuse for me to stop looking. I continued living at the cabin alone."

Snowflakes began to drift down from above. I pulled the thief's balaclava up over my mouth and nose to warm my breathing air. The higher we climbed, the colder it got.

"One day, in the wintertime, I was out looking for whatever game might have braved the weather," my father continued. "I heard something rustling in a snowbank. Thought I'd gotten lucky and stumbled across a rabbit. I almost shot at it. Good thing I didn't. It turned out to be a kid."

My boot slipped over a tree root hidden beneath the snow. "What?"

"It was a kid," he repeated, finally looking behind him to check on me. I got to my feet by myself. "He was about eight or nine years old, covered head to toe in snow and completely blue in the face. I thought I was too late. He was practically dead of hypothermia, but I pulled him out of the snowbank and rushed him back to the cabin. A few days later, he was back to normal and chatting my ear off."

"I'm totally lost," I said, shaking my head in disbelief. "You found a kid in a snowstorm? Where did he come from?"

"Denver," my father answered matter-of-factly. "He had run away from home. He was a foster kid. Both of his parents died when he was young, and his foster parents abused him. He told me that he couldn't go back, so he ran into the mountains, hoping for something better. I told myself that after he recovered, I would take him back to the city, but I couldn't bring myself to do it. He had bruises all over. Old ones, new ones. Scrapes and scars. I didn't have the heart to send him back to that."

"So you kept him," I guessed.

"I did," he confirmed. "He reminded me of you at that age. Sharp, witty, resourceful. And he had a mouth like a sailor on him. I taught him everything that I taught you. After a while, Sylvester and I were the best kind of team."

I froze in my tracks, taking hold of a sturdy branch to steady myself on the slippery rocks of the mountain face. "What did you say his name was?"

"Sylvester."

"Sylvester," I said. "As in the director of Camp Haven?"

My father unfurled my fingers from the branch, clapped his arm around my shoulders, and led me up the rocks. "Sylvester was never the director of Camp Haven, George. I was. Up you get."

He gave me a leg up over another steep rock face. As I cleared the ledge, I let out a small gasp. The land flattened out in a small clearing, the far side of which looked out over the side of the mountain. A small house, erected from stone and wood, occupied the far corner of the clearing. Wisps of smoke spiraled up from the chimney, leftover from a hastily extinguished fire. I got to my feet, dusted snow from my knees, and approached the far edge. The ruins of Camp Haven were visible below. It was all ash and debris now, flattened by Base One's ruthless attack.

"You've been up here all this time," I said. "You've been watching the camp, haven't you?"

"The rest of the story that Ludo told you is somewhat true," Dad said as he joined me on the ridge. "I figured there were more people like Sylvester out there, people who wanted something different than what Denver and the rest of the world had to offer them. So I started to build Camp Haven, but when the first campers arrived, I couldn't face them. My fear of others held me back. I left Sylvester to judge the best of them—unbeknownst to them, of course—and I appointed leaders as he saw fit. Unintentionally, I made him the mysterious figurehead of the camp. He split his time between here and the cabin at Camp Haven, relaying news and messages to me from the residents."

"I knew something was up with Sylvester. No one had ever seen him before. God, I can't believe it's been some kid living in my old house this entire time." I kneaded the bridge of my nose between my fingers. "Wait a second. You knew, didn't you? If Sylvester tells you everything that goes on at the camp, you would have heard about me showing up. Well?"

Dad bowed his head. "He did tell me. Georgie Fitz shows up at Camp Haven's gates with five other people. I would be lying if I said that I never hoped you would return here after the EMP hit. I knew you would be safe here."

"I asked for a meeting with Sylvester," I remembered. "To ask him about you. He denied it."

"Ah, yes, I'm afraid that was my fault as well," he replied. "I told myself that it was because I couldn't risk blowing my cover, but the truth is that I wasn't ready to face you quite yet. Not after everything that had happened between us. I was simply happy that you had returned to where you belonged."

"Where I belonged?" I scoffed and crossed my arms over the bulky vest of the tactical jacket. "Dad, you practically held me hostage here. Don't you remember what it was like?" I deepened my tone in my best impression of my father's voice. "Always be prepared, George! Get in the bunker, George! Don't make a sound, George! If you do, you're dead. You hear me? Dead!"

The word hung in the air between us, spoiling the brisk freshness of the falling snow. My father, stunned, studied my eyes, the only part of my face that was still visible from beneath the balaclava. I shoved my hands in my pockets and turned away from him.

"Georgianna," Dad began. My full name sounded foreign to

me. No one had called me that since my mother had died. "Is that really what I was like?"

"You don't remember?"

"I remember being vigilant," he replied. "I remember doing my absolute best to make sure that you were always safe. I remember teaching you how to survive on your own."

"But you don't remember the yelling and the terrifying life lessons. Of course not."

"I know I was strict with you," he said. "But I never had any idea how it was affecting you. Is that why you left?"

"I left because I was eighteen, and I wanted to go to college. I wanted to see a part of the world that wasn't the inside of that damn cabin." I scuffed the toe of my boot in the snow, sending a flurry of white plummeting over the ridge's edge. "And you told me that if I went into the city, I would get murdered just like my mother."

"Jesus, George." His chin trembled, and he covered his mouth to hide it. "I'm so sorry. I'm so sorry. You have to understand what it was like for me back then. Your mother's death—"

"I understand now," I said. "I thought about it—what my disappearance must have done to you—every single day that I wasn't up here in the mountains. And I'm sorry too. I was selfish back then. You needed help, and I never showed up to give it to you."

"It's a father's job to take care of his daughter, not the other way around."

"You take care of the people who take care of you," I corrected. "It doesn't matter who they are. I should have done a better job taking care of you."

Silence fell as we returned to gazing out over the ridge. Once again, the burning embers of Camp Haven drew my eye. Darkness clenched around my heart and squeezed tightly. That land was home to a thousand stories, only a fraction of which belonged to me. Some of them belonged to Eirian, who was probably on his way to dead at Base One by now. Other stories belonged to Jacob and Nita and Ludo and Penny. Their stories all had one thing in common. They had all died at Camp Haven.

"This is what's left," Dad murmured, following the black smoke as it rose into the sky. "Years upon years of hard work and dedication. Years of protecting a group of good people. All gone in the blink of an eye."

"You should understand why I have to go to Base one then," I said. "Some of your people are still alive. *My* people are still alive. We have to find them."

"Have you seen Base One?"

"No."

"It's an old abandoned military base," my father said. "I found it long before the EMP hit, before those idiots took up residence there. The place is a ghost town. It's like whoever was assigned there up and left for no reason. There were still cans of food in the storage closets when I checked it out. The thing is it's a ghost town in a fucking fortress. If you thought Camp Haven was hard to get into, you have no idea what you're up against."

"Base One brought down Camp Haven with a couple of souped-up cherry bombs," I reminded him.

"Exactly," he said. "I'll regret not taking that threat as seriously as I should have for the rest of my life, but my point is that they made flattening Camp Haven look easy. And the guy who runs the place is a ruthless motherfucker."

"Buddy?"

"Yeah. Sergeant Major Buddy Arnold."

"Dad, no one named Buddy can ever be as intimidating as they want to be."

"Believe me," he said. "This guy can. You don't want to take a shot at bringing him down."

"I'm not trying to bring him down," I argued. "All I want to do is get my friends back. Eirian and Pippa and Pippa's baby are there. I have to go, and I can't do it alone. Please come with me. Please help me."

He refused to look at me. "I can't do that."

"Why the hell not?"

"Because Sylvester was in the cabin when Base One attacked Camp Haven," Dad said. "And I have to go find out if he's still alive."

2 2

$\mathcal{T}$here was no point in going anywhere or doing anything in the state that we were in. Besides, we couldn't come to an agreement on a course of action anyway. Both of us wanted to conduct rescue missions of sorts, but what was a rescue mission when you didn't know if your targets were alive or dead? The blow to the side of my head was catching up to me. I swayed at the edge of the cliff side, taking hold of a skinny tree to steady myself. My vision swam, and the sight of Camp Haven, ashy and barren below, blurred into abstract shapes of fire and ash. I stumbled forward, dangerously close to the edge. My father caught the back of my new jacket, took my arm over his shoulder, and led me to the little stone house in the clearing. Though it was smaller than the cabin we lived in before Camp Haven existed, it had the familiar touches of the place I used to call home. One of the perks of living off the grid was an excessive amount of free time. Dad had spent his decorating his home with hand-sewn rugs and blankets, crafts carved out of wood or deer antlers, and books that he appeared to have bound himself. There were two beds, each with a fluffy fur comforter, as well as a living space and a tiny kitchen complete with a tap for running water. Dad set me down on the smaller bed and went to tend to the fire. The embers crackled and hissed as he prodded them with a steel poker. He added kindling, and without striking any kind of kit, managed to get the blaze going strong once more. When he stood up, he flinched, groaned, and put a hand to his back.

"Getting old, are you?" I asked.

"I keep in decent shape." He peeled off his raccoon-pelt coat and hung it on a hook behind the door of the house. Beneath, he wore the familiar plain garments that I'd grown used to seeing at Camp Haven, another reminder that he was always closer than I'd imagined him to me. He lifted his shirt, twisting around to see his back. "One of those goons clubbed me with his gun when everything was in chaos. How's it look?"

A solid purple bruise stretched across the lower middle part of his back. I tried not to wince. The injury wasn't a small one. If I'd been hit like that, I would have already been in bed.

"It looks like it could be a kidney injury," I told him. "Are you feeling okay?"

He waved aside my worried look. "I'm fine. Just sore. You hungry?"

I was, but food was the last thing on my mind. I lay back on the bed, running my fingers through the thick furs. This must have been where Sylvester slept when he wasn't working in Camp Haven. My father had adopted a surrogate son while I was away. I wondered if Dad's second child appreciated him more than the first.

"How old is Sylvester now?" I asked him.

"Sixteen."

He busied himself in the kitchen. I heard the faucet run and reminded myself to check out his plumbing system later. His house even had a stove with two burners. He lit them from below, and flames licked the bottom of the pot of water.

"Chicken or fish?" he asked.

"Fish."

"Good call." He put a hat on and pulled on a sweater. "I'll be right back. The ice box is outside. You know, in the ice."

When the door closed behind him, I rolled off the makeshift mattress and stood up to admire my father's handiwork. It was amazing what he could do with limited resources. The house and everything in it was proof of that. I ran my fingers across the rough stone walls, studying the stucco he had mixed to cement everything together. I turned the faucet in the kitchen on and off then ducked under the sink to check the pipes, which appeared to have been appropriated from the salvage at Camp Haven. They led through the stone wall and outside, and I was sure if I followed them, I would find a water tank nearby. Dad had honed his survival skills to a sharp point. He was completely self-sufficient, more so than he had been when he raised me in the woods as a child. Back then, we fetched water from the river in buckets and boiled it over the fire to purify it. Now, my father had his own damn plumbing system.

"It's decent, isn't it?" he said, having returned from his mission outside. He held two fresh trout. How he had found them in this climate, I didn't know. Then again, I knew better than to question my father's proficiency in the woods.

"It's pretty damn impressive," I told him. "How do the pipes work?"

"Gravity."

"Funny."

"It's true," he said. "Gravity and pressure. Took me a while to figure it out. I swore a lot and threw some things, but I got it eventually. I never realized how much I missed indoor plumbing until I saw that faucet flow for the first time."

"Got toilets that flush too out here?"

"Afraid not." Dad chuckled as he began preparing the fish, expertly slicing through the belly and pulling out the entrails. He pointed through the window above the kitchen sink with his knife. "The outhouse is several paces into the woods that way if you need it."

"I'm good."

He continued working, deftly dismantling the trout. He heated another pan, tossed some kind of oil into the bottom, and threw the fish in. The pan hissed and sizzled as Dad took a container from a wood cabinet.

"You still like tea, right?" he asked, peering into the container. "Or did Denver turn you into a Starbucks coffee kind of girl?"

"Tea's fine."

"Oh, good." He scooped a mixture of leaves and herbs from the container, transferred them to the pot of water, and began to stir. The aromas of cinnamon and cloves filled the cabin. "I grew this stuff myself. Did you know you have to wait until a tea plant is three years old before you can harvest the leaves?"

"Yeah, I was there when you planted the first one, remember?"

"Right."

I wandered over to the mantel above the fireplace. Two pictures, each housed in a handmade wooden frame, rested on either end. I picked up the first. It was faded and worn, the colors bleached by the sun that found its way inside through the window, but I recognized it anyway. It was taken a few weeks before my mother's murder. The three of us—Mom, Dad, and me—stood in front of Denver's Downtown Aquarium. It was the last trip that we ever took as a family. I brought the photo closer, squinting at my mother's features, wishing that the picture wasn't so washed out. After all these years without her, I'd forgotten what she looked like. Dad had abandoned all of our photo albums when we'd left the city, as if he didn't want the reminders of his wife's tragic end. Now I saw that my mother and I shared the same oval face shape, arched eyebrows, and inquisitive lips. Other than my purple hair, I was a mirror image of the woman in the photo. No wonder Dad looked at me like he was seeing a ghost. To him, the two dead women of his family had come back to haunt him all at once.

The next picture over was newer, less affected by the sun. It was a Polaroid—strange considering my father had never owned the camera. In it, my father posed next to a young boy who was about ten years old. The boy was tall for his age and impossibly thin, as if he'd hit a growth spurt the second before the photo was taken. He had dark olive skin, deep brown eyes, and curly black hair. He wore cargo shorts and a threadbare T-shirt with sleeves that hung past his elbows. I recognized the shirt, a Big Dogs graphic tee with the slogan "If you can't run with the big dogs, stay off the porch!" printed on the back. Originally, it belonged to my father.

"Is this him?" I asked Dad, brandishing the picture. "Is this Sylvester?"

He wiped his hands and tossed the dish towel over his shoulder. "That's him."

"He doesn't really look like a Sylvester."

"Yeah, I named him that," Dad said, jimmying the fish pan over the burner so that the trout slid back and forth. "He wouldn't tell me his real one. Said he didn't want to be that boy anymore. And Sylvester—"

"Comes from the Latin adjective for 'wild,'" I finished. "I remember. Years ago, you told me that's what you would have named me if I had been a boy."

"Much to your mother's chagrin."

I carried the picture over to him and placed it on the counter next to the stove, right in the line of Dad's eyesight. "Tell me something. If you care so much about this kid, why are you up here filleting trout instead of down there looking for him?"

The lines around his mouth deepened into a frown, but he kept his gaze peeled on the fish. "Don't start, George."

"We're wasting time. They could be dying. Sylvester, Eirian, Pippa—"

"And we'll be dead too if we don't rest before we go down there," Dad said. "Look at you. You nearly fainted outside a few minutes ago. That was one hell of a crack that you took to the head. And when was the last time you slept? By the looks of it, you haven't gotten much shut eye in the past several days."

He was right. I couldn't remember the last time I'd slept for more than a couple fitful hours at a time. At this point, I was running on pure determination.

"Take a nap," he said, nodding at the bed. "The food will be ready when you wake up. Then we can come up with a plan. Being tired and hungry isn't going to get us anywhere."

As he said it, my eyes watered and burned from exhaustion. Each blink grew heavier than the last. I drifted toward the bed. "Maybe you're right."

"I am right."

I sat down on the fur blankets, kicked off my boots, and cozied up. "Just an hour or two. Then we go look for them. Agreed?"

"Agreed."

THE HOUSE WAS DARK, except for the fire in the hearth, when I woke up. Night had fallen. The stove burners had been extinguished. A single cooked trout waited for someone to eat it on the counter next to the sink, along with a mug of tea that I assumed was now cold. I looked at the next bed over. Dad was dead asleep, ensconced beneath the blankets. He had not woken me when dinner was ready, and while I felt more rested than I had in several days, resentment left a bitter taste on my tongue. He had never intended to rush out of his cozy campsite to check on the people that we'd abandoned after the attack. Once again, his own fears stopped him from being a decent person.

I slipped out from under the covers, grabbed my boots, and tiptoed across the room. As I passed the coat hooks, I grabbed my tactical jacket and balaclava, gently collected the rifle, and snuck out through the front door. The hinges creaked, but Dad snoozed on. I sat on the stoop and laced up my boots before my toes could freeze together and fall off. The snow kept falling, as if it magically never stopped in this section of the mountains. When I was all wrapped up, I shouldered the rifle, checked the compass on my watch, and started on my way down. No matter what Dad said, it was my duty to check out Base One for myself.

It was slow going, especially without a flashlight or a torch. The light of the moon led the way, glistening off of the snow. Most of the ground was untouched. The rabbits, raccoons, and other woodland creatures were all holed up out of the cold. The farther I walked, the more I wished to be back in my father's stone home, warm and safe beneath the blankets. Out here, as I navigated the sharp rock ledges, I was more likely to break an ankle or catch pneumonia. I mis-stepped, skidding over the edge of a rock face and landing flat on my back several feet below. The snow did nothing to cushion the fall, which knocked the wind out of me.

"I am an idiot," I muttered to no one in particular as I groaned, rolled over, and pushed myself up to my feet again. "Watch where you step, Georgie. You're no good dead."

Great. Now I was starting to sound exactly like my paranoid father.

As I continued on, I realized I had made another rookie mistake. When my father had led me up the mountain to his home, I wasn't paying attention to our route. I had no idea where Base One was in relation to my position anymore. Every tree looked the same. Every rock was a copy of the one I'd just passed ten minutes ago. Base One was south of here, west of Camp Haven. That was all I had to go.

I wandered on through the woods, this time clocking my

path so that I would remember how to make it back to my father's camp. After an hour or so, with no sign of Base One in sight, I turned around to look at the trail of footsteps that I'd left. Maybe it was safer to go back. Getting lost in an unfamiliar part of the forest was one of the easiest ways to get dead.

"Ten more minutes," I told myself. "You get ten more minutes, and if you haven't found any clues by then, swallow your pride and go back to Dad."

I trekked onward, squinting through the darkness for a hint of humanity. Just as I was about to give up and turn around, a dark spot in the snow caught my attention. I leaned closer. It was a fresh droplet of blood. And up ahead. Another few drops. I followed the trail, all of my senses now at attention, until the smell of burning wood tickled my nose. A small fire burned in a clearing up ahead. I approached as close as I dared before ducking behind a cluster of holly bushes, peering through the leaves for a better look.

It was one of Base One's soldiers, a man with blond hair and red cheeks that I didn't recognize. He had cleared the snow from a patch of ground around the fire to sit down. His bloodied pant legs were rolled up to reveal an open wound in the back of his calf. From the looks of it, he'd caught a bullet in the muscle there. As I watched, he bit down on a stripped stick that had fallen from one of the trees, doused the wound with what I assumed was some kind of drinking alcohol, and reached into the bullet hole with his bare fingers. A mangled yell made its way past his clenched teeth, but the pain was justified. He fished the bloody bullet out in a matter of seconds and flicked it across the snow with an air of disgust. Then, to further impress me, he took a needle and surgical thread from his nearby bag and began to stitch up the hole in his leg.

From what I could see, he had two weapons on his person. The first was a big ass tactical knife that lay open beside his first aid kit. The blade was covered in blood, like he'd used it to cut away the ruined parts of his flesh. The second was a handgun in a thigh holster, which he had unbuckled from his pants in order to tend to the wound. The gun now rested on the flat stump of a fallen tree, within arm's reach of the soldier. I retreated from my hiding place, circled the camp until I was behind the man, and advanced again. The crackling fire and the soldier's muttered swear words covered up the sound of my footsteps through the snow. When I was close enough, I grabbed the gun from the stump and shook it free of the holster.

"What the hell—?" the man said, but before he could look my way, I locked my arm around his neck, tipped his chin up, and pressed the handgun to his jaw. "Ow! Go easy on me, would you?"

"You didn't tense," I said, noting the relaxed set of the soldier's shoulders. Anyone else in such a precarious position would have panicked.

"That's because I'm about to do *this*," he said, and reached up over his head to grab the back of my jacket. Before I could react, he hauled me over his shoulder and slammed me down in front of him, right into the fire. Sparks scattered everywhere as I rolled free and patted the smoking fabric of my jacket. A metallic click echoed through the clearing. Somehow, without ever leaving his seat on the ground, the soldier had gotten the gun from me during his little trick.

"That wasn't very nice." He leveled the gun at my foot instead of my head. We were mere feet apart. He could blow me apart if he wanted to. Instead, he just observed me with mischievous, navy blue eyes. "Do you mind tell me why you jumped an innocent man camping in the woods."

"Innocent?" I threw a handful of frozen dirt at him. It bounced off the insignia on his jacket, but he didn't bat a single eyelash. "Innocent, my ass. You're from Base One."

Realization opened up his expression. "You're one of them, aren't you? From Camp Haven?"

"Yeah, one of the only ones that survived."

"I'm sorry."

"Don't apologize to me!"

He lifted his gun a little higher as my voice echoed through the trees. "Be quiet."

"That little pistol won't do much against my rifle," I said.

"You'd have to get it off your back first," he pointed out. "By the time you do that, I could already have fired two kill shots. One through your head and one through your chest. I really don't want to do that. If you would just let me explain—"

"Explain what?" I challenged. "How Base One decided that their people were more important and valuable than ours? How you marched into a peaceful camp that probably would have *shared* our supplies with you if you had only had the decency to ask? How you murdered innocent men, women, and children for no reason other than to show off an unnecessary amount of power?"

"I didn't murder anyone!" His chin quivered, as if a flood of emotions threatened to spill forth from between his lips. He set the gun in the snow and kicked it over to me with his good leg. "There. Does that help? Will you listen to me now?"

"The knife too."

He folded the blade into its sheath and tossed it over the fire. I caught it one-handed then sat down across from him.

"I used to be a Marine," he said, returning to his leg. He tore open a sterile bandage, positioned it over the stitched wound, and taped it down. I wondered where he'd gotten the medical supplies in his first aid kit. "Before all of this shit hit the fan. Got an honorable discharge a few years ago, but I never really got back to a normal life. I was always a bit of a loner, so when that damn EMP went off, I didn't have anyone to look after. I decided my best bet was to get out of the city, head up into the mountains. I found a few of my old unit buddies along the way who had the same idea. They said they'd heard a rumor about an old base up in the Rockies that the Army was using for emergency purposes. They were recruiting able men and women to join them."

"Sounds sketchy," I said as I turned my palms inward to warm them up over the fire.

"It was," the man agreed. "But at the time, I didn't really have too many other choices. We headed up to Base One, got cleared, and joined the ranks. If I had known about the Sergeant Major before then, I never would have set foot in that place."

"Buddy Arnold."

"You've heard of him?"

"Only in passing. Keep talking."

"Buddy's unhinged," he said, rolling his pant legs back down to cover the bandaged wound. He zipped up his jacket. "Talk about a man drunk on power. He runs Base One like a damn prison. The civilians that live there are scared shitless of him. A lot of the soldiers are too."

"So why stay?"

"Because the other option was certain death."

"I want to know why he wanted to attack Camp Haven," I said. "We hadn't done anything wrong. We weren't interfering with Base One. Why kill everyone there?"

"Were you there for the first raid too?" he asked. "At the med bay?"

"Yeah."

"Base One was ill-prepared for this sort of thing," the man went on. "Buddy was so focused on gathering weapons and other defensive supplies that he didn't think about much else. Like sickness. Someone came in with a bug. Next thing you know, we were all half-dead from it. Camp Haven was the closest source for medical supplies, and you've probably already guessed that Buddy doesn't like to share."

"How many people are there at Base One?"

"Five hundred, give or take."

I let out a low whistle. "Holy shit."

"Yeah, so it gets kind of hard to keep everyone happy," he said. "When Buddy suggested we take down Camp Haven in its entirety, I outright refused. I was one of very few. Most of the guys wouldn't dare to stand up to him."

"And yet you still have a bullet hole in your leg," I reminded him. "How did you manage that if you didn't storm Camp Haven with the rest of your friends?"

"Buddy shot me," he answered, gritting his teeth. "As punishment for defying him. Then he told our medical team to leave the bullet in my leg as a reminder of my mistakes. That was the last straw for me. I snuck out when the night guards switched shifts, climbed up here, made camp, and now here we are."

"What happened to being afraid of dying out in the wilderness?" I asked.

"I figure I'll take my chances," he replied. "I served my country already. I did my part. Buddy is the worst kind of military guy. I knew guys like him in my own unit. They take pleasure in torturing others, all while they hide behind a mask of patriotism. It's bullshit, and I refuse to be a part of it." He pulled a can of Vienna sausages from his pack and popped the lid off the tin. "You want one?"

"I'll pass."

"Suit yourself," he said, fishing the first sausage out of the preservatives with his fingers. "So what's your story? You made it out of Camp Haven alive and out of Base One's hands. From what I know, that makes you and me the only free people out here."

My pulse pounded faster. "You've seen other survivors?"

"Yeah, I was in the hospital at Base One when they brought

everyone in," he replied. "They didn't look great, that's for sure—"

"Did you see a tall man with dark curly hair and bright green eyes?" I interrupted. "He's about six foot three. Wiry build. He was wearing a dark gray sweater and a black coat."

He chewed thoughtfully on his canned sausages. "I'm not sure. They brought a lot of guys in."

"What about a teenaged girl?" I pressed. "Blonde hair, brown eyes. She would have had a newborn baby with her."

"Oh, I remember her!" He brightened, strangely happy to have information to offer to a woman that had just held him at gunpoint mere minutes ago. "She was a feisty one. Told the C.O. that she'd chop his balls off if he so much as got near her baby."

"That's Pippa," I said. "She's like my little sister. Is she okay? What's going to happen to her?"

"She seemed fine." The soldier took another bite out of a sausage, spraying juice across his chin. "Got a couple of scrapes on her face that our med guys cleaned up. The baby was deemed healthy too, once she finally let someone take a look at him."

"Her. The baby's a girl."

"My apologies. Anyway, I'm sure she'll be fine. Base One is a lot gentler with the ladies," he said. "They'll give her a job in camp, like washing laundry or something. As long as she keeps her nose down, she'll be okay."

I heaved a sigh. "That's the problem. Pippa isn't the type of girl to keep her nose anywhere but as high in the air as she possibly can. What about the men? What happens to them?"

"Two options," he said, holding up his peace fingers. "First, if you're lucky, you impress them. They'll make you a private, bottom of the barrel. Then you go through an expedited training process before joining the ranks. Or second, you don't impress them or you make trouble. In that case, it's the worst kind of grunt work for you. And believe me, you don't want to have to be the person that cleans out Buddy's personal shitter for him. You just don't."

"Where's Base One in relation to us?"

He jabbed a thumb over his shoulder. "Back that way a few miles." He looked up from his sausages. "Oh, no. Is that what you're doing out here all alone? You're looking for Base One. Honey, take my word for it. You don't want to find it."

"My friends are there."

"And there they'll stay," he said. "You're better off out here on your own if you can survive it. Stay away from Base One."

"Why are you still protecting it?" I demanded. "I thought you hated the place."

"I do," he insisted, finally setting the sausage tin down to speak to me over the fire. "Honestly, I don't give a damn what happens to Buddy and those other assholes. For all I care, you could call in an airstrike to blow the place apart, but I got the feeling you don't have that happy power. Listen to me, lady. If you want to survive, you'll do the smart thing and turn around. Forget about your friends. Save yourself."

"I can't do that. I can't leave them there. They're all I have left."

He sighed, leaned against the fallen log behind him, and plucked the last sausage out of the can. "I figured as much. The guards switch shifts every six hours. That's your best bet of getting in. Go through the main gates. They don't use them often because they think it's too obvious. And if you see a guy with a shaved head, biceps like the devil's, and a voice like a can opener, run in the opposite direction."

"Buddy Arnold?"

"Buddy Arnold."

"Thanks." I stood up, dusting dirt from the seat of my pants. I hesitated then returned his gun and knife to him. "That way, right?"

He nodded. "Good luck out there. I hope you find your

friends. You seem like a decent person, even if you did hold a gun to my head."

I shook his outstretched hand. "You're not so bad yourself. What's your name?"

"Aaron."

"Nice to meet you, Aaron," I said, walking about from his campfire. "I hope to see you around."

"Whoa, wait a second." He twisted around to watch me go. "You're not going to tell me your name?"

I walked backward through the woods to keep an eye on him. "I'll make you a deal. If we meet again, I'll tell you my name."

"Oh, we'll meet again."

I grinned and waved, leaving the soldier at his camp. It was reassuring to know that not everyone at Base One ran on power-hungry bullshit, but I couldn't let my guard down. Not until Buddy Arnold had been taken care of.

I followed Aaron's directions toward Base One. This time, I found plenty of hints that I was heading along the right route. Trails of footsteps crisscrossed in the snow. Smeared bloody handprints decorated some of the bark on the trees, as if an injured hostage needed a shoulder to lean on and was never offered one. Farther along, I found the remnants of my father's crossbow victims from earlier that day. The bodies had been collected from the woods. There were marks in the earth from where the living soldiers had dragged their dead comrades to whatever fate Buddy Arnold deemed appropriate for them. I followed the tracks down the incline of the mountain until the ground leveled out. A stone platform jutted out from the trees, beyond which a line of lights illuminated the night sky. I flattened out on my stomach, crawled toward the platform's edge, and looked out.

"Holy shit," I whispered

Neither Dad nor Aaron had exaggerated the sheer size of

Base One. It was a stone fortress built in a small valley between the higher walls of the mountain, stretching at least half a mile in each direction. Guards walked along the top of the ramparts, guns at the ready to fire at anything that moved, but the interior of the camp was quiet and still. Everyone—including Buddy Arnold, I hoped—was asleep in bed, but as soon as I made to shift away from the edge, a hand came down on my shoulder.

*a*ron's knife was still in my pocket. I whipped it free and whirled around, but my attacker knocked the blade out of my grip with frustrating ease. I scrambled across the snow for the weapon, all too aware that I didn't have time to bring the rifle into a decent position to defend myself.

"George, stop! It's me. It's Dad. Amos."

I rolled to a halt. Sure enough, my father stood in the clearing with me, armed once again with his crossbow. "Dad? Shit, you scared me to death! I thought you were someone from Base One."

"If I was, you would already be dead," he said, sitting next to me. He looked out at Base One, his nose wrinkled as if he had caught a whiff of something mightily unpleasant. "I should have known that you would come out here the first chance you got. You're still the same kid, never thinking about the risks."

"Except I'm not a kid anymore."

"You sure are acting like one," he replied. "Leaving in the middle of the night. Heading into the dark alone and unprepared."

"I brought my rifle."

"And you couldn't raise it quickly enough to defend yourself against me or that lonely soldier you found back there in the clearing."

"You followed me?" I asked, incredulous. "You know, Dad, this is one of the reasons I left you up here in the first place. It isn't normal—"

"You got lucky with that guy," he said, adjusting his seat on the ground to get a better look at Base One's enormity. "He could have killed you if he wanted to."

"Not everyone wants to kill me."

"No, but you can't blindly trust strangers in the woods either." He picked up the knife from where I'd dropped it and handed it back to me. "Call me paranoid. That's fine. But now we're in a situation where paranoia could save your life, so for once, just once, could you please listen to me?"

I tucked the knife into one of the pockets of the tactical jacket. If it weren't for my father's presence, I probably would have tried to return it to Aaron. Dad had plenty of knives to choose from, and I'd accidentally taken an important survival weapon from the repentant soldier. But if I mentioned the internal guilt to Dad, he would accuse me of being soft once more.

"Are you convinced now?" he asked.

"Of what?"

He gestured to Base One, sweeping his hand wide across his chest to emphasize the sheer size of the rival compound. "That your run-of-the-mill rescue ideas won't fly in a place like this. You're heard it from multiple people now, one of which has had firsthand experience with Buddy Arnold."

The thing that irked me most was that he was right. The scale of Base One was too massive for me to tackle alone. I had no intel, no team, and no way to get inside. Sheer determination wouldn't cut it for this mission. I needed some kind of edge, and I had no idea how to get one.

Dad lightly bumped my shoulder. "George, I know how much these people mean to you. I know you feel like you can't leave them at Base One in good conscience, but think of it this way. They're safe for now. They have a place to sleep, food to eat, and clean clothes to wear. Who knows? Maybe Base One isn't so bad after all."

"Weren't you eavesdropping on my conversation with Aaron back there?" I asked him. "He said the civilians there are treated like crap. He left because he couldn't stand to live there anymore. He would rather be alone in the woods."

"That's what he said anyway."

"You think he was lying?"

"I saw a soldier in the woods with a serious injury and a gun to his head," Dad replied. "He would have said anything to placate you as long as you didn't shoot him."

"I thought you said I didn't have a shot."

He huffed and squinted up, suddenly interested in the moon's position. "It could have gone either way." He caught the look on my face. "Don't smirk at me. Do you want my help or not?"

The snow crunched beneath my boots as I sat back on my heels in surprise. "You're going to help me?"

"Like I said, you haven't changed." Dad pulled a scope from a bag over his shoulder, mounted it onto his crossbow, and lifted it to eye level, scanning Base One from one end to the other. "I know that if I don't help you, you'll come up with some hare-brained scheme of your own to get in, which will probably not go the way you planned it to, and you'll end up hurt or dead, alone without your friends."

"Wow. Such faith you have in me."

"On the contrary, I have the utmost faith in you," he said. "I don't doubt your abilities. After all, I taught them to you, though I am slightly surprised you didn't brain dump all of that information when you left the mountains for the city. Proud of you, George."

My cheeks and neck grew warm. I cleared my throat, grateful that the cover of night hid my pink color. I had grown accustomed to living without parental approval. I'd even tricked myself into thinking that I didn't need it, considering I didn't have parents around for most of my life, but the moment invoked memories I'd forgotten about, ones from happier times before my mother died.

"Here's the deal," Dad said, lowering the crossbow and returning his gaze to me. "First things first, we need to go back to Camp Haven. Weigh the circumstances for me, would you? You know that your friends are at least alive. I have no idea if Sylvester made it out of there. Besides, there could be other survivors that the Base One soldiers overlooked. My responsibility, first and foremost, has to do with taking care of Camp Haven. Can you understand that?"

I looked my father over. Even in the dim light of the moon, I could make out his genuine concern. It was etched into every line on his weathered face. Maybe I'd been wrong before. Maybe he had changed. After all, he had built an entire compound to take care of a group of people that he considered similar to himself. He cared about them, and the fact that so many of them had been lost to such an act of violence was sure to be hurting him on the inside.

"Fine," I agreed. "We'll go back to Camp Haven. We'll find Sylvester. Then what?"

"Then we can deal with Base One," Dad replied. "Three heads are better than one anyway. Maybe Sylvester will have a few ideas about how to get an advantage over these guys."

"You think a sixteen-year-old could take down a military fortress?"

"Don't underestimate him. He's a savvy kid," he said, packing up the scope again. He patted me on the back.

"Remember what you were like when you were sixteen? He's ten times worse."

"Gee, thanks."

"Come on, George. Let's get back to the house. We hit Camp Haven at daybreak."

AT FIRST LIGHT, after a sturdy breakfast of leftover trout and dried fruits, we layered up, armed ourselves, and headed out. This time I paid attention to the terrain, noting our path down the mountain just in case I ever had to make it back up on my own. It was a decent use of my time considering my father and I ran out of safe conversation topics within five minutes of our departure. There was plenty to talk about. The problem was that anything and everything dredged up moments from the past that we weren't keen to acknowledge.

"Cold up here, isn't it?" Dad grunted as he hopped down from a rock ledge. "I always forget how cold it gets every winter."

I jumped down and landed with my knees bent. "Freezing."

Dad tugged on a lock of lilac hair that had escaped my hat. "So tell me about this hair. I'm curious."

"Like I said, it was a dare," I replied, repositioning my hat so that it covered more of my ears. "I hosted a talk radio show in the city. You have to find some way to get listeners to tune in. We were trying to raise awareness and cash for a campaign that focuses on treating mental illness." We hiked on together, our boots crunching through the snow in unison. "So we came up with this plan. For a donation, listeners could dare us to do whatever they wanted. The amount of the donation matched the severity of the dare. Once the dare was complete, the listener donated the cash. I got a hundred bucks for the head shave and another thirty for dyeing it purple. Then I kept the crazy style because I liked it."

Dad chuckled and ran his hand over the short buzz cut that he maintained himself with a straight razor. "I gotta hand it to you, George. You always knew how to get a conversation started. A radio show, eh? What did you talk about?"

"Everything," I said. "But mostly I wanted to inform other people my age. My generation isn't the type to turn on the news or read the papers. We like to be entertained and informed, which isn't necessarily a bad thing. I talked about politics, current events, elections at every level, and a little bit about whatever was happening in Hollywood at the time to keep everybody on their toes."

"Hollywood," my dad muttered. "How do you think all those famous actors and actresses are faring now?"

I stepped over a large, loose root that protruded from the snow. "I'm sure some of them had bunkers somewhere. It wouldn't surprise me."

"Did you ever talk about something like this on your show?" He made a controlled slide down a steep but short hill, landing on his feet at the bottom. "What to do in the event of an apocalypse?"

"Once or twice." I slid after him, using one gloved hand to keep myself on course as I slipped across the snow at top speed. "Most listeners weren't interested in it. Our numbers dropped during those shows. We don't have a whole lot of preppers tuning in. I guess most people like to ignore the possibility of this sort of thing actually happening. We all figure that it won't during our lifetime."

My father swept ice from the back of my jacket, shaking his head. "Ignorance."

"Blissful," I reminded him.

"Yeah, until the whole world has gone dark, and you're out here in the wilderness all alone without the faintest idea of how to get a fire started."

"Not everybody thinks the way you do, Dad."

"I thought the city might have changed you," he said, his shoulder bumping against mine as we continued our hike. "I thought you might have intentionally forgotten the things that I taught you. When the EMP hit, my first thought was you. I thought you'd be dead."

"Still kicking."

"You made it up here on your own," Dad said. "And you brought five other people with you to safety. That's an impressive feat."

My mind wandered to those five people. Four of them were dead from one calamity or another. It made me all the more eager to rescue the remaining fifth.

Dad cleared his throat. "So... were any of those people particularly, er, special to you?"

"Uh." I side-eyed him, but he kept his gaze forward. "You mean like romantically special?"

Even with a scarf and a hat and the collar of his coat turned up, his blush was visible. "Well, I mean, sure, if that's what it was, but you know, special in the general sense of the word too." He wiped his brow and heaved a sigh. "I'm just interested in what you got up to during these past several years, but if you don't feel like telling me, I guess that's your right."

His stooped shoulders encouraged me to share. He just wanted to know what his daughter had been doing with her life for the nine years that he'd missed.

"Jacob Mason," I said. The name already had a weight to it. He was gone now, leaving only his name for people to remember him. "We met in college. We were never quite right for each other—we came from different worlds—but we were together long enough to get engaged."

"You're engaged?"

"Not anymore," I replied, scratching my left finger out of habit. I'd left the ring behind in our apartment in the city. Now, I wished I still had it, if only to commemorate Jacob. "The stress of getting out of the city was too much for us. Jacob saw me shoot a man, and he realized that he didn't know about a huge chunk of my life. It disintegrated from there. By the time we made it to Camp Haven, we had already broken up."

"I'm very sorry to hear that."

"It's okay." I kicked a mound of snow and watched it splatter everywhere with a simple sense of satisfaction. "It was hard at first. We were both mad at each other, but I think we were actually kind of friends toward the end there."

"Were?"

"He died," I said, trying not to picture that moment in my head. "He jumped on a grenade during the attack to protect us. Next thing I knew, he was just gone."

There was a moment of silence. Dad didn't say he was sorry for my loss. I was glad for that. If he apologized for every person that I'd lost in the last few months, the word would lose all meaning.

"The other people were Jacob's mother, father, and little sister," I rushed on. I ticked their names off on the fingers of my gloves. "Penny, Jove, and Pippa. And my friend Nita. Pippa and her baby were the only ones that survived the attack."

Dad ducked under a tree branch but didn't quite clear it. It dumped a load of snow down the back of his jacket. "You mentioned Eirian too, but he was already a member of Camp Haven when you arrived here."

"He was one of the first people that I met here," I explained. "I liked him right away. You know when someone simply has good vibes? It was like that. He was always working hard but never lost his positive attitude. He made me laugh, and he helped me build the radio tower for the camp without knowing anything about it."

"Seems like a good guy."

"He was—is," I corrected myself, remembering that I hadn't lost everyone in the attack on Camp Haven. "That's why I can't leave him at Base One. He's too important to me. Pippa too. I have to get her back for Jacob."

I stopped short when another glance through the trees offered me a look at the charred remains of Camp Haven. The thick barrier that protected the compound had been blasted apart. Most of the buildings were torched. The Bistro and DotCom had survived the worst of it, most likely because Base One hadn't wanted to ruin the supplies stored there. The med bay, where I'd witnessed most of the attack, had a huge hole in the side where the grenade had gone off. The entire camp was littered with rubble and bodies. The dead wore expressions of shock and terror.

I emptied my stomach off to the side. My father waited patiently several feet away, and when I'd finished, he pretended not to know what I'd been doing. He did, however, hand me his canteen. I took a swig of water, rinsed my mouth, and spat on the ground.

"Good to go?" he asked.

"Let's do this."

We stepped over what was left of Camp Haven's outer wall and into the compound itself. I forced myself to look at each face that lay on the ground. They defended each other as best as they could, and they deserved recognition for that sacrifice. I took down their names in a small notepad that I'd borrowed from my father's house. If there were bodies missing, the survivors might still be out there somewhere, whether at Base One or in the surrounding woods. Wherever they were, I was determined to find them.

"I haven't been down here since we first started welcoming other people in," Dad murmured, turning over a collection of roof shingles with the toe of his boot to check beneath them. "Back then, the only buildings here were the cabin and the Bistro, which also doubled as the community center. Everyone slept in tents they had brought with them from the city. It was breathtaking to see them build this place from the ground up. Sylvester brought me all of the plans for approval. Every time they proposed something new, I doubted that we could find the material to get another building up, but they always managed to make it happen." His eyes glistened with trapped emotions. "I knew them all from afar, through Sylvester's stories. They were my family, my responsibility, and I allowed this travesty to happen."

"You didn't know," I said, kneeling beside a woman to check her pulse. Nothing. I moved on. "Base One didn't have any reason to attack us like that. It was a power play by a mad man. You couldn't have predicted that."

"I should have put more security measures in place," Dad said. "I should have suggested that they build a reinforcement barrier alongside the outer wall. I should have—"

"Dad."

"George, I'm at fault—"

"No, it's not that," I whispered, yanking him behind one of the walls of the women's dormitory that was still standing. "I think I heard something."

Both of us went still, hardly breathing as we peeked around the wall, Dad's head stacked on top of mine. There, near the doors of the med bay, two Base One soldiers poked around in the mess.

"God damn it," Dad growled. "These bastards are everywhere."

"What are they still doing here?" I said. A bubble of rage inflated in my chest as one of the soldiers flipped up the shirt of a woman on the ground and made a rude gesture. His friend's raucous laughter echoed eerily through the demolished campground. "Shouldn't they be back at Base One by now?"

"I guess Buddy Arnold wanted to make sure no one slipped through the cracks," Dad replied. "Maybe he doesn't want people like you out here looking for revenge."

"Too damn bad," I muttered.

Dad brought his crossbow up. "Say goodbye, boys."

"Wait!" I hissed.

He lowered the bow an inch. "What?"

"Is this who we are now?" I asked him. "Are we going to kill everyone that crosses our path?"

"George, are you seeing these guys?" he said. "They're out here picking through our remains, disrespecting the dead. They murdered our people."

"Yeah, they suck," I agreed. "But if we kill them point blank, then we're just as bad as they are."

Dad ground his teeth together. "Fine. You have a point. Let's get close enough to take them out... gently. But they're damn lucky that you have a finer conscience than me. Ready?"

"Ready."

At the same time, we darted out from behind the wall to run to the next bit of cover, splitting up. Dad went right, and I went left, but when I crouched behind a fallen support beam, I knew that something was wrong. I glanced around the beam. The two men weren't standing near the med bay anymore.

"No visual," I whispered to Dad. "You?"

He checked. "Nope. Stay alert."

A gun cocked near my ear. "Hello, darling."

It was the soldier that had mimicked violating the dead woman. He had managed to sneak up on me and now stood with his feet planted on either side of my figure as though to make sure I had the perfect view of his crotch. His friend stood over Dad, the nose of his rifle against my father's ear.

"Little tip," he said. "Next time you're planning to ambush someone, don't discuss tactics within earshot. Your voices carried."

"This one's old," the second soldier said as he prodded my father with the gun. "Buddy won't want him. We should just kill them both."

355

The first soldier leaned down and took my chin. "And waste such a pretty face?"

"Do whatever you want with her," said the second soldier. "But I call dibs on this guy's crossbow."

The first soldier's head snapped up. "If he has a crossbow, he's got to be the guy that killed the unit in the woods. Oh, this is too good." He looked down at me again. "Don't worry, honey. I'll be gentle."

"Little tip," I said. "Don't stand with your weakest parts exposed."

I drove my foot up between his legs. The soldier dropped his gun and crumpled to the ground with a groan, but the dirty hit wouldn't keep him down for long. I grabbed a piece of concrete from the rubble and slammed it into his temple. He immediately blacked out.

"Don't move!" the second soldier shouted, still aiming his gun at Dad. "Don't come any closer, or I'll shoot him!"

I raised my hands above my head, showing him that my gun was not at my disposal. "Come on, man. It's two against one now. Let him go, and run back to Base One before Buddy realizes that you're missing."

The soldier's mouth went slack. "How did you know—?"

He didn't get a chance to finish his sentence. Dad grabbed the nose of his gun and yanked him forward. The soldier lost his footing, and Dad easily flipped him onto his back. Then he took a cue from my book and knocked the soldier out with a piece of rubble. He dusted his hands off and sat back on his heels.

"Thanks for distracting him," he said. "I wouldn't have made it if I was out here on my own."

"Thanks for not killing him."

"You asked nicely. Let's keep moving."

We combed through the buildings, on the hunt for trapped survivors, but found nothing but more death. I recognized every face. Ludo and Jax had left this world hand in hand, both of them splayed out near DotCom. Nita's body still rested in the hallway of the med bay, where a shooter had taken her out from behind. If she had been positioned a little bit off center, the gunner would have taken me out instead. I closed her eyes before catching up with Dad.

"We need to clean this place up if we're ever going to rebuild it," I said, wiping moisture from my eyes. "All of these bodies are going to poison the ground and the water supply."

"Let's focus on what's in front of us for now," Dad said, leading the way out of the med bay. Outside, he gazed up at the cabin on the hill. Unlike the other buildings, it had survived mostly intact, with the exception of a few bullet holes that ripped splinters from the logs.

We walked up the hill with heavy feet and low expectations. I had not yet returned to my childhood home despite living mere inches from it for the past few months. I wished that Dad's charade with Sylvester hadn't kept me from exploring it again. The front door was bashed in. Base One had raided the place. The handmade furniture was overturned, the cabinets were open and barren, and the linens had been stripped from the beds. Dad searched every corner of the place, but there was no sign that a sixteen-year-old boy had been here during the attack.

"Damn!" Dad said. "Where are you, Sylvester?"

"What about the bunker?" I asked him. "Camp Haven never used it, but if you raised Sylvester like you raised me, he would have known it was there. He could have waited out the attacks there."

A glimmer of hope crossed Dad's face. "Genius. Let's go check."

The entrance to the bunker was at the bottom of the hill, across from DotCom, but a large wooden support beam, charred at either end, lay across the doors. If someone was inside, they wouldn't be able to get out on their own. Dad grunted as he tried to shift the beam himself.

"Give me a hand, George?"

I took the other end of the beam and lifted it up. Together, we hauled it away from the bunker's entrance. Dad brushed snow from the metal ring that served as a handle and yanked the rusty door upward. It creaked open, and we peered into the darkness below.

"Got a flashlight?" I asked Dad, stepping inside. "I'll go check for him."

He handed over a hand crank lantern. "Be careful."

The bunker was the stuff of nightmares. There was nothing down here. It was all gray reinforced concrete that could probably survive a trench war. I shuddered as I lifted the lantern and squinted into the gloom. This place brought back claustrophobic memories.

"Sylvester?" I called, my voice echoing off the walls. "Are you in here? It's Georgie, Amos's daughter."

I reached the opposite end of the bunker, but there was no sign of another living, breathing human being there. I jogged back toward the square of light at the entrance and climbed out.

"He's not down there," I told Dad, breathing hard as I slammed the doors shut. If I never had to go in the bunker again, it would be okay with me.

"Did you check all the way in the back?" Dad pressed.

"Yes. He's not there."

"Damn it!" Dad slammed his fist against a crumbling wall, sending it tumbling over. "Damn it, damn it, damn it!"

"Dad, calm down," I said. "There's no sign of his body, so that's a good thing, right? Maybe he got out of here before Base One could get to him."

"Or he's buried under a pile of rubble somewhere."

"Possibly."

I pulled the balaclava off my mouth and nose to take an unfiltered breath of air. The fabric bunched around my neck, pressing against my throat like a tightening noose. I took it off entirely and shoved it into my backpack. As I zipped the pack up again, something on the ground caught my eye.

"Hey, Dad. Look."

It was an unlit match, the red head of it bright against the white snow. A few feet away, another crimson dot stood out against the terrain.

"It's a trail."

24

The matches were spaced at roughly five-foot intervals, leading through the wreckage of Camp Haven, past the demolished front gate, and into the woods below. We paused where Camp Haven ended and the tree line began. As far as the eye could see, the matches continued down the mountain.

"Do you think it's Sylvester?" I asked Dad, shielding my eyes from the sun as it pierced through the clouds.

"It could be," he said. "But I don't understand why he would go down the mountain instead of up. Why didn't he just return to the house?"

"Maybe it wasn't safe to do so," I suggested. "What's the plan?"

Dad shrugged his shoulders so that his backpack rested more comfortably. "I guess we follow the matches. Even if it isn't Sylvester, someone laid them out for a reason. We might as well see if we can help them."

Without looking back, we started down the mountain, picking up the matches to use for ourselves as we went. The trail wound through the trees in a zigzag pattern to make up for the steep elevation. As we followed it farther into the woods, the distance between each match began to lengthen, as if the person dropping them had started to run out of trail markers. Eventually, the trees began to thin out and the ground leveled off. Dad stopped short, though there were still a few matches ahead of us.

"I don't like this," he said. "We're nearly to the bottom of the mountain, too close to the city. Sylvester would never have come down here. It's too dangerous."

From our position, I could see the buildings at the edge of Denver, looming toward the horizon. Like Dad, I had no desire to return there. There was too much strife and devastation to behold. I preferred the quiet safety of the mountains, but my curiosity prodded me forward.

"There are only a few more matches," I said. "We've come this far. There's no point in turning back now. Besides, what if it is Sylvester, and he's hurt out here, and we don't bother to look for him? We can't risk that."

Dad rubbed his fingers against each other, like wiping dirt off of them, in a nervous tic. The fabric of his gloves whispered together. "I suppose you're right. We should try and pick up the trail where it left off."

"Good. We're agreed." I walked forward, picking up the remaining matches out of the snow save for the very last one. It lay right at the edge of the tree line. Beyond that, there were no signs of the person who had dropped it.

"No footsteps," Dad said, examining the surrounding snow. "No other tracks."

I had to step out of the shadows in order to reach the final match, but as soon as I did, I knew that I had made a mistake.

Something shifted and clicked beneath my boot. A loop of rope, masked by the snow, caught around my ankle and tightened. I was yanked off my feet as the trap's counterweight dropped, and I dangled upside down, fifteen feet above the ground.

"George!" My father checked the rest of the area for other traps before looking up at me. "Are you okay?"

"A little woozy," I replied as the blood rushed to my head. The rifle slipped from my grasp and landed in the snow below. My backpack hung heavily around my neck. "Otherwise, I'm fine."

Dad checked the counterweight, a large sack of sand tied to the opposite end of the rope, and chuckled.

"What's so funny?" I demanded, but it was difficult to sound authoritative while I swayed back and forth from the rope with a burning red face.

"Oh, I'm just having a laugh at you," Dad said, fiddling with the knot that attached the rope to the counterweight. "If you had taken my advice, you wouldn't have stepped into that trap."

"And we wouldn't have a lead on Sylvester either," I shot back. "Can you hurry up? I feel like my head's going to explode."

As Dad whipped out a knife to make quicker work of the rope, I revolved slowly on the spot, turning toward the city then toward the woods then back to the city again. When Dad was in my sights again, his back to the city as he sliced at the rope, my breath caught in my throat.

"Dad, look out!"

It was a moment too late. A wooden baseball bat crashed across Dad's head, dropping him instantly to the ground. A group of five individuals, all wearing solid black from head to toe, had snuck up on us from the city. One of them took up Dad's position at the counterweight, peering up at me as he worked the rope free. In an instant, I plummeted toward the ground and landed in the snow. The fall knocked the breath out of my lungs. Before I could scramble to my feet, I was surrounded.

"She's definitely one of us," one of the cloaked people said.

"And the man?"

"They're traveling together," said the first. "It would be a gesture of good faith to bring them both in. She'll be more accepting of us that way."

"I'm sorry," I said, staring up at the masked faces. "Who are you?"

I received no answer, but rather got a blow to the back of the head with the same baseball bat that had taken out my father.

THE ACHE at the base of my skull disrupted my unintentional slumber, and my surroundings slowly swam into view. I lay in a fold-out metal cot with a thin mattress and scratchy blankets. The pillow beneath my head stank of goose feathers that had gotten wet and never dried out properly. The room was small and had no windows, more like a place for storing cleaning supplies than a bedroom. The outer wall was made of weathered gray stones, which meant the building was older than most of the others in Denver.

I touched my fingers to the bruise on my skull and winced. Whoever had swung the bat had gotten a nice piece of me. The skin was tender to the touch, and it hurt to look in either direction.

"You know, for once, a good 'please' might be nice," I grumbled as I sat up. "Instead of a head bashing."

"I couldn't agree more," another voice said from outside the door. There was a small window with no pane through which the voice spoke. "Unfortunately, others here feel that we need to take certain precautions to keep ourselves as safe as possible."

"Who are you?" I asked, experimentally rolling my neck out to either side.

The door opened, and a tall woman around my age entered the room. She had short dark hair and wore thick black glasses. She wasn't armed, and as far as I could tell, she didn't have any weapons on her person. I guess she wasn't expecting me to attack her in my current state, but even so, I found it ballsy that she didn't arm herself in these uncertain times. For good measure, I checked the room for my own weapons, but they had been confiscated from me while I was unconscious.

"My name is Caroline," the woman said, extending her hand to shake mine. "You're safe here."

I batted her hand away. "I was already safe before you nutcases came along and hit me over the head. Where's my father?"

"In the next room," she replied. "He, too, is recovering from his head wound, but he hasn't woken up yet."

"Well, did you check if he has a concussion?" I asked. "If he's still unconscious, you could have hurt him a lot worse than you hurt me."

"Our medical expert has examined both of you and declared that your wounds are superficial."

My head throbbed again. "Superficial, my ass. Where the hell are we?"

"You're in a church in Denver," Caroline said. "It's our safe house."

"And who exactly do you belong to?"

A man poked his head into the room. Like Caroline, he appeared to be a normal civilian. "Hey, Caroline? If she's awake, Marco wants to see both of them in the main hall."

"Thanks, Max," Caroline replied. "We'll be there in a few minutes."

Max took note of my aggravated expression. "Do you need some help?"

"No, I got it. Thanks."

"Alrighty." Max disappeared, leaving me and Caroline alone again.

"Okay, you need to fill me in," I said to her, attempting to stand. She rushed to my side and helped me up. "What the hell is going on here? Why did you bring me here?"

"I wasn't a part of the hunting party," Caroline said, looping my arm over her shoulder. "And as far as who we are, I can't tell you. That's for Marco to fill you in."

"Who's Marco?"

"You'll meet him in a few minutes."

The corridor outside my temporary bedroom was made of the same gray stone. Stained glass windows lined one side of the hallway, but each one was boarded up with two-by-fours and other pieces of scrap wood. My father emerged, supported by Max, from the next doorway. His eyes were a little cloudy, but he brightened when he saw me.

"George! You're alive."

"Of course she's alive," Caroline said. "We're not murderers."

"Could have fooled me," Dad muttered.

"Marco will explain everything," Max said.

"*Who's Marco?*"

Neither one of them answered. Instead, they continued to haul us down the corridor until we reached the door at the end. We pushed through to the other side, navigated a small passage, and emerged on the stage in the belly of the church. A group of thirty to or so people gathered in the pews below, each wearing an eager expression. The church itself had not been altered much, though it had been stripped of any religious affiliations, like the drapings over the altar, that were easily removable.

"What the hell...?" I muttered, looking out at the sea of faces as Caroline led me to a pair of chairs in the center of the stage. "This isn't some kind of ritual sacrifice, is it?"

"No, silly," Caroline said, sitting me down. "Sit tight. We're going to start in a few minutes."

Max helped my father into the chair next to mine. They didn't tie us down or secure our hands like I expected them to. If I wanted, I could spring up from my seat and make a run for it. Chances were I wouldn't get very far. The throbbing bump on the back of my head and the crowd below would probably stop me before I could reach the exit doors. I exchanged a glance with my father and saw the same truth in his eyes. We were going to have to wait out the madness for now.

A middle-aged man separated himself from the crowd and stepped up onto the stage. He was shorter than average, with wispy black hair swept back from a deep widow's peak. Like the others, he wore sensible clothing for the scenario outside: heavy duty cargo pants, an athletic sweatshirt, and black work boots. There was nothing to set him apart from the others besides the obvious respect that the rest of the crowd had for him. They fell silent as he approached us, as if waiting for him to approve of our presence.

"Welcome," he said, spreading his arms wide. "My name is Marco Coats. Please introduce yourselves to my family."

"Uh," I said. "I'm Georgie Fitz."

"And I'm her father, Amos," Dad finished. "Do you mind telling us exactly what's going on here?"

"Certainly," Marco answered. "We've rescued you."

"I don't think bashing us both in the head and taking us to an unfamiliar part of the city counts as rescuing us," I pointed out. "In fact, we were doing just fine. We have people of our own to get back to, so if you could just point us in the right direction—"

"It's not safe," Marco interrupted. "Outside these walls is a wasteland. Denver is in ruins, as is the rest of the world. I hope you will accept my apology for your injuries. It was important for us to relocate you without cluing you in on our location, just in case things don't work out."

"What things might that be?" Dad asked.

"Let me back up for a moment," Marco said. "It might be easier if I explain things from the beginning. You see, we are the Denver Legacies."

The crowd chattered as he announced their title. Some people even let out little whoops of enthusiasm.

"I'm sorry, the who now?" I asked.

"We are the few and far between who survived the destruction of the United States," Marco clarified. "We are the sons and daughters of the new world. We are the ones who were chosen to restart humanity."

Silence fell as he finished declaring the group's purpose. I let out an involuntary snigger. "Chosen by whom exactly?"

Marco lifted his palms to face upward, as if calling down a higher power from above. "By fate. By destiny. And you are one of us."

"What a load of bullshit," Dad said, rolling his eyes. "You do realize that you aren't the only group of people who survived out there, right? Humanity doesn't need to be rebuilt. It's still out there."

Marco's attention on me wavered, and he shifted his focus to my father. "Are you not a believer, sir?"

"A believer of what?" Dad said. "Whatever crap you've come up with to make yourselves feel better about the end of the world? No, I'm not."

"That's all right," Marco replied. "Many of our number were skeptical when they joined us. Once you recognize the advantages of being a Legacy, you will begin to understand our way."

"What exactly is your way?" I asked, wishing more and more that I hadn't been stripped of my weapons on the way in. If I had my rifle, Dad and I would already be out of here. "I'm a little confused."

"We are a community," Marco said. "We care for each other. We provide for each other. We carry the weight of this burden for each other. We search for survivors on the outside and bring them to the safety of our home."

When he put it that way, the Legacies didn't sound much different from Camp Haven. They were a group of people that had banded together in order to survive the effects of the EMP blast. They relied on each other, just as the members of Camp Haven had. The only strange part was this whole "chosen by fate" gag that Marco was spinning.

"Marco, no offense, but we have our own community," I said, trying to keep my voice as level as possible. "And we desperately need to return to it."

"Shh," Marco said as he put a finger to his lips. "There is no need to make up stories. We accept you here. You're one of us. We would like you to sit for the togetherness ritual."

"The what? Listen, Coats, is it?" I wasn't in the mood to play nice with this guy. I reserved first name basis for people I actually respected. "I'm not making up any stories. There are other survivors out there, people that I care about, and I can't hole up all nice and cozy in your church just because you think you're some kind of chosen one."

The entire congregation shifted forward as I stood up from my chair. I swayed, still groggy from the head injury, and Marco took the opportunity to plant me in a seated position again.

"You're confused." Marco traced my the outline of my cheek with his fingertip. "We are the only ones left on earth. You must stay here and become a Legacy like the rest of us."

"Don't touch her," Dad warned him.

"Perhaps you have misunderstood our intention," Marco continued as if he hadn't heard him. "We are not here to harm you. We are here to help you. Once we perform the togetherness ritual, you will be free to go about your business here as you see fit. You will have access to our food and clothing stores and a warm bed to sleep in. You will be a part of our family."

"We don't want to be a part of your damn family," Dad said.

"Wait a second," I cut in. "If we participate in this ritual, then we can do whatever we want?"

"As long as it benefits the Legacies," Marco said. "But yes. This isn't a prison. You are a free member of society."

"Okay," I said. "I'm in."

"George!" Dad threw me a shocked look. "What are you doing?"

"You heard him," I replied. "We're safe here. We would be

provided for. Come on, Dad. Warm food, a bed to sleep in at night. Sounds pretty good, right? We didn't have any of that out there in the woods."

Dad finally caught on to my scheme. It would be easier to hatch an escape plan from the Legacies' hideout once they trusted that we were a part of their group. Otherwise, they would be anticipating our rebellion. Dad gave me a slight nod.

"You have a point," he said, for Marco's benefit rather than mine. "It would be nice to stay warm for a while."

"See?" Marco smiled widely, displaying straight, white teeth that would make any post-apocalyptic dentist proud. "You're already beginning to understand what the Legacies do for one another. Shall we perform the ritual?"

"Er, what exactly does this ritual entail? Not that I'm necessarily against it," I added hastily at the look on Marco's face. "It's just that I'm a little hesitant to perform blood bonds or something like that, what with the state of the world at the moment. You understand, right?"

Marco's chuckle echoed through the church. "My dear girl, you continue to think us barbaric. The ritual is more of a welcoming ceremony. It's a simple linking of the hands, and once you complete our circle with us, then you are a Legacy yourself. No blood bonds required."

"Oh, thank goodness."

"Are you quite ready then?"

Caroline and Max took the stage again to help us out of the chairs and down the stage steps. The other members of the Legacies spread out, forming a loose circle. Marco stood to our left, Caroline and Max to our right.

"Let us join hands to welcome Georgie and Amos Fitz to the Legacies," Marco announced, and he extended his right hand across his body to grasp the left hand of the member next to him. One by one, the Legacies linked themselves together, working their way around the circle toward us. Max reached for

Caroline's hand, Caroline reached for Dad, and Dad reached for mine. Once Dad and I were connected, Marco offered his free hand to me. His palm was smooth and cool. When I took it, he loaned me what he might have thought was a warm smile, but his brilliant teeth made the expression look more lethal than welcoming.

"We are one," he said to the crowd.

"We are the Legacies," everyone replied.

Then, hands still linked, everyone lifted their arms and flipped around to face the outside of the circle. Once everybody's arms were uncrossed, we were permitted to drop each other's hands and roam free of the group.

"Congratulations," Marco said to us, patting first Dad then me on the back. "We're happy to have you here. If you like, Caroline would be happy to take you on a tour of our home. She can also find you extra sweaters if you like. It gets quite drafty in here."

As he drifted away to talk to the other Legacies, Dad leaned in and muttered in my ear, "Now what? We're no closer to finding Sylvester."

"Now we take the tour," I whispered back, "and figure out what the best way is to get the hell out of here."

Caroline approached us with a smile. "You ready for the tour?"

Dad pasted on a similar expression. "As we'll ever be."

THE CHURCH WAS A LARGE CATHEDRAL, complete with rectory and attached school. The Legacies only used bits and pieces of it for themselves. The place had room for several more people to move in. Each member of the group had a choice between their own bedroom and bunking in the group dormitory that was once meant for teenagers on religious retreats. Dad and I chose to stay in the rooms that we were assigned in, since the main hallway had an exit door at the end of it. Like Camp Haven, the church had been broken up according to usage. Caroline showed us the kitchen, where a few of the Legacies prepared lunch for the group, the community center, where several others played games or read books to keep themselves busy, and the storage rooms, where we picked new sweaters to replace the ones that we had ruined during our hike in the woods. Thankfully, my tactical jacket was still intact.

"Can I ask where you put our weapons?" I said to Caroline. "Those are incredibly important to us."

"You won't need them here," she replied. "We don't allow weapons on the premises. We have a no-violence policy."

"Unfortunately, policies don't always keep violence from happening," Dad chimed in. "I'd feel a lot safer with my crossbow in hand."

"Guns make people nervous," Caroline replied. "And you are safe here. Once you get to know the others, you'll realize that we're all just trying to protect one another." We arrived back at our rooms. "Do you have any other questions for me?"

"Nope," I said. "Thanks for the tour, Caroline."

She checked her watch. "Lunch will be served in the community center in a few minutes. You're welcome to eat there or pick up your food and eat elsewhere. See you then."

"Thanks," Dad added.

As soon as she turned the corner toward the community center, I faced my father. "All right, let's get the hell out of here."

"What about my crossbow?" he asked as I ushered him toward the exit door at the end of the corridor. "It's not like those things are just lying around. We can't go out there unarmed."

"I recognize this church," I told him. "It's toward the edge of the city, and if I'm not mistaken, there's a sporting goods store around the corner."

"That place will be completely cleaned out, you know that."

I peeked in the window of each door as we passed it, hoping that we might happen upon wherever the Legacies hid the rest of our things. "Do you want to find Sylvester or not? We have to get out of here as soon as possible. That means sacrificing our weapons. All we have to do is make it out of the city alive. Then we can go back up to Camp Haven and raid the stockroom there. I'm sure we can find a few leftover rifles."

"If Base One didn't raid the weapon stash too," Dad said.

The exit door was only a few paces away. "Guess we're taking our chances—whoa!"

Dad grabbed the back of my jacket and yanked me away from the door that I'd just pushed open. I caught my breath and took another look at the outside, wondering if I'd been seeing things correctly. Sure enough, there was a massive pit, at least ten feet deep, directly beyond the doorstep. At the bottom, jagged pipes and debris promised a painful landing. If Dad hadn't pulled me back, I would have strolled right into the hole.

"That's not intentional, right?" I said, trying to slow my panicked breathing. "I mean, it probably happened because of the EMP, don't you think?"

"EMPs don't cause big holes to open up in the ground," Dad said. "This was definitely intentional. No wonder all of the Legacies are so buddy-buddy. They don't have an option. Marco Coats has trapped them here."

25

J spent the rest of the day checking every exit in the building. It was a difficult feat, trying to avoid the Legacies who freely roamed the church, but I managed to make it to each door by dinner time. Every single one of them was inaccessible. Either they were boarded up or there was some kind of booby trap on the opposite side. Rationally, I knew that this might be the Legacies' way of protecting the church from potential threats, but what with the cult mindset that Marco inspired, I was more inclined to believe Dad's point of view. Marco Coats was trying to keep the Legacies from getting out.

I skipped lunch, but when dinner rolled around, I figured it was best to keep myself fed. Not to mention, I was curious to see what kind of meals that the Legacies came up with. Back at Camp Haven, we spent months gathering wild game and other food sources to make sure that we were prepared for winter. Were the Legacies on par with Camp Haven's talents?

In the community center, I joined the short line of people waiting to be served and looked out at the tables. Dad was already working on making friends. He sat at a table with a few Legacies that were closer to his own age, looking quite at home as he scooped soup from his bowl. This was our plan now, to blend in as best as we could in order to get information from the people around us. I just didn't expect Dad to be the one to pull it off so quickly. He had suffered from agoraphobia for half of my life, but if he was a stranger to me, I never would have known. He chatted lightheartedly with the others. The only evidence of his discomfort was the way he rapidly tapped the heel of one boot beneath the table, restlessly jiggling his leg up and down.

The food was canned. I could tell by the mushy texture of the noodles in the soup, as well as the dull color of the green beans. The Legacies weren't quite like Camp Haven then. They got their food from somewhere else, which meant that they would eventually run out of it.

With my tray in hand, I looked around the community center for a place to sit. Half of me wanted to join my father at his table, but I knew I wouldn't fit in with older crowd of Legacies. I spotted Caroline sitting on her own at a table in the corner, her face buried in a book. I headed toward her.

"Mind if I sit here?" I asked.

She glanced up. "Not at all."

I pulled out the chair opposite her and got comfortable. She immediately returned to her book, brow furrowed in concentration. "What are you reading?"

She lifted the book so that I could read the title. It was Cat's Cradle by Kurt Vonnegut.

"That's seems appropriate," I said. "Isn't that book about a made-up religion and the end of the world?"

Her eyes lifted from the page. "The Legacies haven't made up their own religion."

"You guys made camp in a church."

Caroline sighed, bent the corner of her page to mark it, and closed the book. "Look, I know this place seems weird, okay? I thought the exact same thing when they brought me in, but in my opinion, it's better to be alive and weird than normal and dead. Wouldn't you agree?"

I lifted a spoonful of soup like a toast to her words. "I guess you have a point. How long have you been a part of the Legacies?"

"About a month," she replied. "I was nearly dying of hypothermia a few blocks from here. If it weren't for them, I would have been just another body on the street."

"So do you believe in all of this stuff?" I asked her, blowing cool air across the surface of the soup. "Do you really think that the Legacies were chosen by some higher power to repopulate the earth?"

She made a face. "I have no urge to help repopulate the earth with any of the people here, but I'm happy to go along with whatever Marco believes if it means I get food to eat and a warm, safe space to sleep at night."

"So you don't believe it?"

Caroline looked around to make sure that no one else was within earshot. "No one says this out loud, but most of us don't buy into all that chosen ones stuff. Some do—the older folks mostly—but I think that's because it's easier to have something to believe in at the end of the world rather than constantly reminding yourself that nothing really matters. If I have to call myself a Legacy and participate in silly group meetings to earn my place here, then I'm okay with that."

"That's a relief," I said. "I'm glad someone here had the same idea that I did. My dad and I have been living in the mountains ever since the EMP hit, but our camp got trashed and we ran out of supplies."

"So you came into the city to look for more?"

"Not exactly." I let the noodles on my spoon splash back into the bowl and fished out a piece of chicken instead. "Hey, I couldn't help but notice that all the exits are blocked off here. What's up with that?"

"Marco says it's to protect us from people trying to get in from outside." She broke a piece of cornbread in half and offered it to me. "Here, eat this. It's more appetizing than the soup."

"Thanks. Do you believe Marco?"

"To a point," she replied. "Honestly, I have no desire to go outside—there's a protected courtyard here if I want to get some sun—so it doesn't bother me much. Besides, I don't see a reason why Marco would want to keep us in here."

"Maybe he likes feeling powerful," I suggested.

"I don't doubt it."

"So if no one goes outside the church, where does this food come from?" I tried a bite of the cornbread. As promised, it was much easier to stomach than the bland, sodium-laden soup.

"Some of it was already here in the church's cache," she replied. "I guess the rest of it comes from outside."

"So between foraging for expired cans of food and looking for other survivors to add to your number, there are certain members of the Legacies that are allowed outside?" I asked, pretending to be absorbed in the chemical makeup of my cornbread. "How exactly do they make it in and out of the church without jumping into one of those pits that Marco's dug outside every door?"

Caroline picked up her book again and hid behind it. "I don't really know. I don't ask questions. I just live here."

I licked my spoon clean and used it to lower the book a few inches so that I could see Carolina clearly again. "That was a lie."

"How do you know?"

"I'm good at reading people." I leaned across the table and lowered my voice. "Listen, Caroline. You seem like you have a decent head on your shoulders. Can I share something personal with you?"

She perched the book on the edge of her lunch tray, still angled so it looked like she was reading it, and nodded.

"When I said that my dad and I have been living in the

mountains, I meant that we were staying at a self-sustaining compound home to about a hundred other people," I told her. "A few days ago, a rival camp stormed the place. Most of my friends are dead, and the others are missing. We followed a trail to Denver, hoping to locate one of them, but the Legacies took us before we could find him. He's a sixteen-year-old boy by the name of Sylvester. Have you seen or heard of him?"

She shook her head. "I usually keep to myself. I only helped bring you in because there aren't a lot of women here my age. If they brought a kid in, I haven't seen him."

"I just find it suspicious that the trail we were following ended right where the Legacies set up an overhead trap," I said, leaning back in my chair with a sigh. "Any thoughts on that? If the Legacies are so altruistic, why are they setting snares to collect more people?"

"How do you figure it was the Legacies?" she asked. "Someone else probably set that trap, and the Legacies saved you from it."

"Their heroic appearance was a little too coincidental for me," I replied. "Can you be straight with me? How do the Legacies get in and out of the building?"

Caroline fixed me with a hard stare. "I can't mess up here. Marco isn't all hugs and kisses. I've seen him kick people out of the church before for not adhering to the Legacies' standards."

"I won't tell a soul that you helped me," I promised.

"You swear?"

"I swear."

"Fine." She closed her book. "There's a group of Marco's closest friends that go out at night. My guess is they scour the city for extra food and supplies. They're damn good at it too. So far, we haven't run out of anything. From what I've witnessed, the exit is on the second floor of the rectory."

"The second floor?"

She shrugged and polished off the rest of her cornbread in

one bite. "My room is on the first floor. I hear them go up there, and then it's just silence until they come back. A second floor exit is the only thing that would explain it."

"Where's your room?"

"On the east side of the building," she replied. "The main staircase is blocked off though. Marco tells everyone that the wood steps are rotting."

"So there's another way up then?" I pressed.

"Yeah," she replied. "But you're not going to like where it is."

"Try me."

"It's just a guess," she said, "but I think they go up through the bell tower, the entrance of which is next door to Marco's bedroom."

Of course. The bell tower was situated in the worst place for sneakiness. I'd noticed the entrance near the back of the church during the welcoming ceremony, but hadn't thought much of it.

"I don't suppose Marco joins the other Legacies outside for their evening jaunts?" I asked.

"Nope. He waits for them to get back."

"Great," I muttered. "So I'll have to distract Marco somehow, follow his team up into the bell tower, get out of the church without being noticed—"

Caroline put her fingers in her ears. "Can you stop? I don't want to know how you plan to break the most basic of the Legacies' rules. That way, if they question me about it, I can honestly say I have no idea."

I put the last quarter of my cornbread on her tray before standing up with my own. "You've earned that back. Thanks for the tips."

I scraped my dishes clean and stacked the lunch tray on top of the others near the trash can. Then I passed by the table where my father sat, where he and his new friends guffawed over one joke or another.

"George!" he said, clapping me on the back. "I want you to

meet some of these fine folks. This is Jeffrey, Bing, and—wait for it—his name is George too!"

The other George, a muscular man with fading tattoos and a motorcycle gang-style beard, grinned and winked at me. "Your dad's a kick, sweetheart! You know he hasn't watched a football game in over fifteen years? We're catching him up on the odds. I'm thinking it's the Patriots again this year. God, I hate those bastards."

"Too bad the EMP put the NFL out of business," I said. "I don't think the Superbowl is going to happen anytime soon."

It was the wrong thing to say. Clearly, the older men at this table were living in an augmented version of reality. They preferred to believe that everything would go back to normal in a few weeks or months rather than face the truth of living in this church, eating canned food, with Marco Coats as their leader for however long it took to rebuild the city.

I cleared my throat. "But what the hell do I know? Dad, can I borrow you for a minute? I need to talk to you about something."

"Sure." Dad collected his tray, which he had polished clean of food. Somehow, he had managed to choke down all of his soup. "See you around, fellas."

"Find us for dinner, Amos," the other George said. "I'd like to hear more of your survivor tales. It's like a reality TV show."

"Will do, George."

I ushered Dad away from the others. We were among the first to leave the community center after lunch. Apparently, the Legacies were so starved for interaction with the outside world that they supplemented it with each other's presence instead. Just in case, I pulled Dad into a storage closet to keep our impending conversation from wayward ears.

"Did you find out anything from those guys?" I asked.

"Not yet," he replied. "I was buttering them up. All I figured out was that the three of them were part of the first group of Legacies, the ones that supported Marco from the start."

"That's good!" I said. "I'll know who to follow tonight."

"Tonight?" Dad bumped up against a broom and knocked it over. It ricocheted loudly off the storage room's door. "What's going on tonight? Who are you following?"

"Caroline told me that a group of Legacies goes out every night to look for food and supplies," I explained. "Apparently, they leave in and out through the bell tower and an exit on the second floor. I'm going to spy on them tonight. There's something fishy about this place. Denver is totally wrecked. I find it hard to believe that they've found enough food to feed everyone here without running into any trouble."

"I thought we were trying to get out of here," Dad said. "Not debunk the mystery of the Legacies' storeroom."

"We are," I agreed. "But I like to know what type of people I'm breaking bread with."

"Hang on," Dad said. "Isn't the entrance to the bell tower right near Marco's room?"

"Yeah, that's what I need you for."

WE PLAYED it safe for the rest of the day, engaging with the other Legacies as they went about their business at the church. Most of the time, they simply tried to keep busy. They worked far less to keep their compound running than we had in Camp Haven. What with all the canned food, there was hardly a kitchen to maintain. They didn't dry and store fresh meats or vegetables. Everyone cleaned their own space, and the Legacies kept a schedule of whose turn it was to clean out the toilets at the end of every day to avoid arguments. In their downtime, the Legacies played cards, read books, organized group sports or games in the courtyard outside, or hung out in the community center to drink tea and instant coffee. All in all, I had a hard time fathoming how laid back this group of people was about the current state of the world, but I also envied how easily they lived in comparison to those outside the church.

When dinner rolled around, a delicious meal of fried Spam and canned peas, I found Caroline in her corner, reading again. She was one of the few people who kept to herself at the church. When I sat down at her table without asking, she raised one eyebrow as she peered at me over the book cover.

"This is going to become a habit of yours, isn't it?" she asked.

"Hey, I thought you wanted friends," I said. "You were the one who told me that there weren't a lot of women here your age. I'm just trying to fit in."

"What's the point?" But she set her book down next to her tray of nearly finished food anyway. "You're leaving as soon as you can, aren't you?"

I pushed the cubed Spam around the tray, trying to convince myself to eat it. "I thought you didn't want to know."

"I don't."

She fell silent. Without conversation to occupy my mouth, there was no avoiding the Spam. With a wrinkled nose, I brought a cube of meat up to my lips and bit down. Shockingly, it wasn't as terrible as I thought it would be. In fact, it tasted like the bacon I used to mix into my omelets when I still had access to fresh eggs and a working stove.

"If you're going tonight, you should be extra careful," Caroline said.

"Why is that?"

"Because it's a new moon."

I speared another cube of Spam. "So? What, are the Legacies reverse werewolves or something?"

"No, but I think they take advantage of the darkness," Caroline explained in a low voice. "They always come back with more supplies after a new moon."

"Isn't that a good thing?"

"Maybe for the rest of us," she said. "But the last few times those guys have come back from a new moon night, they had blood on their hands."

I missed my mouth with the fork, and the Spam splashed into the mushy peas. "Now we're getting somewhere."

WHEN DARKNESS FELL and most of the Legacies had retired to their rooms, I crouched in my bedroom with my ear against the door, listening for any sign of movement out in the corridor. Around midnight, the sound of footsteps justified my aching knees. I peeked through the window. A group of five men, some of which I recognized from lunch that day, trotted past my room toward the main part of the church. They wore crude riot gear—chest plates, gauntlets, and helmets—made from whatever materials they had on hand, and each of them carried a gun in a holster around their waist. To finish off the strange look, each man wore a pair of black goggles around their neck.

"Night vision," I muttered. "Where the hell did they get those?"

I counted to thirty once the men had passed my door. Then I knocked a pattern against the adjacent wall that separated my room from my father's. Thankfully, it was made of plywood and particle board rather than the stones of the outer wall. A few moments later, my father knocked back, and I heard the door to his room creak open. I met him in the hallway.

"Look what I found," he said, handing over a nine millimeter handgun.

"Where did you get that?"

"From the other George," he replied, chuckling. "It was almost too easy. At dinner, I told him that I was always a gun guy. He showed me right to the room where they keep all of the weapons. He thought we were bonding. I couldn't swipe your rifle or my crossbow without getting noticed though. This is all I got."

"Is it loaded?"

He produced two clips from his pocket. "Here. Use it wisely."

I loaded the gun, ditched the empty clip, and slipped the spare one into my back pocket. "Thanks, Dad. This makes me feel a whole lot safer."

"I still don't like the idea of you going out there alone."

"What choice do we have? Are you ready? We're going to lose track of the Legacies if we don't hurry."

"Give me five minutes," he whispered, continuing down the hall. "As soon as you hear the diversion, make a run for the bell tower."

"What's the diversion?"

"You'll know it when you hear it."

He disappeared into the shadows at the end of the corridor, and I hid in the doorway of my room to wait. The next few minutes were excruciating. Every creak and or groan from the old building sent another shot of adrenaline rushing through my veins. I had no idea what I was doing here, or what would happen if and when I made it all the way up the bell tower and out of the church. All I knew was that I had to get out of the Legacies' compound before Marco Coats found a way to keep me and Dad here forever.

A sharp series of small explosions interrupted my train of thought. I ran down the corridor and ducked into an empty room close to the church's main hall. Marco's room and the bell tower were a little farther along, but the sounds were loud enough to rouse the Legacies from their beds, and I didn't want to draw attention to myself once they left their rooms. Sure enough, sleepy faces began to emerge from the hall to look around for the source of the noise.

"What is that?"

"Is that a bomb?"

Marco Coats himself ran right past my hiding spot, down the corridor toward his charges. "Everyone back to your rooms, please! There appears to be a disturbance in the courtyard. Remain inside."

As the Legacies took the advice of their leader, I ducked out of the empty room with a chuckle. Marco wasn't as quick on the uptake as everyone thought he was. I could tell from the poppy explosions that Dad hadn't done anything too dangerous. He'd simply rigged a couple of cherry bombs, which were completely harmless unless you got too close.

The entrance to the bell tower was locked from the opposite side. I rolled my eyes, checked that the hallway was clear, and aimed a massive kick at the door. The lock popped free, and the door sprang open. I stepped inside, closed the door behind me, and looked up. A rickety set of stairs wound around the inside of the cylindrical tower. At the very top, the church bells rested silently. It was a long way up.

"Ugh, please tell me I don't have to make it all the way to the top," I mumbled as I took the stairs two at a time. A few flights later, it became obvious that there was no entrance to the second floor from this area. Either Caroline was lying or misinformed. I continued all the way up, my legs aching in protest, and looked out of the first of four windows that allowed the bells' solemn tones to reach the rest of the city. From this height, it was easy to orient myself. The church was a few miles from the edge of the city. It wouldn't take long to reach the woods once we found a way out of the Legacies' grasp.

The drop from here to the ground was too far for the Legacies to jump. Rappelling down the bell tower was pretty much their only option, and I was relatively sure that the Legacies weren't doing that every night. I checked the next window, the one closest to the roof of the building.

"Bingo."

A rope ladder hung from the window, leading back down to

the lower eaves of the church. Carefully, I lowered myself through the window and hooked my feet through the first rung of the ladder.

"Don't look down, don't look down," I muttered as I began to climb down the ladder. I glanced at my boots to check the position of the next rung and accidentally got a glimpse of the space between me and the ground. I jerked my eyes back up. "Shit, I looked down."

When my feet landed firmly on the roof of the rectory, I let out a big breath. From here, I could see the parking lot of the church. Five people jogged across it. The Legacies' salvage party. If I didn't hurry, I would lose them.

The window directly beneath me was open. I lowered myself over the edge of the roof, dangling from the shingles, and kicked my legs back and forth to swing toward the window. Once I had enough momentum, I let go of the roof and jumped into the open window, rolling to a stop in the hallway. I got to my feet and followed the corridor to the opposite end. Another window. Another ladder.

"Here we go again," I said. Thankfully, this was the last leg of my escape. The ladder led into the parking lot. I sprinted across it, trying to catch up with the rest of the Legacies while keeping light on my feet. Caroline had been right about the new moon. The city was beyond dark. My eyes struggled to see the ground in front of me. I carried a flashlight on my belt, but I feared the light might expose me if I turned it on. No wonder the Legacies carried night vision goggles. As I cleared the church's property, I had to slow down or risk tripping over something in the dark. I paused, listening for the Legacies instead of looking for them. A tin can tinkled in the alley ahead.

"Way to go, Jeff," the first man said. I recognized his voice. It was the other George, Dad's new friend from lunch.

"It's just a soda can."

"Lock it down, will you? Let's keep moving."

I followed the voices, catching sight of the Legacies' silhouettes as they crept through the alley. It was slow going. I had to keep hidden, which meant trailing the group at a safe distance. I lost them once or twice in the shadows of the streets. The farther we traveled from the church, the more I wished I'd put a little more thought into my plan.

"There."

The Legacies stopped so suddenly that I almost knocked over a garbage can in my haste to find another hiding spot behind them. I crouched behind the can, listening to their whispered conversation.

"I see three," the other George muttered. I had no idea what they were looking at. The only thing in the area was an old gas station with all of its windows bashed in. "Anyone else?"

"No, boss."

"Let's go."

The other George and his team crept toward the gas station. They spread out, two to the left, two to the right, and one in the center. I slipped from my garbage can cover and snuck to their last position to watch. George silently counted down on his fingers. Each Legacy drew his gun. When George put his last finger down, they burst into action.

"Go, go, go!"

The team leapt through the windows of the gas station. Inside, three people sprang up from where they had been sleeping on the floor.

"Put your hands up!" Jeff ordered, brandishing his gun. "Hands up!"

The three people, two men and a woman if my limited vision wasn't deceiving me, obeyed. The other Legacies looted the gas station, tearing it apart until they found a small stash of nonperishable foods hidden beneath the register.

"Got it, boss!"

"Please." The woman's wavering voice carried out to my hiding spot. "Please, don't take our food. That's all we have left."

George shrugged. "Sorry, lady. We got people to feed too. You know what it's like. Every man for himself out here."

"You son of a bitch," one of the woman's companions snarled in George's face. He lowered his hands and stepped into George's personal space. "Who the hell are you to come in here and steal our food? Get the hell out!"

"I don't think so."

The man seized George by the throat. A second later, a gunshot went off. I flinched, and the woman screamed as the man crumpled to the floor. He was dead. George lifted his gun.

"Anyone else?"

The second man stepped forward, putting himself between George and the sobbing woman. George aimed at his head.

"Stop!" I yelled, springing up from my hiding place and sprinting toward the gas station. I leapt through one of the windows, grabbed the barrel of George's gun, and ripped the weapon out of his hands. "Stop, stop! They're innocent people!"

In the next second, the other Legacies aimed their own guns at me. I lifted the other George's weapon level with his head. Stalemate. He raised his hands.

"You're Amos's daughter," he said. "We just brought you in yesterday. What the hell are you doing out here?"

"Stopping you from killing anyone else," I replied, breathing hard. "These people are in the same boat that we are. They're trying to survive, and you're taking what little supplies they have for your own comfort. It's wrong."

"That's life," the other George snapped. "Give me back my gun."

"No."

One of the other Legacies aimed a sharp kick to my hamstring from behind. The muscle cramped, and my knee gave way. George pried his gun from my grip and patted me down.

He found the nine millimeter in my belt, along with the spare clip.

"I told Marco that you were going to be trouble," he said, sliding my gun into a spare holster. He grabbed me by the arm and hauled me to stand. "Get up. We're going back to the church. I love being right. Fellas, get the rest of the food and head out. We're going to have to call it an early night."

He pushed aside the survivors of the raid, who were too stunned by the violent robbery to do anything but watch as the Legacies dragged me outside. The church's bell tower loomed in the distance. My teeth clenched together as the other George pushed me through a mound of trash. I thought about climbing the numerous ladders of the church with the Legacies' supervision.

"Great," I muttered. "This should be a grand old time."

---

26

*G*etting back into the church was not a pleasant experience. George watched my every step, often grabbing me by the scruff of the neck or the back of my jacket to remind me that he was the one in control here. If the circumstances were different—if Dad weren't still inside the church—I would have figured out a way to knock George unconscious for his rough touch. As it was, I could only spit petty insults at my new bodyguards as they hauled me back to Legacy territory.

"Where's Marco?" Jeff asked when we reached the bottom of the bell tower. "He's usually waiting for us here."

George shook me by the collar of my coat. "Well? Answer the question!"

"How should I know, you bilge rat?" I said. "He wasn't here when I left to follow you morons."

George tightened his fingers around my throat. "Marco's always here. Tell me where he is before I strangle you right here and leave you in your father's bed for him to wake up next to in the morning."

"Fine," I gasped, eyes watering as they bulged out of my head.

George released me, and I massaged my bruised throat. "We set off a diversion in the courtyard. He's probably out there cleaning it all up."

George hauled me down the corridor. Before we could reach the courtyard, Marco himself came jogging in from outside.

"George!" he said, his eyes darting from the leader of the salvage group to me at their center. "What on earth? You should still be outside! Why do you have the girl with you?"

George kicked me down and deposited me at Marco's feet. "She followed us. Saw what we were doing."

"Oh, dear."

"You're full of shit," I said to Marco, forcing my aching legs to stand. "You preach all this crap about how the Legacies are the chosen ones, and then you send your men out there to kill innocent people and steal their supplies. Tell me, Marco, what makes those people matter less than the ones you've collected here?"

I didn't bother to keep my voice level. It rose and wavered, drawing the sleeping Legacies from their rooms for the second time that night. My father emerged from his bedroom as if he had been sleeping there all this time.

"What's going on?" he said, stepping between me and Marco. "What have you done to my daughter?"

"Nothing yet," George said. "But she broke the rules. That means she has to be punished."

I sidestepped my father to confront Marco again. "I want an answer, Coats. Why save some and condemn others? What criteria do you judge your survivors on?"

"You're delusional," Marco said calmly. "We are the only ones left. We are lucky to have—"

"Luck has nothing to do with it," I replied. "I watched your men go out and kill someone over a few cans of food. Do the rest of the Legacies know how you're feeding them?"

From the expressions on the faces that lined the hallway, I assumed that the answer was no. Marco's serene smile slipped.

"Not every person is fit for membership with the Legacies," he said. "They are chosen based on their ability to rebuild humanity."

"So you admit it then," I challenged. "*You're* the one choosing these people, not some bullshit version of fate or destiny. I bet you wished like hell that you hadn't chosen me."

Marco's eyes never left mine. "Gentlemen? Would you be so kind as to escort Miss Fitz to the main hall. I'm afraid George is right. She must accept the consequences of her actions. The Legacies do not tolerate disbelievers or insubordination."

"I don't think so," I said, and I drove my elbow up behind me, catching the other George under the chin. His teeth cracked together, and he dropped his gun to cradle his jaw. At the same time, my father aimed a blow to Jeff's solar plexus. Jeff doubled over, and Dad relieved him of his weapon as well. We fired in unison as the other Legacies attempted to restrain us. I caught Marco in the foot and another bodyguard in the leg as I sprinted down the corridor.

"Stop them!" Marco screamed, cradling his bleeding foot on the ground.

The Legacies closed in, chasing after us in their pajamas. We raced for the exit door at the other end of the corridor.

"What about the giant pit on the other side?" I yelled to Dad.

"Get ready to jump!"

He reached the exit first and swung the door open. I readied myself to leap off the edge, but it turned out that I didn't need to. Someone had laid wooden planks across the gap in the ground, creating a safe bridge from one end to the other. I ran across it.

"Dad, come on!"

When my father was clear, I yanked the wooden planks out of place so that they fell into the pit below. The Legacies piled up at the door, trapped in the church by their own doing. We left them there to stare at our backs as we ran away.

"This way," I said, gesturing around the back end of the church. "We need to get back to the mountains."

"Well, that was a kick," Dad huffed as we jogged through the alleys. I flipped on my stolen flashlight since we weren't lucky enough to have night vision goggles. "Though I kind of wish you'd given me a heads up. I'm not exactly dressed for hiking." He was wearing pajamas and boots, though he'd had the sense to steal a jacket from one of the Legacies on the way out.

"What a waste of time," I said. "That place was useless. I can't believe we got stuck in there for an entire day."

"I can't believe we made it out," my father said. "I'll be honest, I didn't think we were going to make that jump. It's lucky someone laid those boards over that pit."

"Yeah, lucky," I mused. "Either that, or someone else knew that we needed an alternate exit strategy."

"You think you made an ally in there?"

I thought of Caroline, quiet but stalwart. "Maybe. This way."

While Dad could find his way through the woods in a heartbeat, he wasn't the best at navigating the city. I led the way through the dark alleys and trash piles. Denver wasn't improving. It was stuck in its mourning process. It had been a few months since the EMP had taken out the country's entire electrical grid. I would have thought that recovery teams might have made it out to the major cities by now, but walking through Denver was like picking through a wasteland. It was less chaotic than it had been a few weeks ago. Either that, or we were close enough to the borders not to run into anyone too violent. Not many people had survived in the city. Those who had were smart enough to stay far away from others. We gave the few survivors that we collided with a wide berth, and they afforded us the same courtesy. Behind a dumpster, I found a stash of men's clothes that were about Dad's size. The pants were too long and dragged beneath the heels of Dad's boots, but they were better than the flannel pajama bottoms that he had left the church with. As he dressed and put his new gun away, he let go of a gusty sigh.

"I'm really going to miss that crossbow."

"Dad, it seems unhealthy to mourn a weapon," I said, peeking around the next corner. The trees were visible from here. We were getting closer and closer to home. Funny that I considered a camp in the woods my safe space now. It was like going back in time.

The space between the buildings gradually widened until there were no structures left between us and the wilderness. Once we reached the trees, we walked along the woods' border to look for the last match. I also kept my eyes peeled for other hidden traps. We didn't have the time to waste escaping it. It had snowed since the last time we were here, and the match had long since been covered up. Dad's nervous tic—rubbing his fingers together as if there were something stuck to the tips of them—came back in full force.

"I'm sorry," I said. "I know how much Sylvester means to you, but we need to get higher and make camp. We don't know if the Legacies are following us or not."

"You're right." He nodded, hiding his face from me. My father rarely cried. When I was young, he told me that crying was a display of weakness. Even now, upset as he was over Sylvester's continued absence, he didn't allow his waiting tears to fall.

As we headed for higher ground, uneasiness washed over me, an instinctual feeling that someone else's eyes were trained on my back. I scanned the area around us, sweeping the beam of the flashlight back and forth through the trees. The woods were quiet. The animals were gone, having migrated south or hibernating. The moon was absent, and the barren branches of the trees reached out like the fingers of inhuman nightmares. Nothing moved at all, so I tried to convince myself that the feeling of being watched was all in my head.

Our strength waned halfway to the ruins of Camp Haven.

We cleared a spot of snow, started a fire, and hunkered down for the night. We found fresh water at a half-frozen river nearby, but we had no food and no blankets to keep ourselves warm, so we huddled together and kept close to the fire. My toes felt like icicles in my boots and I wished for the warmth of Dad's stone house high above, but I eventually dozed off out of sheer exhaustion.

A few hours later, I woke up to the sound of a loud splash in the distance. The river's steady gurgle floated through the trees, but it was punctuated by faint cries of help. I shook my father awake.

"What?" He shot up from his prone position and looked around with bleary, wild eyes. "What is it?"

"Someone's out there," I whispered. "Near the river."

We listened for a moment. Another stressed whimper made its way into our campsite. Dad stood up, shook off the snow that had settled on his coat, and drew his gun. I followed suit, and we jogged silently through the trees toward the river, following the cries downstream.

The water came into view, gray and icy as it rushed down the mountain. The current was strong enough to float large chucks of ice along like miniature icebergs. I swept the beam of the flashlight along the river, but the cries had stopped, and there were no signs of the person who had made them. Then, out of nowhere, a dark-haired boy broke through the surface of the water a mere five feet from where we stood on the bank. He drew in a desperate gasp of air before the current overtook him again.

"It's Sylvester!"

We broke into a sprint, following Sylvester as the river swept him swiftly downstream. The current was so rough that he struggled to keep his head above the water. Occasionally, a block of ice slowed his descent, but we weren't fast enough to pluck him from the river. Each time we got close, he disappeared, and we lost track of him again.

"We need to get ahead of him," I called to Dad, who ran alongside his surrogate son and shouted encouraging words. I looked downstream. Sylvester was rapidly approaching a drop in the river up ahead. It was a short fall, but the rocks in the water below would make for a rough landing. A massive tree had fallen over right before the river dropped off, its trunk propped over the water. "Stay with him!"

"George, where are you going?"

I sprinted along the bank as fast as I could, scrambling over large rocks and squeezing between the trees that lined the river. I ripped through the dead branches of a low bush, drew ahead of Sylvester, and put on a final burst of speed. When I reached the fallen tree, I pulled myself up by its roots to the makeshift bridge over the water. Then I flattened out on my stomach, the bark rough through my clothes, and dangled my hand over the river. Sylvester was heading right toward me at a breakneck pace.

"Grab my hand!" I shouted.

Sylvester reached out. For one heart-stopping second, I thought that the river would rush him right past me and over the rocks, but my adrenaline kicked in. I seized Sylvester's wrist, and he took mine, locking our hands together as the current tried to drag him off. With all of my upper body strength, I hauled him out of the river and dragged him onto the log by the back of his sopping sweater. He trembled violently as I half-carried him off of the tree and laid him down on the bank.

Dad caught up with us and knelt beside the teenager. "Sylvester!"

The kid's lips were blue, and his face was so drained of color that the veins beneath his eyes were visible. "D-D-Dad?"

My stomach plummeted at the word. This kid had been calling my father his for the past several years. I wondered if he had had a more pleasant upbringing than my own.

"You're alive," Dad gasped, catching the boy up in a hug. "Oh, thank God. I thought you were dead. I thought you didn't make it out of Camp Haven."

Sylvester tried to reply, but his chattering teeth made it impossible for him to form full sentences. "S-s-still h-h-ere."

"We need to get him back to camp," I said. "He's freezing."

Dad picked Sylvester up from the ground and carried him through the woods in his arms. Sylvester's long limbs, which he had not yet grown into, dangled from Dad's grasp, as though he didn't have the strength to control them. At the camp, I hurriedly stoked the fire to encourage a bigger flame. We got Sylvester out of his damp clothes, laid them out to dry, and dressed him in Dad's spare pajamas from the church. Even so, he shivered so much that he looked like he was trying to vibrate into a different dimension.

"His pulse is racing," I muttered, pressing two fingers against the inside of his wrist. I picked up his hand. The tips of his fingers were turning blue. "Dad, he's hypothermic. We have to find a way to warm him up and fast."

Dad held Sylvester closer, using his own body heat to warm his son, and stared up the incline of the mountain. "The house is too far away. We'll never make it up there in time."

"The city's closer," I said. "I can run back in and find supplies."

"No." Dad rocked Sylvester back and forth like an oversized child. "It's too dangerous for you to go alone."

"I have to," I said. "Do you want him to die?"

"N-not d-d-dying," Sylvester muttered.

"I hate to break it to you, kid, but you will be if we don't get your temperature up as quickly as possible," I told him.

"What makes you think you'll be able to find anything useful in the city?" Dad challenged. "The place has been picked clean. You would have to raid someone else's camp, and that's asking for trouble. Even then, you'd have to find a camp to raid first."

"But we already know of one," I reminded him. "The Legacies."

It seemed counterintuitive to return to the group of people that we had just spat in the face of in order to ask for help, but Sylvester's condition left me with no other option. I couldn't let the kid die. It would bury my father. As I traversed the city, following the same path in that we had taken out, I kept a lookout for anything I could make use of. Unfortunately, all I could find were a few pages of old newspaper, good for bunching up to use as personal insulation, but not the best for warding off hypothermia. The church loomed ahead. Candlelight glowed in one or two of the windows, but the rest of the building was dark. After the excitement of our escape, I hoped that Marco Coats and his minions had taken the rest of the night off.

I circled the church to look for the best way in. The bell tower was off limits. There was no way I could take a shot at getting past Marco's bedroom twice in one night. Ultimately, I decided on the door that we had used for our own hasty exit. The wooden planks that someone had so kindly dropped for our escape plan were still there, propped up against the edge of the pit. All I had to do was haul them out of the hole and position them across the top of it again. I tiptoed across the rickety boards and pressed my ear against the door. There were no sounds on the other side, so I cautiously entered the building.

The hallway was deserted. Marco hadn't bothered to station guards anywhere. Perhaps the bullet hole in his foot had distracted him from his leadership abilities. Either that, or he had lost all of the competent ones in the fight. Smears of blood stained the floors and walls. The majority of it had been mopped up, but the Legacies couldn't entirely erase the losses they had

ALEXANDRIA CLARKE

suffered that night. Maybe it would make them think twice before killing other people for their own benefit. I doubted it.

I crept down the hallway, keeping light on my toes, and knocked on a door that was a few rooms away from my temporary bedroom. A face peeked out through the window. Caroline's eyes widened. She drew the door open, grabbed the front of my jacket, and yanked me inside.

"What the hell are you doing back here?" she whispered. "Are you insane? If Marco finds out that you stuck around, he'll kill you!"

"I'm pretty sure Marco was a dentist in his former life, so I don't think he has the stuff for murder."

"I wouldn't be so sure," Caroline said.

"He's got a bullet hole in his foot," I reminded her. "He wouldn't be able to catch me anyway. I need your help."

She let out a small laugh. "You need *my* help? No way. My reputation is already on the rocks here. If they figure out that I was the one who told you about the salvage group and the bell tower, I'm dead meat. Not happening."

"But it was you, wasn't it?" I asked her. "You were the one who set the planks down over the pit outside the exit door. You knew that we would need another way to get out of the church."

Caroline paced back and forth, but the room was so small that she had to change direction after every three steps. "Fine. Yes, it was me."

"So you've already helped me once," I said. "You're not one of them, Caroline. You're not really a Legacy. You put someone else before yourself because you saw that they were in trouble and needed help. That's an amazing quality to have, and it would be great if you could access that quality again."

"What do you need anyway?" she asked. "I thought you would be halfway up the mountains by now."

"We were," I told her. "And then we found the person that we came down here to look for. The only problem is that he fell

398

into a freezing cold river and now he's dying of hypothermia. We need supplies. Clothes, food, warming blankets if you have them. Oh, and our weapons back. My dad loves that stupid crossbow."

Caroline stopped pacing to cross her arms and fix me with a steady stare, as though she was trying to figure out if helping me again would be worth the hassle.

"Please, Caroline. The kid's only sixteen. He doesn't deserve to die out there in the cold."

She slid her feet into a pair of slippers and drew a coat on over her pajamas. "Fine. Follow me. And be quiet, for Pete's sake."

"Thank you so much," I whispered.

We snuck out of the room and hurried up the hallway. Caroline's slippers were silent against the stone floors, but the thump of my boots echoed if I moved too quickly. She shushed me multiple times, but we made it to the storage rooms near the community center. Caroline moved swiftly, searching through cardboard boxes full of spare clothes. She stuffed everything into an empty duffel bag.

"We don't have warming blankets," she muttered, as she rolled up a wool comforter and added it to the duffel bag. "But we do have a ton of those disposable hand warmers. If you use enough of them, you should be able to get his body temperature back up." She located the box of said warmers and dumped them into the duffel.

"Did I mention how grateful I am to you right now?"

"Yeah, yeah. Keep moving."

She led me to the kitchens next, where she plucked cans and boxes from the shelves. We couldn't take too much. Otherwise, Marco and the others would notice that someone had stolen from them. After the kitchen, I followed Caroline to another room with a locked door. She knelt down and picked the lock with a hair pin from her pocket then twisted the handle free. It was the weapons room, stocked full of stolen guns and other explosives.

"I didn't peg you for a lock picker," I said, searching the room for Dad's crossbow and my rifle. There were rows upon rows of pistols, rifles, grenades, and body armor. No weapons, my ass.

"I got kicked out of military school a while back," she replied. "But not before I learned a few useful skills."

"What did you do to get kicked out of military school?"

"You don't want to know."

"Aha!" I grinned in triumph as I extricated Dad's crossbow and bolt quiver from the other weapons on the wall. My rifle was nearby as well. I loaded it with the ammunition from the Legacies' stash. Then I slung the crossbow across one shoulder, the bursting duffel over the other, keeping my hands free to aim the rifle if need be.

"Got everything?" Caroline said. "Let's get you out of here."

Easier said than done. Marco, his foot wrapped in several layers of bandages, waited for us on the other side of the door with a gun in hand.

"Heard your door open, Caroline," Marco said, glaring at her. "We'll talk about the punishment for your treason later."

On a whim, I locked my elbow around Caroline's neck and dragged her away from the door to the armory. She struggled against my grip, clawing at my arm, as I placed the rifle against her temple.

"Relax, the safety's on," I muttered to her under my breath. Then I spoke to Marco and his cohorts in a clearer tone. "Don't blame her. I forced her to show me to the storage rooms. I threatened to kill her. Unless you want another dead Legacy on your hands, I'd back the fuck up and let me out of this hellhole."

Marco hesitated, his eyes darting between my cold expression and Caroline's terrible face. I had to give him credit. He obviously cared about her. Otherwise, he would have already taken the shot. I backed slowly toward the hallway that led to the safest exit. Marco, leaning heavily on his good foot, limped after me, his gun trained on my head. I grinned as I moved swiftly into the next corridor. He couldn't keep up with me.

Unfortunately, he wasn't the only one awake. I failed to check the next hallway for danger and ran straight into the chest of another Legacy. The man was massive. The top of my head didn't even draw level with his chin.

"Oh shit."

"Stop her!" Marco yelled. "She's stolen from us!"

I released Caroline and ducked under the monstrous man's outstretched arms before they could close around me. That was the best thing about fighting an opponent that was larger than you. It took them a lot longer to move their bulk around. I darted around to the man's left, but he stuck his foot out at the last second. My boot caught, and I went flying, landing face first on the stone. I heard rather than felt my nose break. There was no time to contemplate the stars flashing in front of my eyes or the blood streaming down my chin. I scrambled to my feet and rushed for the door, but Marco had caught up with me. He yanked on the duffel bag, the strap of which tightened around my neck. I choked against it, then whirled around and aimed a punch down the center of Marco's face. Another crack echoed against the stone walls, and the skin of my knuckles split as they made contact with Marco's nose and teeth. He released his hold on me and doubled over with a groan.

"You broke my nose, I break yours," I said, spraying him with blood. "Guess that makes us square." I paused at the exit door to look back at Caroline, who had convinced the other Legacy not to follow me. "You're better than this place. If you ever want to get out of here, come find me."

With that, I leapt over Marco's quivering form, kicked open the exit door, and escaped into the black night with my haul.

2 7

*B*y the time I made it back to the campsite, Sylvester was bundled up in the rest of Dad's clothes, and Dad was down to his long underwear. The fire roared dangerously bright. If anyone else was camping nearby, they definitely would have spotted us. It was a risk that Dad was willing to take to save Sylvester's life. When I stepped into the clearing, he raised the handgun.

"Dad, it's me!"

"Jesus, George. Your nose!" He dropped the gun and wrapped his arm around Sylvester again. The kid's eyes were hardly open, like he couldn't make sense of the world around him. "Did you find anything?"

"As a matter of fact..." I dropped the duffel to the ground, along with the rifle and the crossbow. "I did."

"My crossbow!" Dad said. "How did you get all of this?"

"With a little help from the same person that got us out of there in the first place." I ripped open the duffel back and threw a pair of snow pants and a jacket to Dad. "Put those on. How's he doing?"

"He's hanging in there," Dad said, only moving from

Sylvester once I had come to take his place. "But his body temperature is still too low."

I ripped open a packet of hand warmers and placed them at even intervals over Sylvester's body. Then I wrapped him in the wool comforter and tucked it in until he looked like a gray, over-sized human burrito. I stuck another warmer into a knit hat and pulled it on over Sylvester's head.

"There we go," I said, rubbing the kid's arms to help get the blood flowing. "We'll get you warmed up soon, kid. Don't worry."

"Come here, George," Dad said. "Let's have a look at that nose."

I left Sylvester's side to let the hand warmers do their work and joined Dad near the fire. He doused the corner of a spare T-shirt with water from the canteen we had filled at the river and began dabbing at my nose. The blood had dried up and caked around my nostrils and chin. Dad worked to clean it off, trying to avoid jostling the break.

"It's not too bad, but we're going to have to set it if you want to breathe properly for the rest of your life," Dad said, rinsing the blood off the T-shirt for the third time. "You ready?"

"No."

He took my face in his hands and placed his thumbs on either side of my nose. "Counting down from three. Three, two—"

He shoved upward before he got to one, and my face felt like it might explode from the pressure, but when the bone popped back into place, I felt immediate relief.

"Ow."

Dad examined his handiwork. "Sorry. It'll have to do for now."

"I'm okay with that." I dug through the duffel bag and tossed him a can of Spaghettios. "Eat that. You look pale."

He punctured the top of the can with his knife and slurped

the mushy noodles out of the roughly cut opening. I opened my own can and tapped it against his.

"Here's to a disgusting breakfast and a beautiful sunrise," I said, lifting the can up. The sky was just beginning to lighten, and the horizon was a beautiful lilac color.

"Here's to you," Dad added. "I can't believe you pulled that off. I'm assuming that Marco was the one that gifted you with the broken nose?"

"One of his big, dumb Legacy bros, actually," I said. "Don't worry. I made sure Marco and I had matching wounds before I left."

Dad chuckled. "Good. He deserves it. Thank you."

I fished a wayward piece of pasta from the lip of my can. "For what?"

"For risking your life to save Sylvester's," Dad said. "You don't know him at all, and you willingly put yourself in danger to make sure that he was all right. Twice. First at the river, then at the church."

"Well, I know how much he means to you," I muttered. "Found family is just as important, sometimes more, as the people who you're related to by blood." I checked on the kid again, relieved that he had finally stopped shivering. "The important thing is that we got Sylvester back. One down, two and a half to go."

"And a half?"

"Pippa's baby."

"Ah." He took another chug of pasta.

"You're having second thoughts, aren't you?" I asked him.

"About what?"

"About figuring out how to get my friends out of Base One."

"George—"

I plunked my half-empty can into the dirt. "I knew it. I knew I couldn't count on you for something like this. I held up my end of the bargain, Dad. I put off rescuing my friends so that we could go back to Camp Haven and find Sylvester. Well, we found him, and he's safe, so now it's your turn to help me for once in your goddamn life."

Dad wrapped another coat around himself. "George, I'm doing my best here, okay? I'm trying to be realistic."

"You promised!"

Sylvester stirred. "Dad?"

Dad wasted no time in taking the opportunity to put off our conversation. He rushed to Sylvester's side. "Hey, buddy. You had us scared shitless for a while there. How are you feeling?"

"Hot," the kid muttered. Thankfully, his lips were beginning to pink up again. He rolled side to side, his arms trapped beneath the blanket. "Why am I wrapped up like a crazy person in a psych ward?"

"You were hypothermic," I told him, untucking the corners of the blanket to free his arms. "We were trying to get your body temperature back up to normal."

Sylvester grasped my hand in his, and I was grateful to note that his skin was warm against mine. "You saved me. You're the one that pulled me out of the river."

"Yeah," I said. "Do me a favor though? Avoid any half-frozen bodies of water from here on out, okay?"

"You got it."

"What happened out there, Sylvester?" Dad asked. "When did you get out of Camp Haven? Were you the one that left the trail of matches down to the city?"

Sylvester took the can of Spaghettios from Dad and swallowed a mouthful. "Slow down, Dad. My brain's still thawing out. I left the cabin and got into the bunker as soon as the explosions went off. I probably should have tried to find a way to save a few of the others, but I was honestly too freakin' scared. I waited down there until the explosions and the screaming stopped. When I finally came out, Camp Haven was a graveyard." His eyes glazed over as he stared into the fire, and I knew that he was watching his memories rather than the flames. "I didn't know what to do. The soldiers had taken the survivors north, toward your house. I couldn't make it up to you without them noticing me. And I couldn't stay in Camp Haven either. I figured the only way to survive would be to find supplies in the city, so I headed down. I dropped the matches in case something went wrong. You'd know where to find me."

"Except you weren't there," I reminded him.

"Yeah, I ran into some trouble," he said. "Someone had set up a trap. I noticed it before I walked into it. The person who set it didn't like that. They chased me away from the city, but I lost them in the woods."

"The Legacies," Dad muttered, rolling his eyes. "What happened next?"

"Got lost," Sylvester said. "I spent the day trying and failing to retrace my footsteps. Then I heard your voices in the woods. The only problem was that you were on the opposite side of the river. I had to try and cross it somehow."

Dad flicked Sylvester's ear.

"Ow!"

"That was stupid," Dad said, wagging his pointer finger in Sylvester's face. "I can't believe you willingly jumped into a half-frozen river. Don't ever do that again."

"I wasn't planning on it." Sylvester rubbed his ear and looked up at me. "Who are you exactly? You look familiar."

I exchanged a look with Dad, who shrugged before returning to the campfire with a new can of food.

"I'm Georgie," I told Sylvester. "I'm *his* daughter."

Sylvester's brown eyes widened in surprise. "The one that got lost in the woods when she was eighteen. I thought you were dead!"

"Is that what he told you?"

"No, I just—" He faltered, glancing between me and my father's broad back. "Wow, you're really pretty."

That got a laugh out of me. "Nice deflection, kid."

"What happened to your nose?"

"I lost a fight with the floor. On your behalf, I might add."

Sylvester winced. "Sorry about that."

"Don't sweat it." I looked at my father again, who ate quietly near the fire, and lowered my voice. "Listen, I need you to do me a favor."

"Anything," Sylvester said. "You saved my life."

"You know the people who attacked Camp Haven?" I asked him. He nodded. "They were from another camp, a military operation that the soldiers call Base One. They took the Camp Haven survivors back to their compound, and now two of my friends are trapped there."

Sylvester's brow wrinkled with concern. "That's terrible."

"I agree," I said. "I want to get them out, but Base One is practically impenetrable. I can't get in there alone. Dad promised to help me, but now he's going back on his word."

Sylvester finished the last bite of pasta and then tossed the empty can across the camp. It hit my father's back, bounced off, and rolled away across the dirt. I flinched. Apparently, subtlety wasn't Sylvester's thing.

"Hey!" Dad scolded, turning round to face us. "What was that for?"

"Is it true?" Sylvester demanded.

"Is what true?"

"Did you promise her that you would help save her friends?"

Dad's face grew red. "Sylvester, you don't understand the risks involved—"

"Life out here is all risks," Sylvester said. "Especially since the EMP went off. That doesn't mean that we back down from helping our friends. In fact, it should inspire us to do the exact opposite. If there are people from Camp Haven trapped at this Base One place, then I want to get them out."

"Sylvester—"

"That's our family, Dad," the teenager pushed on. "We introduced each and every one of those people to Camp Haven. I watched them build the compound from the ground up. They're our responsibility. We can't leave them there."

"I understand that," Dad said with the air of a man placating a child. "But there's too much at risk. Besides, if we rescued all of the Camp Haven survivors, what would we do with them? Camp Haven is gone, and I certainly can't fit all of you in my house."

"So we'll rebuild," Sylvester suggested.

"It took years to make Camp Haven what it was," Dad reminded him. "And it's the middle of winter. We don't have the supplies to keep everyone safe. Right now, they're better off at Base One."

"I don't believe that," I said. "Everything I've heard about Base One has been negative. The man I met in the woods earlier— Aaron—he told me that Buddy Arnold runs that place like a prison. The civilians *and* the soldiers are terrified of him. We can't let our people live in fear."

"See?" Sylvester said. He had started shivering again. I tugged the wool comforter up to his chin. "Come on, Dad. We have to go save them. You promised."

"All right, fine!" Dad threw his hands up in defeat, accidentally tossing canned pasta into the air. "We'll go to Base One to look. *Just* to look. If we can figure out a safe way to get in to talk to someone, I'll consider following through with it."

"I guess that's all I can ask for," I said.

DAD and I took turns keeping watch as we slept through the morning. Sylvester was determined to get moving, but we persuaded him to catch a few more hours of shuteye. He was a hardy kid. His brush with hypothermia hadn't dampened his spirits, and we continually had to remind him to take it easy. When the sun was high enough in the sky to warm the tops of our heads, we packed up our things, scattered the remains of the fire, and headed up the mountain. We bypassed Camp Haven, taking the long way around to avoid seeing the destruction of our home again. It was agreed that we needed to return to Dad's house before we proceeded to Base One in order to eat something other than canned noodles, make sure that Sylvester was in good health, and prepare ourselves for what we might find at the military camp below.

Sylvester, despite his gusto, fell into his bed as soon as we arrived home, pulled the covers over his head, and immediately began to snore. I sat on the floor and tugged my boots off, flexing my toes. They were cold and sore from walking all day. As I massaged the soles of my feet through my socks, Dad lugged a bucket of water to the stove.

"I'm going to warm this if you want to wash up," he said. "How's your nose?"

"Holding steady."

Dad lit the fire beneath the stove burner, flicked out the match, and glanced at Sylvester. "He likes you."

"He isn't very difficult to please."

Dad chuckled lightly. "This is true. His outlook on people varies greatly from mine. He thinks that everyone deserves kindness and respect until they prove that they don't."

"That's very noble of him."

"I don't know where he got it from," he replied. "I certainly didn't teach him that."

"No, of course not," I said. "The classic Fitz way is blatant mistrust from introductions."

I meant it as a joke, but Dad didn't smile or laugh.

"You can take the bed," he said, dipping a soft washcloth into the warm pot of water to wipe the dirt and grime off of his arms. "I'll sleep on the floor."

"Dad, I didn't mean it like that—"

"It's fine."

He shut himself off, his expression neutral and nonchalant as he continued to go about his business. Despite our reunion, there were things from the past that haunted us both. It would take a lot more time than a few days to rebuild a relationship that was never rock steady in the first place. It was doubtful that we would ever fully put our family drama aside, but second chances didn't come around often.

"It's hard for me," I admitted. I kept my voice low, telling myself that it was because I didn't want to wake Sylvester. In truth, I didn't know how to say these things to my father out loud. "Seeing you with Sylvester. You're warm and fatherly. You weren't like that when I was a kid. I see that you've changed, and I'm proud of you, but there's a part of me that's jealous of Sylvester for getting what I always wanted." Dad stopped moving but remained silent, leaning over the kitchen counter as if he needed it for moral support. "I'm trying to get used to the new you," I went on. "It's going to take some time. I'll do better tomorrow. And you can have the bed. I know your back bothers you sometimes."

I took the spare blankets that I had stolen from the Legacies and layered them on the floor next to Sylvester's bed. Then I hunkered down and pulled the covers around me in a tight hug. I was almost asleep when my father finally responded.

"I love you, George. You know that, right?"

"Yeah. I know, Dad."

THE NEXT MORNING, we pretended that the previous evening's conversation had never occurred. Dad made breakfast—dried berries, mashed tubers, and sizzling rabbit meat—for the three of us. We ate around the fireplace and drank Dad's homemade tea. Sylvester kept us entertained with all sorts of stories from his years with Dad. As we laughed at his impressions of my father, I almost forgot about the problems that lay beyond our campsite. It was so refreshing to spend time with family—since Sylvester already felt like a brother—that I dreaded returning to reality. Eventually, when our plates were clean and the fire smoldered lower and lower, we had to face the challenge ahead.

We prepared ourselves for every possible outcome, arming ourselves with weapons from Dad's shed. He had collected lost gear—hunting rifles, knives, and the like—from unlucky hikers over the years. I dressed in multiple layers, unwilling to get caught out in the cold again, and pulled the tactical jacket on last. The Kevlar patches were still intact, even after the jacket had taken a few beatings. If Base One started shooting at us, I had a little padding.

To my surprise, Dad didn't argue when Sylvester announced that he would be accompanying us. After yesterday's strife, I had expected Dad to tell the teenager that he wasn't well enough, or that approaching Base One was too dangerous.

"There's no point," Dad muttered to me as we watched Sylvester pocket a handful of snacks. "It's useless arguing with him."

"I can hear you!" Sylvester said.

"Get a move on, kid," I told him. "We have places to be."

We made it to the outlook over Base One in record time. The snowfall had let up momentarily, and it was warmer that it had been yesterday. I pulled off my hat as we surveyed Base One's gargantuan territory, enjoying the crisp breeze that played with my hair.

"Holy shit," Sylvester said, scanning Base One from one side to the other.

Dad cuffed him over the head. "Language."

"Sorry, but holy shit."

"Yeah, it's big," I said.

"Big is an understatement," Sylvester replied. "You didn't tell me that Base One was the size of Jupiter."

"You scared?"

"No!"

"Kids, stop fighting," Dad said dryly. "This was your idea, so what's the plan?"

"Well, we obviously can't lay siege to the place." I studied the base's structure, taking note of each man stationed at the entrances. The main entrance—the one that Aaron had advised I use if I wanted to go inside—was at the far side, opposite of our position. "We would never make it out alive."

"Three against five hundred are not encouraging odds," Dad agreed. "Not to mention, this place is built like a fortress. We could never sneak in."

"No, we couldn't."

"So we're agreed?" Dad asked. "There's no point in risking our lives here?"

"I said we couldn't sneak in," I replied. "I never said that I couldn't walk in through the main gates."

Dad and Sylvester, on either side of me, turned to stare at my face as if to check if I was serious or not.

"You're kidding, right?" Sylvester said. "You want to hand yourself over to them?"

"Absolutely not," Dad said.

"We need intel from the inside," I argued. "The only way to get it is if we have someone *inside* Base One. If I give myself up, I can walk right into Buddy Arnold's camp without a problem."

"And what happens if they shoot you on sight?" Dad challenged.

"They won't," I said. "I heard them talking about me after the Camp Haven attack. They know who I am. They know that I can use the radios. They need me."

Dad rested his hand on my shoulder. "There's no way I'm letting you walk in there alone."

I shook him off. "You can't stop me. I'm going in, whether you like it or not. Now you can either stick around and help me or you can pretend that I don't exist."

Dad and I stared at each, locked in a silent argument. Sylvester's eyes darted between the two of us as though he were watching a particularly entertaining ping pong match. He elbowed Dad in the side.

"Uh, Dad?" he said. "No offense, but you're a dick if you don't agree to help her."

"Language!" My father and I said at the same time.

Sylvester raised his hands innocently. "If you don't help her, I will."

"Sylvester, that's not necessary—" I began.

"Fine," Dad said.

I looked at him in shock. "Fine? You mean…?"

"Like I said, I can't let you do this alone," Dad said. "I assume you've been working on this idea for a few days now. What do you need me to do?"

I grinned, pulled a fully functioning two-way radio from out of my bag, and handed it to Dad. "Listen for my signal."

J circled around Base One through the woods, wanting to stay hidden until the last possible second. I'd left my weapons with Dad and Sylvester. There was no point in bringing them when the soldiers would confiscate them as soon as I set foot in their camp. Additionally, I'd shed a few layers beneath the Kevlar coat. It was all part of the plan. The fortified walls of Base One were taller up close. They towered over the land, casting long shadows far across the ground. I watched the main entrance from the trees, my heart pumping loudly against my rib cage. Six men patrolled this entrance alone, the one that Aaron claimed was loosely guarded. There was nothing else to do but present myself. I just had to gather to courage to do it. With a deep breath, I stepped out of the forest and began walking toward the front gate as slowly as possible. It wasn't long before the first guard noticed my black jacket against the stark white landscape.

"Twelve o'clock," he called to his cohorts, raising his gun at a ready position.

I lifted my hands above my head as the other guards

converged. "Please," I said, forcing my voice to tremble. "I need help. I have no food or water. I'm hurt. Please help me."

To really sell it, I sank to my knees before the soldiers could reach me. The first one stopped a few feet short, and I looked up at him through damp eyelashes.

"Jesus, your face," he said. "What the hell happened to your nose?"

"A rock fell while I was hiking this way," I lied. "I couldn't move out of the way in time. Do you have a medical team here?"

"Yeah," the soldier said, lowering his gun a little. "They can fix you up."

"Wait a second, Galt!" Another soldier approached us from the main gate. "I recognize her. She's from Camp Haven."

"So what?" Galt asked. "We took in the other survivors. Why not her?"

"I'm not saying we don't take her in," the second soldier said. "The bitch got away from us the first time. I'm saying we take her straight to Buddy. Pat her down. Make sure she doesn't have anything sharp or explosive on her."

"Take it easy, Douche."

"For the hundredth time, it's Deutsch!"

"Whatever." Galt let his rifle rest against his hip, helped me up from the ground, and checked me over. "Sorry about this," he muttered, running his hands up my inner thighs. "It's protocol. She's clear!"

Galt and Deutsch took me by either arm, but while Galt was gentle in escorting me inside, his partner squeezed so tightly I thought I might lose circulation. The massive gates rolled open to allow us entrance, and we walked right into Base One.

Despite the size of the compound, it felt crowded. Soldiers and civilians alike rushed from place to place in a frenzy of activity. The buildings were blocky and gray, built from old architectural plans. The outer walls made every point in the camp seem claustrophobic. No matter where you stood, they closed in on you from above, trapping you in place. Base One was not like Camp Haven. There was an aura of fear in the air, a bitter tang that you could taste on the tip of your tongue. As the soldiers ushered me along, I couldn't help but notice the wide-eyed stares pointed in my direction. The civilians' expressions seemed to warn me of issues to come.

I was shunted into one of the boring gray buildings, where the inside was no better than the exterior. The walls were painted sterile white, and each door was marked with bold capital letters. Galt and Deutsch pushed me through one labeled "Processing." More soldiers waited in the next room, which was completely empty save for a showerhead mounted to the wall.

"This is going to suck," Galt said to me under his breath. "I'm sorry in advance, but after this, it's not so bad."

"What are you talking about?" I asked him.

He didn't get the opportunity to answer. Without my consent, three female soldiers stepped forward and began stripping me out of my clothes. I didn't protest until they reached the last layer, but they pinned my hands down and relieved me of even my underwear. Goosebumps erupted across my skin as one of the women physically examined me from head to toe.

"Bend over and cough," she ordered.

Aaron was right. This place was like prison.

Once the soldiers had finished their preliminary inspection, they turned on the showerhead and shoved me under the battering stream of water. I coughed and spluttered as they scrubbed me raw with a bar of awful-smelling soap, roughly washed the oil and dirt from my hair, and rinsed me off. After drying off, Galt returned with a neatly folded pile of clothes. He averted his eyes from my body as he handed them to me.

"I guessed the sizes," he said. "You're almost out of the woods. We're heading to the medical unit next. Hopefully they can do something about your nose."

Shivering, I shook out the clothes. They had provided me with a pair of loose gray cargo pants and a matching button up shirt. Most of the civilians wore similar outfits topped with a puffy winter jacket. I got dressed as quickly as possible, grateful for any kind of defense against the soldiers' probing gazes. Once I had finished, Deutsch reached out to take me by the arm again, but Galt stepped in.

"I got it," he said, taking my elbow gently. "You can stay here. She's had enough of you gawking at her."

As Deutsch glared at us, Galt escorted me from the room and down the hall. The medical unit was through a different door, but it was no warmer than the previous room. Everything was white and sterile. A soldier with bright orange hair examined a file behind the front desk, his feet propped up on another chair.

"Whaddaya got?" he asked carelessly, popping bubble gum between his teeth. He glanced over the file. His boots fell off the desk and hit the floor. "It's you!"

"Kalupa?" I said in disbelief. Sure enough, it was the tall, gangly soldier that I'd spared in the woods a few days ago. I was glad to see that he hadn't suffered at the hands of Buddy Arnold for being the only survivor in his unit.

"Wait a second," Galt said. "You guys know each other?"

"No," Kalupa answered, too quickly for it to be considered the truth. He cleared his throat, straightening the already neat files on his desk. "I mean, not really. She—uh—"

"I saved his ass," I replied for him.

"*This* is the chick you saw in the woods?" Galt asked Kalupa, laughing deep in his belly. "Dude, she's tiny! I thought you said she took out an entire team on her own."

"She did!" he insisted. Apparently, he hadn't told the rest of them about my father's presence in the forest that day.

Galt shook his head, still laughing, and knocked Kalupa over the head. "Oh, Kalupa. You're a riot. She needs vaccinations. Oh, and can you have a look at her nose? It's pretty fucked up."

When Kalupa stood up, the top of his head nearly brushed against the low ceiling. Out of habit, he hunched over to avoid making contact. He opened a nearby cabinet to take out latex gloves and a syringe of clear liquid.

"Roll up your shirt sleeve," he said, fixing a needle to the syringe.

"Hang on a minute," I replied. "Camp Haven gave us vaccinations too. What if yours and theirs are contraindicated?"

"We administered this vaccine to all of the Camp Haven survivors," Kalupa said. "None of them had any problems with it."

"What's it for?"

He pulled the cap off of the needle with his teeth and spat it out. "Typhoid."

"*Typhoid?*"

"Relax," Galt said. "We mostly have it under control."

"*Mostly?*"

Kalupa wiped my arm with a cotton swab. "Can you hold still please?"

The needle punctured my skin, and Kalupa pushed the plunger down. He tossed the syringe into the trash can and patted my arm.

"All done."

I inspected the prick in my skin. "Where did you guys get all of this stuff?"

"Here and there," Galt answered.

I glared at him. "You don't have to be coy. Base One burned my home to the ground in order to steal our supplies. I guess you did the same thing to other compounds, right?"

Kalupa took my face with surprisingly gentle hands to inspect my nose. "Base One had a few things on hand when we got here. I wasn't a part of any other raids. Did you set this yourself?"

"Yes."

"Nice job," he said, impressed. "It's mostly just swollen. I can splint it so that it stays in place and give you some painkillers."

"Don't waste them," I replied. "The pain doesn't bother me."

"Whatever you say, hard ass." Kalupa rifled through another drawer of the cabinet to look for the nose splint. Under his breath, he asked Galt, "Hey, uh, does Buddy know she's here yet?"

Galt took a fresh set of paperwork from a file cabinet and began filling it out. "Probably. Deutsch was on guard with me when she came in. He seemed pretty adamant about delivering her straight to Buddy."

"Great," Kalupa muttered. "Questioning is going to be a bear."

"What's your name, honey?" Galt asked me.

"Georgie Fitz."

He scribbled it across the top of the paperwork. "And what exactly did you do to piss off our beloved comrade?"

The scene from the night that Camp Haven went up in flames replayed in my mind. Eirian, Pippa, and I had made it out of there and into the woods alive, only to be chased by a group of Base One's soldiers. They had separated us from each other, and four or five guys had kicked me to the ground. My father showed up with his crossbow then, mercilessly taking out the soldiers around me. Only one of them escaped. Deutsch's black hair and beady eyes were suddenly familiar to me.

"I embarrassed him," I answered.

"Good," Kalupa said, gently setting the splint across the bridge of my nose. "He's an ass. You're better off avoiding him if you can. Now, listen. Mostly everybody here is a jackass. You've probably figured that out already. It's Buddy's doing. At Base One, you either prove that you're ready for anything or you fall to the bottom of the pile."

"Where are you at?" I asked him.

"Somewhere between rock bottom and too useful to treat like absolute dirt," Kalupa replied as he taped the splint down. "I'm one of the only people who showed up to Base One with any kind of medical experience. Buddy knows he can't mess with me, but after that fiasco a few days ago, I'm definitely on his shit list. Stick around Galt. He'll keep you out of trouble. Somehow, he's got Buddy in his back pocket."

Galt grinned, dug into the cargo pockets of his pants, and pulled out a Snickers bar. "It's only because I found a truckload of these on the way up to Base One. They're Buddy's favorite." He tossed the candy bar to me and raised a finger to his lips. "Shh. Don't tell anyone where you got that."

I unwrapped the Snickers bar and took a savage bite out of it. It had been months since I'd had real chocolate. My taste buds had grown used to the organic, home-grown food we had at Camp Haven, and the candy was too sweet. I wrinkled my nose and inspected the wrapper.

"Not good?" Galt asked.

"Too sweet," I said, handing it back to him. He chomped down on the leftovers and shrugged.

"Galt, can you not?"

"Sorry."

"As I was saying," Kalua went on, examining his handiwork as I wiped caramel off my chin, "Buddy's an ass, and so are his cohorts. They're going to want to question you. Deutsch is probably on his way to pick you up right now."

"Question me about what?"

"About what happened after you and your friend shot up my entire unit."

"Oh." I pasted on a sheepish expression. "Yeah, sorry about that."

Kalupa tossed the extra first aid supplies back into the cabinet. "Don't apologize. You did what you had to do. But I highly recommend that you don't tell Buddy that you weren't working alone. Paint it like you were scared for your life. You killed those men because you thought that they would kill you first if you didn't. That's your story. Stick to it. Otherwise, you'll be detained in some tiny room for however long we're stuck in this hellhole."

A barrage of knocks hammered on the door to the medical unit, and Deutsch let himself in before Galt or Kalupa could grant him access. His black hair, usually greased against his scalp, was disheveled and sweaty, as if he had run across the base and back again.

"Oy," he said, taking me by the arm. "You idiots have had her long enough. She's wanted in questioning."

"I'm coming with," Galt said.

Deutsch put his hand on Galt's chest to stop him. "No, you're not. I brought her in. She's mine."

"She's not a piece of property." Galt swiped Deutsch's hand away with a little too much force. Deutsch tried not to wince. "And for the record, I was the one who picked her up in my sights first, *Douche*. Get the hell out of my way."

Glowering, Deutsch finally backed down, rubbing the new welt on his hand. Galt led me from the room with a gentle hand on my back, keeping himself between me and the other soldier. I waved to Kalupa, who waved back with a sad look on his face. If Base One had more guys around like Kalupa and Galt, maybe it wouldn't be such a terrible thing to be stuck here after all.

"Listen," Galt muttered close to my ear so that Deutsch couldn't eavesdrop on us. "Chances are, questioning is going to suck. Stay calm. I'm going to be there the entire time."

Galt and Deutsch escorted me down the long, white corridor, through a back door, and into another building that was no warmer than the last two.

"Jesus, this whole place is a maze," I murmured.

"It's so intruders can't find their way around," Deutsch announced.

"I don't suppose you could get lost, could you, Douche?" Galt asked.

"I swear to God, if you call me that in front of Buddy—"

Galt whirled around and grabbed Deutsch by the collar of his uniform. "Buddy's coming to questioning? Why didn't you bother to tell me this before?"

Deutsch scrabbled to free himself. "Get off me! She killed an entire unit. Of course, he'd want to see her!"

"You know what happens to the women that Buddy interviews," Galt snarled, his face inches away from his adversary's. "They're practically falling apart at the seams by the time he's through with them."

"I won't fall apart," I said.

"See?" Deutsch finally wrestled out of Galt's grip. "She's totally fine with it."

"For now."

The third building seemed to be full of offices. I peeked into a few of the open doors as we passed by them and caught sight of soldiers working at their desks or goofing off instead. Most of them glanced up at me, intrigued by the newcomer. In that sense, Base One was similar to Camp Haven. It got boring to live the same life day after day. Any kind of news broke up the monotony, even if it was only for a couple of seconds.

"Hiya, Galt," one of the soldiers called through the doorway, craning his neck for a better look at me. "Did you find a stray?"

Galt kept his gaze straight forward. "Sure did. See you later, Kips." When we were clear of that particular office, Galt whispered in my ear. "Remember that guy's face. Don't interact with him. He's one of Buddy's favorites."

"Let me get this straight," I whispered back, keeping an eye on Deutsch to make sure he kept his back turned to us. "I should only make friends with the guys that Buddy hates?"

"Basically."

"Kalupa said Buddy likes you."

"I'm the exception to the rule. Eyes front, Deutsch!" he barked to the other soldier, who had looked over his shoulder as our muttered conversation reached his ears. "This doesn't concern you."

"Just because you outrank me doesn't mean I can't make your life a living hell," Deutsch challenged.

"I'd like you see you try," Galt said. We reached a new door, this one closed and locked. Galt fiddled with a ring of keys on his belt. "Come on. In here."

The interrogation room, for lack of a better title, was the least welcoming out of all of Base One's interiors, and that was saying something. It was bare except for one small table and a rickety chair. The far wall had a black mirror set into it, one of those windows that people could hide behind while they studied you unabashedly. I glared at my reflection, wondering if Buddy Arnold was standing on the other side, and fought the urge to raise my middle finger to the glass.

"Keep a cool head," Galt said, leading me to the chair. He unhooked a water canteen from a loop on his cargo pants and set it down on the table in front of me. "Everything goes a whole lot smoother if no one yells."

"How many people start yelling?" I muttered.

The door opened again to allow someone else entrance to the room, a man so tall and muscular that I couldn't collect his appearance all at once in the tiny interrogation room. Galt and Deutsch backed up against the wall, each snapping to attention, shoulders back and hands flat against their thighs like wind-up toy soldiers. I looked the man up and down, from boots the size of small barges to the crown of his shiny bald head. He had rolled the sleeves of his uniform up to emphasize the bulge of his biceps. Each of his long legs were about as thick as the tree trunks in the forest outside. When my gaze reached his face, I found a permanent sneer across his mouth, a jaw so boxy and square that it could have been shipped through the postal service, and a raised, ropey scar that cut diagonally from the middle of his forehead, across the lid of one piercing green eye, and down the rest of his cheek. This had to be Buddy Arnold.

2 9

*B*uddy Arnold's breath smelled like tinned anchovies, as if he had popped open a can just prior to his entrance and snacked on the tiny fish for the sheer pleasure of feeling the bones crunch between his teeth. The stench alone was enough to incite an intense sense of displeasure at Buddy's presence, but the sparkle in his eyes as he recognized me made my blood run cold. He smiled with only half of his mouth, as if the nerves in the other half had been destroyed by some unfortunate incident. I tried to square my shoulders and keep his gaze, but as his crooked smirk grew wider, my fight or flight response told me to flee as fast as possible. Unfortunately, that wasn't an option.

"You," he said. That was it. He remained standing, shoulders back, his hands loose and easy at his sides. This was a man who did not fear opposition. He invoked too much unease in those around him, and no one dared to test his show of strength.

"What about me?" I replied. Dry. Empty.

"Oh, ho!" Buddy spread his arms, looking first to Galt then to Deutsch. "She's a feisty one! Tell me, which one of you brought her in?"

"I did, sir," Galt and Deutsch replied at the same time. Galt rolled his eyes as Deutsch, too eager, bounced on the balls of his feet.

Buddy snapped his fingers. "Deutsch. Out."

Deutsch immediately stopped bouncing. "But, sir—"

"Out!"

The soldier didn't dare refuse a direct order from his superior, but as he followed Buddy's finger to the door, he grumbled under his breath about the lack of respect at Base One.

"What did you say?" Buddy challenged.

"Nothing, sir!" Deutsch slipped out of the interrogation room, but I doubted that he would return to his post outside the front gates of Base One. Presumably, he would join whoever else was watching the interrogation from the other side of the reflective window.

Once Deutsch was gone, Galt spoke up. "Sir, Deutsch was out in the field during the incident."

"Yeah, yeah," Buddy said, digging a finger into his ear and flicking away whatever came out on the tip of it. "But Deutsch is a blithering, ass-kissing idiot. Besides, I assume he's already told you his account of what happened in the woods that day?"

"Yes, sir."

"Then we're squared away." Buddy planted one hand on the table beside me, his enormous palm flattening out against the metal surface. "Allow me to introduce myself. My name is Sergeant Major Buddy Arnold."

"I know who you are," I told him. "And I would appreciate it if you respected my personal space." To emphasize my point, I jabbed at the pressure point on the inside of his elbow. His reflexes were too quick for me to make contact, but it got him out of my immediate area. Galt hissed, and when I caught his eye, he shook his head once to either side.

Buddy, who had taken a step back from the table to evade my

unprovoked attack, nursed a pretty sneer, but when I challenged him with a stare, the expression morphed into his signature lopsided simper.

"From my understanding," he began, "you have come to Base One to take advantage of our hospitality. Were I in your position, I might afford my hosts a little more respect."

"Can we cut the shit?" I said. "We both know that Base One isn't as reputable as it claims to be."

"Meaning?"

"Meaning if your operation was officially approved by the United States government, it would have been more obvious," I replied. "I'm not blind, *Buddy*. This whole place is outdated, from the equipment to the uniforms. Your guys are dressed in gear from the eighties. If this place were legit, the Army would have figured out a way to deliver updated accommodations to you."

"Perhaps you haven't noticed," Buddy said, "but we're in the middle of a national crisis, and in the Army, we use what we have on hand."

"Really? And what would the Army think about you and your soldiers marching into a camp of innocent civilians and burning the place to the ground to steal their supplies and eliminate competition in the surrounding area?"

Buddy glared at me. "Camp Haven was an accident."

"Bullshit."

"Speaking of which," he continued, unbothered by my accusation, "we have you in this room for a reason. You could be tried for murder considering you killed several Base One soldiers that night."

"Out of self-defense," I replied. "If you want to talk about death, go back to Camp Haven. The place is a graveyard. Bodies everywhere." I rose from the chair, unable to remain seated any longer in this man's abominable presence. In the corner, Galt shifted his stance, unsure what to do, but Buddy lifted a hand to keep him at bay. "You killed my family, my friends, the only people I had left in my life. When your soldiers tried to capture me, I believed that no good could come of it. It was my life or theirs."

Buddy crossed his arms and studied me, his eyes roaming up and down my body as if he were trying to figure out how one woman from the city in her late twenties had managed to take down multiple trained soldiers. "We never had any intention of killing you, Miss Fitz."

I cocked my head. "You know my name?"

"I've been watching Camp Haven since the blast went off," he said. "I thought we could learn from their ways. They got along well, but the place was practically Amish. Then you showed up, and I watched as you convinced those bozos to set up a working radio tower. That was when I knew I needed you at Base One."

"You want me to build you a radio tower?" I asked, confused.

"Base One already has a tower," Buddy said, "but it's been out of service for quite some time now. I need you to get it working so that we can contact the authorities in DC."

"What makes you think I would do anything for you?"

Buddy stepped into my personal space, looming over me. His crossed arms brushed against my chest. "Because I know how women like you operate. Base One isn't just home to a bunch of soldiers who murdered your people. There are innocent civilians here, civilians who I'm sure you care about." He examined a fleck of dirt beneath his fingernail. "You have one week to get the radio tower up and running. If you can't manage that, I'll pick one civilian a day to torture on your behalf. Is that understood?"

There it was. Buddy's lack of humanity. Everyone had warned me about it, from Kalupa to Galt to the soldier in the woods a few days ago, but it had taken a good five minutes for Buddy to pull it out of his back pocket and put it to use. Buddy was a corrupt man, drunk on power and fear mongering, which made the place that he commanded, Base One, a corrupt establishment. The people here were no safer than on their own in the woods, and I was the only one who could do anything about it.

"It's unrealistic to expect me to fix the tower in a week," I said, keeping my voice low so as to not anger Buddy further. "I don't even know what's wrong with it, or if Base One has the supplies I'll need to repair it."

"One week," Buddy repeated. "Perhaps my incentive will encourage you to work as diligently as you did at Camp Haven."

"Incentive? It's a threat!"

"Semantics." He snapped his fingers. "Galt! Show Miss Fitz to the tower so that she can examine it. Your week doesn't start until tomorrow morning," he added to me. "Eat something and get a decent night's sleep. Then you can start working. See? I can be reasonable."

"Reasonable, my ass," I growled, taking a step toward Buddy with clenched fists. Galt grabbed me around the waist before I could do anything stupid.

"All right then!" he said as he escorted me away from Buddy. "Let's get moving, Miss Fitz. I'll give you a tour of the compound." He steered me into the hallway and out of the building through a back door.

I squinted as my eyes adjusted from the dim oil lamps indoors to the bright natural light of the sun. A gust of wind turned up the collar of my new uniform. "So that's Buddy Arnold?" I asked Galt as he pointed us toward the center of the camp.

"That's him."

"I can't wait to punch him in the face."

· · ·

I SPENT the remainder of the day with Galt. We inspected the radio tower first. It sat in the direct center of Base One, and the control panel was at the very top. We had to climb up a rusted rickety ladder built into the side of the tower to get up to it. The control room was tiny, and the windows had been busted out, either by weather or vandals, long ago. There wasn't much to stop you from tumbling over the edge of the tower if you happened to trip. The view was amazing, so long as I didn't look directly toward the ground. Up here, I could almost pretend that I lived in the sky with the birds. I was level with the tops of the highest trees and could see all the way to the smoky ruins of the city. In addition, from this height, I could map out all of Base One. I scanned the grounds, trying to commit the layout of the compound to memory as quickly as possible. The knowledge would undoubtedly come in handy later.

The tower itself, thankfully, wasn't beyond repair. It had mostly been sabotaged by exposure to the elements. The equipment was outdated, but I could make it work. Little did Buddy know that I needed a functional radio as much as he did. It was the basis of my rescue plan, and Buddy had given me exactly what I needed to bring him down once and for all.

"Can you fix it?" Galt asked. "Please tell me you can fix it."

"Oh, yeah," I said, examining a control panel. "I can totally salvage this piece of crap."

Galt, it turned out, was quite useful. He was the best soldier I could have asked for to get me around Base One on my first day. He pointed out important buildings—like Buddy's quarters—and shortcuts from one end of the compound to the other. He introduced me to soldiers like himself and Kalupa, men who had been shanghaied by Buddy to complete his deeds for a shot at survival in a post-apocalyptic world. I memorized their faces. These were the men who I could go to for help once shit hit the fan. At the end of the day, after Galt had taken me to the mess hall for dinner, he led me to the women's barracks.

"It's not much," he said, leading me through the rows of bunk beds. Every single one was occupied. Women and children alike stayed here, some of them sharing mattresses to make room for others. Their eyes followed us as Galt showed me to a top bunk at the very end of the room. "Buddy freed this one up for you."

"What do you mean, he freed it up?"

"Don't ask. Lights out is in twenty minutes. I'll see you tomorrow."

Galt left, and I was alone with the other female civilians of Base One. I climbed up into the top bunk and sat against the wall, dangling my feet off the edge of the bed. Every face was turned toward mine. I scanned each one, hoping to see someone, anyone, who had made it out of Camp Haven alive. The women averted their eyes as soon as I met their gaze, but once I moved on to look at the next face, I felt their stares again. I didn't recognize anyone. Pippa wasn't here either. I leaned over the bed to address my bunk mate, a woman in her thirties with short dark hair and thick shoulders.

"Hey," I said. "I'm Georgie."

The woman glanced up from a book she was reading and smacked my outstretched hand like a fraternity brother greeting his friends. "Addison. Nice to meet you."

"What happened to the woman who had my bunk before?"

"We prefer to remain ignorant on that front." She set her book aside and looked up at me. "How'd you get here?"

"I walked in," I replied, unwilling to share the entire answer. "Is this the only dormitory for women, or are there others? And where do the men sleep?"

Addison pulled the sleeves of her thermal over her hands to keep them warm in the drafty bunk. "You didn't see outside? There are about ten barrack buildings, four for women, six for men. Why?"

"I'm looking for someone," I said. "Two someones, actually. A seventeen-year-old girl named Pippa and a tall Welsh guy named Eirian. Sound familiar?"

"All the guys look the same to me," she replied. "I can't help you there. There's a Pippa staying in the medical unit with a baby. Is that her?"

Relief rushed through me. "Yes. Is she okay? How do you know her?"

"I work there," she said. "I used to be an EMT before all of this garbage happened. She's hanging in there. Stress plus postpartum depression is screwing with her. That's why she stays there."

"Can I see her?"

"She's off-limits," Addison said. "No visitors."

"Of course," I grumbled. "Can't you get me in?"

"No offense, but I don't know you," she said. "And I'm not about to break protocol to get me in to see some random girl. Sorry about that."

She returned to her book, and I knew that the conversation was over. Nobody at Base One wanted to be associated with a rule breaker. It might bring Buddy's wrath down on them. I rolled over and stared at the ceiling, where someone had carved their initials into the plaster.

"Lights out!" someone shouted from outside the barracks.

All at once, the women blew out the oil lamps near their bunks, and the barracks plunged into darkness. The lamp above my bed remained lit. Addison kicked my mattress from below.

"Put that shit out," she whispered.

I blew on the flame, extinguishing the last bit of light in the room. Then I waited. In a matter of minutes, the women stopped rustling around to get comfortable as they fell to sleep one by one. Mismatched breathing patterns filled the barracks like a light whispering wind, occasionally punctuated by a snore or mumble. Wide awake, I looked out of the window that was level with my bed. Base One's guards remained on duty, patrolling the top of the wall, but the grounds themselves were empty. Silently, I slipped out from beneath my rough blankets and leapt down from the bunk, landing in a low crouch on the floor. As I pulled on one of my boots, Addison stirred and sat up.

"What are you doing?" she hissed.

"Go back to sleep."

She snatched my other boot away from me before I could get it on the other foot. "Whatever you're thinking of doing, stop right now. If you get caught out there, they'll take you to Buddy Arnold. Believe me, you don't want to meet Buddy Arnold."

"I've already met Buddy Arnold," I told her. "And he doesn't scare me. Now give me my boot back."

She held it behind her back. "No."

"Listen, if I get caught out there, you're going to be the first person they ask if you know anything," I said. "Do you want to know what I'm doing to tell them or would you rather pretend that you were asleep this entire time and this conversation never happened?"

Addison hesitated then reluctantly handed the boot over. "I hope you know what you're doing."

"Never."

Once I had both shoes on, I snuck out of the window above my bunk and dropped to the ground outside. The snow was black and icy, and I was grateful that Base One had let me keep my own boots rather than issue the shitty ones that everyone else here had to wear. I never would have been able to quietly navigate the compound in the flat-footed soles of the camp-issued footwear.

I stole from dormitory to dormitory, peeking in through the windows to get a look at the people inside them. The first three next to mine housed the rest of the women. I skipped quickly over those and continued to the men's buildings. Here, I spent a little more time, pressing my face to the windows to scan each bed for the person I was looking for. Finally, in the last barrack,

I caught sight of a tuft of wavy black hair. I rapped lightly on the window nearest. The person rolled over, dislodging the blanket from his face.

"Eirian," I breathed. He wasn't entirely awake yet. I checked to make sure that no guards had snuck up behind me and knocked on the window again. This time, Eirian blearily opened his eyes and looked up. I waved and grinned. He scrambled out of bed and shoved the window open.

"Georgie!" He cupped my face and peppered kisses across my mouth and cheeks. "You're alive!"

"Shh." I could help but smile as I leaned into his warmth. "Don't wake the others."

"But how did you—? Where have you been? Why are you here?"

"It's a long story," I told him, holding his hands between mine. "Did you think I was going to leave you in here?"

"I didn't know what to think," Eirian replied. "Pippa's in the medical unit. They won't let me see her—"

"I know."

"Jesus, Georgie." He leaned his forehead against mine. "I know it's only been a few days, but I missed you so much. What are we going to do?"

"You're not going to do anything," I said. "Keep your head down. Pretend you don't know me. I've got this under control."

Eirian gave me a wry look. "What exactly are you planning?"

"You'll see."

OVER THE COURSE of the week, I did everything in my power to get the radio tower up and running. I spent almost every minute from dawn until dusk in the open air of the control room, wiring circuit boards and toying with my limited supplies. Galt supervised me each day, but he often grew tired of the unfailing cold by midmorning and kept watch from the ground instead.

This suited me just fine. The control room felt crowded when Galt's gun was present, even though I knew it would take an uncontrollable circumstance for him to feel compelled to use it. I worked diligently, sending Galt on errands through the camp when I needed some tool or piece of equipment. Each night, I reported to Buddy Arnold, and each night, I lied about my progress. My goal was to get the tower operational as soon as possible, but I had no plans to update Buddy with the reality of my progression. I pretended that the tower was too far gone for me to repair it in a week, allowing my voice to waver and my eyes to fill a little more with each report. Buddy grew more and more agitated with every notification, and he reminded me on a daily basis of what would happen if I did not succeed by the end of the week.

When I wasn't in the tower, I gave Galt the slip to roam Base One on my own. After the first three times, Galt stopped scolding me for my behavior. We entered into a silent agreement. He didn't ask, and I didn't lie. During my outings, I trailed the higher ranked members of Base One, skulking around corners and hiding in the shadows as I listened to their conversations. Most of the time, all I heard were lamentations about the food in the mess hall or the lack of beautiful women on base, but one evening, I gathered a piece of information that I could actually use to my advantage.

Halfway through the week, after I had finally gotten one of the control panels to respond to my work, I celebrated by stealing a muffin from the mess hall and hiding in the pantry as a pair of soldiers raided a stash of MREs. The first one, Kips, was the man that Galt had warned me about when I'd first arrived at Base One. The second, a skinny guy with a rat face whose last name was Rios, I had rarely seen without Kips by his side. They were two peas in a pod, and both of them worshipped Buddy like he was a god. As I munched silently on my muffin, crouched behind several massive bags of white rice in the pantry, I listened to their conversation, which they didn't bother to keep quiet, and watched them through the slits in the pantry door.

"So what's Buddy's deal with the radio tower?" Rios asked Kips as they dug through the neatly stacked MREs with no regard to organization. "Why does he want to get it working so bad?"

Kips examined a label on one of the meals before tossing the package over his shoulder. "He says he wants to contact one of his old superiors. The guy's apparently been stationed in DC for the last couple of years."

"So Buddy thinks he can get help for us out here?"

"I don't think it's help that Buddy's interested in."

Rios paused in his demolition of the MRE pile. "What do you mean?"

"I've known Buddy for years," Kips said, ripping open one of the meals. He took one thing from inside and tossed the rest in the garbage. "We were in basic training together. He moved up the ranks fast. Always the perfect soldier. Then one day something fucking snapped in him."

"And?"

"And he killed one of our guys when we were out on a mission," Kips said. My stomach dropped. Suddenly, the muffin didn't taste so good. "Shot him right in the back and kept shooting until the rest of us pinned him down. He was dishonorably discharged, but before they could do anything else, he disappeared."

"If he was dishonorably discharged, how is he the Sergeant Major of Base One?" Rios asked. Kips shot him a look, and realization crossed Rios's face. "Oh. No one here knows that he was discharged, do they?"

"Nope, and if you tell anyone, I'll kill you." Kips voice was light, but the threat was real. "Buddy's a fucking nutcase, but let me tell you, I was glad to see him out here. No one else would have made it this far. No one else would have gotten this place running again. My guess is he wants to get ahold of our old unit leader and get him to change his story about the shooting. Otherwise, Buddy's going to be arrested as soon as the legit guys find this place."

"Yeah, but what are the chances that's going to happen anytime soon?" Rios said, finally locating an MRE that he was satisfied with and setting it aside to eat later. "The entire United States is down for the count."

"Buckley Air Force Base is up and running," Kips said. He opened a package of cereal and ate a handful straight from the box. He spat the soggy wheat pieces onto the floor. "Ugh. Stale. Anyway, Buddy's patrols found out that the guys at Buckley are working their way through Denver. Eventually, they'll make it into the mountains, and when they do, they aren't going to be pleased to find Buddy at the helm of Base One. Buddy has no intention of turning this base to Buckley's control. He likes being in charge."

"Sheesh," Rios said. "And I thought *you* had problems."

Kips threw the box of cereal at Rios's head. "Shut the fuck up."

THREE DAYS LATER, my week was up. The day was coming to an end. It was now or never. With Galt on the ground, I had privacy up in the control tower. I'd already been informed that Buddy was on his way to inspect my handiwork. I'd managed to get the radio functioning, but damned if I was going to let Buddy send out the first message. I sat up in the tower, freezing and alone, and broadcast as far as I could. I kept my voice low as I repeated my message over and over again, as many times as I dared, hoping that it would get picked up by its intended recipient. Thankfully, the wind carried my voice away from the camp below. Galt and the other soldiers remained oblivious to my success with the radio.

A loud metallic creak warned me of Buddy's imminent arrival as he and Galt climbed the ladder to the control room. Quickly, I set aside the mouthpiece and ripped a wire out of place so that the broadcasting feature was disabled, but the radio itself still picked up frequencies. Buddy climbed into the control room, head bowed so that he wouldn't bump it on the low ceiling.

"Well?" he demanded. "Your one week is up. Is the radio working or shall I draw names out of a hat to determine who to waterboard first?"

I turned up the volume on the speakers so that Buddy could hear the static coming through them. "We're up and running. All I need to do is wire the mic so that you can broadcast."

"And why haven't you done that yet?"

I lifted the frayed wire. "Because I'm working with shit. Get me a new wire, and you can send your broadcast to DC stat."

Buddy narrowed his eyes and snatched the wire from my hand to examine it. Then, without another word, he marched toward the ladder to leave the tower. I let out a sigh of relief. It would take them hours to find another coil of wire. I'd hidden all of it that I could find inside the mattress on my bunk. We were safe from Buddy's outgoing message, and hopefully, the mic issue would buy enough time for what I needed to happen. Suddenly, the radio speakers crackled and a voice rang through the control room.

"This is Senior Airman Hogan of Buckley Air Force Base responding to your S.O.S. call," the voice said. "Do you copy?"

For the longest minute of my life, Buddy and I stared at each other from across the tiny control room, listening to the Airman repeat his message as he waited for us to reply. Slowly, he walked back to me, his steps precise and controlled. He looked at the radio speakers, then back to me, then to the busted wire of the microphone.

"What the hell have you done?" he said calmly, and then he grabbed me by the front of my shirt and launched me out of the tower's shattered window.

30

*T*he first thing I felt upon waking up was a shooting pain up the side of my torso and through my shoulder. When I opened my eyes, everything was a blurred at the edges. White walls trapped me against a hard, lumpy mattress. I tried to sit up, but my head throbbed and pulsed with every beat of my heart.

"I wouldn't do that if I were you."

I turned my head to follow the familiar voice, hardly daring to believe it, but there was Pippa Mason, in all her glory, sitting in the bed next to me. She rocked a small bundle of blankets that rested in the cradle of her crossed legs. Like everyone else, Pippa had changed a great deal over the past several months. Not long ago, she was an average high school senior at a private Catholic high school, captain of her field hockey team and bound for the Ivy Leagues once she delivered her unexpected baby and handed her over to a family that was ready to raise a child. Pippa had been the epitome of blonde and preppy, never seen without makeup or a manicure. Now, there were dark shadows beneath her eyes, her fingernails were short and dirty, and she had cut her hair short to her chin—with a knife, if the jagged edges were any indication—to keep it out of her face. To top it off, there was no family around to raise her baby. The newborn was solely Pippa's responsibility.

"I would hug you," I croaked, "but I'm having trouble remembering which of my limbs are which."

"You look like hell too," Pippa said.

"What happened? Did you see?"

She looked over her shoulder, checking the medical unit for other people. "I thought you were dead when they brought you in. Blood everywhere. Your shoulder was swinging out of its socket. It was gross."

That explained the makeshift sling that trapped my arm close to my body. Talking to Pippa helped clear my mind. I took note of my injuries, checking on the extent of the damage. I wiggled my fingers and toes. One fractured pinky, but otherwise all right. My torso had taken the extent of it all. My ribs ached in protest with the smallest movement, sending shooting pains through my lungs and making it hard to breathe, and my shoulder, which someone had popped back into place, felt like it might make another attempt at escape.

"I didn't even know you were here," Pippa said. "What the hell happened out there? How's the rest of Camp Haven?"

"It's gone," I said. "Everyone's dead or trapped here. I came for you and Eirian, but I think this has all spiraled out of control. Have you seen Buddy?"

"Buddy Arnold? The guy who runs the camp? I don't even know what he looks like. Why would he ever set foot in the medical bay?"

"Because he's the one who pushed me out of the radio tower," I growled, ripping an IV needle out of my arm. I didn't trust Base One's drugs at all. "I've been here all week. Buddy made a deal with me to get the radio working, but he wasn't pleased when he realized what I did with it."

"What did you do?"

Before I could answer, an ancient speakerphone mounted in the corner of the room buzzed to life. "Attention, Base One civilians," a voice announced. "This compound is now on lockdown. Our security has been compromised. Please do not panic. As long as you follow the lockdown protocol, no harm will come to you."

A wide grin spread across my face. "That," I told Pippa. "That's what I did."

Pippa stared at me like I was crazy. "Georgie, what's going on?"

"We're getting out of here," I declared, throwing the sheets off of my legs and using all of my willpower to pull my aching limbs out of the bed. My clothes were folded neatly on a nearby chair. I shed the medical unit's gown and got dressed. "How long was I out for?"

"Several hours."

"We need to go." I tossed her my tactical jacket. "Put that on and tuck Athena inside. It's big and warm enough for the both of you."

Pippa looked down at her baby, who gripped her mother's index finger with her whole hand. "Athena?"

"That's what I call her," I said. "Did you change the name?"

She shook her head. "I like Athena. It's strong."

"I agree. Come on. Let's get moving."

It was easier said than done. Every step I took was punctuated by a sharp stab in the chest as my broken ribs reminded me of the trauma my body had been through earlier that day. I needed to be in bed, to let myself heal, but the window of time to get out of Base One was too small to waste. I had to know what was going on outside. I ushered Pippa toward the door of the medical unit, but it flew open and nearly smacked me in the face as Buddy Arnold entered from the other side.

Immediately, I put myself between Buddy and Pippa, forcing the younger girl away from the monstrous man. He strode forward, took me by the collar of my shirt, just as he had when he had thrown over the edge of the tower, and shook me until my brain rattled against my skull.

"What have you done?" he demanded, spittle flying from his mouth and spraying my face. "Base One is surrounded. You've put all of my people at risk?"

"Surrounded by who?" I challenged. "Real military men?"

He threw me against a cot, and I yelped in pain. Buddy wasn't done. He stood over me and leaned down. "I'm going to make you wish you'd never been born, Georgie Fitz."

"Not if I have anything to say about it," Pippa said, and she smashed an oil lamp over the back of Buddy's head.

The blow hardly fazed him, as enormous and hard-headed as he was, but it gave me enough time to scramble beyond Buddy's reach. He thundered after me as I overturned cots and bedside tables to put more obstacles between me and him, but his powerful legs crushed the furniture beneath his boots. He caught up with me as we rounded the door to the medical unit again, dragging me up from the floor as Pippa watched in horror from the other side of the wrecked room.

I dug my nails into Buddy's hands as they enclosed around my throat and squeezed, but it was no use. My airway closed off, my eyes bulged and watered, and my toes left the ground as Buddy lifted me into the air by my neck. Bright spots of light danced in front of my eyes as the rest of my vision blackened. Was this it? Was this the end? Had I done enough to save the people of Base One from Buddy's wrath, or would I die in vain?

When the pressure around my neck suddenly vanished, I slumped to the floor and gasped for air, massaging the bruises at my throat. A loud *thwack* caught my attention, and I looked up just in time to see Eirian land a savage uppercut to Buddy's chin. He didn't stop there though. He threw punch after punch in vicious combinations, his fists flying so quickly that my brain didn't process where they landed until after Buddy's reactions.

He had caught Buddy by surprise. It was the only reason that he'd managed to gain the upper hand in the fight. Eirian aimed one last jab to Buddy's jaw. The larger man spun around like a top, lost his footing, and crumpled to the floor.

"Move," Eirian ordered, picking me up from the floor. His knuckles were covered in Buddy's blood. "Pippa, get Athena and let's go!"

As Buddy rolled over, groaning, the four of us escaped from the medical unit. Outside, Base One was unrecognizable. Men and women in real military uniforms flooded the entire compound. Half of them rounded up Base One's counterfeit soldiers, who would face the consequences for posing as members of the Army. I spotted Kips and Rios lined up with the others, their hands bound with zip ties behind their backs. The rest of the military officers directed Base One civilians toward evacuation routes that led out of the compound.

"What is all this?" Pippa asked, staring around in wonder.

"It's a rescue mission," I replied, beaming with pride.

"You're doing, I'd guess?" Eirian said, grasping my hand in his as we joined the line to leave Base One. "I figured there was a reason Buddy pushed you out of the radio tower."

"What can I say?" I grimaced as my ribs protested our steady walk, but nothing could stop me from grinning at each real soldier we passed by. "I told you I'd get you guys out of here."

"How did you do it?" Pippa said.

"Sent out a couple of broadcasts while I had the chance," I replied. "I knew that there was a legitimate Air Force base nearby that was helping Denver out. I figured it might be worth a shot to get ahold of them."

"You're a damn genius."

We shuffled through the gates of Base One. In the woods, the Air Force base had set up an organizational checkpoint, alphabetically by last name, for all of the survivors.

"Pippa, go get yourself and Athena checked in," I told the

younger girl, pointing to the Airman who was taking note of those with last names starting with M. "Then come find me."

"What about you?" she asked.

"Don't worry about me," I said, waving her off. "Go, go." I kept a smile on my face until she left, then immediately crumpled. "I need to sit down."

Eirian helped me to the ground, propping me up against a tree trunk that was out of the way of the Air Force's process. The day's ordeal had taken everything out of me. I was exhausted, and I didn't think I would make it one more step on my own.

"I'll get you some water," Eirian said. "Stay right here. Don't move."

"Like I could if I wanted to."

He disappeared into the crowd, and I stretched out to watch the organizational attempt from afar. After the civilians checked themselves in, they piled into a convoy of working Humvees, which led away from the looming walls of Base One and down the mountain face. A deep sense of satisfaction stole through me, momentarily easing the discomfort of my injuries. It had been mere days since everyone and their brother had told me that I had no hope of infiltrating Base One. No one had believed that I could do it, not even my father, and yet here we were. Not only had I gotten Eirian, Pippa, and Athena out, but I had brought Base One to the attention of people who could really help the civilians.

"Georgie?"

I turned around at the sound of my name and broke out a smile. My father had found his way down to the evacuation site. A pair of binoculars dangled around his neck. He had been watching this entire time. If I knew him like I think I did, he'd been watching Base One ever since I arrived here the week prior.

"Hi, Dad."

He rushed forward and dropped to his knees to hug me, but stopped himself when he got a better look at my injuries. "Jesus, kid. What did you do to yourself?"

"I'll heal," I said, patting his shoulder. "I did it though. I saved them."

"I know. I'm so proud of you."

"Where's Sylvester?"

"At home," Dad said. "I wasn't sure what the situation was going to be like out here, but you've certainly outdone yourself. Where are they taking everybody?"

Another truck—old enough to have evaded the effects of the EMP—drove off with another load of survivors.

"No idea," I said, letting my eyes flutter shut. I was so tired. All I wanted was a real bed and a decent night's sleep. "But it's better than Base One. Better than having Buddy Arnold looming over their shoulders every minute of every day."

And then there was Buddy's face, beaten and bruised, looming over my father's shoulder with all of his teeth bared. Somehow, he had gotten out of Base One unnoticed. He yanked my father's crossbow out of his grip and launched it through the trees. Before Dad could react, Buddy drew a long hunting knife out of its sheath and pressed it against Dad's throat. A droplet of blood welled up beneath the blade.

"Don't!" I cried, struggling to stand and failing to do so.

Buddy backed up as I crawled toward him, taking my father with him. "So this is the guy that murdered all of my men in the woods that night, is it? What perfect justice, Miss Fitz, that he happens to be your father. Poetic even."

"I swear, if you touch him—"

"You'll what?" Buddy asked with a laugh. "You can barely move. What are you going to do? Drown me in your tears?"

"I'll kill you."

Buddy's lips tilted up in that lopsided smirk that I hated so much. "Oh, Miss Fitz. I'd like to see you try."

And then he drew the blade across my father's neck.

"No!" I yelled. Dad's eyes widened as blood spurted from his neck. Buddy dropped him, and he fell to his knees in the mushy snow. I crawled over to him and pressed my hands to the gash, but there was too much blood. In a few seconds, it coated my hands like thick red paint. "Help!" I screamed, tearing through my vocal chords. "Help us!"

"See, Georgie?" Buddy said, wiping my father's blood off of his blade. "If there's one thing you'll learn from all of this, it's that life isn't fair. Get used to it."

I launched myself at Buddy, forgetting that I was injured from head to toe, that he was a massive man trained in several different forms of combat and that I was a radio host that just happened to have a few extra survival skills. Nevertheless, it took him by surprise. I raked my nails down his face, opening a new wound parallel to his old scar. He growled and threw me to the ground next to my father, where I fought to catch my breath. Buddy raised his foot, his boot poised over my skull as if he mean to stomp it into the ground as his final stand.

And then a bullet lodged itself in the direct center of Buddy's forehead. Pippa—Athena in one hand and a revolver in the other —stood on the opposite side of the clearing. She didn't lower the gun until Buddy's body landed splay-legged on the forest floor with a resounding crash. He was dead, but I didn't care. All I cared about was my father, bleeding out from the wound in his neck.

"Georgie," he rasped, taking my hand and pressing it to his heart. "I'm so sorry for everything, but I want you to know. You have to know. I love—" He gasped as another gush of blood spilled from his neck. "I l-love…"

He never finished his sentence.

FIVE YEARS LATER

Pippa stood on the riverbank alone, watching the icy water pass her by. The current was sluggish and slow here. During the summers, this was where we spent the sunniest of days, swimming in the chilly water to cool off. But it was winter again, and winter always brought a few painful memories along with it. Pippa drew a lighter from her pocket, flicked it on, and lit a candle. Then she knelt down by the river's edge and set the candle in the water. It floated on the surface, buoyed up by a small balloon of Pippa's making, and sailed down the river like a ghost into the purple dusk.

I stepped up to Pippa's side. "You okay?"

"It's the anniversary," she said, keeping her eye on the candle-light as it drifted down river. "Of their deaths."

"I know."

She leaned her head against my shoulder, and I put an arm around her. "Do you ever think about it?"

"All the time."

She lifted her head to gaze up at me. "Do you ever feel bad about the people that you killed to stay alive? We considered

449

them the enemy, but someone else could be burning candles from them."

"If I didn't feel any remorse, I would wonder if I was human at all anymore." I swept her blonde hair away from her face. Usually, we didn't talk about these things. The past was in the past, and we were all keen to move on from it. And as far as I knew, there was only one person that Pippa had ever killed. "Do you regret shooting Buddy? Is that what this is about?"

"I don't regret it," she said. "He killed my brother."

The memory of Jacob flitted in and out of focus in my mind's eye. Pippa was the only surviving member of the Masons. That was our world now. We had fractured bits and pieces of other people's families, and we tried to fit the jagged edges together to form a new unit, like taping the broken glass of a picture frame back together.

"Hey, you know what else today is?" I asked Pippa, anxious to get away from the more morose subjects. "It's your daughter's fifth birthday, and she's impatiently waiting for you to get back to the homestead so that she can open her presents and eat some cake."

Pippa smiled. "All right. Let's go."

After Base One had been evacuated, we had decided not to accompany the rest of the survivors to the Air Force base. Instead, we returned to the ruins of our home. Camp Haven was nothing like it used to be. We had safely and respectfully disposed of the bodies. Then it had taken us months to clear out the debris. When we began to rebuild, we started out small. Eventually, Camp Haven was reborn, this time with new and improved features. Not only did we rebuild the cabin with a larger floor plan, but we wired it with electricity and indoor plumbing on our own. The process was slow, and it involved a plethora of foul language, but now Camp Haven had running water and light switches, which was more than enough to make up for our trouble.

Denver recovered from the EMP at an infinitesimal pace. Slowly but surely, the United States was trying to get back to normal. A few of the blown transformers had been replaced with new ones. Hospitals and emergency services were up and running. Giant grocery stores had been replaced by modest daily markets, where local farmers and other small businesses sold their homemade goods to those less crafty. We visited these markets often. Camp Haven's soil was perfect for growing organic fruits and vegetables, and we couldn't possibly eat all that we produced on our own. We traded our wares for things we couldn't get up in the mountains, like first aid supplies and gasoline for our generators. It was a new way of life, but after everything settled down, I began to realize that I was okay with this slower, more organic version of living. It made me focus on the things that were really important.

"Mama!"

A tiny blur collided with Pippa's knees, and Pippa leaned down to pick up her daughter and swing her around in wide circles. Athena was the epitome of the Mason family's genetics. She had bright blonde hair and inquisitive brown eyes, and while she resembled Pippa around the nose and mouth, the shape of her face belonged to her late Uncle Jacob. Like the rest of us, Athena had found herself part of a family that was not necessarily related by blood, but by mutual love instead.

Eirian jogged across the homestead, his boots crunching in the fresh layer of snow that had fallen in the dark hours of that morning. "Sorry," he said with a grin. "She got away from me."

I kissed him hello. "Thwarted by a five-year-old, were you?"

"To be completely fair, she's got really long legs for a five-year-old."

"Uncle Eirian's slow," Athena declared, head lolling about on her shoulders as she recovered from the dizziness induced by Pippa's wide arcs. "He doesn't pick up his feet."

Eirian pinched Athena's pink cheek. "I let you win, kid."

"Nuh-uh!"

"Uh-huh!"

"All right, separate, you two," Pippa said, setting her daughter on the ground. "I swear, Eirian. Sometimes I wonder if you're five years old too."

Eirian proudly squared his shoulders. "They say to never lose your inner child."

"Mama, I want to open my presents!" Athena said, tugging on Pippa's hand. "Please? Pretty please? Pretty please with Uncle Eirian's dignity on top?"

"Okay, she's way too advanced for a five-year-old," Eirian muttered. "Who's teaching her this stuff?"

Pippa finally gave in. "Okay, okay! Your presents are in the cabin, and so is your cake. Do you want some cake too?"

Athena jumped up and down with joy. "I love cake!"

"Who doesn't?" Eirian said. He took Athena's other hand. "Let's go stuff our faces, lovebug."

I chuckled as Eirian and Pippa swung Athena between them, her feet rarely touching the ground. Together, we went up to the cabin, where smoke puffed out of the chimney and floated across the clear blue sky. The inside was toasty and warm. We stamped the snow out of our boots and shed our jackets near the door. Athena made a beeline for the kitchen, where a pile of presents sat on the table next to a homemade cake. She reached for the first one, but someone jumped out from behind the kitchen wall, scaring Athena away from the table.

"Rah!" Sylvester roared, holding his hands up like a monster's claws. "I am the guardian of the birthday presents! You shall not pass!"

Athena recovered from her fright, giggled, and threw a fake

punch at Sylvester's mid-thigh, the highest part of his body that she could reach. "They're my presents, you beast!"

Sylvester pretended to double over in pain, moaning dramatically. "Oh, gods of thunder and lightning! Why have you forsaken me? I am vanquished!"

He lay on the floor and flopped over, tongue sticking out of his mouth. Athena propped one foot on his hip and struck a power pose, only for Sylvester to flip over and tackle her.

"All right, all right!" Dad emerged from the adjacent room, carrying more presents under one arm. Sylvester and Athena froze as he frowned down at them, one hand perched on his hip. "How many times do I have to tell you two? No tussling in the house!"

"Sorry, Grandpa Amos."

"Yeah, sorry, *Grandpa*," Sylvester added, untangling himself from the five-year-old.

Dad smacked his surrogate son over the head. As he stepped into the sunshine streaming in through the open window to set the rest of the presents on the table, the light reflected off the shiny scar across his throat. Five years later, and I still couldn't believe that he had survived Buddy's murder attempt. Sometimes, I wondered if something stronger than luck and science had brought him back from his near-death experience.

"So, Athena," he said, leaning down to look the little girl in the eye. "Which present do you want to open first?"

She pointed to the biggest one on the pile. "That one!"

"That one's from me," I told her. "I hope you like it."

Athena ripped away the brown paper to reveal a bow that I had made by hand and a quiver of arrows. The weapon was fit to her size. It would teach her the basics of handling a compound bow in the future, but she couldn't do any real damage with it.

"Cool!" she exclaimed, tugging experimentally on the string.

"Really?" Pippa said to me. "A freaking bow?"

"What?" I replied innocently. "She's a Greek goddess. She needs a weapon. Besides, the arrow tips are padded."

"Open mine next," Eirian said, sliding a present across the table toward Athena.

Sylvester shoved Eirian out of the way. "No, do mine! It's better than Uncle Eirian's, I promise."

"Everyone relax," Dad said, raising his hands to command silence. "Everyone's presents are awesome… but you all know that Athena's going to like what I got her the best."

The table exploded in a roar of playful arguments. I grinned, leaning into Eirian as he made his case, and watched my found family duke it out, each catering to a five-year-old who had them all wrapped around her little finger. Life wasn't perfect. All of us had lost people and things that were important to us, but we pushed through. We made it out of the foggy depression together, and the chorus of laughs stitched together the frayed pieces of our mending hearts.